REMAIN SILENT

REMAIN SILENT

JAMIE DENTON

BRAVA

KENSINGTON PUBLISHING CORP.
http://www.kensingtonbooks.com

BRAVA BOOKS are published by

Kensington Publishing Corp.
850 Third Avenue
New York, NY 10022

Copyright © 2007 by Jamie Denton

All Kensington titles, imprints, and distributed lines are available at special quantity discounts for bulk purchases for sales promotions, premiums, fund-raising, educational or institutional use.

Special book excerpts or customized printings can also be created to fit specific needs. For details, write or phone the office of the Kensington Special Sales Manager: Kensington Publishing Corp., 850 Third Avenue, New York, NY 10022. Attn. Special Sales Department. Phone: 1-800-221-2647.

Brava and the B logo Reg. U.S. Pat. & TM Off.

ISBN-13: 978-0-7582-1014-2
ISBN-10: 0-7582-1014-0

First Kensington Trade Paperback Printing: November 2007
10 9 8 7 6 5 4 3 2 1

Printed in the United States of America

REMAIN SILENT

Chapter 1

LAUREL JENNINGS DETESTED funerals. Her dislike was even more profound when the interment consisted of someone close to her, someone vitally important in her life. That particular list, which was short to begin with, had now been reduced by one more.

She recognized the faces of many of the mourners, most were from the occasional social function her business partner had insisted she attend. They were old, boring, and disgustingly rich, but they'd kept her art restoration business flourishing, so with a grudge, she'd gone whenever Jonathan had insisted. No one would force her to be sociable now.

It would all be over soon, she thought, shifting her gaze from the simple pine casket with the Star of David etched onto the top, to the rabbi. She wouldn't be putting in the obligatory appearance at the Linton home following the graveside service. Johanna Linton, Jonathan's mother, had made that point patently clear. Instead, she would escape the bloodthirsty stares of Jonathan's family and mourn in private the loss of her business partner and dear friend. Until then, she'd maintain the status quo by remaining on the fringes and keeping her distance.

Distance was easier than involvement. Involvement required an emotional investment and risks she was no longer willing to take. Experience had taught her only her work was worthy of that kind of investment. Her work couldn't betray her. At least not the kind she performed now. Four years ago, it'd been a different story . . . and another unhappy ending.

Laurel bowed her head as the rabbi issued the final blessing over the casket, automatically crossing herself after the final *Amen* before she realized her mistake. The gold of her Rolex caught the sunlight. A surprise gift from Jonathan when he'd landed the St. Giovanni's restoration project. Had it only been a year ago? Jonathan had been so happy. The restoration of the *Gates of Paradise* had been a major coup, one she'd never dreamed would belong to Artifacts. But Jonathan had worked his magic and made it happen, catapulting them to worldwide recognition, and within a matter of weeks, they'd had more work than they could handle.

She let out a breath and quashed the memories. As she turned away, her black Italian heels ripped into the soft, damp grass. Quietly, she walked away and headed across the cemetery to where her car was parked while the mourners paid their respects to Jonathan's family. She'd already said her final good-byes to her dear friend. There was no need to do so again.

She adjusted her dark sunglasses and looked toward her car. For a brief second, she stilled, her fight or flight instincts warring for domination. After a slight moment's pause, she continued forward, her head held high. She could run, but they'd easily catch her, so why bother? Fighting she was accustomed to, it was as familiar to her as being alone. Besides, she'd known they'd come. It had been inevitable.

"This is rather dramatic," she said in a cool, calm voice intentionally devoid of emotion when she neared the front end of her sleek, silver Jag where the two detectives waited for her. Determination straightened her spine. She wasn't about to let Detectives Pete Teslenko and Gino Scanlon see they'd rattled her.

They'd questioned her for hours following her discovery of the body, and she hadn't fallen apart once. Not when they'd searched Artifacts, nor when they'd conducted an extensive search of her home. Keeping her emotions buried inside was a habit born from necessity, and her toughest survival skill she'd managed to hone to a fine polish over the years. To allow the overzealous detectives to witness how much their presence at Jonathan's funeral upset her wouldn't only be a waste of time, but a drain on valuable energy she suspected she would desperately need to see her through the next few hours. Besides, it went against everything she'd ever learned since she was ten years old. There was no reason to break from tradition at this point.

Teslenko and Scanlon looked at each other, speaking some silent dialogue she had no hope of understanding. She'd studied their faces and habits during those long, relentless hours of interrogation. Studying people was her business, especially when she knew without a doubt she'd be fighting for her freedom—perhaps even her life.

"Tell me, gentlemen. Is arresting me at Jonathan's funeral for the benefit of the family, or could it be for something as tasteless as the camera crew that showed up ten minutes ago?"

Detective Scanlon, an aging, portly fellow with a weathered face and more salt than pepper hair, stepped forward. His faded blue gaze was narrowed and cold. "Laurel Jennings," he said, slipping a pair of handcuffs from the leather pouch attached to his belt, "you are under arrest for the murder of Jonathan Linton."

Despite her determination to remain detached, hearing the words still made her flinch. She swore under her breath, then turned and handed her Fendi bag to Detective Teslenko as if he were nothing more important to her than a lackey to do her bidding. She'd known this was coming, she just hadn't known when, or expected it to happen so soon. Based on what she'd learned from observing Scanlon and Teslenko, two of L.A.'s finest, she should've known they'd arrest her at the funeral in front of not only Jonathan's family, friends, and business associates, but the Channel 4 news team as well. She didn't put it past the two glory seekers to have tipped off the press themselves about her impending arrest in the first place.

The murder of Jonathan Linton, one of the Beverly Hills social set, was news. Big news. The list of Lintons was indeed powerful, from a studio head all the way up to the nation's capital. When one of their own was brutally and viciously murdered in cold blood, the news not only made headlines, but warranted a sound bite or two during the commercial breaks of prime time.

If it bleeds, it leads.

This one bled all over the place.

Scanlon reached for her right arm. "You have the right to remain silent."

She watched helplessly as the mourners filtered into the parking area, their attention locked in her direction. They looked on in varying degrees of shock, surprise, and even a few not-so-surprised observers, as Scanlon slipped a chilled silver handcuff over her wrist.

The television reporter rushed them, shouting instructions to the cameraman.

"You have the right to an attorney," Scanlon continued, his voice as cold and emotionless as his eyes had been.

The reporter from Channel 4 thrust a microphone in her face. "Dr. Jennings, did you murder your business partner, Dr. Jonathan Linton?"

"If you cannot afford an attorney . . ."

Laurel struggled to keep her breathing even. *Don't show*

them anything! She silently repeated the mantra, shutting out the drone of Scanlon's voice as he issued her Miranda rights.

The ratcheting sound of the cuff pierced her concentration as Scanlon secured her left wrist. Her steady breathing faltered.

Getting nothing from her, the reporter peppered Scanlon with questions. "Detective, is Dr. Jennings being charged with the murder of Jonathan Linton? When will she be arraigned?"

Teslenko, Scanlon's much younger, cocky partner stepped in front of the reporter while Scanlon led Laurel across the blacktopped roadway. Amid the sea of Jags, Mercedes, Beemers and limos, the shit-brown, state-issued Chevy was anything but nondescript. The door creaked when it opened and Scanlon helped her inside. He shoved it closed, then signaled for his camera-preening partner.

She was going to jail. For a murder that, if Detective Teslenko was to be believed, had death penalty written all over it.

She'd need an attorney. A damn good one, too, because if the district attorney managed to get a conviction, he'd make sure she fried.

The general population of the Inmate Retention Center consisted heavily of drug dealers, gang bangers, and small-time crooks as well as some of the county's most notorious criminals. Overcrowding, under-staffing and inside deals occurred with such regularity, no one paid attention any longer. Just because the residents of the county cooler were behind bars didn't mean their illegal activities had waned, slowed, or dissipated, and were often enabled by the very men and women paid by the taxpayers to run herd over the underbelly of society.

The large, imposing multi-million dollar complex was

Laurel's new home away from home. She fought to control the fear twisting inside her. Having become adept at hiding her emotions years ago, she didn't worry about anyone knowing she was afraid. There had been situations in her past more frightening than what she was about to face. Neither the loud slam of the steel door, nor the finality of the computerized lock clicking into place made her flinch or show a speck of what was really going on inside her.

With her head held high and her back as straight as a refurbished six-hundred-year-old pilaster, Laurel walked in front of the female guard down a narrow corridor decorated in solid concrete. Turning right where the guard indicated, she entered a large dressing room area without frills, or privacy, more reminiscent of a locker room, sans the lockers. A young girl, dressed in a gray shirt and pants that resembled a doctor's scrubs, slid off a backless stool and tossed a dog-eared romance novel on the high counter. The kid looked no older than sixteen, with short-cropped black hair and the tattoo of a tear drop just below her left eye. Laurel didn't care to know the significance of that tattoo.

"You a six?" the kid asked, then, without waiting for an answer, crossed the room to a shelf containing Laurel's new wardrobe. She glanced down at Laurel's feet. Her brows rose a notch and a covetous light entered her dark brown eyes. "What size?"

"Five and a half," Laurel answered, vaguely wondering how this young girl recognized top quality, designer shoes. She seriously doubted someone with a tear drop tattoo shopped at Neiman's on a regular basis. Until recently, Sears had been considered high dollar to Laurel.

The trustee handed her a stack of gray then dropped a washed out pair of slip-on sneakers on top of the pile. "Strip down. Keep your bra and panties." Her tone was indicative of a recitation by rote. "Put the rest of your clothes in this bag. It'll be tagged and returned to you if you're released. You gotta take a shower then the guard will search you before you dress. You don't have to wash your hair, but you have to wet it through."

Laurel kept the guard and the trustee in her line of vision and did as instructed. The soap smelled of disinfectant, didn't lather worth a damn, and was just as worthless in removing the remaining ink stains from her earlier fingerprinting.

None of it mattered. She'd lived through worse and survived. She'd do so again.

She finished with the sorry excuse for a shower, then turned to find the guard watching her. Damn. She used to be better at looking over her shoulder. Somewhere in the past few years since leaving Boston, she'd gone soft. The illusion of safety did that to a person.

She wanted a towel, something to wrap around her hair and wipe away the water chilling her skin, but from the surly look on the guard's face, she had a feeling her request wouldn't be well-received. After suffering the indignity of a cursory body search, she was ordered to dress, handed a scratchy, woolen blanket and a man's black pocket comb before being ushered out of the dressing room through another series of buzzers and metal doors.

They were putting her in with the general population. For the first time in her life, the whiz kid who'd graduated high school at the age of fourteen, obtained a Ph.D. in chemistry from MIT by the age of eighteen, and achieved her second doctorate, in Art History, from UCLA after leaving Boston for good, was no one special. Laurel Jennings was nothing more than just another sorry story in gen pop.

The L.A. county jail didn't have a special wing for geniuses. No one cared that she'd once been responsible for dissecting antibodies that would save the lives of hundreds in the event of chemical warfare. No one gave a damn this wasn't the first time she had blood on her hands.

"This way." The guard prodded her with the tip of her baton, urging Laurel through the final doorway.

She kept her eyes on the back of another female guard, following her past a row of cells on the right, and dirty, barred windows on the left. The noise level hummed with conversation, televisions, and surprisingly, laughter. The guard stopped in front of an open cell door. So did the conversation of the five women occupying the ten-by-ten cell.

Using the tip of her baton again, the new guard pointed to a bunk against the far wall. "In there," she ordered in a harsh voice, then waited for Laurel to precede her into the cell. "Ten o'clock is lights out. Meals are at six, twelve, and six. You miss chow, that's your problem. Showers and head are through that door."

That door consisted of an open doorway in much the same layout as the drab cell. Three walls, metal bars, and no privacy.

Laurel nodded, then dropped the blanket on the vacant lower bunk once the guard left. The other women stared at her, but she ignored them and spread the blanket over the stained, bare mattress, determined not to think about the lack of sanitation.

"You're gonna have to pay for that bunk, Honey."

Laurel let out a sigh and turned, facing her new cell mate. Great, she thought. She wasn't here two minutes and already she was starring in a cheap remake of Corman's *The Big Doll House*, the kind that played on cable well after midnight.

When Teslenko and Scanlon had arrested her, she'd tried not to think about what could happen to her in jail. She was tough. She could handle it. In fact, she seriously doubted anything the burly woman standing center stage planned to dish out could be worse than what she'd already suffered in her life. From the long line of foster homes after her mother's death, to a betrayal so devastating her life had been forever changed, a night or two behind bars would be a breeze.

She lifted her chin a notch. "Sorry, but I left my platinum Visa card at home." She turned her back on the woman, dismissing her.

"I ain't looking for money, Honey."

Laurel sighed again and turned back around, nailing the woman with a narrowed gaze. "I really don't give a damn what you're looking for, so back the fuck off."

The nearly six foot, easily two-hundred pounds plus convict in desperate need of a lip and chin wax had the audacity to laugh. "Oooh, tough little bird, aren't you? Let's see how tough you are after I get what I want."

A slender woman with hair as black as midnight and eyes to match slid off the top bunk above Laurel. "Lay off her, Billie."

"Keep out of this, Rodriguez." Billie shot Rodriguez a heated glance before shifting her attention back to Laurel.

Billie took a threatening step toward her, but Laurel held her ground, her chin inching up another notch. The three remaining cell mates stared with a mixture of awe and excitement. "This is between me and Miss High and Mighty."

"I've already been charged with one murder," Laurel said, keeping her voice low, cool, and emotionless, and she hoped, threatening. She gave a careless shrug she was nowhere near feeling. Whatever worked. "One more doesn't much matter to me at this point."

Behind her, she heard Rodriguez's sharp intake of breath. "No shit?"

Laurel kept her attention on Big Burly Billie. "No shit."

A scrawny woman with pasty skin and the most lifeless brown eyes Laurel had ever seen, swung her feet to the floor and stood beside Billie. "Self defense?" the woman asked. "Right?"

Laurel slowly shook her head. "Wrong." God, she prayed she was playing out this scene right. She was on her own, and fighting for her life—again. And in more ways than one. "Cold blooded. Pre-meditated. Capital murder."

Laurel took a step toward Billie and tipped her head back to look directly into the woman's startled hazel eyes. "It's your call," she said in the same cool, careless tone that belied the trembling of her insides. "You can sleep in your bunk tonight or a pine box. I really don't give a rat's ass."

Chapter 2

DAMON METCALF BREATHED in the crisp, cool air of the Montana evening before lifting the stoneware mug to his lips. The calendar proclaimed spring, but Mother Nature had other plans if the light coating of snow covering the mountainous landscape was any indication of her cantankerous mood.

Deafening quiet surrounded him. The only break in the silence came from the brook that flowed along the edge of his property. He liked it this way, the quiet, the early signs of dusk settling over the rugged landscape. No congested freeways with bumper-to-bumper traffic. No noisy courtrooms during morning arraignment call. No loud hum of the district attorney's office still in action at the end of a long day.

He let out a weary sigh and propped his backside against the log railing. He sipped the strong, black coffee and watched, amused, as a pair of chubby squirrels went to battle over a pine cone that had fallen from a nearby evergreen. Oh yeah, he liked it this way—provided he ignored the stab of regret that walking away from a fast track career occasionally caused him.

He'd left his old life behind. He'd walked away without a backward glance, leaving behind a stellar career, friends, and even what was left of his family, all because he couldn't face himself in the mirror. Yet, after eighteen months, the sounds, the smells, even the sweet rush of adrenaline remained fresh in his memory. Unfortunately, so was the bitter taste of his ambition. As fresh as the nightmare he'd had just that morning.

All these months later, and he still awoke in the middle of the night in a cold sweat, blood roaring in his ears, and his heart pounding beneath his ribs. By now he'd have thought the constant chills that crept up on him would have waned, but considering the vividness of the dream that had been haunting him all day, he didn't believe he'd ever be able to put the past completely behind him.

So many memories. So many nights lying awake in his bed because anything was better than seeing the blood-soaked sidewalk.

He looked down at his comfortable, scuffed boots. For the flash of an instant he saw rich, blood red footprints across the wooden deck.

His footprints.

Willing away the images took effort. After a moment, only the wood planks of the deck, scarred with age, remained.

He glanced into his half-empty mug. Maybe he should've gone with the scotch he'd been contemplating. Or maybe added a shot or two of Bailey's to his coffee. Better yet, he should drink himself into oblivion, past the point of giving a shit. Maybe then he'd manage a night of dreamless sleep.

Regrets weren't all that had driven him from the warmth of his log home this evening. All day long he'd been plagued with a keen sense of dread that he hadn't been able to shake. Or maybe it was foreboding? He didn't have any answers.

His head started pounding. He squeezed his eyes shut against the pain. As usual, the pounding only increased.

Because he couldn't face what he'd done? Or maybe because he didn't like what he'd become? The answers springing to mind sent off another round of tiny pin hammers to his already pounding head.

Would it ever end?

Probably not. At least as long as the blood of Kendra Tarragona and her four-year-old daughter remained on his hands and seared in his conscience.

With a grunt of self-disgust, Damon pushed off the railing and strolled down the stone steps before he gave into the lure of a scotch-induced stupor. Following the worn, dirt foot path around the cabin to his workshop, he shoved open the heavy door and slipped inside, breathing in the deep, rich scents of wood oil and sawdust. The calm he sought evaded him.

He walked into the small office off to the left of the converted bunkhouse, flipped on the light, and dropped into the squeaky leather chair behind the handmade oak desk. The desk had been the first project of his "new" career after he'd traded in his code books for woodworking tools. Instead of studying precedents and arguing case law before the judicial system, he designed furniture. He spent his time building custom pieces, refurbishing antiques and dickering his prices good-naturedly with the local residents of Bozeman, Montana. He wasn't stinking rich, but he was more than comfortable. More importantly, all he managed to kill these days were a few trees.

Escaping the law had been easy. Unfortunately, he still had to face himself in the mirror on a daily basis, something that hadn't become any easier with the passage of time.

He settled down to work on the plans for an armoire he was designing and tried to lose himself in the creative process. The haunting images or that sense of dread gnawing at his gut refused to fade completely, but he eventually managed to ignore them—until the fax machine setting on the lateral filing cabinets behind his desk whirred to life, jerking him back to the present.

He checked the clock on the far wall, surprised to realize he'd worked well past nine o'clock. Once the fax stopped humming, he spun his chair around to view the transmission.

Stunned, he stared in disbelief at the first of the four sheets he'd plucked from the paper tray. The copy of the photograph was grainy and of poor quality, but he'd recognize that face anywhere.

Laurel.

He read the headline of the accompanying *Los Angeles Times* article three times before the words finally sank in, and still, he couldn't believe what he was seeing:

LINTON MURDERER ARRESTED

He read the article, then looked back at the photograph of Laurel again, carefully taking in the details. He couldn't see her hands, but he could tell she was handcuffed as someone assisted her into the back of an unmarked police vehicle.

Her stoic expression made him frown. Classic Laurel, he thought. A sight all too familiar.

Still, it just couldn't be possible. Laurel? Arrested for murder?

"Bullshit."

Laurel didn't have it in her to commit murder. Especially not one as brutal as the article implied.

Or did she?

Who knew better than he did exactly how cold and detached she could be? He also knew how passionate, loving, and caring she could be.

No, it just wasn't possible. No way could she have murdered Linton. He didn't believe it for a second.

People change.

Didn't he know it.

They hadn't spoken since he'd walked away, from his career, from his way of life, because he'd effectively cut himself off from anyone or anything that remotely reminded
him of the past. She may have been the one to call it quits
long before his ambitions ruined him, but that didn't mean
he didn't still care about her.

He briefly closed his eyes to shut down a new surge of
memories better left alone. He and Laurel had been over for
a long time. Four years to be exact. They'd been friends long
before they'd become lovers, and he'd foolishly believed they
could return to their former status quo. He'd been wrong
because what relationship had remained had become severely
strained. When he'd told her he was leaving Los Angeles for
good, she hadn't tried to talk him out of his decision. In
fact, he could've sworn she'd been relieved.

He opened his eyes and looked at the photograph again.
"Jesus, Laurel. What have you done?"

He read through the last two pages of the fax. He quickly
scanned the copy of her booking sheet, charging her with
murder in the first degree. The final page consisted of a
handwritten note asking *Isn't this* your *Laurel?* She hadn't
been *his* Laurel for long time.

The note also indicated Laurel's arraignment was scheduled for the day after tomorrow. From the large, bold scrawl,
he suspected the sender was male. The note wasn't signed,
nor was there any identifying information on the faxed pages.
It was illegal, but so was jaywalking. People did it all the
time.

Curious, he picked up the handset on the fax, then punched
*69 into the key pad. Not surprisingly, a voice recording in-
formed him the last number to call his line was restricted.

He replaced the handset, then scrubbed his hand down
his face. Before he could question his motives, he booted up
his computer and made travel arrangements for the next
available flight to Los Angeles. He didn't stop there, and re-

served a rental car and booked a room for a couple of nights at the Westin Bonaventure. The hotel was downtown, close enough to the criminal courts building and the Inmate Retention Center to make it a convenient choice.

Laurel wouldn't want him there, of that he had little doubt. But she needed help, if only to retain a damn good defense attorney for her.

His body hummed with a surge of anticipation that could only be caused by his decision to return to LA. What was he thinking, willfully walking back into the lion's den?

God help him, he hadn't looked so forward to anything in months. Eighteen of them to be exact.

Assistant District Attorney Alan Rosen sipped his second and last cognac for the night from the comfort of his study. CBS hadn't even carried the story of the hottest murder investigation since the Simpson case, and all NBC had bothered to run was Teslenko's sorry ass when they'd arrested Laurel Jennings.

"Grandstanding dick head," he muttered. He flipped over to TIVO to check the recording of the local ABC broadcast.

The Linton murder was a career maker, and it was all his. He hadn't checked CNN yet, but he suspected news of the arrest would be national by now. Tomorrow at the latest. And if not, he wasn't above calling a press conference himself to start the media train rolling.

Shortly after the new year when District Attorney Yates had announced his plans for retirement, the political movers and shakers had approached *him*, Alan Rosen, about running for the top prosecutorial seat. A few years as D.A., followed by a bid for the Senate, and from there, who knew?

He'd been preparing for such an opportunity for as long as he could remember. He'd risen above the sweat and calluses of his blue collar roots by attending the right schools, marrying the perfect politician's wife, all the way down to his two extremely photogenic sons currently away at an Eastern boarding school. Alan Rosen was the American dream personified.

A self-satisfied grin curved his mouth. Yes, who knew?

Straightening, he temporarily set aside his ambitions and opened the investigation file he'd spent the better part of the evening reviewing. He had means and opportunity. He had fiber samples, hair samples, and even blood evidence. He had Laurel Jennings's fingerprints all over the murder weapon. Hell, he had everything but a solid motive and a signed confession. And best of all, Jennings had no verifiable alibi.

Motive wasn't a necessary ingredient to prove murder. But it sure would make it easier to convince the jury that a death penalty conviction was the only possible decision on a charge of murder in the first degree.

Last he'd heard, she had yet to request an attorney, but Laurel Jennings was no pauper, not by a long shot. He practically salivated at the thought of going up against any one of the city's A-team defense counsels. The bigger the name, the better the coverage. All part of the machine he planned to manipulate that would go a long way in guaranteeing him a political future beyond the prosecutor's office.

He flipped through the photographs of the murder scene he'd reviewed at least a hundred times already, stopping when he came to a 5x7 publicity still of his prime suspect that Detective Scanlon had appropriated from the university where Jennings taught graduate courses part-time. She was a looker, he'd give her that much. But according to Teslenko, Laurel Jennings was one ice-cold bitch. Cold enough to butcher a grown man, obviously.

Rosen couldn't argue with Detective Teslenko's assessment. He knew the Jennings woman, not intimately, but they did occasionally move in the same social circles and he'd made her acquaintance. The last time he'd seen her had been at a charity auction with the victim. She might be a nice little trophy to show off at cocktail parties, but in bed, he'd bet she was as responsive as a corpse.

It was her eyes, he decided. They were a spooky shade, not vibrant enough to be called violet, more like a deep shade of lavender. "Spooky," he muttered, then polished off the last of the cognac.

But was she cold and calculated enough to commit murder, at least in a jury's mind? That was what he had to prove beyond a reasonable doubt to twelve men and women and two alternates. And without motive, his job would be that much more challenging.

In his experience, murders like Linton's happened for one of two reasons—to cover up another crime or betrayal, whether real or perceived. Had Linton betrayed Jennings? Something had to have caused the Ice Queen to snap. Or was her reason for killing Linton nothing more simple than greed?

Rosen shrugged. He'd figure it out—one way or another. His job was to get a jury to convict. And this one was capital—for the simple reason that Jennings profited from the death of her partner. How difficult could it be to prove that Jennings's only motive for killing her business partner was to gain total control of a company that had quadrupled its profits in less than a year's time? Men, and women, have killed for less.

Her attorney would raise arguments as to why she wasn't guilty. But once he proved otherwise, it'd be a snap to convince a jury the little lady deserved nothing less than being strapped down cruciform style with a needle full of good-night-sweet-ice-queen-juice shoved into her arm.

Lucky for him, his ambitions demanded nothing less.

"Conner, you need to see this."

Conner Tillman didn't bother to look up from the data

he was reading as his wife, Evelyn, stormed into the den amid a flurry of silk and an overdose of Estee Lauder. Everything was important to Evelyn, from Macy's semi-annual sale to the local animal shelter's need for funds, or whatever charity she'd become involved with that week.

He let out a patient sigh when she snatched the remote control from the glass-topped cocktail table. She pressed the button, turning the television to the Fox News channel.

She pointed to the wide screen television set. "It's Laurel," she said, her voice mingled with equal parts alarm and dismay. "Oh my God, Conner. It's really her."

Now she had his attention.

Conner set the research notes from the department head of the Massachusetts Research Institute's bio-tech division aside and whipped off his reading glasses. "Turn it up, dear." He leaned forward on the butter soft leather sofa, watching the taped footage in stunned silence as Laurel Jennings was led away in handcuffs and assisted into the backseat of an unmarked police vehicle.

Although he'd kept tabs on her since she'd left the Institute, he hadn't actually seen her in years. Like a good "daughter," she sent the obligatory holiday and birthday cards and gifts, and Evelyn always received a phone call the third Sunday of every month. Always in the afternoon, always when Laurel knew he would be on the golf course or at the driving range.

Laurel had certainly changed from the gangly, shy teenaged prodigy they'd taken into their home into a stunningly beautiful young woman. The world could've been hers, too, if she hadn't turned her back on the Institute. He never should have let her leave, but the ultimate decision hadn't been his.

Little did she know, the decision hadn't been hers, either.

Evelyn settled onto the sofa beside him, shaking her head.

Her disbelief and dismay were evident, as the reporter told of the investigation into the murder of Jonathan Linton that had led to Laurel's arrest.

"Can't you do something?" Evelyn asked. "Do you think we should go to her?"

Conner didn't answer. His mind was elsewhere, digesting the facts and the reality that after four years, he could very well have just been handed the opportunity to bring Laurel and her beautiful mind back to the Institute where she belonged. Back under his control.

Laurel's departure from the Institute had cost him. He might still be regarded as the head of MRI, but his position had suffered for a time when the directors made the decision to allow Laurel to leave. She'd been his responsibility, and in their eyes, he'd failed the Institute.

Her coming to live with him hadn't been an accident, either, but she'd never known. No one had, not even Evelyn, who'd unwittingly brought Laurel to his attention. His wife had flourished in her role as foster mother to the shy, but brilliant fourteen-year-old girl who'd been recruited by MIT. Big Brother had been watching and waiting for the right opportunity. When the time had been ripe, actions had been taken and the responsibility had fallen to Conner to mold the young prodigy to suit the needs of the Institute.

He'd played his own role to perfection, as well. The caring father figure. The concerned champion to an emotionally damaged young girl. It had taken some time, and a whole lot of patience, but Laurel had eventually blossomed under his carefully constructed guidance, even if he couldn't rightfully accept all the credit himself. Evelyn's loving nature had played an important role in Laurel's emotional well-being, and his wife had done a stellar job of creating a safe haven for the girl. But he'd been the one responsible for grooming her for her place at the Institute, albeit indirectly. When Laurel had come to him and said she'd wanted to go to work, he'd pretended to pull a few strings and gotten her a job as a lab assistant to the one man Conner had trusted, his oldest friend, Scott Metcalf.

At first, not even Scott had been aware of the machinations surrounding Laurel, and Conner had made the drastic misjudgment of trusting Scott with the truth. That knowledge had eventually cost Scott his life, and nearly cost Conner his career.

But all that was about to change.

Evelyn's hand grasped his. "Isn't there something we can do for her?" she asked, her voice laced with concern. Dear, sweet Evelyn. After nearly forty years of marriage, she still had no clue.

He turned his hand in hers and laced their fingers together in a gesture he knew she'd find comforting. "I'll make a few phone calls."

Conner still had power, with or without the backing of the directors. A little ingenuity would be in order, of course, but he knew how to play the strings to perfection. Before long, Laurel Jennings would be back where she belonged— under his total and complete control.

And there wouldn't be a damn thing she could do about it.

Chapter 3

IN FULL LOTUS position, hands on her knees with her palms upraised but her eyes wide open, Laurel took in long, slow measured breaths and stared at the painted cinder block wall. Seated in the center of the bunk atop the prison-issue scratchy blanket, she attempted to meditate.

Attempt, being the operative word.

She'd never fully mastered the theory of clearing her mind. Her brain simply didn't work that way. So she did what she always did in her quasi-meditative state—she made lists.

Tonight, however, she had only been able to conjure one list, and it definitely ran on the short side.

Who wanted Jonathan dead?

Not a single suspect sprang to mind for one simple reason—everyone adored Jonathan. At least everyone she knew who knew Jonathan, from their clients, to the vendors who supplied Artifacts, and especially their meager staff at Artifacts.

Jonathan had possessed a certain charm that even she hadn't been immune to, and he'd had a talent for convincing her to do things she'd rather not. Like the time he'd persuaded her to attend a wrap party for one of the biggest budget films his uncle's studio had produced in years. She honestly hadn't seen the purpose, not to mention that she'd never felt comfortable at parties. Small talk was another art she'd never mastered. But Jonathan had cajoled her until she'd been unable to deny him. Damn if he hadn't walked away from the party with a commission, too, for one of Hollywood's most famed and revered, if more temperamental, actresses who'd hired them to restore an original Chippendale highboy. The job hadn't paid all that well, but the actress had been so pleased, they'd received several referrals as a result. Small jobs, all, but what Jonathan had liked to call their bread-and-butter commissions. It'd been those smaller commissions that had kept them afloat in the early days of Artifacts.

No closer to a list of possible suspects, she blew out a steady stream of breath and glanced around the dim cell. Lights out, she'd discovered, was merely a figure of speech. The only differences between lights on or out were the television sets, hanging from support brackets to the walls outside the cells, no longer blaring to a wide variety of channels, and a quieting of the general population by several decibels. The lights had been dimmed a degree or two, casting a strange, vapor-like jaundiced glow, making the dreary cells even more bleak and depressing.

A pair of over-washed sneakers suddenly appeared in Laurel's line of vision, followed by the long, slender legs of Rodriguez as she slid from the upper bunk. Without invitation, she climbed onto Laurel's mattress and sat.

"You'll get used to it," Rodriguez said in a hushed tone, but loud enough to be heard over the snuffling snores of Big Billie. Her fifth cellmate, a petite blonde they called Liza, whom she'd learned was awaiting trial on the charges of manufacturing and trafficking methamphetamine, slept quietly on the lumpy mattress above Big Billie's lower bunk. The other cellmate, she'd discovered, the one with the pasty face, was pulling a sixty-day stretch for criminal trespassing.

"God, I hope not," Laurel answered quietly.

Rodriguez shook a Marlboro from a crumpled pack, then graciously offered a cigarette to Laurel. "The first night is always the worst."

Laurel declined Rodriguez's generous offer. If she'd learned anything about life behind bars in her first hours of incarceration, it was that tobacco of any kind was the end-all-be-all of inmate currency. It bought extra blankets, shampoo, clean towels. Even tampons, which were considered contraband for reasons beyond Laurel's comprehension.

Laurel looked at the other woman. "Can I ask what you're in for?"

"I was set up."

Naturally.

Her second lesson—everyone was innocent.

"Asked the wrong guy for a date," Rodriguez expounded, then drew deeply on her cigarette. "Got ninety days with time served for solicitation of an undercover cop."

"A sting operation?" For some reason, Laurel thought those were a product of Hollywood, or something done on special editions of *Dateline* or *20/20*. But then she didn't normally associate with criminal types, either, so what did she know? Apparently, not so much.

Rodriguez's wide mouth split into a grin. "Maybe you're not so green, after all."

Laurel shrugged. "Lucky guess." She watched television. It was her one true vice. She found it helped quiet her mind, especially in the middle of the night when the demons haunted her the most. She had a new food dehydrator and a set of kitchen knives guaranteed to never dull to prove it, too.

"You get props, girl. Handling Billie the way you did. Impressive."

"She backed down first." She hadn't really done anything except stand up to the burly woman. If she'd wanted to,

Billie could've easily pulverized Laurel. Maybe that wouldn't have been such a raw deal. At least she could've spent the night in the infirmary where she might have been able to catch a few hours' sleep. Where she wouldn't be so afraid to close her eyes.

"Never let the bastards know you're afraid of them," Rodriguez offered sagely.

"What makes you think I was afraid?" So much for her pulling off the tough-chick act.

"You ain't never been in jail before. Ain't the type."

No, but she'd been a prisoner, only a different kind. "Oh, and what type is that?"

Rodriguez drew on her cigarette and regarded Laurel through a ribbon of blue smoke. "Prim. All proper like. Smart, too. You talk like a professor or somethin'."

"That obvious, huh?"

Rodriguez flicked an ash over the side of the mattress onto the floor. "It's written all over you."

Wonderful. Just what she needed. A bull's-eye taped to her ass in a place where backstabbing, the literal kind, was second nature.

"So you really kill a guy?"

Laurel shrugged. "That's what they say."

"But you didn't do it." Skepticism filled Rodriguez's black-as-midnight eyes.

"You sure about that?"

Rodriguez gave her a sly grin. "Like I said, you ain't the type."

"The evidence the D.A. has says otherwise."

According to Detective Scanlon, they had DNA, opportunity, even her fingerprints on the murder weapon. But they were so wrong. She had no reason to kill Jonathan. He was her business partner, her best friend. And if the gossips were to be believed, her lover.

"You'll get off," Rodriguez theorized after stubbing out her smoke on the metal bunk frame. "You got money, you get off. Got a lawyer yet?"

Laurel thought about that for a moment. She had money, but no lawyer, not even the law firm Artifacts kept on retainer for various contractual matters. She'd contacted Howard Barnes when she'd been arrested, but he'd informed her that it would be a conflict of interest for his firm to represent her in a criminal matter for which she was accused of murdering one of his clients, and that his firm didn't practice criminal law. Considering the fat retainer check she'd signed just a month ago, his attitude had irritated her. When she'd promptly pointed out the absurdity of his statement, reminding him that she, too, was one of his clients, he'd at least promised to refer her to another firm, albeit reluctantly.

She hoped like hell Howard kept his word. At this point, she had no other choice as it was all the hope she had to cling to at the moment.

"I'm working on it," she told Rodriguez.

"Make sure you get a good one or like me you'll get stuck with whatever overworked, piece-of-shit public defender has morning roll call when you're arraigned."

"That's bad?"

"Ninety days with time served and I didn't even flash my tits? You tell me," Rodriguez said cynically. "How hard would you work when the pay's the same whether your client does jail time or not?"

"There is such a thing as taking pride in one's work." A philosophy she and Jonathan had lived by.

Rodriguez's soft laughter did nothing to mask the years of bitterness from a life of hard times and disappointment. "Maybe on your planet. On the third rock from the sun, reality bites."

Laurel let out a sigh. She had a feeling her reality was going to bite hard enough to leave scars. Big, nasty, ugly ones.

"When will you be released?" Laurel asked.

"Day after tomorrow," Rodriguez answered. "First thing I'm doing is heading across town for a Tommy burger."

Sounded like heaven to Laurel, even if she didn't have the slightest clue what a Tommy burger was all about. Anything was better than the carb-ridden slop which was supposedly beef stroganoff they'd been served at dinner.

"You got a name?" Rodriguez asked her.

"Laurel Jennings," she said. "Doc—just call me Laurel."

"I'm Cha-cha." Rodriguez extended her hand, which Laurel shook.

"Cha-cha?" Laurel didn't want to think how Rodriguez had acquired that particular moniker.

The other woman smiled sheepishly. "Carlotta."

Laurel smiled back. "It's pretty."

Carlotta, aka Cha-cha, shrugged her slender shoulders, then scooted off the mattress. "You tell anyone and *I'll* kick your ass." The threat fell short due to the half smile still hovering on her full lips.

"Get some sleep," Cha-cha added before climbing back up on her bunk. "You're starting to look like shit, Jennings."

Laurel didn't bother to enlighten Cha-cha that it was physiologically impossible to appear thus. All she'd receive was a blank stare anyway, so why bother? Instead, she stretched out atop the thin blanket, kept her eyes open and tried to quiet her racing mind.

Bastard. That's what they would call her baby. A love child. A bastard. Born on the wrong side of the blanket. No doubt there were other names and clichés she'd exorcised from her memory, but no one would dare call the heir apparent anything but rich.

Her baby, *their* child would have its rightful place in the Linton family tree. All she had to do was keep it together and keep playing it smart.

There were worse things than being called a few cruel names, but nothing compared to being dirt poor. Nothing more frightening than not knowing where to sleep at night, or where the next meal was coming from . . . or what she'd had to stoop to in order to get that meal.

Thankfully, those days were behind her. She'd come far, and it hadn't been easy, but she'd done it with only her wits to guide her. A little ingenuity went a long way.

She let out a long, slow, even breath to keep the demons at bay. She tipped her head back and looked up at the stars overhead in the cloudless midnight sky, dimmed by the bright lights of the city. If she believed in God, she might have found comfort in knowing *He* was watching over her and her baby. But she gave up on that deity years ago. What kind of God allowed a person to suffer like she'd suffered?

She tugged the expensive wool coat Jonathan had given her for her birthday last winter, pulling it tighter. How she missed him. The way his brilliant blue eyes sparkled when he smiled. The gentle way he treated her. How could things have gone so wrong?

He'd said he loved her. And he'd lied. She shouldn't have been surprised. They all lied—eventually. Another fact of her sorry-assed life she'd learned at an early age.

Standing on the soft ground above his grave gave her an odd sense of comfort. A chilled spring breeze ruffled her bangs just as she was convinced she'd felt a feathery, light flutter in her tummy. Her breath caught and she placed her leather-gloved hand against her flat abdomen. Standing over Jonathan's final resting place, she took the movement as a sign. An omen of good things to come, an omen that she'd made the right decision this time. An even better life, which she deserved and had every right to attain for herself and her unborn child.

Their unborn child.

She had plans. Big plans. When the cops arrested Laurel

Jennings right there at the funeral, she had known she'd never have a better opportunity to make her next move. Without that snobby bitch's interference, she and her baby, *their* baby, stood a chance at real happiness. She didn't know what, if anything, Jonathan had told that bitch about their relationship, but as long as the cops kept Jennings locked up, her chances of getting what rightfully belonged to her were unlimited.

She might not have the Linton name, but she had the Linton heir. And it didn't get much better than that for someone like her.

Provided she kept it together and kept playing it smart.

The beauty of insomnia was that it gave Gino Scanlon time to think. The problem with thinking was that it fed his insomnia like a thirsty drunk falling off the wagon.

For the last three hours he'd lain in bed, his mind running through the facts of the Linton murder investigation again and again. He dissected every piece of evidence until he couldn't think about it another minute.

Dammit, he'd done his job. They'd made an arrest. The DA was happy, and ADA Rosen was damned near orgasmic at the possibility of a conviction. The victim's family was pleased that justice was being served. So then why was his gut churning with acid that had nothing to do with the cold pizza he'd chowed down in a sorry excuse for supper?

Because something stank. And it sure as hell wasn't the stench of the city filtering through the open window of his downtown, third floor apartment, either.

He rolled up from the bed and sat on the edge, no closer to an answer than when he'd arrested Laurel Jennings. With his elbows braced on his knees, he hung his head in his hands and briefly considered popping open the bottle of sleeping pills the doctor had prescribed for his insomnia, just to escape the torment he'd witnessed in her big-eyed gaze that so belied the cold exterior she showed him. Fifty milligrams would garner him at least four hours of dreamless sleep, but he'd feel like shit come morning, and he'd still have no answers as to why the investigation continued to nag him.

He lifted his head and looked at the cordless phone resting on the night stand next to the alarm clock. The large red digits proclaimed the hour past midnight. Not that he had anyone to call, at this hour, or any hour for that matter. If it weren't for the occasional wrong number and telemarketers, the only time the damn thing rang was when the department needed him. He hadn't spoken to his ex-wife in months, not since she'd gone and married that sap of a semiretired insurance salesman. His kids wouldn't be too thrilled to hear from him, either, especially at one-twenty-eight in the morning.

He pushed off the bed and headed into the bathroom to take a leak. The countdown to his retirement had begun. With less than four months left until he turned in his shield and collected his pension, he was officially a short timer. Then what the fuck was he supposed to do with himself?

Retired cops fell into three categories. Either they didn't have the guts to leave the life behind them and became pathetic, aging private investigators, or they bought sail boats and cruised up and down the coast bored out of their skulls, or they swallowed the lethal end of a pistol and bought the farm with a self-inflicted terminal case of lead poisoning.

Since he got seasick standing in the shower too long, he supposed he would join the pathetic group that couldn't let go and either join forces with another retired cop, or maybe even start up his own PI firm. He'd take grunt work from the legal eagles, hiring himself out to track down and interview witnesses, search for missing persons and follow around deadbeat dads or cheating husbands. It sure as shit beat that third category.

Without turning on a light, he walked through the darkened apartment and into the kitchen where he yanked open the fridge. More cold pizza, a carton of half eaten sweet-and-sour pork, dried out fried rice and a six pack of soda awaited him, along with a couple of shriveled oranges and a quarter slab of moldy cheese. He chucked the dried-out fruit and rotten cheese into the garbage can, then snagged a can of caffeine-free Diet Coke. Maybe he could get to know his grandkids when he retired. Only God knew how he'd pull that one off since his son and two daughters barely spoke to him, and when they did, he was left feeling like he'd just interrogated a star witness to a crime.

He lowered his girth into a cheap vinyl kitchenette chair and drummed his fingers on the veneer table top in time to the rhythmic ticking of the analog clock above the stove. He'd investigated enough crime scenes to know a random killing when he saw one, and as far as he was concerned, the Linton murder didn't come close. One of the ugliest cases of a slice and dice he'd seen in his long career. In his opinion, it'd been personal. Damn personal, too, based on the horrific state in which they'd found the body.

Acid continued to churn in his gut, followed by an unfamiliar chill that shot down his spine. The evidence had pointed to only one person, and the arrest they'd made had been based solely on that evidence. But what had driven Laurel Jennings into a murderous rage? According to the witnesses he'd questioned, Jennings and Linton had been tight. What made someone as cool as she seemed snap? He wasn't buying Rosen's greed theory. It didn't fit. Even when he factored in the lack of a solid alibi, no sign of forced entry, and the most damning of all, Jennings's fingerprints all over the murder weapon, the murder still made little sense, but he'd had no choice but to arrest her.

Jennings might be the cold and distant type, but did she really have what it took to basically tear a grown man to shreds? Linton had been no puny runt, but an athletic, six-foot-plus guy. In Gino's mind, none of it added up, regardless of the evidence. Still, the murder had been personal. That had to count for something, didn't it, even if he couldn't figure out the why?

Four hours of dreamless sleep suddenly sounded like a good idea. He took a swig of soda and wandered back to the bedroom, popping the lid off the bottle of pills. He dropped down atop the covers and waited for the acid churning in his gut to absorb the pill and deliver him into a blissful, drug-induced sleep where unanswered questions couldn't haunt him.

Chapter 4

B Y THE TIME Damon's plane landed at LAX the following afternoon, doubt had settled around him like a too tight wool coat on a hot summer day. Stifling, not to mention uncomfortable as hell.

He inched along the 405 freeway and wondered again at the wisdom of his decision to come back. It wasn't like Laurel had asked for his help, for crying out loud. She hadn't even called him. Not that she would. She'd chew off her own foot before she asked anyone to lift a finger for her. Stubbornly independent, that was Laurel, all right. To a fault.

Which was the exact reason he'd taken it upon himself to hop on the first flight out of Bozeman that morning and come running back. Back to a place he swore he hated. Yet here he was, back amid the smog, the crowds, the grime, and especially the crime that had once been the mainstay of his livelihood.

Laurel would hate him being back even more.

The wisdom of his decision? What wisdom?

He cranked up the radio, a classic rock station he secretly admitted he missed, and changed lanes to catch the ramp for the 110 freeway. With a flick, he tossed his sunglasses onto the passenger seat. A dull reddish haze currently overcast the early afternoon sky, but he suspected the cloud cover would soon part for yet another bright sunny day in good ol' Southern California. The home of Dodger dogs, Laker games, traffic jams, and Disneyland. He supposed he did miss attending the occasional football game, but the Raiders have given up on L.A. to return to Oakland and even the Rams had bailed to St. Louis, so what was the point?

He didn't bother with a map. Whatever he may have forgotten about traversing through the maze of freeways in the southland could be made up simply by following the signs. He was, after all, in Los Angeles.

He probably shouldn't have bothered with finding a hotel, either. Chances were Laurel would take one look at him and tell him to take a hike. But as of this morning's phone call to the court clerk, no attorney of record was on file for the defense in *State v. Jennings*. He had his doubts about the cream of the criminal defense crowd lining up to represent the woman accused of murdering the nephew of one of L.A.'s most powerful families. A smart lawyer, or an ambitious one, certainly didn't bite the hand he hoped would one day scratch his back. Which made Damon the perfect lawyer for Laurel. He had nothing to gain, or lose.

Still, she could refuse to allow him to represent her, which he fully expected. That was her right. A stupid move, but her right just the same. For all he knew, he could be back in Bozeman tomorrow. Back to the peace and quiet.

Back to pretending he wasn't bored out of his skull.

"Jennings!"

Laurel swung her feet to the floor and looked over at the guard. "Yes?"

"Your lawyer's here."

Relief flooded her as she slid off the bunk. Despite her eyes being grainy from lack of sleep, the pounding of her

head from insufficient levels of caffeine to sustain her throughout the day, and her nerves being stretched to the limit, she
couldn't help feeling as if things were looking up for the
first time in the past twenty-four hours. The glimmer of
hope she'd clung to throughout the long night had paid off.
Howard Barnes had kept his promise.

"Remember what I told you," Cha-cha whispered to her.
"Tell him to ask for O.R."

Laurel nodded and followed the guard past the long row
of cells and through the same series of locked doors she'd
passed upon her arrival yesterday. In a matter of moments,
she'd finally meet with her criminal defense attorney. She
had no idea who Howard had retained to represent her, but
at this point, she didn't much care. From her vantage point,
she was hardly in a position to be too selective.

All she wanted at the moment was sweet, blessed freedom.
On that score, she wasn't about to hold her breath, despite
Cha-cha's jailhouse advice about requesting she be released
on her own recognizance. Last she'd heard, people arrested
for murder one were rarely sprung from the slammer to
await trial, especially without bail. Even O.J.'s highly publi-
cized "Dream Team" hadn't been able to get their contro-
versial client released.

Still, she couldn't completely give up hope. With any luck
whatsoever, her attorney might be able to get her out on
bail. However astronomical the sum, it'd be worth every
cent. During the long hours stretched out on her bunk in the
puny cell she'd come to one solid conclusion, she had to get
out of there. Someone killed Jonathan and it wasn't her.
And unless she could determine who would want her business partner and dearest friend dead, she'd very likely spend
the rest of her life in jail for a crime she didn't commit.

At the end of another long corridor, the guard instructed
her to turn left despite the sign indicating that the visitor's

area was located in the opposite direction. Federal law didn't provide for prisoner privacy, but because she was meeting with her attorney, she'd at least be afforded the illusion of such due to attorney-client privilege.

"Wait right there," the guard said in a bored tone as Laurel approached the last heavy metal door on the right.

Laurel did as instructed, waiting while the guard unlocked the door, then peered inside. After a brisk nod, Laurel entered the spartanly furnished, windowless room.

The door clanged shut behind her and she flinched. The clang of metal, and the dread she felt clear to the bottom of her soul whenever she heard the loud, despondent sound, weren't things she'd ever become accustomed to, no matter how many years she might have to spend behind bars.

With nothing else to do but wait for her lawyer to show, she walked to the table, pulled out one of the metal folding chairs, and sat. Time ticked by slowly. She knew because she watched the black-framed clock on the wall ahead of her.

2:34 P.M.

She drummed her fingertips on the imitation wood grain surface of the cheap table. Who wanted Jonathan dead?

2:35 P.M.

She slumped back against the cold metal seat. Not a single person she could think of, no matter how many times she attempted to summon a list of possible suspects. Everybody loved Jonathan.

Well, someone hadn't. But who was what she needed to find out if she hoped to be acquitted.

2:35:30 P.M.

She crossed her feet at the ankles and let out a long, drawn out sigh. God, why had she gone back to Artifacts that night to talk to Jonathan? Why hadn't she just called him instead?

2:36:15 P.M.

Another twenty seconds ticked by when she finally heard the scrape of the guard's key in the door. She instantly sat up straighter, folded her hands in front of her on the table, and vainly attempted to appear serene. A next to impossible task when her insides were jumping and twitching with a combination of fear and nervousness.

The door pushed open and she stared in absolute shock and disbelief. Damon? Here? How on earth was it possible? How did he even know she was in trouble?

Bad news travels fast.

"Hello, Laurel," he said once the door clanged shut again.

Once again, she flinched. Although, she was unsure whether from the loud clang of the metal door slamming closed or the sound of Damon's velvety deep voice. It'd been months since she'd last seen him, a meeting that hadn't gone very well, either. In fact, it'd been a disaster.

"What are you doing here?" she blurted.

His left eyebrow rose a fraction as he crossed the small room and set a legal-sized pressboard folder on the table. "Now is that any way to greet an old friend?"

He remained standing, and she frowned. She wasn't sure what was expected of her. Should she stand? Was it appropriate to give him a hug? She suddenly felt as awkward as a teenager.

"Is that what we are now? Old friends?" They'd been more than that, and they both knew it. Once upon a time she'd believed him capable of hanging the moon and stars. But that was a long time ago. The moon and stars had other keepers, ones capable of more than she'd ever imagined. Which was why she and Damon could never be "friends." It wasn't safe—for him.

"I'd like to think so," he said as he reached for her hand, tugging gently to pull her to her feet.

Still stunned by his presence, she didn't think to offer a

protest when he pulled her to him and slipped his arms around her, holding her close. For the breath of an instant, she stiffened, uncomfortable with the physical contact of another human being. How long had it been since someone had touched her? Even with her superior brain power, she had trouble calculating the exact time and place.

Damon only tightened his hold on her until she eventually relaxed. For the moment, she pretended they really were old friends. That she wasn't in jail for murder, that she'd never had to lie to him to end their relationship. In those moments she pretended she really was safe in his arms, that no one would be aware of her every move. She gave in to the fantasy that *they* wouldn't know Damon had returned to L.A. just to see her because she was in serious trouble.

While the stolen moments slid away, she greedily took the comfort he offered in the gentle warmth of his embrace. So strong. Sure. Protective. So what if it were all nothing but a fantasy? It was her fantasy, dammit.

Much sooner than she wanted him to, he loosened his hold and settled his hands on her shoulders. "Are you all right?" he asked.

She nodded. The caring and compassion in his eyes tripped her pulse. Something lodged in her throat. Her heart, perhaps? She didn't doubt it.

He searched her face, his expression full of concern. "You're sure?"

She nodded again, not trusting her voice not to betray her.

"Is there anything I can get for you?"

A tremulous smile tugged her lips. "Freedom," she whispered, the single word thick with emotion.

"I'll do my best." He smiled then, one of those full blown, heart-stopping ones that always made her pulse race just a little bit faster. It might have been four years since they'd been lovers, but that didn't mean she'd ever stopped loving him, not completely, anyway. Oh sure, she'd gotten over him. She'd had no choice. But there was always a part of her heart reserved for him, no matter what.

Which was why he couldn't stay. She couldn't allow it. She still cared for him too much to let him risk his neck for her. The world was a better place with Damon in it, even if he couldn't be in her world.

Needing space and time to think, she stepped away from him and returned to the cold metal chair. "Why are you here, Damon?"

He took the chair opposite her. "Because you need a lawyer."

"And you know this because . . . ?"

He flipped open the pressboard folder he'd brought with him. "It's all over the news, Laurel," he said without looking at her.

"I thought you quit practicing law."

He slid a pen from his pocket and looked at her. "So did I," he said.

Was it her imagination or did the color of his eyes actually brighten slightly? With anticipation, she wondered? Apparently she wasn't the only one living with regrets.

"And you were a prosecutor, not a criminal defense attorney," she reminded him.

"True. But you know what they say—the best defense attorneys are all former prosecutors."

Another time, another place, she would have smiled at his arrogance. Today it only made her nervous.

He pulled a yellow legal pad from the file folder and uncapped his expensive-looking pen. "Your arraignment is scheduled for tomorrow morning."

"How did you know?"

A half smile tipped up one corner of his mouth. "I picked

up the court's file before coming here. I'll have a copy of the DA's file in the morning before your arraignment. I need to see the evidence they—"

"No," she said, frowning. She shook her head. "I meant how did you know that I didn't have an attorney?"

"Does it matter?"

"To me it does."

"A little birdie faxed me."

Her frown deepened. Who would do such a thing? And why? It wasn't like she had an unlimited supply of friends who were rooting for her. Quite the opposite.

A chill of fear chased down her spine and settled with dread in her belly, weighing her down. Her own personal Big Brother.

The bastards were always watching. At least she assumed they were, making certain she remained silent. But if that were indeed the case, why would they advise Damon, of all people, of her current situation? It didn't make sense. He was the last person they'd want her associating with, and she had the broken heart to prove it.

She stood so fast, the chair tipped and clattered to the floor. "You can't represent me."

"Yes, Laurel. I can. It's not like my license to practice—"

"No," she blurted. "I won't allow it." She wouldn't allow them to hurt him, too. Not Damon. *That* she couldn't handle.

He leaned back in the chair and crossed his arms. "And you have so many other options," he said sarcastically. "I didn't exactly pass a bunch of hungry defense attorneys lining up outside to represent you."

Agitated, she moved around the small space, but with nowhere to go, she returned to the table, picked up the chair and sat. God, she'd give just about anything for some fresh air. Clear her head so she could think straight. And come up with another convincing lie he'd believe.

"Howard Barnes is sending someone to represent me."

Damon's gaze turned skeptical. "Sure he is."

"He promised." Reluctantly, but a promise was a promise.

"Yeah, and he obviously lied."

"You don't know that."

"Come on, Laurel. Even you're not that naïve."

"You're wrong about Howard. His firm has represented Artifacts from day one. He'll keep his promise."

"How did you come to hire Barnes's firm to represent Artifacts?"

"One of his other partners is Johanna Linton's personal attorney."

"I rest my case."

"What do you mean?"

"Barnes isn't going to do you any favors, Laurel. Not if he hopes to keep all those Linton billable hours in his firm." Damon leaned forward and pinned her with his gaze. "It's either me or whoever is covering arraignments in the PD's office tomorrow. You could get lucky. Maybe you'll get some bozo fresh out of law school hoping to make a name for himself. Win or lose won't make much of a difference, not that he'll be any threat to Rosen. Notoriety is notoriety, right? Just make sure they spell his name correctly in the papers."

You'll get stuck with whatever overworked, piece-of-shit public defender has morning roll call.

She didn't know which was worse, some greenhorn hoping to build a career—the overworked piece of shit Cha-cha warned her about—or Damon. It didn't matter. She was screwed unless she got out of this hell hole. Period.

"Okay," she said. "You can represent me at the arraignment, but then you have to promise to find me a good criminal defense attorney. I don't want you representing me."

Something in his gaze shifted and those glorious green eyes that once looked at her with so much caring and affection turned as hard as stone. He nodded abruptly and stood, scooping up documents they hadn't even discussed, returning them to the folder.

"I'll see you at the arraignment then." He turned and walked to the door where he rapped heavily against the small glass pane.

She hated that she'd hurt him, but she'd had no other choice. She absolutely could not allow him to represent her. Not if she cared about him, and dammit, she did. She'd never stopped.

"Damon?"

For a moment, she thought he was going to ignore her, but then he finally turned to look at her.

The coldness in his eyes chilled her. Although it pained her, she knew she was doing the right thing—for both of them. "You didn't even ask me if I did it?"

One eyebrow lifted slightly. "You might be guilty of a lot of things, Laurel, but murder isn't one of them."

Omar Mendocini was a pretentious man. Fabrizio Renaldi knew this about his employer. Understood it, since he, too, possessed a certain level of pretension himself. In truth, the idiosyncrasies of any of those who employed him were usually of little consequence just so long as he was paid the money promised him in a timely manner. Not so this time. Mendocini was near broke, not to mention desperate, which made the Florentine banker a risk.

Fabrizio paid the room service bill in cash, then added a substantial tip, culling a smile from the bleary-eyed deliverer. Silently, Fabrizio waited until the door closed before attending to his meal.

With the television tuned to CNN, he took a seat at the small dining table and concentrated on opening the bottle of Chianti he'd ordered with his dinner. He pulled out the cork, then set the bottle aside to allow the wine sufficient time to breathe before plucking the silver dome from the heavy platter covering his dinner. Bending forward, he breathed in the rich aroma of charbroiled steak, new potatoes, braised baby green beans, and creamed peas. He smiled. For dessert, he'd ordered a thick slab of chocolate cake.

He so enjoyed when his work brought him to America. The food choices never failed to please him, although he did tend toward standard American fare when in the States. Twenty-four-hour room service pleased him even more.

He poured himself a glass of wine, then cut into the thick steak, murmuring his approval when the meat's juices flowed onto the platter. A perfect medium rare. Just the way he liked it.

With a late night replay of Larry King's earlier broadcast for company, he ate his dinner. Fabrizio considered himself a nocturnal creature, more so by nurture than nature. The cover of darkness suited his line of work, although on occasion he was called to perform during the light of day. As a thief, he much preferred the shadows.

He'd been contacted by Signor Mendocini two days ago through the usual channels and had gone as requested to the Mendocini palazzo in Florence to meet with the banker in private. Even meeting a potential employer at his home wasn't all that out of the ordinary, particularly a man as pretentious as Mendocini. What had been unusual, however, was the nature of the banker's request—to erase all evidence of his connection to Jonathan Linton.

Three days ago Linton had been murdered. His business

partner, Laurel Jennings, had been arrested and charged with the crime. These were mere details—none of which were Fabrizio's concern. He didn't care who had killed the reproduction expert or even that the man had been murdered. Nor did it make a difference to him if his employer was responsible for the murder, which was entirely possible. He'd been hired to eliminate evidence of Mendocini's connection to Linton, or more accurately, proof of the deal Mendocini had made with the devil.

On the long flight from the continent to the United States, he'd given the job before him considerable thought. He was unconcerned with security issues. A man of his experience was well-versed in various security systems, electronic surveillance, alarms, and such. He'd reviewed the security plans for Artifacts upon his arrival and had no concerns in that regard. The fact that the places he'd be required to search were quite possibly under police surveillance was but a minor inconvenience. Nothing to cause him so much as a moment's hesitation. He was just that good.

Two things did concern him, however. First, was Mendocini's ability to pay. The first payment, in American dollars, had been deposited into the numbered account as promised. But Fabrizio knew enough about Mendocini, and his finances, or recent lack thereof, to have more than a passing concern about seeing the remainder of his fee—not to mention the bonus promised him if he recovered the funds Mendocini had paid Linton for his unique services.

Second, and most important, Fabrizio was a Florentine, and the fraud Mendocini had perpetrated on the people of Florence appalled him. Even a thief of his caliber had standards, and while he was responsible for the theft of several of the world's priceless works of art, he considered what Mendocini had done to his beloved St. Giovanni's as a personal affront.

He would complete the job he'd been hired to perform.

Then he would take whatever steps necessary to assure the people of his homeland were not robbed of their pride. If that meant exposing the pretentious Omar Mendocini and bringing shame and ruin to a centuries old family steeped in Florentine history, *questo è la vita*.

Chapter 5

WITH HER HEART pounding, Laurel walked single-
file behind the other female prisoners into the parti-
tioned area of the courtroom usually reserved for members
of the jury. During morning arraignment, the jury box served
as preferential seating for persons in custody. She needed a
shower, her own clothes, and a decent meal, preferably not
one overloaded in carbs and seriously lacking in flavor. And
most important, that sweet blessed freedom Damon promised
he'd try to win for her.

She sat as the guard instructed her to do and took the
seat in the far corner of the second row of elevated seating.
Immediately, she searched the courtroom for Damon. Her
heart sank when she spied Scanlon sans his cocky partner,
Teslenko. He was probably there to make sure she got hung
out to dry for a crime she didn't commit. He could choke on
a donut for all she cared. She had more important things on
her mind. Like where in the hell was Damon? Had he changed
his mind? Had her insistence that he not represent her eventually taken hold during the long hours of the night? No,
he'd be there. He wouldn't turn his back on her. That was
her M.O., not his.

She refused to panic. At least not yet. He could've gotten

caught in traffic. The elevator could be stuck between floors. Maybe he had to go buy a tie because he forgot to pack one. She knew she was being ridiculous, but any number of reasons might explain his absence. A temporary absence, she hoped.

God, when had she become such a pathetic hypocrite? She knew the answer. Four years ago, to be exact.

The court clerk called the first case and she blew out a breath filled with relief that it wasn't hers. If they called her case, she'd simply ask for a few moments until her attorney arrived. And he would. This was Damon, after all.

Twenty minutes later, she felt fairly confident she could muddle her way through the arraignment process on her own if Damon failed to appear. As Cha-cha had related, the public defender she'd observed was indeed overworked and rather passionless.

The process appeared simplistic enough. The judge's clerk called the case, the charges were read into the record, then the accused entered a plea. Simple. If the defendant pled not guilty, the prosecutor and defense attorneys haggled before the judge over bail or whether or not the accused deserved to be released O.R. If the judge declared the accused unfit to be released, then he or she was held in custody until trial, usually set within a matter of weeks. A plea of guilty or *nolo contendre* dispensed of the matter quickly or continued it to a later date for sentencing, depending upon the severity of the crime or even the criminal history of the accused.

She lacked a criminal history, but unfortunately, there hadn't been a single murder case called before the court for her to analyze. She'd hoped to gauge the judge's rulings to give her a better idea of whether she'd be sprung. She had a business to run, classes to teach, a murderer to find. Jonathan had a meeting scheduled at the end of the week with the curator of the Natural History Museum she'd need to cover, not to mention her own speaking engagement in Chicago at the Field Museum on computerized restoration techniques. She imagined if she were given freedom, there would be restrictions and limitations on travel. Like not being able to leave the state.

She'd worry about that later. Right now, walking out of jail was high on her list of priorities.

The court clerk rattled off a series of numbers. "*State of California vs. Laurel Olive Jennings,*" the middle-aged woman called out as she handed a file to the judge.

Laurel's knees shook when she stood. *Damon, where are you?*

"Alan Rosen appearing for the state, Your Honor."

Laurel recognized the deputy district attorney from television newscasts. If the guy wasn't out to condemn her for Jonathan's murder, she might've found his distinguished good looks and commanding presence somewhat attractive. He was tall, broad shouldered with dark hair and a sprinkling of gray at his temples. And he wanted her ass.

Oh, Damon, where are you?

The judge cast his tired gaze in her direction. "Miss Jennings, do you have an attorney?" he asked in a bored tone.

"Doctor," she corrected the judge, only because the title made her feel more confident. She needed all the help she could get at the moment.

"Excuse me?"

"It's Doctor Jennings," she said. "Not Miss."

"Well, then, *Doctor* Jennings," the judge said with a mild hint of sarcasm, "do you have an attorney?"

Laurel swept the courtroom again with her gaze, studiously avoiding making eye contact with Scanlon, then looked back to the judge. "Yes, sir."

"And where is he or she?"

Good question. "Running late," she improvised, and hoped she hadn't just lied to a superior court judge.

"Your honor," Rosen spoke up, "the state shows no attorney of record for the defendant."

The judge looked irritated. "Let's give her the benefit of the doubt for the moment, Mr. Rosen. I'll recall the case in twenty minutes."

Now Rosen looked irritated and shot her a scathing glance. Laurel didn't much care. After all, the guy wasn't exactly on her side of the nasty equation she suddenly found herself on, now was he?

The door to the courtroom opened. Laurel breathed an immediate sigh of relief. Damon.

She looked at the judge. "He's here," she blurted, interrupting the clerk as she attempted to call the next case.

He's here. Oh thank, God. He came.

Her pulse rate accelerated. Nerves. Anticipation. Relief. She didn't much care. Damon had arrived. That's all that mattered. Well, that and regaining her freedom. Once free, she'd find an attorney and who really killed Jonathan. In that order.

Rosen turned, his expression going from irritation to shock, then boomeranging back to annoyance at the sight of Damon. In fact, he looked mildly intimidated, sending Laurel's confidence level up a notch. Not that it should make a difference. After the arraignment, Damon was history. She could have it no other way.

The judge waved Damon forward. He crossed the bar and shouldered his way through the sea of attorneys hovering around the defense table. "Damon Metcalf appearing for the defense, your honor."

"Glad you could join us, Mr. Metcalf. Does your client understand the charges?"

Damon glanced her way and she nodded. What wasn't to

understand? Jonathan was dead and everyone thought she did it.

"How do you plead, Dr. Jennings?" the judge asked her.

"Not guilty," she said in a clear, firm voice. She wasn't dammit. She'd never hurt Jonathan. He was her friend and she'd loved him. To think that she'd kill him was ludicrous.

"The defense requests the defendant be released on her own recognizance," Damon told the judge.

"The state objects, Your Honor," Rosen countered. "Due to the severity of the charges, the state requests the defendant be remanded until trial."

"Doctor Jennings has no criminal history," Damon argued. "She has strong ties to the community, a profitable business, she—"

"I realize you've been out of practice for a while, counselor, but your client profited from the death of Mr. Linton, thereby making this a capital murder case."

Damon looked at her sharply. She shrugged. She had no idea what Rosen was talking about. If anything, her business would suffer because of the loss of Jonathan.

To the judge Rosen added, "Doctor Jennings is a flight risk. She has connections throughout the world. To release the def—"

"That's enough, gentlemen," the judge intervened with an impatient lift of his hand. "Bail is set at one million dollars. The court will accept a bond, provided the defendant agrees to remain in the state and surrenders her passport to the court."

A million dollars? She didn't have that kind of money. She wasn't destitute by any means, again, thanks to Jonathan, but she didn't have a million dollars sitting around. Her business was worth a great deal, but Artifacts was a corporation. She simply couldn't go withdrawing a million bucks from the bank for personal use, even if she was the only living shareholder.

Damon glanced her way again and she nodded. What was she going to say? No?

The clerk rattled off a series of dates that Damon noted in the file he'd carried into the courtroom with him. He turned to leave and Rosen said something to him she couldn't hear. He brushed past the prosecutor and spoke to the bailiff, who nodded in response, then signaled to the female guard watching over her and the others still awaiting their chance at freedom.

She glanced in Scanlon's direction and was momentarily stunned by his reaction to the turn of events. The bastard had the audacity to smile.

Without a word spoken, Laurel was led from the courtroom to another small room with barred windows and brown-speckled industrial tile. The large metal door clanged shut leaving Laurel two choices, either sit in yet another cold metal chair at a scarred wooden table or look out the window to the courtyard below where prisoners were transported to and from the courthouse.

She opted for the window and waited for whatever was going to happen next, wondering how in the world she was supposed to raise a million dollars from behind bars.

With one phone call, she thought. One she knew she'd never make, no matter how far out of control her life became.

Not since leaving Boston had she allowed another person to decide what was right for her. She lived her life her way, with no one telling her what she should or shouldn't do. Where she should work, live or what to do with her free time were her decisions, and hers alone. In her personal life, the only opinion that mattered was her own.

No one was in charge of Laurel, except Laurel. And it was nothing but a lie.

A fat lot of good her diligence at pretending had done. Once again, all because of a set of circumstances she'd had no part of, her life was so far out of control it was scary, spinning in a downward spiral with dire consequences. And there wasn't a damn thing she could do about it except play the wait-and-see game, then adapt accordingly. There were no footholds, no magic grips for her to latch onto and at least make an attempt to pull herself out of the disaster her life had become—again.

With a sigh of disgust, she moved away from the barred and grime-smeared window in time to see a new guard's face appear in the small glass opening on the door. The lock turned and the heavy door swung slowly open to reveal her past.

Damon shouldered his way around the guard's bulky frame and entered the drab, sparsely furnished twelve-by-twelve room. He looked pointedly at the guard until the door clanged shut.

Memories she hadn't allowed herself to call to mind yesterday when she'd seen him came crashing through the barriers she'd worked long and hard to erect. The two of them swinging from a rope tied to an ancient oak tree and splashing into the pond on the property at his parents' summer home when they were kids. Learning how to skip rocks, discovering the delights of sitting in silence amid a field of wildflowers, watching the hummingbirds flit from one place to the next in search of nectar. Sprawled on her back in the summer grass with her eyes closed, listening to the cacophony of bees buzzing nearby under the hot sun. Damon had taught her there was more to life than textbooks.

A socially inept, self-conscious seventeen-year-old girl, already in a graduate program at MIT, asking her best friend to teach her how to French kiss. Then, later when they were older, making love to the man she'd fallen crazy in love with.

Memories. Sweet memories of a time before betrayal, before the disillusionment had set in and cynicism became the norm. Cherished memories of carefree days spent with her closest, and probably only, friend in the world at the time. Sensual memories of the adults they'd become—until she'd had no choice but to send him away.

If only, she thought.

She hadn't allowed herself to cry. Not when she'd discovered Jonathan's ravaged body in the workroom at Artifacts, and certainly not at his funeral. Nor had she shed a tear when Scanlon and Teslenko had arrested her, or once during the two long nights she'd spent on her bunk in the county jail, with only her own morbid thoughts and Big Billie's snores for company. She wouldn't now, either, but lordy, she was as close to the verge as she'd been in a very long time.

As much as she wanted to bolt across the room and fly into his arms, she refused to seek the comfort of something familiar that would only be torn away from her later. Besides, what good would it do? Just as soon as he retained counsel for her, he'd be back in Bozeman.

Instead, she breathed in Damon's rich scent, committing the faint woodsy aroma to memory. "Thank you," she said awkwardly.

"We got lucky," he said as he approached. He dropped the file on the table and frowned. "Are you all right?"

She nodded. "I will be," she said. "Now." She still couldn't believe he'd managed to get the judge to agree to release her on bail. She'd been granted a miracle. Now she could only hope her luck held because she figured it'd take one more miracle for her to find out who really did kill Jonathan.

"Let's sit down," he suggested. "We don't have much time."

She drew back a chair and sat. Damon took the one opposite her, opened the file, and pulled out a yellow legal pad. "The first thing we need to do is get you out of here," Damon said, not looking at her, but at the notes he'd scribbled on the pad during her arraignment. "I called a bail bondsman before I left my hotel. He should be here any minute."

"I don't have a million dollars," she told him. Thanks to Jonathan, Artifacts had done exceptionally well the past year. She even had a couple of sizeable bank accounts and a relatively lucrative investment portfolio thanks to the success Jonathan had brought Artifacts, but she wasn't a millionaire by any stretch of the spreadsheet.

Damon glanced up from his notes. "You don't need a million bucks, Laurel, just one hundred grand. The bondsman will use your condo in Westwood as security."

"It's not free and clear."

"Doesn't have to be," Damon said. "You got a hundred grand you can get your hands on?"

"Not from behind bars."

"The bondsman will have a few forms for you to sign to authorize a transfer of funds."

She nodded. Whatever it took to gain freedom, she didn't care. She'd gladly hand over every last asset in her name. No way could she spend another night in that horrible cramped cell.

"Your defense isn't going to be cheap," Damon continued. "A capital murder case can run into the hundreds of thousands. You got that kind of money lying around? In addition to making bond?"

She might suck at relationships, but she was an ace at managing her personal finances. "Yes," she told him with a nod. She hadn't exactly expected her defense to be free.

"In addition to the bond money, I'll need about fifty grand

to retain an attorney for you. Provided I can find someone decent willing to take over your defense."

She was confused. "You walk in with fifty grand, I doubt you'll have a problem." She hoped. She'd signed a check for half that amount to Howard Barnes and he hadn't even bothered to send someone to talk to her.

"Don't be so sure." Damon looked at her fully then, and for the first time she noticed subtle changes. His idealism may have faded long ago, but what struck her now was the vibrancy of his green eyes. And of course, he was still as gorgeous as ever, all wide shoulders and lean-hipped stride. His thick sable hair was a tad longer than she remembered, too, but the fire and passion that had always burned in his eyes and had all but vanished was back. And that had her worried.

She couldn't, wouldn't be his cause. "Just don't be thinking that you'll represent me," she said and meant it. "Some lawyer out there will want the job."

"You hope."

Did she ever. "You want to help me? Then find me a lawyer."

A dark look entered his eyes and his features simultaneously hardened to granite. After a moment, he let out a hefty sigh and set his pen down atop the legal pad. "Look, I haven't practiced law in a year and a half, Laurel. I really have no desire to return, either. I'll do my best to find a top criminal firm to handle your defense, but I don't want you to get your hopes up." He leaned back in his chair. "I'll arrange for your release, retain counsel, and then I'm back on a plane to Bozeman in the morning. Happy?"

Not really. For a girl with serious trust issues, Damon really was her first choice at a time like this. Problem was, it wasn't him she didn't trust. "Yes."

Disappointment momentarily clouded his gaze. What

had she expected? That he'd thank her for refusing to allow him to represent her?

He turned his attention to the file in front of him and rifled through the small sheaf of papers. "Sign this," he said, sliding a printed document in front of her. "It's a limited power of attorney that'll allow me to secure the funds to pay the retainer for your defense."

She picked up the sleek pen, still warm from his touch. She signed where he'd indicated and listed several account numbers he'd need to access.

The lock on the heavy metal door turned suddenly. She shifted in her seat to see the most scruffy, burly-looking creature she'd ever encountered, enter the small room. Damon stood and crossed the room to shake the big-as-a-grizzly man's hand. "Good to see you, Burke. Thanks for coming on such short notice."

"Long time, Metcalf." Burke, who had to be at least six-and-a-half-feet tall and practically as wide, spoke in a small, tinny voice. He sounded as if he'd swallowed helium.

"Laurel, this is Burke Spring. He's going to see you get out of here."

Spring? Oh, who was he kidding? How utterly ironic.

"I wish I could say it's a pleasure," Laurel said politely, taking the beefy hand Burke extended. The giant's touch was surprisingly gentle.

"Under normal circumstances, Dr. Jennings, I'm sure it would be," Burke said in that cartoon character voice. "I have some forms you'll need to sign, to set up the transfer of funds and allow for the lien on your property." He took the seat Damon had vacated and got to work pulling forms out of a plain manila folder.

Damon gathered up the papers she'd already signed for him. "How long before you think she'll be released?" he asked the bondsman.

"It'll take a couple of hours for me to get the paperwork through the clerk's office, then it just depends on how backed up they are in lock up." Burke checked his watch and shrugged. "Should be no later than four, four-thirty. Maybe six, tops."

Damon nodded. "I'll try to be waiting for you," he said to Laurel. "Call me if things move faster than anticipated." He rattled off his cell phone number, which she easily committed to memory.

"Where are you going?" she asked him. God, she hated that she sounded so desperate, but she figured a woman with a capital murder charge hanging over her head was entitled to a little desperation. She understood Damon had business matters to attend to on her behalf, but she realized she really didn't want him to leave her.

He rapped on the door and waited for the guard to respond. "To find you a damn good lawyer."

She already had a damn good lawyer—if only she could have him.

"Next of kin?"

Laurel shook her head. "None," she told Burke. At least not legally.

He looked up from the form he'd been completing. "I need a name, Dr. Jennings."

She shrugged. "Damon Metcalf."

"He's your attorney of record."

Not for long.

"I'm sorry." Normally she'd give him Jonathan's name, but as he was six feet under, he no longer qualified. Any of the people she'd once considered close enough to be listed as her next of kin, with the exception of Damon, were dead, or dead to her. Not exactly a stellar track record.

"No parents, no siblings?" Burke asked.

"My mother died when I was young." She'd become a ward of the state of Massachusetts, flitting from one foster home to the next until she'd been placed with Conner and Evelyn Tillman.

"There's no one," she told Burke.

He let out a big sigh. "Okay, then. What about business associates?"

Again, she'd have given him Jonathan's name. "Stacy Owens," she said. "She's the go-to-girl at Artifacts." Jonathan had been interviewing for another assistant, someone without an art degree to free Stacy up from handling the administrative end of the business.

Burke nodded his big grizzly head and jotted down Stacy's name along with the phone numbers Laurel recited from memory. She also provided him with the name of the head of the art history department at UCLA where she taught graduate courses two evenings a week in addition to the Friday afternoons she kept office hours advising her grad students.

The heavy metal door opened. "Time's up," the guard announced. "The prisoners are being sent back to lock up."

Burke asked Laurel to sign another couple of forms, then gathered up his papers, and stood. "Don't worry, Dr. Jennings," he said in that strange little voice. "We'll have you out of this hell hole today."

Laurel stood and offered her hand. "Thank you, Mr. Spring."

"Burke," he said, swallowing her small hand in his enormous one.

"Burke," she repeated and offered a thin excuse for a smile. "Call me Laurel."

The big man nodded, then quickly departed. Once again, she found herself alone until the surly guard returned for her.

She walked to the grimy window to look out into the

pitiful excuse for a courtyard below, all blacktop and black-and-white Department of Correction buses used for transporting the accused. She'd always been alone, so she didn't understand why the thought of being so now filled her with such sadness.

She let out a sigh. The old cliché about reaping what you sow finally made sense to her. She made herself a promise. If she ever got out of this mess, the first thing on her list of things to do was harvest herself a wider circle of friends. As had become the norm for her lately, the list of exactly how she planned to accomplish that feat, however, remained pitifully empty.

Chapter 6

THE LAW OFFICES of Crossen, Jacobs and Gable weren't unlike any number of the multitude of other law firms located in the heart of the Wilshire District that Damon had visited that afternoon. Just one more high-rise office, decorated with polished mahogany-paneled walls, gleaming brass fixtures, and a reception area tastefully overdone with high-priced antique reproduction furnishings and upholstered in deep jewel tones. Just one more law firm on a short list leading nowhere fast.

Crossen, Jacobs and Gable held one exception, Damon thought wearily, Joss Jacobs. His last hope at finding Laurel decent representation. If Joss refused to represent her, he'd have no choice but to succumb to his B-list of lawyers and firms still suitable for a decent defense. Decent, but not the best.

Laurel deserved better than decent. Hell, her life depended on it.

He could use some food. He could use a drink, too, and not necessarily in that order.

He checked his watch. Eighteen minutes and counting.

His frustration continued to mount. In the four-and-a-half hours since he'd left Laurel in Burke's capable hands, he'd attempted to call in favors from seven of the best criminal defense attorneys with a Los Angeles or Beverly Hills address. Only four had agreed, or were available, to see him. In the end, it had made little difference. He'd received the same bullshit response—conflict of interest.

Damon was running out of patience, and out of lawyers who owed him favors. He hadn't yet found a single firm that didn't represent a Linton in some matter or another, directly or indirectly. Laurel couldn't have been accused of offing some nobody schmuck. Oh no, she had to go and get herself charged with the murder of a relative of one of the southland's most powerful families.

Leave it to Laurel to never do anything half-assed.

The last firm he'd been to was one of many on retainer for Monarch Studios, headed up by none other than Jonathan's uncle, Abe Linton. The one before that had been retained to probate the estate of David Linton, none other than the former chairman of the board for Linton Development, the company responsible for transforming the San Fernando Valley into a sea of identical, over-priced tract homes and profitable strip malls.

The results from the first two firms on his short list had been pretty much the same. The minute he mentioned Jonathan Linton's name, he'd essentially had the door slammed in his face.

The heavy mahogany door separating the reception area from the guts of the law firm opened. A statuesque brunette appeared wearing a short red skirt just this side of decent. "Mr. Metcalf?" At his nod, she smiled sweetly and said, "Mr. Jacobs will see you now."

Damon left the plush reception area and followed her down an industrial-carpeted corridor, past a glass-walled conference room overlooking the L.A. skyline into a windowless maze of cubicles filled with legal secretaries and paralegals who showed him little-to-no interest. Telephones jangled. Printers hummed. Conversation buzzed throughout the busy office. He experienced the tiniest pang of . . . regret?

Not a chance.

Relief?

Yes, definitely relief, he decided, following the sway of the brunette's slender hips. Relief that he no longer held any interest in the operation of the legal machine. He was through with endless hours of paperwork and legal arguments. No more morning arraignments for him, or figuring out how to be present in two courtrooms simultaneously. No more reluctant witnesses afraid to testify against guilty-as-sin defendants. No more thinking himself infallible.

Laurel was right. He was the last lawyer in the world who should be representing her.

The brunette held open the door to a corner office and motioned him inside. Damon stepped past the brunette just as Joss came out from behind his desk, his hand outstretched to Damon in greeting.

"Nice place," Damon said, summoning a grin for his old friend as he shook Joss's hand.

"Doesn't hurt that the old man's name is still on the letterhead," Joss quipped.

Joss had no reason to play the role of modest attorney. He and Damon went back a long way—all the way back to a frat house at Northwestern University. Since that time they'd remained close, even though they often argued opposite sides of various legal issues before the criminal courts. Nepotism hardly played a role in Joss's success, the man possessed a brilliant legal mind, and he couldn't help wondering if the old man's influence hadn't played a role in Joss's abdication from criminal to corporate law.

"What brings you back to town?" Joss asked, indicating an ox-blood leather guest chair. "Finally get tired of all that communing with Thumper and Flower?"

Damon's grin slipped to a half-hearted smile when he spied the framed photo of two dark-haired little girls with Santa on the credenza behind Joss's desk. The *Bambi* reference finally made sense.

"A friend is in trouble," he told Joss. "You still know your way around the criminal courts, or has corporate law made you soft?"

Curiosity immediately lit Joss's direct gaze. So, the switch to corporate law wasn't Joss's choice, after all.

"Must be some friend to drag you back to L.A."

Damon simply nodded. What else could he say? His departure might have been abrupt, but it'd been no secret. In fact, it had been public. Damn public.

"She needs an attorney. A good one," he said meaningfully.

Joss's grin widened. "You've come to the right place. What's the charge?"

There was the arrogance Damon remembered, and had been counting on. "Capital murder. Trial begins in six weeks."

Six weeks filled with discovery, investigation, legal research, and hours spent preparing motions, all geared to shatter the prosecution's case against Laurel. Although he hadn't yet had time to read a scrap of the state's evidence against her, he knew in his heart she was the last person on earth capable of murder. Still, Rosen's words as Damon was leaving the courtroom continued to ring in his ears—*Your bitch is gonna fry.*

"That's quick, even for a criminal trial." Joss frowned suddenly. "Who's prosecuting?"

"Alan Rosen."

Joss shook his head, his disgust apparent. "Jackass. I never could stand that son-of-a-bitch."

"Get in line," Damon agreed. "The investigation's already making headlines. Rosen is going to turn this one into a career-maker."

That sinking feeling in the pit of his stomach, which had nothing whatsoever to do with lack of sustenance, returned. *Your bitch is gonna fry.*

Joss turned to the laptop on the desk return beside him and pulled up his electronic calendar system. After a few mouse clicks, he said, "Six weeks, right?"

"Yeah," Damon said and opened the file he'd brought with him. "Pre-trial motions are due June fourth. Jury selection starts on the eleventh."

"I'll have to move a couple of things, but it looks good," Joss said turning back to face Damon. "Who's the defendant?"

"Laurel Jennings," Damon said, and waited for the proverbial slamming of the door.

"The Linton murder?" A definite note of surprise lined Joss's voice.

"That's the one," Damon answered. The acid churning in his stomach burned.

Joss leaned back in his cushy chair and regarded Damon thoughtfully. "Laurel Jennings is the friend?"

"Yup," Damon said. He didn't need to elaborate. He and Joss went back a long way and Joss knew about his relationship with Laurel. At least superficially. "She needs a good criminal defense attorney, Joss."

"Yeah, well, I wish you luck finding one," his friend said. "There's no way I can represent her."

Damon let out a frustrated breath. "Let me guess," he said. "Conflict of interest."

Joss nodded. "The firm represents The Linton Foundation, Damon. The decedent's mother is the chairman of the board. I'm sorry."

"Is there a firm in town that doesn't represent a Linton?" he wondered aloud and closed the file.

"Did you try Gilardi's office? He's a whore, especially if the press is involved."

"His partner handled Caroline Linton-Marlboro's third divorce."

"I'm sorry, buddy. I wish I could help."

"Yeah, me, too."

Joss gave him a curious look. "How many favors you try to call in so far?"

"You're my fifth."

Joss chuckled and shook his head. "Gee, thanks for the vote of confidence."

"No offense."

"Ah, hell, none taken." Joss stood and circled the desk, indicating the meeting had come to an end.

Just like that, Damon was back to ground zero.

"I really wish I could help out," Joss said.

"So do I." Damon stood and walked with Joss to the door.

Joss paused, his hand stilling over the door knob. "Look Damon," he said, turning to face him. "We've been friends for a long time. You didn't hear this from me, but your client is up shit creek."

"So I'm gathering," he said.

"No, you're not hearing me. She's up a creek and the Lintons have the monopoly on paddles."

"Meaning there isn't a lawyer in southern California gonna take this case off my hands."

Joss nodded. "All you might find is someone with nothing to lose."

"And practically guarantee Laurel's conviction," Damon added.

"Exactly."

Damon muttered a curse. He knew Joss was right. He'd even warned Laurel of the possibility. The Lintons were just too powerful. They even had a U.S. senator in their goddamn family tree.

"How long you gonna be in town?" Joss asked, opening the door.

"I'm not sure. I might be flying back to Bozeman as early as tomorrow."

"Too bad," Joss said. "I've got a pair of tickets. Clippers. Courtside tomorrow night."

"Maybe next time." They both knew there wouldn't be a next time.

With nothing else to do but leave, he shook Joss's hand again, made some noise about it being good to see his old friend, thanked him for the information, and headed for the exit.

Another door slammed in his face. Another dead end.

Dread churned sharply in Damon's gut along with the acid already simmering there. Laurel would pitch a fit, but she'd just have to get over it. At this rate, she would be lucky to get stuck with an overworked, out-of-his-league public defender who either didn't give a shit or would be so intimidated by Rosen or the Lintons, a death warrant would be waiting for the judge's signature before the case even made it to the jury for deliberation.

The last thing he wanted was more blood on his conscience, but he was out of options. Unfortunately, so was Laurel. She did have an attorney. One Damon Metcalf, Esquire—whether she liked it or not.

Metcalf was back. Damn. He'd always hated that son-of-a-bitch.

Alan Rosen tossed back the scotch in his glass and signaled for the bartender to bring him another while quietly swearing a blue streak. He didn't for a minute doubt his own meteoric rise in the D.A.'s office would never have been possible if Metcalf hadn't walked out after the Tarragona fiasco.

And now the sanctimonious bastard was back.

What the hell was he doing here? he wondered. How did he even know the defendant?

He had no immediate answers. But he'd get them. He always did.

Pushing another twenty to the edge of the bar, he impatiently signaled again for the bartender just as his cell phone vibrated in his pocket. He ignored it in favor of more scotch when the bartender showed up with a refill.

It made little difference to him which side of the case Metcalf was working. He wanted him nowhere near the Jennings prosecution, and now the son-of-a-bitch was listed as attorney of record for the Ice Queen.

"Fucking prick," he muttered, then downed half the contents of his second scotch of the day.

He needed a win on this one. Badly. He'd be damned if his near-perfect record would be marred at this stage of the game. Especially now. The Lintons were too powerful, and he had to make an impression. A lasting impression, the right kind of impression, if he had any hope of gaining the public and financial support promised to him. Indirectly, of course.

He had to make certain the Jennings bitch fried. A conviction would practically guarantee him the top job in the next election. A death penalty conviction would guarantee backing with Linton money. But if Metcalf defended Jennings, he couldn't count on a slam dunk, either, because the bastard was just that good, even if he hadn't seen the inside of a courtroom in months. Hell, he'd already gotten the bitch bail, and all he'd done was show his goddamn face.

Shit. Metcalf-one, Rosen-zilch. Not quite the stellar beginning he'd been shooting for. Not even close.

His cell phone vibrated again. He considered the remaining contents of his drink, and thought about turning the damn thing off completely. He needed to think, and he did that best with a tumbler of room-temperature scotch in his hand. Instead he reached into his pocket and checked the display. RESTRICTED.

He hit the call button anyway. "Rosen," he answered, his tone brusque.

"Laurel Jennings just made bail," a deep male voice intoned.

"Who is this?" Rosen demanded.

"Someone concerned for your future, Mr. Rosen," the caller said, then hung up.

Alan stared at the now-blank display for a moment, then carefully slipped the phone back into his suit pocket. In one gulp, he polished off the last of the scotch, then swiped the change from the twenty off the bar. A five slipped from his grasp and floated to the hardwood floor. He ignored it, staring instead at the trembling of his hands he had a feeling no amount of scotch could calm.

Laurel paced impatiently in front of the bank of telephones inside the crowded waiting area of the county jail. Anything was better than being locked up behind bars, but she wanted as far away from this horrible place as humanly possible.

Her heels clicked on the asphalt tiles as she continued to pace, doing her best to avoid the multitudes waiting to be called for visitation with their prisoner of choice. She didn't belong here, that much was obvious from the curious stares from the throng of people in the waiting room.

Impatience bit at her hard. Twenty minutes ago she'd called Damon's cell phone and left a message, informing him she'd been released. He still hadn't shown. Where the hell was he?

Since the battery in her cell phone was dead, she fished another quarter out of the bottom of her designer handbag and turned toward the phones again, nearly tripping over a young mother with a sleeping baby in a bulky stroller.

The woman gave her a sour look.

"Excuse me," she muttered as she side-stepped the stroller.

Asking for help, even for something as simple as a ride home, wasn't easy for her. For almost as long as she could remember, she'd been an independent soul. Whether because she'd been an only child or the cause stemmed from the circumstances which she'd found herself thrust into at the age of ten, she couldn't exactly say. She knew only that depending on no one but herself was the wisest course, and the safest. The only way she knew how to at least attempt to control the chaos.

She made a decision. If she didn't get away from this place she'd go nuts.

She dropped the quarter into the slot and dialed Damon's cell. After four rings, her wasted effort was rewarded with his voice mail.

"Hey, it's me again," she said. "I'm taking a cab, so just meet me at my condo." She let out a little impatient puff of breath. "Please."

She had no idea where her car might be, if the detectives had had it impounded, or if it was still sitting in the parking lot at the cemetery. She supposed a call to the police station would solve that little mystery, but she had no desire to speak to anyone in law enforcement at the moment. Right now her goal was to make it home in one piece, have herself a hot shower, some decent food, then she'd see about locating her car. And come up with a list for putting her life back together, one that included a guarantee she'd never have to spend so much as another nanosecond behind bars ever again.

Her decision made, she headed for the exit in search of a taxi. In the movies, there was always a cabbie waiting by the curb hoping for a fare. Maybe luck would be with her for a change and that little piece of Hollywood fantasy would serve as a convenient slice of reality. Maybe she'd even find Damon waiting for her.

No such luck.

Shielding her eyes from the glare of the late afternoon sunshine, she scanned the curbside. Her reality really did bite. Not a single cab driver within miles, or Damon for that matter. Unfortunately, she did recognize the shit-brown Chevy and the heavyset detective leaning his tremendous bulk against the front quarter panel of the passenger side.

She planned to ignore him. And then he pushed off the car and approached her.

"Detective Scanlon," she said coolly. "To what do I owe this displeasure?"

"Aw, come on, Doc. Is that any way to greet the man about to save your ass from a pricy cab ride to Century City?"

"Westwood, actually. And thanks, but no thanks." She turned and started walking. To where, she didn't have a clue. She didn't exactly frequent this part of the city on a regular basis. Ever, in fact.

Scanlon appeared at her side. "I'd really like to talk to you."

She picked up her pace. "Isn't there some rule about you not being allowed to consort with the enemy?"

"You're not the enemy, Dr. Jennings."

"Funny, but I don't see it that way. You did arrest me."

"I was doing my job," he countered, struggling for breath.

She stopped, not because she took mercy on the out-of-shape detective. She glanced up and down the street. Not a single cab in sight. Damn.

"By arresting an innocent woman?" she asked. "Bet you scored some serious brownie points for that one."

She didn't relish walking back inside the waiting room to call a cab, but with her cell dead, she didn't have many choices if she hoped to get home any time soon.

"Look, we didn't have a choice. The evidence—"

"Is flawed."

"The evidence doesn't lie," he countered.

She looked at Scanlon curiously. "Then why are you here, Detective? Certainly you didn't come just to remind me you think I'm guilty. Or is curbside harassment a service you provide to all the criminals you put in jail?"

He glanced toward the car, parked almost a block away now, then back at her. Kindness shown in his eyes, taking her off guard.

"Let me take you home," he said patiently. "We can talk."

"Why should I?"

"Because Dr. Jennings, I don't think you're guilty, either."

Chapter 7

SHE STOOD NEAR the open window with her hand resting protectively on her abdomen, hoping for a cooling breeze to stir the stagnant air of her second floor walk-up, yet dreading it at the same time. The greasy aroma from the chicken joint below nauseated her. The Mexican bakery on the corner could be counted on for some hunger-stirring aromas, but this late in the afternoon, Martinez's was closed.

Varying styles of music warred for domination from the shops lining the busy city street below, from heavy metal to hip hop to gangster rap. A young mama pushed a baby stroller through the swarm of hookers hawking their used wares and drug deals going down. She would not raise her baby in this shit hole. Her baby, their baby, would have better.

She missed Jonathan so much she felt an ache deep in her chest. That gentle smile of his, the twinkle in his eyes. The sexy little wink he'd give her when he was certain no one was looking.

Sighing, she turned from the window and walked to the sofa she'd picked up from a second-hand store and sat. She suspected the sofa was more third-, or even fourth-hand, but it no longer mattered. Soon she would have new. New everything for her new life, once she set the wheels in motion first thing tomorrow morning. Everett P. Sharpe owed her a favor, and she planned to collect.

She smiled at the irony. Oh, she'd collect, all right. In more ways than one.

Propping her feet on the cheap, imitation walnut coffee table, she picked up the remote and tuned into the Channel 7 news. This morning she'd caught the early morning broadcast of one of the local news breaks during *Good Morning America*. That bitch was supposed to have been arraigned today and she was hoping for news on the outcome. Only one person stood between her and the life she deserved, and she needed that bitch to rot in jail for the rest of her life.

Fifteen minutes later, all she knew was that there'd been more drive-by shootings in South Central and the weather pattern wouldn't be changing for another five days. It was only mid-April, and already the southland promised to be just as stifling as always. Maybe she would move. Relocate to Seattle. Sure, it rained a lot, but the weather was cooler and the winters weren't all that harsh like they were in the east. She could afford to move into Microsoft country now. Or would soon, she thought with another smile as she smoothed her hand over her tummy.

She'd spent so many years fantasizing about a better life, the possibilities were nearly overwhelming. Which life should she choose? The one that starred her as a successful owner of racehorses? Or maybe the one where she lived in a lifestyle of socialite luxury on Park Avenue with a summer house in the Hamptons and annual trips to exotic European locales? And there was the one where she turned all her fantasies into best-selling novels from her quiet country home. She'd become a recluse, like Hemingway, or maybe she'd live larger than life like ol' F. Scott. She might even decide to stay in L.A., buy a place in Malibu where the weather was cooler, and sit on her deck and paint seascapes. And shop. On Rodeo Drive, of course.

"Laurel Jennings, the state's prime suspect who only yesterday was charged with the murder of Jonathan Linton, is being freed today on one million dollars bail. Assistant District Attorney Alan Rosen could not be reached for comment. Trial has been set to begin with jury selection for June eleventh. Kevin McElvoy reporting live from the Los Angeles County Criminal Courts Building for the Channel 7 news team. Back to you, Ann."

Fury swelled inside her as she stared at the television screen. Free? They let the bitch walk?

"No!"

"Kevin, wasn't Ms. Jennings charged with capital murder? Isn't it uncommon for the court to set bail?"

"True, Ann," McElvoy confirmed. "According to our source in the district attorney's office, Jennings profited from the death of her business partner, therefore qualifying the murder as capital. From what we've learned, there's a clause in the business agreement between Jennings and Linton that supports the DA's case for capital murder." The field reporter looked at the notes in his hand, then back at the camera. "Should one of the partners predecease the other, the deceased partner's holdings in the company they co-owned, Artifacts, an art restoration business located in the Wilshire District, reverts to the surviving partner. And it appears to be quite an inheritance. Dun and Bradstreet records indicate Artifacts is valued at over ten million dollars."

"Yet the court still allowed bail?" the anchor questioned. "That seems highly unusual."

"It is, Ann," McElvoy agreed. "However her attorney, former L.A. prosecutor Damon Metcalf, argued that Jennings has no criminal record and has successful ties to the community."

"Very interesting, Kevin," Ann replied. "You'll keep us updated. And in other news . . ."

She turned off the television, her fury turning white hot. Ten million dollars that belonged to her. To her baby.

She stood, her entire body shaking with the force of her rage. Her legs trembled as she walked from the drab living room down a dingy corridor into her minuscule bathroom. With her hands braced tightly on the sink, she looked at her reflection and knew what she had to do.

She had no choice. She had to end the bitch.

Many of the preeminent scientific minds in the world called the Massachusetts Research Institute home. Scientists employed by the Institute were responsible for some of the greatest advances made in AIDS research as well as various cancers and other debilitating diseases. In recent years, the Institute's top medical scientist had become one of the premier leaders in stem cell research.

But the Institute had many faces. The one shown to the public was strictly that of a medical research facility striving for cures to the world's diseases. But while important works were indeed being conducted in the field of medical research by the Institute's top researchers, it was all nothing more than an elaborate cover for the Institute's true purpose.

Beneath the façade, the Institute was by far the government's first line of defense against chemical warfare. But more importantly, and unknown to but a select few, the Institute served as the first line of *offense* in the development of the country's chemical weapon arsenal.

Conner Tillman was one of those select few.

He drove his Cadillac Escalade up the winding, paved roadway toward the executive parking garage of the Institute. At the guard shack, he showed his identification card, then waited for the guard to produce the electronic thumb print scanner which would grant him access once approved.

He'd been summoned. He'd known it would only be a

matter of time before the directors were fully aware of the possible benefits of Laurel's arrest, or the ramifications. Not that Conner was overly concerned with the dangers of her arrest. No risk existed to connect the Institute to Linton's murder—except for Laurel. They simply weren't responsible.

The guard produced the credit card-size scanner. Conner placed his right thumb on the electronic pad.

"Good evening, Dr. Tillman," the guard said stoically once the green light flashed. "Will you be staying long tonight, sir?"

"Not too long." He produced a smile for the guard. "Old age must be catching up with me. I forgot something in the office," he lied easily.

Too easily, he thought. Once upon a time, he would've been appalled by how easily the lie had slid from his lips, but too many years of ambition, and a few too many cover-ups in the name of national security or scientific progress, had changed him.

"Very well," the guard said with a brief nod. He returned to the shack and within seconds, the electronic wrought-iron gates swung open.

Conner drove through the gates and headed directly to his parking space on the third level reserved for upper level executives and the directors. He left his vehicle, noted the number of limos and SUV's, and after passing through several more security measures, he finally made his way to the top floor boardroom where the directors waited for him.

A pair of Marine guards flanked the doors to the boardroom. The guard to the left remained absolutely still, while the guard to the right swiftly opened the door.

Conner stepped into the darkly paneled boardroom. Four of the five directors, indicative of their leadership equality, were seated at the large, round rosewood table, centered in the room. The fifth director approached him, his hand extended in greeting.

"Thank you for coming at such a late hour, Conner," the director said, shaking his hand.

"No problem," Conner answered.

The director motioned toward the table and Conner crossed the thick, plush carpet and took the only available seat at the table. "Would you like something to drink?" another of the directors offered.

Conner declined. He wasn't fooled by their apparent congeniality. He wouldn't have been summoned if they were about to pat him on the back for a job well done. If that were the case, he'd have arrived at the Institute tomorrow to find he'd been promoted or perhaps he'd have received a notification slip from his bank advising him of a wire transfer.

"Very well," another of the directors stated. "Conner, we're concerned by the recent events surrounding Dr. Jennings."

"I'm sure I don't need to remind you this could become a very unfortunate circumstance for all of us," another of the directors, the eldest and most powerful of the group, stated.

"I'm aware of the ramifications, sir," Conner told him. The identities of the directors of the Institute was a closely guarded secret. The fact that all five of them were now present spoke volumes of their collective concern.

The youngest of the directors—if fifty-something could be considered young—gave Conner a hard stare. "She never should've been allowed to leave in the first place," he said coldly. "She knows too much."

"Calm down," the man to his left said, placing a hand on his counterpart's shoulder. "Conner is aware of how important our work is here." He then looked to Conner. "Our concern is what Dr. Jennings could offer by way of a plea bargain."

Yes, Conner had considered this as well. It had been all he'd thought about since hearing of Laurel's arrest. If faced with the death penalty, which he understood was Assistant

District Attorney Rosen's goal, she may offer information about the Institute, and in particular her knowledge of the directors' identities, in exchange for a reduction in her sentence.

"She must be silenced," the youngest member of the distinguished group stated.

"I understand your concerns, however Dr. Jennings is a gifted scientist. The work she did for the Institute resulted in some of our most successful advances," Conner said. "Wouldn't our purpose be better served if she were once again under our control?"

The younger director made a sound of disgust, his opinion on the matter crystal clear. The others looked on with interest.

The elder of the group asked calmly, "How so, Conner?"

"If Dr. Jennings is convicted, we could very easily have her under our control again. She would essentially serve her sentence here, with us."

"We're not running a prison," the younger director argued. "This isn't Club Fed, either."

Conner smiled. "No, of course not. But we have the capabilities of arranging her release into the Institute's custody." These were five of the most powerful men in the country. They could move a mountain if they wanted, with nothing more than a phone call or the push of a button.

"I understand the great things Dr. Jennings has done, and can continue to do, for the Institute under the right circumstances," the most powerful of the group said, his voice soft yet resonant. He sat with his hands clasped together in front of him, his head angled slightly to the side as he looked directly at Conner. "We all know the supreme importance of the work she did for us. She could once again be one of our most valuable assets, and that is something to consider when making our decision on how to handle this very delicate situation. However, your plan does contain a serious flaw. We have no way of ensuring Dr. Jennings will even be convicted."

Connor smiled. "Actually, sir, that's not entirely true. . . ."

"Where's my car?" Laurel asked Scanlon as he headed up the on ramp of the 101 freeway.

"Police impound lot," he said, merging into the heavy rush hour traffic of downtown Los Angeles. "Standard procedure. Someone breaks into your car or steals it, the department gets sued."

The mentality of lawyers and juries never failed to amaze her. No doubt just that had occurred and it had cost the department a bundle in legal fees defending such a lawsuit.

"And how much more is that going to cost me?" Her bank accounts were already one hundred and fifty grand short. Not that another few hundred would hurt her, but the inconvenience of having to rescue her car from an impound lot annoyed her. She had enough to do, like put her life back together. And figure out who would've wanted Jonathan dead.

"Tomorrow I'll arrange to have it released to you."

"Gee, thanks."

He shot her a quick glance.

Suddenly, she felt guilty. "I apologize." She wasn't accustomed to being so rude. Stress, she thought. Facing a murder conviction made a girl a little edgy. "Thank you," she said, softening her tone. "I appreciate it."

His answer was a brief nod of acknowledgment. "Nice ride," he said. "You have it long?"

"The Jag?" she asked. At his nod, she said, "A few months."

"Business must be good."

"Yes," she answered after a moment, wondering where this conversation was heading, and if it were even legal. "It has been."

"I hear Artifacts has some impressive commissions like *Gates of Paradise*. The *Gates of Paradise?*"

"Jonathan has an uncle who knows someone on the board of St. Giovanni's," Laurel answered. "Do you know the history of the doors?"

Scanlon checked the rearview mirror, flipped on the turn indicator, and moved into the fast lane. An oxymoron during rush hour. They'd barely moved ten yards in as many minutes.

"If I remember my humanities," he said, "weren't the original doors to the baptistery of St. Giovanni's commissioned something like six hundred years ago?"

"In a manner of speaking. It wasn't an actual commission so much as it was a prize in a contest. And it's not the east doors of the baptistery themselves that are priceless, but the ten bronze relief panels created by Lorenzo Ghiberti. They were so beautiful, the doors were dubbed the *Gates of Paradise*."

"Didn't he compete against Brunelleschi?"

"Very good, Detective."

"We're not all a bunch of gorillas," he said. "Some of us can even write our own name."

She managed a small smile. "There's a scandal for you," she added. "A lot of ink has been spilled about the competition between Brunelleschi and Ghiberti and how Ghiberti was awarded the commission. But you're not interested in a lesson in art history, are you Detective?"

"No, I'm not," he answered, changing lanes again as traffic finally started to move forward at a decent clip. "I'm interested in how Artifacts came to receive a commission like that."

His answer surprised her. "Why?"

Scanlon shrugged, but she wasn't buying his noncommittal response. "I dunno," he said thoughtfully. "Just seems like a pretty important job for a little unknown company like Artifacts."

"As I said, Jonathan's family has a lot of contacts."

"Enough to suddenly put your company on the map and fill your bank account with a whole lot of green."

"Capitalism. It's a wonderful thing," she answered sarcastically.

Scanlon didn't respond and they drove the next few miles in silence. Laurel kept her gaze on the sea of red tail lights ahead of them as they neared the interchange that would take them to Westwood.

Money, she supposed, could be a strong motive for murder. Perhaps Scanlon wasn't being generous after all in offering her a ride home. Perhaps what he was really after was a reason she might have killed Jonathan.

"You think I killed my business partner because we'd gained a reputation for restoring classical works of art and were suddenly making more money than we knew what to do with?" She shook her head. "Ever hear the one about biting the hand that feeds you?"

"You ever hear the one about wanting it all for yourself?"

"I've told you before," she said, her tone turning icy. "Jonathan wasn't only my business partner, he was my friend. I had no reason to kill him."

Scanlon braked as traffic slowed. "He also was your lover."

"You believe everything you hear?" she asked. "Jonathan and I are . . ." Jonathan wasn't anything. He was dead. ". . . *were* friends." Not that she expected him to believe her.

She let out a weighty sigh. "You already know all this. You said you didn't think I killed Jonathan. What was that about?"

"You're right. I don't think you killed him."

A slight break in traffic had them inching closer toward the speed limit again. Scanlon took the off ramp that had them nearing Westwood.

The setting sun blazed in deep, blinding hues of burnished red and gold. She dug into her bag and pulled out a pair of Oakleys. "Then why did you arrest me?" she asked, slipping on her sunglasses.

Scanlon pulled his own sunglasses from the front pocket of his shirt. "Because the evidence points to you."

She let out another sigh. "And the evidence never lies."

"That's right. Your fingerprints were on the murder weapon. Hair and fibers from the suit you were wearing were found on the body. The vic's blood was on your clothing. You had access to Artifacts."

"I own the place," she reminded him.

"You have no solid alibi for the time period after you left the university until you arrived at Artifacts."

He had her there. She'd taught class that night, then afterward had spent a couple of hours in her office at the university reviewing project proposals from her students. Alone. Instead of going home as was her habit, she'd gone to Artifacts to talk to Jonathan, who'd promised her he'd be working late. She'd honestly been surprised to see his car in the parking lot, and even more surprised to find his butchered body on the floor of the workroom.

"But you still don't think I did it? Even though the evidence says otherwise and my alibi is paper thin."

Scanlon shot her a quick glance. "Motive, Dr. Jennings. You said it yourself. You had no reason to kill your business partner. And why would you? He was making you money. A lot of it. Greed could be a very strong motive for murder, but you wouldn't have all those important commissions without Linton."

"That's right."

"You ever wonder where all that money came from?"

"From the commissions we earned. Not only did we have the *Gates of Paradise* restoration, but several important museum pieces as well. The restoration for priceless works of art doesn't come cheap. It's an extremely tedious and delicate process."

"You sure?"

"What are you saying? That Jonathan was involved in something illegal?" The idea was preposterous.

Or was it? Not that she actually believed Jonathan could be involved in anything illegal, but *something* had been distracting him the past few months. He'd missed several appointments in recent weeks and she'd even had to take over on a couple of projects he'd been responsible for just so they could make their promised deadline.

"I'm saying anything is possible," Scanlon said.

"No," she said, and shook her head. "Not Jonathan."

"How well did you know Linton?"

The term straight arrow existed because of people like Jonathan Linton. He didn't do drugs, didn't gamble, didn't chase women. As far as she knew, their work at Artifacts was his sole reason for living. If he'd had any one fault, she supposed his dedication and drive to see Artifacts become hugely successful would have been it. Which was why his lack of focus the last few weeks before his death had worried her. Once upon a time, she'd worried that his determination bordered on obsession, but in no way could he have stooped to illegal activities to ensure their success.

Or could he have? Who understood better than her that people weren't always what they seemed?

Lintons never failed because it wasn't an option. How many times had he told her those very words?

"He was one of the few people in this world that I trusted," she finally answered. And she meant it.

"You don't trust too many people, do you?"

"No," she said, then pointed toward the sign ahead on the right. "This is my exit."

"Why is that?"

Her stomach clenched. Hunger pangs, she tried to convince herself, but knew that was nothing but a lie. "How many people do you trust?" she answered.

Thankfully, all he offered by way of reply was a grunt, which she took as an acknowledgment. As they neared the end of the off ramp, she motioned for him to turn left. The rest of the ride was spent giving him directions to her condo.

By the time they pulled into the parking garage, the sun had set. She instructed him to go to the fourth level where her condo was located. He pulled into the visitor's slot near the elevators, but the garage was darker than normal. The light, she noted, was out again, casting the area around the elevator in dark shadows.

"Thank you for the ride," she said as she unbuckled her seat belt. "I appreciate it."

"I'll walk you to your apartment. Make sure you get in okay."

Her hand stilled and she gripped the handle of her bag. "That isn't necessary."

Scanlon let out a rough sigh. "I'm an old-fashioned guy, Doc. Humor me, okay?"

Despite herself, she smiled and accepted his chivalry as graciously as possible. She didn't want to like Scanlon. She didn't think they were supposed to be talking, either, and figured her attorney, whomever that may be, would have an opinion or two on the matter. But learning that the detective didn't think her guilty of murdering Jonathan had to be a piece of worthwhile information, regardless of the legalities of the issue.

She dug her card key out of her purse and used it to gain entrance to the main corridor on her floor and led the way down the hall to her unit. She made a right at the far end, followed by a quick left into an alcove where her unit and another were located. She stopped cold.

"You leave this open?" Scanlon asked, shouldering his way past her. He pulled his service revolver from the shoulder holster under the jacket of his cheap suit.

He looked at her, and she shook her head.

"You wait here," he said, lowering his voice, then inched toward the door, his gun drawn.

Using his foot, he slowly pushed open the door. He moved quickly then, drew his weapon in front of him and said in a cold deadly voice, "Make one move asshole, and it'll be your last."

Chapter 8

"PUT YOUR HANDS behind your head, real slow like," Scanlon ordered from the doorway. "Down on your knees."

Laurel remained what she perceived as a safe distance behind Scanlon as he entered her condo with his gun drawn. She walked slowly into the marble-tiled foyer and stood just beyond the entry to the living room, staring in shock, not at the intruder, but at the absolute destruction of her home.

The safe haven she'd been craving since Scanlon had first slipped the cold handcuffs over her wrist at the cemetery, looked as if it were now nothing more than a garbage dump. The place had been trashed beyond recognition. No, not just trashed. Worse. It'd been ruthlessly ransacked.

"Whoa, just take it easy."

Laurel immediately recognized Damon's deep, velvety voice, and walked the remaining distance into what was left of her living room.

"Do it," Scanlon demanded harshly. "Now."

"Detective, stop."

Scanlon kept his gaze, and his gun, aimed at the back of Damon's head. "You know this jerkwad?" Scanlon asked.

"Yes. He's not a jerkwad. He's my . . . attorney," she said eventually. He wasn't really, only technically. Unless as he'd predicted there wasn't a lawyer in southern California willing to take her case. "Detective Scanlon, this is Damon Metcalf, formerly of the district attorney's office?"

"We've met before," Damon said.

"Ah, hell." Scanlon immediately holstered his weapon. "Sorry about that Metcalf. Just doing my job."

Damon muttered something in response to Scanlon's apology that Laurel didn't catch. After a moment's pause, he finally shook the hand Scanlon extended in belated greeting. She could only imagine Damon wasn't too happy about having had a gun aimed at his skull.

"How did you get in here?" Scanlon asked Damon.

"I know where she keeps the spare key," he explained. He stepped around the frame of the remains of her cocktail table, his loafers crunching on shattered glass. "I haven't touched anything, and used my cell to call 911 to report the break in."

Laurel looked around her, her heart breaking. Just about everything she owned had been ruined. The sofa, an eighteenth century reproduction, had been shredded, as had the cushions of the authentic Queen Anne chairs she'd refinished and reupholstered herself. The glass tables had been shattered, every reproduction vase smashed, paintings were sliced, prints ripped from their frames and torn in half. Books, including the few leather-bound first editions she'd kept in an antique barrister case, were strewn about the room, the pages ripped from the leather bindings, their covers sliced. Even her phone and the remote controls to her television and stereo system had been smashed, as well as the electronics themselves.

She knelt down to inspect a pile of CDs and DVDs. Every last one had been removed from their protective cases. "Who would do something like this?" she whispered around the lump lodged in her throat.

Damon approached her and she looked up at him. A

sympathetic expression encompassed his handsome face. "Laurel—"

She raised her hand to stop him, stood abruptly, and walked away. She didn't want to hear useless platitudes right now. She wanted her life back.

In the dining room, the cherry wood table lay on its side, the top deeply gouged. The cushions had been ripped from the matching chairs and shredded in the same manner as her sofa and living room chairs. The light fixture had been pulled from the bracket, the globes all removed and broken, as had the contents in the beveled glass curio. The few serving dishes she'd collected had also been destroyed, but surprisingly the cherry buffet hadn't been toppled.

With dread, she entered the kitchen. Her hand went to her throat as she surveyed even more damage. All the drawers had been pulled from the base cabinets, their contents dumped onto the wood-planked floor. The cabinet doors stood open, her dishware and cookware a shattered mess amid the cutlery, kitchen towels, and utensils on the floor. The trestle table was littered with canned goods and boxed items, some had even been opened and dumped. The sick bastard had even emptied the contents of her refrigerator and freezer.

"Has anything been taken?" Scanlon asked from the doorway.

Laurel shook her head. "No," she said. "I don't think so." Not that she could really tell if anything had been stolen. To her it appeared as if destruction, rather than theft, had been the goal.

Mission accomplished.

Damon moved past her and pulled a pen from his pocket. Using the tip, he poked at a package of freezer-wrapped pork chops on the table. "These are still frozen," he said, looking over at Scanlon. "Whoever was here, hasn't been gone all that long."

Laurel started to tremble. The shaking started in her hands and zipped along her body until her knees felt weak. She looked around for a place to sit until she could find her bearings again, but every piece of furniture she owned had been damaged and was unusable.

She grabbed the counter for support. Tears welled in her eyes, blurring her vision. They could lock her up, take away her freedom, and somehow she'd find a way to survive. Although she'd never been incarcerated until yesterday, she'd once lived the life of a prisoner. The only difference this time was she wouldn't be living under the illusion of freedom.

She pulled in a shaky breath and tried to steady nerves that felt as if they'd been scraped raw. She'd get through this. She had to. What other choice did she have?

But good grief she could use a good cry. Even when she'd discovered Jonathan's ravaged body or when they'd put him in the ground, she kept the tears at bay. But to see everything she owned so thoughtlessly destroyed, on top of everything else she'd already been through, was just too much.

Not only were the people she loved taken from her, just about everything she owned had been destroyed. She squeezed her eyes shut. No, she would *not* cry. Not now. Not ever.

Maybe later.

It's just stuff, she reminded herself. One insurance claim later, and most of what she'd lost could be replaced or restored. Not true for the people she'd lost in her life. There was no magical form with a dotted line to bring them back.

She opened her eyes, drew in a deep, much steadier breath and let it out slowly. Scanlon looked uncomfortable. Damon looked annoyed.

"You going to be all right?" Damon asked gently.

Not trusting her voice not to betray her emotions, she nodded.

Scanlon left the kitchen, only to return seconds later. "No

sign of forced entry," he said. "How many keys you got lying around, Doc?"

"Just the one, plus the one Jonathan had," she said, a little amazed her voice didn't quaver. "I also keep a spare at Artifacts."

"Who would have access to the key?"

"Stacy Owens," she answered. "She's our admin assistant."

"Anyone else?"

Laurel thought for a moment before answering. "We were going to hire a new go-to-girl to free Stacy up for more of the artistic work we do, so we've had some applicants come through the past couple of weeks."

"What about clients?" Scanlon asked.

Laurel shook her head. "No, no one."

"Do you have a maid service?" Damon asked her.

She shot him a get-real look. "No," she said. "There is a cleaning crew that cleans our offices, though. But I keep my desk locked at night."

Scanlon nodded, then pulled his cell phone from his pocket and dialed. "I'll get the crime scene unit out here. I wouldn't get your hopes up about them finding anything. Whoever did this was damn thorough."

"You mean we shouldn't count on uncovering any fingerprints?" Laurel asked him, but he'd already turned away from her and was busy talking on his cell.

"Probably not," Damon answered. "Laurel, I'm sorry."

She shrugged in response because she didn't know what to say. It wasn't his fault.

He moved closer to where she was leaning up against the counter. She caught a teasing whiff of his aftershave. He smelled woodsy, the way she imagined the Montana countryside would. Such a silly thing to think about when her life was literally a shambles.

"Is it possible someone was looking for something?" he asked her.

She shook her head, then looked at the mess on the trestle table. "What? What could someone possibly be looking for here?" She looked back at Damon. "Pot roast? Yogurt that's outlived its shelf life?"

His answering smile was just a quirk of his lips. "You can't stay here," he said.

"Yeah, I kinda figured." She supposed she should check into a hotel for a few days. She wasn't stupid and suspected this was no random crime. Whoever did this could very well come back. As much as she'd like to rip the offender's cold heart right out of his chest with her bare hands for invading and destroying her home, her sanctuary, she wasn't all that anxious to come face to face with someone carrying that big of an axe to grind.

"I need to call my insurance guy."

"Okay."

"Do you think they'll let me take some clothes?"

"If not, we'll go buy some."

Great. More expense.

She tucked her hands into the side pockets of her skirt. With the toe of her shoe, she pushed away a can of chicken noodle soup and watched it roll under the table. "I think I'm afraid to go into the bedroom."

"I can do it for you. Just tell me what you want."

Want? Where did she begin? Her life back, for starters. "Thank you, but I'd rather do it myself." The idea of Damon pawing through her underwear drawer just wasn't something she wanted to think about. The image just stirred up too many memories better left alone.

"You don't have to, you know," he said.

She envisioned his large, now work-roughened hands sliding over the silks, satins, and lace of her panty drawer. Next, those same hands, gliding over her hips, splayed over her abdomen, his long fingers dipping beneath the elastic band.

She cleared her throat. "Actually, I do."

Damon nodded his understanding. She doubted he had so much as a clue.

In the living room, she heard Scanlon's voice, followed by another, deeper male voice. The uniforms must've arrived. "Do you think my life will ever be normal again?"

"Eventually."

She had her doubts.

"Where were you?" she asked, pushing off the counter. "I called."

"Out in the valley. Looking for a lawyer."

"Any luck?"

"Nope. You're a pariah."

She let out a sigh. That's what she'd been afraid of. "I see you haven't lost your charm."

His lips curved slightly at her sarcasm. "Just trying to keep it honest."

"Why don't you try being my friend instead?"

His hand settled on her arm. A responding tingle shot along the surface of her skin. "I am your friend, Laurel. That's why I'm here. But we do need to talk. Later."

Not knowing what to say, she nodded, then walked away.

In the living room, she found Scanlon talking to two uniformed policemen. "CSU is on their way up," he said as Damon came up beside her.

"I'd like to get some clothes."

"That's not a good idea, ma'am," the taller of the uniformed officers answered. "The crime scene needs to be preserved."

This wasn't a crime scene, it was her home, she wanted to shout, but nodded obediently instead and kept the rebellious thought to herself. What good would it do for her to break tradition and become hysterical now? She'd just expend more emotional energy that she suspected she'd be needing for whatever obstacles she had yet to face. And with the

way her life had been going the past few days, she'd be wise
to expect plenty more hurdles yet to clear. Better to reserve
what little she had left, because she'd be needing it, of that
she was certain. If she'd learned anything in her short life,
she knew if she waited long enough, inevitably that proverbial other shoe would eventually drop. And with the way
her luck was going, she'd better duck.

While Damon gave his statement to the uniformed officers a
few feet away, Laurel stood nearby in the corridor, her back
pressed against the wall for support. She would've loved to
sit down somewhere, take a load off, but given the state of
her furnishings and with the crime scene technicians doing
their job, comfort was a luxury that would have to wait.

She hadn't seen much of Scanlon since the crime scene
people showed up twenty minutes ago. He'd told her not to
leave, not that she had anywhere to go.

She'd had yet to check out her bedroom or either of the
bathrooms to see what kind of damage had been done
there, but after what she'd already witnessed, it didn't take
much for her to imagine the worst. She wouldn't be at all
surprised to find all of her clothes had been ripped to shreds,
as well. What she couldn't imagine, however, was who could
be responsible.

She let out a weary sigh. It'd been over four years since
she'd left the Institute. What could they possibly want with
her now?

Damon had suggested someone might have been looking
for something. Other than the sentimental variety, she didn't
have anything of real value. She did own a small, quarter
carat diamond ring that had belonged to her mother, but
most of her jewelry consisted of estate pieces that wouldn't
garner more than a few hundred bucks on eBay.

She didn't keep a desktop computer at home, and her
laptop was still locked in the trunk of her car, which was

parked in the police impound lot, according to Scanlon. The stereo, television set, and DVD player hadn't been taken, but destroyed, as had the artwork that had once adorned her walls. Those were nothing more than unnumbered, mass-produced prints or the few paintings she'd purchased from various starving-artist sales in the area. She couldn't afford the priceless real art they reproduced or restored at Artifacts, even with the money she'd accumulated due to their recent success.

Still, she couldn't help wondering, was the devastation to her home personal? Who could possibly hate her that much? She didn't think Jonathan's family could be responsible. This was simply all too low budget and seedy for a family as rich and powerful as the Lintons. No, their revenge would be much more subtle, and effective.

After Damon's oh-so-charming pariah reference, she suspected their power was already fast at work. This wasn't rocket science. If he'd gone as far as the San Fernando Valley looking for a lawyer to represent her, she figured there wasn't a decent or reputable attorney within three counties willing to risk their financial future by representing the woman accused of murdering a Linton. She was screwed.

The elevator bell dinged in the distance. More cops, she thought. Or worse, Scanlon's partner. She didn't like Detective Teslenko. The man was a condescending, sanctimonious prick, but then he wasn't exactly her number one fan, either.

At this point, she was very close to being beyond caring about anything but her own comfort. Her feet hurt, her back ached, and she was in need of sleep, food, and a change of clothes—and not necessarily in that order. She really would have loved to sleep in her own bed tonight, but that option was definitely out of the question now.

Well, at least she still had her work. She'd go mad for certain if she didn't have something other than the upcoming trial to occupy her mind.

Laurel turned her head as the distinct sound of flip flops neared. Seconds later, her assistant, Stacy Owens, rounded the corner and rushed toward her, stopping abruptly when she spied the two policemen still questioning Damon a few feet away.

A blend of curiosity and concern lit Stacy's golden brown eyes. "My God, Laurel. What's going on?" she asked. "I thought the police already searched your place last week?"

"They did," Laurel answered.

Stacy attempted to peer into the open door, but Detective Scanlon suddenly appeared in the foyer, his bulk an effective block of any glimpse to the damage inside.

Laurel pushed off the wall and straightened. "Someone broke in and trashed the place," she said when Stacy looked back at her. "What are you doing here?"

Not that she was foolish enough to dissuade the moral support of someone who'd braved rush hour traffic for her, but she was fairly certain Stacy lived a good hour's drive away. With the way Laurel's luck had been going, she seriously doubted her assistant had battled the worst of the Los Angeles freeway system just to bring her good news.

Stacy swung the oversized bag slung over her shoulder to the floor, then knelt down and starting digging through the contents. "I've been trying to call you since I heard you'd been released," she said, her attention on the bag. "Didn't you get my messages?"

"No," Laurel said. "The battery in my cell went dead and the phone in my apartment was broken, along with just about everything else."

"Ah-ha!" Stacy exclaimed. She stood and thrust a small stack of messages at Laurel. "None of it's good," she said, lowering her voice. "We've had four of our future projects pulled. The Field Museum came up with some bullshit excuse about a scheduling conflict and canceled your seminar. And that jerk from UCLA, the head of the Art History

Department, got his Jockeys in a knot when he couldn't get in touch with you. He finally left a message with me this morning."

Laurel briefly closed her eyes. She didn't need to look at the messages in her hand to know why Nicholas Benjamin wanted to speak with her. "He's cancelled my classes."

Stacy nodded, her rich, short-cropped auburn curls bobbing up and down with the movement. "'Until further notice', he said." She let out a sound of disgust. "Lying bastard."

"Until further notice?" Laurel scoffed. "More like until I'm proven innocent."

"It isn't fair, if you ask me," Stacy said sympathetically. "What ever happened to innocent until proven guilty?"

That's what she'd like to know, too. She read a couple of the messages Stacy had handed her and shook her head. "I've only been charged with the crime, not convicted, and already Artifacts is losing clients."

"I'm so sorry, Laurel."

"There's nothing to apologize for."

Why did everyone feel the need to say how sorry they were for her misfortune? Shit apparently did happen, just as the bumper sticker prophesized, only it was happening to her so fast she could barely catch her breath.

She crumpled the messages. "Artifacts will be fine," she told Stacy. At least she hoped so. She didn't know what she'd do if it were taken away from her. With her background, she undoubtedly had options, but they held no appeal to her any longer. Artifacts had become her life.

Stacy frowned. "I'm not worried about my job." She put her hand on Laurel's arm. "I'm more concerned with how you're holding up through all this."

Laurel shrugged and pulled her arm away from Stacy's touch. "As well as can be expected, given the circumstances."

She wasn't comfortable talking about herself. Never had been. Stacy had been employed by Artifacts since they could afford to hire an assistant, and in the past two years, Laurel rarely spoke to her about anything but the work they did. What little she did know of Stacy's personal life, she'd learned in passing from Jonathan, and that wouldn't fill a chemist's beaker.

But that didn't mean she didn't care about Stacy. She did. A great deal, in fact. Expressing her concern, however, had never been easy for her, something which had garnered her a reputation of being cold and distant. Which was why it made no sense to her that someone would try to ruin her. She wasn't close enough to anyone to evoke that kind of emotion.

She frowned suddenly. What if the break-in *was* indeed personal, for whatever misguided reason? Didn't it make sense that whomever had broken into her home might decide to do the same to her business? Or what was left of it?

"I want you to stay away from the office for a while," Laurel said. "Consider it a bonus to your existing vacation plan."

"Do you think that's a good idea?" Stacy asked. "If we close down, what kind of message will that send to our existing clients?"

Laurel didn't care. Stacy's welfare was too important. "I think it'd be for the best. For the time being."

Stacy stuffed her hands into the back pockets of her jeans. "I can work at home." The little white top she wore inched upward, revealing a small gold hoop.

A belly button piercing? Laurel never would've guessed.

"That isn't necessary. I want you to take some time off." And do what? Laurel had no idea what Stacy did for fun.

"I've been working on the plans for the Hamilton reproduction," Stacy continued as if Laurel hadn't spoken. "It's all computer generation at this point. I'll stop by the office on the way home, pick up my discs and laptop. It's no trouble."

"No!" She blew out a stream of breath. "Don't. Please."

"We can't afford to be late on any of our existing projects now," Stacy argued. "Not after the cancellations we've had already."

"We're going to be fine," Laurel reiterated. "But I really don't want you going to the office."

Stacy frowned again. "Talk to me, Laurel. What's going on?"

Laurel didn't want to frighten Stacy, but neither did she want to put her at risk. Jonathan had been murdered—at Artifacts. Her home had been thoroughly ransacked and essentially destroyed. Call her paranoid, but she had a bad feeling anyone connected to her wasn't safe. No way would she allow Stacy to put herself in harm's way. "This break in might have been personal."

Understanding immediately lit Stacy's gaze. "And you think it might be dangerous at the office?"

"Yes. Stacy . . ." Out of the corner of her eye, she saw Damon and the two officers approach. Damon stopped, but the uniforms walked past them and into the condo to speak to Scanlon. "I couldn't handle it right now if anything happened to you, too."

Despite the gravity of the situation, Stacy grinned at her. "I always knew you had a heart under that cool exterior."

"We can go," Damon said once the cops were out of earshot.

Scanlon spoke to the two officers, then walked out into the corridor. "We're going to call in a couple more uniforms and canvas the building," he said to Laurel. "See if anyone heard anything."

He didn't sound too convinced, and Laurel couldn't blame him. She didn't really know much about her neighbors other than the young couple in the unit down the hall. The only reason she knew them, at least in passing, was because she'd met up with their Scottish terrier who preferred the potted palm near the elevator to the actual palm trees in the dog park across the street from the condominium complex. Given the state of her frozen foods strewn about the kitchen, the break in hadn't occurred all that long ago while most of the residents in her building were probably at work.

"This is Stacy Owens," Laurel said, grateful for the interruption. "She's our . . . she's Artifacts' assistant," she corrected. There was no more *our*. She was Artifacts now. "Stacy, Damon Metcalf, and you know Detective Scanlon."

"Detective," Stacy said curtly. She gave Damon a quick once over and smiled appreciatively. "You're representing Laurel?"

"So it seems," he answered.

"For the moment," Laurel added.

Scanlon frowned. "I thought you were counsel of record?"

"Temporarily," Laurel said.

"Temporarily?" Scanlon jammed his hands into the front pockets of his trousers. "You do realize Rosen is going for capital murder, right?"

"I'll find a good lawyer."

Damon rammed his hand through his hair, then rubbed at the back of his neck. "We'll discuss this later."

She gave Damon a hard look. "But you—"

"Later," he interrupted roughly.

She shot him a look of annoyance. He gave her one right back, then shifted his irritation to Scanlon. "And why are you suddenly on her side?" Damon asked the detective. "You're the one who arrested her."

"Detective Scanlon doesn't believe I'm guilty," Laurel said.

Damon crossed his arms over his chest. "You willing to say that on the stand?"

Scanlon's answer was a lift of his heavy shoulders. "You know how the system works."

"I need to call my insurance guy." She had her own ideas on how the system worked, and not much of it was in her favor. "And see about having someone clean up the mess."

"Why don't you let me take care of it for you," Stacy offered. "You've been through enough the past couple of days."

"Thanks, but no. I can do it."

"Let me do something to earn my paycheck," Stacy said with a hint of laughter in her voice.

"It's probably not a bad idea," Damon added. "You look like hell, Laurel."

Stacy fished through her enormous bag again. Once she produced her cell phone, she thrust it at Laurel. "Call the insurance company. I'll wait for him to show, then find a cleaning service."

Laurel looked at Damon, who nodded in agreement. She took the phone and dialed her insurance agent's number from memory.

Laurel took a few steps away when the insurance agent answered on the second ring. After explaining the situation and giving Carl Stacy's cell phone number, she hung up then called and made reservations for herself and Damon at the Beverly Hills Hotel so she'd be closer to Artifacts. Associating with him could be risky, but she'd rather have him close so she could make certain he was safe.

"Where will you be staying?" Scanlon asked her when she handed Stacy back her cell phone.

"I booked a couple of rooms at the Beverly Hills Hotel," she answered.

"That's probably a good idea," Scanlon said. "Stay away from here for a few days."

"Why?" Stacy asked, dropping her cell phone into her purse. "I'll make sure it's cleaned up by tomorrow."

"Because," Laurel said, "Detective Scanlon also believes the break in is personal."

"Hey, I never said that," Scanlon countered.

"But you do," she said. "The damage was too thorough, wasn't it?"

"Let's just say I haven't ruled out the possibility," he answered, albeit reluctantly.

Laurel turned to Damon. "I'll need some things for tonight, and tomorrow I'll need to get my car and pick up a few items from the office."

At his nod, she looked at Stacy. "Carl Kendrick said he'll be here within the hour."

"Who's Kendrick?" Scanlon asked her.

"My insurance agent," she answered. To Stacy she said, "He'll be bringing an adjuster with him. Once they're finished, the cleaning crew can come in."

"If you're going to the office tomorrow, why don't I—" Stacy started.

"Meet me there at ten," Laurel said, and Stacy smiled.

"The crime scene unit is almost finished," Scanlon told them. "So far it isn't looking too good. We'll canvas the building, but unless you have a helpful neighbor, I wouldn't hold my breath, Doc."

A pair of identical depressions appeared between Damon's eyebrows, once again signifying his annoyance. "Surely someone had to have heard something."

"More than likely someone did," Scanlon said, "but you know as well as I do, Joe Citizen doesn't like to get involved."

"Too well," Damon said, then looked over at Laurel. "Ready?"

"Yes." Before leaving, she made Stacy promise not to go near the office until tomorrow. At Scanlon's sharp glance, she added, "Just to be safe."

He nodded, she assumed, in agreement. "I'll wait around with her for this Kendrick to show."

"Thank you," Laurel said. "I appreciate it."

She and Damon turned to leave, but then Damon stopped. "Hey Scanlon," he said. "For the record, anything my client said to you out of my presence is inadmissible."

Scanlon shot him a sour look. "Fucking lawyers."

Chapter 9

SCANLON PULLED HIS cell phone from his pocket and squinted at the display. Rosen. Again.

The prick could go to hell. Officially he was off duty. Even if he were on the clock, he wouldn't be all that thrilled to speak to the pain in the ass ADA.

He silenced the ringer.

The crime scene techies were long gone and Dr. Jennings's assistant had completed the walk through of the doc's condo with a pair of officious-looking ass wipes from the insurance company. They'd left less than ten minutes ago. Owens had mentioned there'd be a cleaning crew showing up, but hadn't been specific of the time. Scanlon didn't much care when they showed up, just so long as he had another look around without the crime scene boys crawling all over the place or Metcalf breathing down his neck.

He'd never been a fan of lawyers, but as far as suits went, he'd always considered Metcalf one of the good guys. He'd been a hard-ass prosecutor, but unlike that pain in the ass Rosen, Metcalf had been fair and honest. That boy could've easily gone to the top, too.

It'd been one hell of a surprise to see him in court this morning on the doc's behalf. He and Metcalf hadn't exactly been the best of buddies, nor had they ever really moved in the same social circles, but they had shared a brew or two after hours on occasion. Even so, he hadn't been aware Metcalf and Jennings were acquainted, let alone close enough friends to bring Metcalf out of his way-too-early retirement.

An interesting turn of events, he thought. A smile tugged at his lips. One that no doubt had Rosen spitting nails, too. It was no secret there was no love lost between Metcalf and Rosen. Tales of their one-upmanship weren't exactly legendary, but they sure as hell made for a good story at the bar after hours.

Scanlon walked over to the shredded sofa and sat on what was left of a tattered cushion. Flipping open his cell phone, he quickly punched in the speed dial code for Teslenko. His partner answered on the second ring.

"Christ, Scanlon," Teslenko grumbled by way of greeting. "Don't you ever give it a rest?"

"You know what they say—no rest for the dumb schmuck with a hunch."

"I hate when that happens."

Yeah, so did Scanlon. It meant long hours off the clock because the brass wouldn't support a cop chasing a hunch on a case they considered closed. "You busy?"

Teslenko's short bark of laughter held no humor. "Would it make a difference if I said I was?"

"Probably not. I'm at Jennings's place," Scanlon told his partner. "How long will it take you to get over here?"

"I could probably be there in thirty. Why? What's going on? Who'd the Ice Queen off this time?"

"Someone broke in and ripped the place to shreds."

"Ah hell. She there now?"

"No, she and Metcalf are at the Beverly Hills Hotel for a few days."

"Must be rough," Teslenko said with a caustic laugh.

Scanlon was well aware of Teslenko's dislike of the doc, but then Pete was one of those cops who subscribed to the guilty until proven otherwise theory. "You coming or not?"

"All right." Teslenko let out a ragged sigh. "I'm on my way."

Just as Scanlon flipped the phone closed, it rang again. Rosen.

Again.

"Persistent prick."

Despite his curiosity, he ignored it. He'd call him back later. Whatever the ADA wanted, it couldn't be good if he was calling so late in the evening.

Probably just wanted to bitch to him about Jennings making bail, Scanlon thought with disgust. As if he'd had anything to do with it. The evidence, or lack thereof, was Rosen's problem now. Scanlon had done his job. Unfortunately, he didn't believe the evidence. And that was becoming Scanlon's problem because as Teslenko had complained, he just didn't know how to let it go.

He stood suddenly, certain he'd heard something in the corridor. Someone approaching?

He walked to the front door, which was still open, and looked into the hallway.

Deserted.

Probably just a neighbor, he thought, although not thoroughly convinced. He leaned his shoulder against the doorjamb to wait for Teslenko to show and kept his eyes and ears open.

This case was becoming more bizarre by the hour. He'd meant what he'd said to the doc. He didn't think she'd killed her business partner, regardless of the evidence. The lack of a strong motive stuck in his mind, because in his opinion, Jennings had no reason to off Linton. By her own admission, Linton was making her a very rich woman. In his experience, you didn't ice the hand that's taken you from a steady diet of Ramen noodles and Kool-Aid to filet mignon and champagne.

The way he saw it, Jennings had simply been in the wrong place at the wrong time. No matter which way Rosen had chosen to stretch that evidence, without a solid motive, the case simply didn't add up to capital murder.

And then there was the break in to her apartment. The total destruction told him the job was more than likely personal. Yet on the other hand, the thoroughness could be an indicator that someone was indeed looking for something. But what, and how was it related to Linton's murder?

The more he thought about the case, the more questions he had. And none of the answers led him to believe Laurel Jennings was guilty.

The elevator dinged. He couldn't see the doors from where he stood, so he didn't know if someone was coming off or getting on, but when no one appeared and he didn't hear the sound of a door closing he suspected the latter. Funny, but he hadn't heard any doors close before hearing the ding of the elevator, either.

He pushed off the doorjamb. Slowly, he ambled down the corridor to peer around the corner. The only occupant of the lobby area was a Scottish terrier lifting his leg on a potted palm near the elevator.

"Where do you want these?" Damon asked.

Laurel sank on the edge of the king-size bed, dropped the packages she'd carried in with her at her feet and toed off her pumps. "Anywhere," she said. "I don't know whether I'm more tired, hungry, or angry because I had to buy all this stuff."

"Probably all three." He set the shopping bags on the bed. "Maybe you should've grabbed a few things from your place, after all." And saved yourself a small fortune, he thought.

She shrugged out of her blazer and looked up at him. Dark circles underscored the exhaustion in her eyes, reminding him of the hell she'd been through the past few days. Which had been reason enough for him not to argue with her over something as trivial as sleeping arrangements when he'd already had a perfectly good room at the Bonaventure. He was picking his battles, knowing he'd have one on his hands over her defense, so he'd simply checked out of his hotel and moved into the room adjoining Laurel's at the Beverly Hills Hotel. Not exactly a bad thing when he worried over her safety given the devastation he'd witnessed at her condo earlier.

"I know, it would've been smarter," she said wearily, "but honestly, Damon, I just couldn't face any more today."

He nodded his understanding. Not only had she suffered the loss of a friend and her business partner, but she'd been arrested and charged with the crime. From what snippets of her conversation with Stacy he'd overheard while he'd been giving his statement to the cops, it appeared as if her business was now suffering as well because of her legal problems. And to make matters even more stressful, what he imagined was the one place in the world where she'd felt safe and secure had been violated in the worst way imaginable.

If it were him, he'd be mad as hell.

He knew all about that proverbial back-breaking straw, and that's what had him worried. For all the strength she showed the world, he knew the real Laurel, had witnessed firsthand the vulnerability she'd learned to keep hidden as a matter of her emotional survival.

She stretched, rolled her shoulders, then reached for the bags closest to her and started pulling out garment after garment. Methodically, she began removing sales tags and separating the items she'd bought into separate piles.

The stop they'd made at Neiman Marcus on the way to

the hotel could very well have been a retail therapy session for all he knew. Lord knew, she'd bought enough crap to pay for a traditional therapy session—at Beverly Hills rates, for that matter. Probably half a dozen times over.

Since she'd reserved them adjoining rooms, he walked over to the door leading to his room and opened it, but would have to go into his own room from the corridor to unlock his side. "Why don't you get settled, take a long hot shower, and then we'll order room service," he suggested. "You must be starving."

"For a decent meal? Absolutely," she said, ripping off another price tag. "I'll meet you in your room in about an hour?"

"Sounds good." He grabbed his garment bag and duffle, then carried his bags to his room, leaving Laurel for the time being.

His own room was an almost exact duplicate of Laurel's, decorated in warm subdued tones of beige, peach, and sage with rich, classic wood furnishings. He'd have been just as happy at the Bonaventure where he'd stayed last night, but even he had to admit The Beverly Hills Hotel was unsurpassed when it came to luxury and service, and one hell of a far cry from his rustic log home back in Montana.

He hung his garment bag in the spacious closet and felt a small twinge of homesickness. He realized how much he missed the towering pines surrounding his property, the big sky, and the clean air. He didn't exactly long for all that solitude, but there was something to be said for what little peace of mind he had managed to find in the months since he'd walked away, even if it was nothing more than an illusion ninety percent of the time.

He carried his duffle to the bed to unpack simply for the sake of convenience since he was unsure exactly how long he'd be in Los Angeles, or even in the same hotel as Laurel if he couldn't convince her he was the only lawyer in the freaking state willing to take on her defense. She needed a lawyer unafraid of the Lintons, one with nothing to lose. She'd never find one better than him to fit that particular bill, but convincing her of that fact wasn't going to be easy.

She didn't want him here, she'd made that clear. Why? is what he wanted to know. Especially when she didn't exactly have all that many people lining up behind her watching her back.

Detective Scanlon doesn't believe I'm guilty.

Then why in the hell had he arrested her?

He walked into the bathroom and let out a weary sigh. Because the ADA had demanded it, that's why. He knew better than most exactly what Alan Rosen was capable of, understood the lengths someone like Rosen would go to for a conviction. Too well, because he'd once stooped to an equally ruthless level.

"Shit."

He dropped his shaving kit on the counter in the bathroom, braced his hands on the cool marble, and looked at himself in the mirror. He wasn't the same cold-blooded bastard he'd once been, he thought. He'd lost his edge.

Sure you have, buddy. Dull as a fucking razor.

So why was his blood humming with anticipation just thinking about going up against such a formidable opponent as Rosen?

He didn't like the answer.

He swore again.

With an angry shove, he pushed away from the countertop and left the elegant bathroom. He crossed the room, picked up the phone and placed an order with room service for a couple of steak dinners and a bottle of expensive wine. He then walked to the mini-bar and opened it, surveying the contents. Plucking a small, double shot bottle of Cuervo

Gold from the shelf, he twisted off the cap and immediately downed the tequila straight from the miniscule bottle.

The booze burned his throat, then settled and blazed in his empty stomach, instantly spreading a relaxing warmth throughout his body. Once upon a time he'd believed in the system. He'd fought hard to protect the innocent and punish the guilty. Until he'd gone too far.

With a grunt of disgust, he tossed the empty bottle of tequila into the garbage can. Briefly, he considered another, wondering how many of those small double shots it would take for him to pass out in a drunken stupor. On an empty stomach, probably not all that many.

Although tempted by the promise of alcoholic oblivion, he grabbed a Coke from the shelf and set it on top of the bar with a snap. He snagged the ice bucket and went in search of an ice machine. When he returned a few minutes later, his mood hadn't improved.

He should have ripped that fax to shreds the second he'd read that headline and seen that damn photograph of Laurel. But he hadn't. And in truth, he wouldn't have either. Oh no, not him. His personal mission in life—protect the innocent, Laurel in particular.

He'd made a goddamn career out of doing the right thing. And what had it gotten him? Nothing but a conscience laden with guilt and far too many sleepless nights filled with memories of two lives cut short. All because he'd been hell bent on seeing justice served.

"What fucking justice?" he muttered. Sure, he might have gotten the conviction he'd been after, but he hadn't been able to stomach the consequences of his actions, so he'd quit. Did he have the stomach now to do what needed to be done when he was Laurel's only hope?

He filled a glass tumbler with ice, then popped the top on the Coke and poured. With the initial buzz and warmth of the tequila effectively killed off by the memories of his ambitions, he considered opening up the mini-bar again and routing out a bottle of rum to add to his soda.

Regardless of the hour, when the memories threatened to swamp him, he usually headed to the workshop and shut his mind off to everything but the process of building a piece of furniture. With no shop handy, the only effective means he could think of to close off the past was massive quantities of alcohol.

A nice diversion, but one he honestly couldn't afford. Not when he had a defense strategy to plan—and a client to convince he was her only hope.

He only hoped they both wouldn't live to regret it.

"So, you tell me," Scanlon said to his partner. "What do *you* see?"

"A fucking mess," Teslenko answered. Carefully, he stepped around the mountain of clothing littering the floor to peer into the barren emptiness of Laurel Jennings's cavernous walk-in closet.

"That's not what I meant," Scanlon said. He stood with his backside against the dresser as Teslenko continued his perusal of the closet. What he wanted was his partner's opinion. Needed him to support his hunch, or rather, tell him that he hadn't gone soft all because of a pretty face and a pair of intriguing eyes fanned with dark sooty lashes.

Teslenko turned back to look at him. "Then you tell me."

"Take a good look," Scanlon said. "You think this is personal?"

Scanlon waited impatiently while Teslenko scanned the doc's bedroom again. Like the rest of the place, both bedrooms, along with the guest bath and the elegant master bath had been trashed.

"Yeah, it does," Teslenko finally answered.

Scanlon sensed a trace of apprehension in his partner's voice. "But?" he pressed.

"That's just it," Teslenko said, slipping his hands into the front pockets of his trousers. "It *looks* personal, but I get the feeling that's the whole point. Like it's intentional."

Scanlon grinned. Teslenko might be a jerk some of the time, but he thought like a cop when it counted. Which is exactly what Scanlon had been hoping for now. "That's what I thought, too. The destruction here is just too damn methodical."

Teslenko went back to the empty closet and peered inside again. "Okay, so maybe someone *was* searching for something." Every last item had been removed from the closet, the dressers and the bathroom cabinetry. Pockets had been torn off clothing, storage boxes and containers opened and emptied of their contents. Even a box of tampons had been torn open and dumped onto the floor. "Any idea what?"

Scanlon let out a sigh. "That, my friend, appears to be the sixty-four-thousand-dollar question."

"In other words, you don't have a clue."

"Just one," Scanlon answered with a slight grin.

Teslenko turned back to face Scanlon and waited for an answer.

"Whatever they were looking for," Scanlon told him, "it's clear to me they didn't find it here." He pushed off the dresser and headed into the master bath, motioning for Teslenko to follow. "Take another look around in here."

Teslenko stepped past Scanlon to examine the master bath for the second time since arriving. After a moment, he shrugged. "I don't get it. What's so special?"

"If they'd found what they were looking for," Scanlon explained, "wouldn't there be items left untouched? Every

single thing in this apartment was tossed." He inclined his head toward a bottle of shampoo that had been sliced in half lengthwise and dumped into the sink. "If this were personal, wouldn't we see more rage?"

Teslenko glanced pointedly to the ravaged shampoo bottle. "I dunno, Scanlon. That looks pretty pissed off to me. What kind of sick bastard slices open shampoo bottles?"

"Someone convinced the doc has something worth hiding?"

"Maybe." Teslenko leaned his hip against the bathroom counter and crossed his arms, a thoughtful expression wrinkling his forehead. "Say you're right. Just what are you planning to do about it?"

"I'll know that when we figure out what they were looking for and why."

"Whoa, hold it a minute. What do you mean *we*? This case is closed."

"Yeah, but the break in—"

"Isn't Homicide's problem."

"Bullshit," Scanlon argued. "This is related to the Linton murder, Pete."

Teslenko shook his head, then shouldered his way past Scanlon. "I fucking hate when you do this, Scanlon," he complained heatedly.

"Yeah, it's a bitch," Scanlon fired back. "Deal with it."

Teslenko let out a ragged sigh. "Look, even if we were given a green light on this one," he said, softening his tone, "have you looked at your desk lately? We have a shitload of cases that have been ignored because of the Linton murder investigation. Ain't no way in hell the Captain is going to give us the go ahead to reopen a case when the prime suspect has already been charged. Especially a case that's as high profile as this one. Imagine what will happen if the

press caught wind of us poking around after the fact. Rosen would shit a brick."

"Screw the press," Scanlon said. "And Rosen. This is somehow related to the Linton murder, Pete. I know it is."

"Maybe so. But without conclusive evidence, you know as well as I do we'll never be allowed to follow up on it. You need more than your gut to take to the Captain."

Scanlon didn't like admitting Teslenko was right, but dammit, he didn't have any other choice. Somehow, the break in to the doc's apartment was related to Linton's murder. He could feel it. Proving it, however, wasn't going to be easy.

But Scanlon was a smart cop. So was Teslenko, for that matter, which was why he put up with the arrogant son of a bitch.

"Cover for me," Scanlon said.

Teslenko frowned again. "What the hell are you talking about?"

"You're right," Scanlon said. "No way the brass is going to approve us working a B&E when there's no homicide involved, or rather no immediate evidence of a homicide."

"More like a homicide investigation that's been solved."

"So says you."

"Me. The brass. The fucking DA's office. And just in case it's slipped your mind," Teslenko added sarcastically, "Jennings was arraigned this morning."

"Yeah, whatever," Scanlon dismissed Teslenko's argument with an impatient wave of his hand. "Look, I know in my gut this is related to Linton and I'm going to find out why."

"Just how do you plan to accomplish this feat? And keep it away from the press?"

Good question. But they'd fucked up, and Scanlon had to

make it right. Laurel Jennings was no murderer, but his gut was all he had to go on—for the moment.

They'd been under pressure since word of Jonathan Linton's murder hit the airwaves. The press had swarmed the DA's office like hungry vultures demanding sustenance. The DA pushed the brass, demanding an arrest. And because shit always rolled downhill, the brass had naturally leaned on him and Teslenko to wrap up the case—yesterday. With his eye more on the pension awaiting him than taking his time and conducting the investigation his way, he'd taken the evidence at face value and made a case against the doc, making everyone up the food chain happy.

Oh sure, he thought, the evidence had led them in that direction, but Scanlon hadn't completely bought it, even if he had ignored it. For one simple reason. It'd been easy. Too easy.

"By doing what we should've done at the beginning," Scanlon said. "We investigated the doc, but no one bothered to look too hard at the vic, did they? He was the Linton golden boy, and we did what we were told and never bothered to look too closely into Linton's background."

"He was what he was," Teslenko said. "A spoiled rich prick who pissed off the wrong person."

"Not quite," Scanlon said with a shake of his head. "He was what the Linton family wanted him to be known as— their golden boy. Come on, Pete. You've been on the job long enough to know that the victim is just as important as the perp in any investigation. We didn't so much as pull a bank record. For all we know Linton could've been racking up gambling debts to the mob."

Teslenko laughed at that. "You're stretching, partner."

Scanlon shrugged. "Maybe, but until we look into who Linton really was, there's a damn good chance an innocent woman could be convicted, and possibly put to death, for a crime she didn't commit. I don't know, Pete," he said. "Is that something you really want on your conscience? I know I don't."

"Who needs a conscience when I have you?" Teslenko let out a long, slow breath. "Okay, partner. I'm gonna hate myself in the morning for asking this, but where do you want to start?"

Chapter 10

LAUREL OPERATED ON auto-pilot, going from task to task, trying not to think too much about anything except the most basic acts of each routine she performed. Silly as it was, just being able to shampoo and condition her hair and shave her legs offered her a sense of comfort. The act of rubbing into her skin the scented body wash she'd picked up at the cosmetics counter at Neiman, filled her with a supreme sense of ridiculous joy. The complementing body lotion nearly made her giddy.

For anyone else the tasks were routine and mundane, but after the past forty-eight hours, to her they were the equivalent of a long-earned extravagance, and she chose to revel in each and every one of them. Who knew washing out a half-dozen new pair of lace panties and a trio of bras in the bathroom sink of the Beverly Hills Hotel could cause such jubilation? After two nights in the county jail, going to the bathroom in private was a reason to party.

She understood that exhaustion, both physical and emotional, played a key role in her current state of mind. Rather than search for that one final burst of energy to fight it, she chose to simply exist in the moment and accept it for what it was—the end of the first leg of a long and arduous journey she had yet to complete.

Once showered, she dressed in a new pair of cotton pajama bottoms decorated with pink kittens chasing balls of bright, colorful yarn. As she dried her hair, she noticed the cotton candy pink camisole hung a little loosely on her body, so she covered up with the little cardigan that matched the mint green bottoms.

Before getting into the shower, she'd utilized the hotel's laundry service and sent most of the items she'd purchased to be cleaned. She didn't even bother to take the added cost for expedited service into consideration when she'd requested the eight-hour turn around time. Since she'd left home with only the clothes on her back, she needed something to wear. She'd been almost desperate in her need to have them laundered before she wore them and attributed it to the time she'd spent in jail.

The thought of jail made her shudder with revulsion. She didn't understand the criminal mentality, especially repeat offenders. Having spent only two nights behind bars had her nervous about getting so much as a parking ticket in the future. Provided she'd even have a future.

She didn't bother with makeup since she'd planned to go to bed once she and Damon had dinner, but she did take the time to remove all the new makeup from the little navy blue-and-gold-trimmed boxes and put them into the fancy cosmetic bag she'd purchased. After applying a light coating of moisturizer to her face, she went in search of Damon.

He'd opened the doors to their adjoining rooms, so she walked right in and found him standing behind the wet bar, his hands braced on the top, his head bent forward. He looked as worn down and beaten as she felt. "Damon? Everything all right?"

He looked up at her, his gaze intent. A frown creased his forehead. "How did this happen?" he asked her.

She continued to cross the thick, plush carpet until she stood on the opposite side of the bar. "Could you be a little more specific?" *This* could be just about anything. Jonathan's death. Her arrest. Damon's return to Los Angeles. Their breakup four years ago or her lame explanation, or even their now sharing adjoining rooms in a luxury hotel. "I have a lot to choose from."

He made a sound that under better circumstances might have been a chuckle. "Never mind," he said, with a shake of his head. "I ordered a bottle of wine with dinner. Do you want something while we wait?"

"Whatever you're having is fine," she said, feeling a tiny bit brave and daring. She was a water-with-a-lemon-twist kind of girl and really not much of a drinker, other than the rare glass of wine whenever Jonathan forced her to accompany him to a dinner with clients. After the week she'd had, a fifth of Scotch in a freeway bag was starting to sound tasty.

She waited in anticipation as Damon filled a crystal glass with ice. She smiled and breathed a little sigh of relief when he pulled the tab on a can of Coke and poured.

"Thank you," she said, when he slid the glass in front of her. She didn't bother to quibble over the fact that he'd poured her a non-diet soda. She figured the sugar rush would do her good and possibly hold her over until their dinner arrived. It'd been hours since she'd last eaten, and even then she'd barely touched the jailhouse fare.

"You're welcome." He picked up his own glass. "Room service should be here soon."

She took a long drink of the soda, draining half the glass. With a quirk of an eyebrow, he handed her the half-empty can. She refilled her glass without comment, then she followed him over to the small seating area near the sliding glass doors.

"Can we open the doors?" she asked as she sat on one corner of the beige-striped love seat. "I feel the need to breathe some fresh air." She wasn't stalling, not really, but she didn't exactly relish the upcoming conversation. He was probably going to insist on representing her, and she couldn't let that happen. Not that she wasn't grateful for everything he'd done for her today, but after tonight, she'd never see him again.

Without comment, he fulfilled her request. "Better?"

She smiled her thanks. "Yes, much," she said, then let out a long, weary sigh. "I guess it'll take a while for that walls-closing-in-on-me feeling to go away, huh?" A feeling she hadn't even realized she'd had until she'd walked out of the county jail this afternoon.

God, how was she going to survive being locked up in prison if she were wrongfully convicted of Jonathan's murder? She'd never been claustrophobic in her life. Now, she was no longer so certain.

"Give it a day or two," he said, taking the chair opposite her for himself. He set his glass on a coaster with the hotel's logo down on the cocktail table between them, then leaned back in the chair and stretched his long legs in front of him.

She didn't know what to say, other than she had her doubts, so she took another sip of her soda. "Despite the circumstances, it's good to see you again, Damon. I've missed you."

Oh yeah, that's telling him to get lost.

"You should come to Bozeman sometime. You'd like it."

She offered him a wry smile. "I'm not exactly sure what my future plans are at the moment, but I'll keep it in mind."

He blew out a stream of breath, then scrubbed his hand down his face. "We should talk."

She nodded before taking another sip of her soda. Ominous words even under the best of circumstances, but he was right. They did need to talk. Or rather, she needed to talk, and fast if she were going to convince him he was the last man for the job of keeping her ass out of jail.

"I didn't do it," she told him. "Damon, you know me.

I'm not a violent person. There's no way I could've killed Jonathan. He was my friend. I loved him."

"No, you're not a violent person, but even the most placid individuals have been known to commit murder." Damon sat up straight suddenly and gave her a level stare. "But you're smart, Laurel. A goddamn genius. Fingerprints on the murder weapon, your DNA found on the body, and no solid alibi to account for your time the night Linton was murdered? Those are not the actions of a smart person."

"I know it looks bad, but—"

"Or maybe," he said, his voice growing hard, "you are smart enough to have crafted it all so the evidence appeared circumstantial."

Her mouth fell open in shock. She couldn't believe he'd dare accuse her of such a thing. "You can't be serious?"

"You've been charged with a capital crime, Laurel. You've been arrested, entered a plea, and now you're going to trial in six weeks. I'm dead serious. And so is the DA."

"But I didn't do it," she wailed. "Why would I kill Jonathan. He was my friend. My business partner." She was supposed to be convincing him to leave, not arguing her innocence.

"Who'd made you a whole lot of money in recent months."

"So I killed him? That makes a lot of sense."

"It does if killing him makes you even richer."

She closed her eyes. Their partnership agreement.

Oh God, how could she have forgotten about something so important?

She opened her eyes and looked at Damon. "I'm as good as convicted," she said. "There's a death provision in our partnership agreement. Artifacts belongs solely to me now that Jonathan's gone."

"How much is the business worth?" Damon asked.

She swallowed. "I'm not sure. I'd have to check with our

accountant to be certain, but probably a little over four, maybe even five million dollars."

"Try ten mil."

She shook her head. "That's not possible." They'd been doing well lately, but not *that* well. Or had they and she just hadn't noticed? Or was that something else that Jonathan had kept from her?

"It is according to what some ambitious reporter got out of your Dun and Bradstreet filing. And in case you were wondering, yes, it does spell motive. With a capital 'M.' It would also explain why Rosen is hell bent on going after the death penalty."

"Oh dear God," she whispered. She never seriously believed the ADA would pursue the death penalty. After all, she was innocent.

She looked at Damon, hoping to see compassion. Instead she saw suspicion in his eyes, and it hurt. Pain and anguish tightened her chest. "It's real, isn't it?" she asked.

He said nothing, just stared at her with those intense eyes, tweaking her heart and stirring something deep inside her. Memories, she quickly decided. Of another time, another place when nothing life-altering stood between them. A time before betrayal had forever changed the course of both of their lives.

"It's not some horrible dream, is it?" she asked. "Or a really bad joke?"

"I'm afraid not, Laurel," he said gently.

Reality had set in for her, and for the first time, she was truly frightened. "I knew all along the death penalty was a possibility if I was convicted, but on some level I think I'd convinced myself they were just trying to scare me," she said. A definite tightness crept into her voice. She drew in a deep breath and let it out slowly, then cleared her throat. "Until now, it had been more of an abstract than actual reality."

Her hands began to tremble and she nearly spilled her drink. Carefully, she leaned forward to set her glass on the table. The camisole she wore gaped, and she caught Damon sneaking a glimpse of her breasts.

He quickly lifted his gaze back to her face and offered up a sheepish grin. She probably should've been insulted, but God help her, despite her current situation, a part of her liked it that he was still interested in her in that way.

Now there was a subject that finally made sense. There'd never been any denying their attraction to each other, or how much they'd once been in love. Although love was no longer an issue, the attraction was still there. She couldn't deny its existence—at least on her part.

She straightened and tucked her hands beneath her bottom. "You see that kind of thing on those cop and news-magazine shows all the time," she continued, "where the authorities try to scare the suspect into confessing. I thought that's what they were trying to do to me, but I had nothing to confess. Damon, I didn't kill Jonathan."

"I don't believe you killed him either. But you can't account for your time. You have no solid alibi."

"I was at the university," she said. "I had a class that night, then I spent some time in my office reading project proposals."

"No one saw you. No one can confirm that you didn't leave immediately after your class. I've read the police report, read Scanlon's account of the investigation. You have no one to back up your alibi. Based on the time factor alone, you had plenty of opportunity to commit murder. Opportunity, means, and now a multi-million-dollar motive. If I fail to convince the jury you couldn't possibly have committed murder . . ."

"I'm as good as convicted."

"Were there any security measures you had to pass through at the university that could place you there at the time of the murder?" he asked, neither confirming nor denying her statement. "Campus security? University personnel? Anyone who might have seen you? UCLA is a big place. Surely someone can provide you with an alibi."

She shook her head. "No," she said, her tone bleak. "Not that I'm aware of. After my class, I saw no one."

Before he could continue with his questioning, a knock at the door sounded. "That's probably room service," he said and went to answer the door.

"Good," she said. "I'm starved."

Once he verified it was indeed room service with their meal, he opened the door. A uniformed waiter wheeled in a cart covered by a pristine white table cloth and laden with silver-covered dishes.

Laurel stood and came toward Damon. "Did you order dessert?"

"No," he said, signing the room service ticket.

"Would you please bring us a couple slices of cheesecake?" she asked the waiter. "One topped with chocolate sauce and the other with raspberries. Fresh, if they're available."

The waiter took the leather-bound room service ticket holder from Damon. "Yes, ma'am," he said, then left, promising to return shortly.

"Screw the calories," she said, her tone defensive. "I need comfort food."

"I didn't say anything."

"Smart man," she said, carrying two of the covered dishes to the round table not far from the wet bar. "It's wise not to argue with a woman who has a death sentence hanging over her head."

"You have a point," he agreed.

He brought the wine and a pair of elegant stemware to the table. While he opened the wine, she retrieved the cut-

lery and remaining items from the cart and went about setting the table.

Once seated, he poured them each a glass of red wine.
"Do you usually return to Artifacts after your classes?" he
asked her.

She sprinkled a liberal amount of salt and pepper on her
baked potato. "Damon?" she asked, then blew out a stream
of breath. "Could we please not talk about this now?"

"We need to discuss the case."

She understood he believed he had a defense to prepare,
and she'd dissuade him of that fact after dinner. But right
now, she was starved, and she didn't want anything to ruin
her appetite.

"No," she said. "Not now. I'm hungry, and if you ruin
the first decent meal I've had in days, I won't be held ac-
countable for my actions."

That made him smile. "Laurel, this *is* important."

"I know that," she said, spreading her napkin over her
lap. "But we haven't seen each other in a while." And she'd
never see him again after tonight, she'd make sure of it.
"Can't my defense wait until after we've eaten? It's not like
this mess is going to miraculously disappear. Cut me some
slack, okay?"

"All right," he agreed, albeit reluctantly from the hesi-
tancy in his voice. "What would you rather discuss?"

She shrugged, then cut into her steak. "I dunno," she
said. "How's your mom? Does she like Florida? What do
you do in Bozeman for fun?"

When he remained silent, she shot him a glance filled
with exasperation. "Gee, Laurel, it's been a long time. How
have you been?"

He smiled again when she rolled her eyes.

"Oh, I see you've cut your hair," she continued sarcastically. "I like it short. Have you lost weight? Seen any good

movies lately? Read any good books?" She wrinkled her brow. "Pick. A. Topic."

He took a drink of wine. "You'd better eat," he said. "You're getting cranky."

"So, how is your mom?" she asked before taking a bite of her steak.

"She's good," he answered, cutting into his own steak. "When I called her last week, she was rushing off to a class. Tae-bo, I think."

Guilt ripped into her. "It's good that she stays busy," she said without looking at him.

"She still misses Dad, but she has a group of lady friends who keep dragging her off to one new class after another. She's taken up stained-glass art, knitting, and china painting."

"I knew about the china painting." A wisp of sadness compounded her guilt. "She sent me a tea cup and matching saucer with purple irises for my last birthday." Unfortunately that gift had been destroyed along with everything else she owned.

"That sounds like my mom, all right. She's joined a knitting club. I now have two drawers full of wool socks."

She knew he'd worried about his mom after his Dad had died. He'd even tried to convince her to move to California, but Kathryn Metcalf was nothing if not stubbornly independent. "She likes Florida, then?"

"Oh yeah," Damon said and cut into his steak again.

"And what about you?" Laurel asked. "What do you do in Bozeman for fun?"

He shrugged. "Not much to do."

"What exactly do you do up there, anyway?"

"Make furniture. Enjoy the peace and quiet. A lot of reading."

"Any reproductions?"

He shook his head. "No, mostly I craft my own designs."

"Too bad," she said, reaching for her glass of wine. "We're always looking for good woodworkers. We have a couple of clients who can't afford to pay for genuine antiques, but they do like period reproductions." Not that she'd ever in a million years use Damon's services, but she didn't tell him that.

"Your business has been doing well," he commented.

"It was a welcome change after those first couple of years when we barely made enough to cover our expenses."

"What changed?"

"Jonathan had heard the Los Angeles County Museum was accepting bids for an important restoration project, so we submitted a proposal and won the bid."

"What was the project?"

A satisfied smile curved her lips. "They have an extensive Rembrandt collection," she told him. "I'm convinced the only reason we were awarded the bid was because of his family's influence. Jonathan's grandmother is on the board of trustees."

"There's no shame in taking advantage of a little nepotism now and then," he said.

"That's what Jonathan said. The Rembrandt restoration was an important job, and before we'd even completed it, more opportunities started coming our way. Important projects, too. Just last month we finished up the *Gates of Paradise*."

"*Gates of Paradise?*"

"St. Giovanni's Church in Florence, Italy. They're actually the east doors of the baptistery and over six-hundred-years old."

"You went to Florence?"

"No, Jonathan went. He actually met with Omar Mendocini, who I'm told is a direct descendent of Lorenzo the

Magnificent, one of the greatest art patrons of the Renaissance. I really would have loved to have gone, but we had too much work. Plus I had my graduate courses to teach, so it just wasn't possible. We did do most of the work here, though."

"They shipped six-hundred-year-old doors halfway around the globe?"

"No, we only worked with the relief panels. Actually, this wasn't a restoration project of the original relief panels, but a restoration of the reproduction."

Finished with his meal, Damon pushed his plate aside. "You lost me."

"The actual doors of baptistery," Laurel said, setting her own plate aside, "were designed by Lorenzo Ghiberti in the fifteenth century. They're stored in a hermetically-sealed vault to protect them. The doors that tourists see are actually a reproduction. Artifacts was hired to restore the reproduction."

"Sounds fascinating."

"The process was pretty incredible. I actually prefer restoration over reproduction because it's about more than art. Science plays a huge role. Chemistry, really, which is my area of expertise. If I walked you through it, your eyes would probably glaze over."

Another knock on the door announced the arrival of the waiter with the dessert Laurel had ordered. "I should have waited," she said when Damon returned to the table with the cheesecake. "I'm stuffed."

"We'll save it for later," he suggested, and took the two plates covered in plastic wrap to the small refrigerator under the bar and placed them inside.

She'd refilled her wine glass and carried it with her to the love seat where she curled up on the end nearest the opened slider. She let out a sigh. "Damon, there's something I need to tell you."

"Can it wait?" he asked. "We should discuss your defense. Trial starts in six weeks. That doesn't give me a lot of time to build a defense."

"That's what I need to tell you. You won't be building my defense." She took a deep breath and let it out in a rush, along with her next words. "You're fired."

He set his wine glass on the table separating them. "I'm what?"

"Fired," she said, more firmly this time.

He stood suddenly to glare down at her. "You can't fire me."

She frowned. "Why not? I'm paying you. I can fire you."

"I haven't taken a dime of your money." He turned and stalked off toward the bar.

She stood and followed him. "What about that fifty grand for the retainer?"

"It's still in your account." He yanked open the mini-bar fridge. "But that's not why you can't fire me."

She folded her arms and waited for an explanation.

He made a sound of disgust, then grabbed a soda from the shelf and shoved the door to the mini-bar closed. "Because," he said popping open the top to the can, "without me, you don't have an attorney. There's no one willing to represent you."

"No one? I find that hard to believe."

"Believe it," he said, then took a swig from the can.

"Fine," she said. "I'll just have the public defender represent me."

"Won't happen," Damon said. "PD's are for the indigent, and you hardly qualify."

"Then I'll pay." She knew she sounded like a bratty kid, but she didn't much care. Damon absolutely could *not* be the one to handle her defense.

"Might as well sign your own death warrant while you're at it."

She narrowed her eyes. "Now there's an idea. I'll just represent myself."

"Why not save the taxpayers a buck and just go right to the gas chamber?"

She did not appreciate his sarcasm. Especially because she was dead serious. Anyone she'd ever cared about was dead. At least one of those had been because of her. She wasn't about to risk Damon, too.

He set his soda can on the counter of the bar. "Look, whoever killed Jonathan is still on the loose," he told her, trying a different tactic. "Your condo has been trashed. I'm not leaving, Laurel. At least not until the nut job responsible is caught."

"Which is exactly why you can't stay," she said, not overly concerned that her own life could be in danger. Maybe because she was already living with the threat of a death penalty conviction hanging over head. "Too many people I've cared about have died. I couldn't stand it if anything happened to you, too."

He stepped close and she breathed in his intoxicating scent. "What is this? You're too logical for superstition."

"I don't care. I'm not willing to risk your life to save my own."

"How noble of you," he said, a gentle smile canted his mouth. "Ridiculous, but noble."

She shrugged. There was nothing noble about it. She couldn't live with the guilt if she were the ultimate cause of his death. "It's not that."

His smile deepened, and so did the shade of his green eyes. "So," he said narrowing the distance between them, "that has to mean you still care about me."

"You know I do." She always had and always would.

A frown appeared on his handsome face, chasing away the tempting smile curving his lips. "Is that why you walked away from us?" he asked.

Just this once, she decided to be perfectly honest with him. "Yes," she said.

Chapter 11

DAMON KNEW THE ethics of the situation could definitely be called into question. Lawyers really shouldn't go around kissing their clients. But that sure as hell didn't stop him from slipping his hand along the side of Laurel's neck and gently guiding her mouth to his.

Her lips were warm and soft beneath his. She tasted as sweet and intoxicating as the wine they drank at dinner. She tasted like home.

She slipped her arms around his neck and brought their bodies together. Memories swamped him. Memories of making love to Laurel.

A curse or blessing? He couldn't decide, but the images floating through his mind haunted him. No, he thought. Not haunted. *Taunted*. Just like her slender curves pressed against him taunted him. Reminding him of what had once been his, of what they could have again if she'd only lighten up.

He angled her head and deepened the kiss.

Sure they could, but for how long, he wondered? Until the trial was over and it was time for him to go back to Bozeman? A temporary affair wasn't exactly his style, and he knew for a fact it wasn't Laurel's. At least the Laurel he remembered, and the woman in his arms was all too familiar to have changed that much. Her touch, her scent. The way her fingers played with the hair at his nape. All classic Laurel.

He skimmed his hand slowly down her back to the curve of her hip. A sexy little moan escaped her lips and she molded her body to his. His libido took off like a rocket.

Desire thrummed through him, effectively diminishing any thoughts he might have about lawyerly ethics. He suspected he was making a monumental mistake in judgment by kissing her, but he'd willingly swallow every ounce of regret in favor of the soulful, silken glide of her tongue exploring his mouth. Actions spoke louder than words, and right now her kiss was saying, "Don't leave me."

He slipped his hand beneath her top, his fingers coming in contact with warm skin. The memories mocking him were as real as it got. He'd been here before—with Laurel. Here, where everything was hot. Demanding. And too damn consuming for him to even consider stopping.

He had no idea where things were headed tonight, but he had a damn good idea where he wanted them to go. Right over to that four-hundred-bucks-a-night bed less than ten feet away.

All too soon, Laurel ended the kiss. She pulled her arms from around his neck and took a step back, followed by another. "We shouldn't."

He could probably give her a dozen or more reasons why he agreed with her, but he only needed one why she was wrong. Because they wanted each other. And because they'd never stopped caring for each other.

Okay, so he had two reasons. He could easily come up with more if she wanted to hear them. Somehow he didn't think she would, though, so he kept those thoughts to himself—for now—because he had a feeling they both knew this wasn't over, not by a long shot.

"We're both old enough to know better," she said. If she

was referring to how they could barely keep their hands off each other when they'd been together, she was right.

"Old enough to know better, but young enough to still give it hell," he said.

She eventually smiled, as he hoped she would. The last thing he wanted was an awkwardness between them. "I meant what I said earlier. I can't have you represent me."

He let out an impatient sigh. "Nothing is going to happen to me."

A flash of panic flared in her lavender eyes. "You don't know that."

He gave a nonchalant shrug. If he didn't make a big deal out of it, then maybe she wouldn't, either. "No one does. Not really. Look, I'm a big boy, Laurel. I know how to take care of myself. But you need a lawyer, and I'm the only one willing to step up to the plate here."

"Deal with it, is that what you're saying?"

She turned and walked to the sliding glass door to peer out into the night and chew on her thumbnail. "I know you think I'm being silly," she said after a moment, "but I feel strongly about this."

He walked to the chair and sat. "I know you do. Nothing is going to happen to me if I represent you. The consequences of you not having representation, however . . ."

"Would essentially be suicide," she finished.

"I'm just sayin'."

"But you feel my fear is unsubstantiated and therefore ridiculous."

"Hey, they're your fears, Mr. Wizard," he said, attempting to lighten the mood. "I'm not trying to minimize your feelings, Laurel. They're real enough to you. I guess that's what counts."

She turned back to face him fully. A deep frown marred the smoothness of her forehead. "Okay," she said. "I'll agree to let you represent me on two conditions."

"That all depends on what the conditions are." At this point he'd agree to just about anything, because he had no intention of walking away when she needed him the most. Whether or not he planned to keep his word on the subject was another matter entirely.

"For one, the next time I fire you, you're really fired, and two, no questions asked."

He leaned back in the chair and propped his foot over his knee. "I'll agree to the first condition, but not the second. You fire me, I have to know why."

He could practically see the wheels turning in that complex mind of hers as she attempted to figure out what he was up to. Or maybe she was trying to figure out how she could get around his condition on her condition. That wouldn't surprise him because he'd bet his license to practice law she was hiding something from him.

"And I'll want the truth," he added. "No cock-and-bull story and none of that 'because I said so' crap. Agreed?"

It took her a full minute to finally cross over to where he sat and extend her hand. "Agreed," she said.

"Good. Now that we have that out of the way, answer something for me." He waited until she sat then asked, "What the hell were you thinking?"

Her eyes widened. "Excuse me?"

"The murder weapon," he said. "What were your prints doing on the knife used to kill Jonathan?"

"I didn't know it was a murder weapon when I picked it up," she explained. "When I arrived at Artifacts that night, I went in through the workroom. The lights were low, like they usually are after hours, and about halfway through the shop area, I spotted the knife on the floor. I didn't even see Jonathan's body right away."

"So you just picked up a bloody knife?"

"Yes," she said. "I did. We have a variety of sharp tools we use in our work, knives included. That's what I thought it was, just one of the tools that had fallen on the floor or was dropped and missed. It happens sometimes. And in the dim lighting, it didn't look like blood. I thought it was paint-stained."

Her explanation sounded logical to him, but he didn't hold out much hope of convincing a jury. Motive, means, and opportunity. The holy trilogy of a slam dunk, and this one had them all.

"All right," he said. "That's it for tonight. Get some sleep. We'll talk more tomorrow."

She stood. Taking her half-full glass of wine with her, she started toward the door leading to her room, then stopped and turned back to face him. "You do believe me, don't you?"

"What I believe isn't important," he said and stood. "It's the jury we need to convince."

She nodded, turned to leave, then stopped again. "I know I might not have given you the impression earlier, but your being here really does mean a lot to me."

Her gratitude made him uncomfortable. "Get some sleep, Laurel."

"Good night," she said.

This time, he stopped her from leaving. "You cut your hair," he said.

She turned back to look at him and flashed him one of her rare high voltage smiles. His trousers suddenly felt confining. "I like it," he said, unsure whether he was referring to the short, sassy cut of her hair or the way that smile of hers made the law the last thing on his mind.

Black ice had killed him. Or so the official report had indicated. But Laurel knew differently. Scott Metcalf's death had been no accident. It'd been a cover up, a plan orchestrated to ensure her silence.

With a groan of frustration, Laurel kicked off the covers.

Although exhaustion pulled at her, the sweet spot where sleep would overtake her continued to elude her. Physically, she was bone tired, but her mind refused to follow the dictates of her weary body. Even after a glass of wine and a heavy meal, she'd been unable to fall asleep or quiet her mind enough to chase away the late night demons haunting her.

And then there was that kiss, the one she kept coming back to and reliving over and over again. Why had Damon kissed her? Kissed her like he'd meant it, too. And why on earth had she kissed him back?

With a weary sigh, she left the comfort of her bed and made her way through the darkened room to the bathroom. Maybe she shouldn't have wasted valuable time arguing with Damon about not wanting him to represent her. She could've made a nice to-do list and discussed her defense. Then, just maybe, she'd have constructive thoughts to occupy her mind rather than wallowing in the past at nearly three in the morning.

She finished up in the bathroom and decided against turning on the television, as was her habit when she couldn't sleep. She even considered sneaking into Damon's room to appropriate one of those heavenly slices of cheesecake he'd tucked securely in the fridge, but she didn't want to risk waking him—or end up in his bed. Not a bad place to be, especially since she wasn't exactly in the mood for conversation, considering the direction her musings were taking her tonight.

Snagging the cotton cardigan from the back of the chair where she'd tossed it before going to bed, she slipped into it, then quietly opened the sliding glass door and stepped out onto the balcony. The air was crisp and cool, the concrete cold beneath her bare feet. She shivered from the chill and rubbed her hands briskly over her arms to generate warmth.

A light breeze rustled the fronds of the tall palms surrounding the elaborate landscaped gardens below. She sat in one of the chairs, pulled her feet beneath her and tugged the little cardigan more tightly around her to ward off the fringes of the breezy night air.

She sat quietly and tried to enjoy the peacefulness of the early hour before the city became alive, but her thoughts still refused to quiet. Who had killed Jonathan? Why hadn't she looked more closely at the knife before she'd picked it up? Why did the people closest to her always end up dead? Had she made a mistake in agreeing to let Damon represent her? Would he end up dead, too?

Usually making her mental lists provided her with insight. In the pre-dawn hour, there were no easy answers. At least none that made any sense, and that bothered her.

She was a scientist. Simplicity and logic were second nature to her. She liked it that way, too, as it allowed her to make sense out of the craziness of life.

She let out a sigh. Had anything in her life ever made sense?

She'd always been far too rational and pragmatic to put much stock in twists of fate, destiny or karma. Oh sure, she'd done the "why me's" just like everyone else whenever her life had been thrown into chaos, but she took comfort in the fact that if she carefully examined each instance separately, every one of them could be explained to her satisfaction. In her own way, she attempted to make sense of the senseless, and it helped her cope.

Her mother's death had been an accident. Some might say it had been a tragic twist of fate that Noreen Jennings had been waiting on that particular corner at that particular moment on a rainy night in Boston when she'd been struck by a drunk driver who'd lost control of his vehicle. In Laurel's mind, fate had nothing to do with the fact that her mother had died. She'd died because a man with too much to drink had chosen to get behind the wheel of his car on a rainy night.

Some might even believe the fates were working toward a greater purpose the night her mother had died. If she'd been alive, then Laurel never would've become a ward of the state and ended up in the Massachusetts foster care system. Never would've been shuffled through a series of foster homes with caregivers who were ill-equipped or didn't care enough to emotionally nurture a child of superior intellect. She didn't believe that mere chance had caused her to be brought to the attention of a particular children's services supervisor who happened to be acquainted with Evelyn Tillman because the two women had served on a committee together to host a charity auction for underprivileged children. It had been nothing more than a chain of events, not some grand plan designed by the fates.

Some might believe that destiny had played a role in bringing her to the care of Conner and Evelyn Tillman, a childless couple who not only understood, but celebrated Laurel's special intellectual gifts. A placement which enabled her to attend MIT after being recruited before she'd graduated high school at the age of fourteen. A placement which could never have happened if her father hadn't walked out shortly after Laurel's birth.

Laurel understood if she hadn't been sent to live with the Tillmans, she never would've known Damon, or his parents, Scott and Kathryn, who were close friends of Conner and Evelyn. But it had nothing to do with fate, destiny or karma. It just *was*, through a series of events over which she'd had no control.

Still, if she hadn't known Damon, she never would've experienced her first real kiss under a summer sky, never would've known the first promise of what passion could be, never would've felt normal for the first time in her life.

Never would've known love and acceptance from such a generous, caring partner. Some might even say that she would never have experienced any of those incredible firsts if it hadn't been for that rainy night in Boston.

Laurel believed that most things in life could be explained by logic. But she also understood that life was messy, and most answers could be explained by choice. Her mother could've chosen not to walk home that night but waited for a taxi instead. Her social worker could've chosen not to discuss Laurel's case with her supervisor but shifted her to another substandard foster care situation. Evelyn Tillman could've chosen not to tell her husband about Laurel. The Tillmans could've chosen not to take her into their home, and she could've chosen not to go to Conner for a job once she'd turned eighteen and was no longer under the auspices of children's services. If she hadn't made that particular choice, she never would've made the discovery that had eventually cost Scott Metcalf his life. And if Scott hadn't died, she might never have ended her relationship with Damon and moved to California where she'd met Jonathan. And maybe Jonathan would still be alive, too.

A sudden chill chased down her spine. No, life wasn't about fate, destiny or karma, it was about choice, and she'd made some bad ones. If she hadn't chosen to go to Scott with her findings, he'd still be alive. But she hadn't known where else to turn, and Scott, not only in his capacity as her official supervisor at the Institute, but a trusted friend, had been the most logical option.

In the end, she'd chosen to leave. She'd wanted out, and they'd let her go, but not without crafting a foolproof insurance policy to guarantee her silence. She'd spoken of her discovery only once, and a good man had been killed because of her. She'd never take that kind of risk again.

She'd done as she was told. She'd kept silent, telling no one of her suspicions and carrying the guilt of Scott's death on her shoulders with her when she'd moved to the other side of the country to start a new life as far away from the scientific community as she could get.

She'd thought she was safe, that the people she loved would be safe once she'd left Boston. But then Damon had taken a position with the LA county DA's office and relocated to California. As much as it hurt them both, she'd made certain he knew they were no longer a couple. And she'd made damn sure Evelyn heard from her about her breakup with Damon, because whatever Evelyn knew, Conner and eventually the directors would, too.

Despite her years of silence, she still couldn't help wondering if the Institute wasn't somehow responsible for Jonathan's murder. Was it possible that his death was one more orchestration designed to ensure her continued silence about the truth behind the Institute's existence?

And if that were the case, why didn't they just kill her and get it over with? Why leave a loose end like herself dangling? Or perhaps the directors had some other, more sinister reason in mind for keeping her alive?

She blew out a ragged stream of breath. She was getting paranoid, and that wasn't like her. Yet, she couldn't stop wondering if there was some connection to a puzzle she hadn't yet solved. On the surface, the Institute was nothing more than a medical research facility which depended heavily on government funding. But it also had another, more secretive purpose, one she'd inadvertently uncovered during her tenure as a bio-chemistry researcher.

She'd been naïve, and under the misguided assumption that her work at the Institute was about saving lives. She'd been wrong. Dead wrong.

"Can't sleep?"

She flinched at the unexpected sound of Damon's sleep-roughened voice. She looked over at him. He stood in the open doorway, shirtless and wearing a pair of battered old jeans slung low on his hips. He had such a beautiful body, she thought. He always had, but maturity made him a worthy competitor of any of the marble sculptures gracing the halls of the world's most famous museums.

"No," she said and frowned. Her life was a mess. What did she think she was doing admiring Damon's body? Looking for a diversion wasn't logical, or simple. Although a little up-close-and-personal admiration would make for one hell of a diversion.

"I didn't wake you, did I?"

"Uh-uh." He stepped onto the balcony and dropped into the chair beside her. "I couldn't sleep, either." Slouching down in his chair, he kicked his bare feet up onto the wrought-iron railing. "I keep wondering, if you didn't kill Jonathan, who did?"

"I've been wondering the same thing," she admitted. Not that she'd ever tell him about the suspicion nagging her. She couldn't, not without putting him at further risk. His being here was bad enough. Besides, what good would it do now to reveal the truth behind his father's death when it would only hurt him? She cared far too much about him to ever cause him, or his mother, any more pain than they'd already suffered.

"I don't want to scare you," he said quietly, "but you realize the break in yesterday is probably connected somehow, don't you?"

"I'd have to be a fool not to," she said. "Do you think whoever did it is the one who killed Jonathan?"

"On the surface, it sure looks that way, doesn't it?" He briskly rubbed his hands over his bare arms. "But I have a feeling it was made to look that way."

"Any idea why?" Which would mean that someone had indeed been looking for something in her home. What, she had no idea. All of her files from the Institute had been confiscated.

"Good question."

She looked over at him. He'd leaned his head back and had his eyes closed.

"There are more questions than answers." She spoke quietly in deference to the hour. "And I don't know where to even start looking for them. Do you have any idea how frustrating that is for me?"

The hint of a smile tipped up the corners of his mouth. "Feeling out of your element, eh, Mr. Wizard?"

A smile quirked her own lips at the use of the old nickname, one she'd earned when she'd shown him how to blow up corn cobs using a few precisely mixed household chemicals. No one had ever called her that except Damon, and she hadn't heard the silly moniker since he'd taken off for the wilds of Montana.

"I don't like not having answers," she admitted to him. "You know that."

"Hmmm," he murmured. "Do I ever."

She looked away. Was he thinking of that warm summer day at his parents' lake house? The time she'd practically begged him to kiss her so she'd know what it felt like to be kissed for the first time? Or maybe a few years later, after they'd gotten involved romantically. She'd experienced plenty of firsts with Damon then.

Goodness no, she thought. They were ancient history. The heat of embarrassment scorched her cheeks just the same.

She cast a surreptitious glance in his direction. His eyes were still closed, but the tenor of the smile gracing his handsome face had changed from teasing to amused.

"Shut up, Damon," she whispered.

He opened his eyes and looked at her. Definite amusement, especially if she factored in the smile he was doing a lousy job of hiding.

"I didn't say anything."

"You don't have to."

"Yeah, but, I remember." In the quiet, his voice sounded all warm and husky. And filled with memories.

She shifted her gaze away from him again. "I was curious, is all," she muttered.

"Insatiable curiosity," he countered.

She couldn't help herself. She smiled. "Like you didn't enjoy every minute of it."

He chuckled softly. "Is it true what they say? That a woman never forgets her first?"

"As much as I hate to be the one to burst your ego," she said, "it's a lie. Probably one created by a man. Like bras or something equally uncomfortable."

"Too bad. I've been told I'm pretty unforgettable."

"Boy, your arrogance knows no bounds, does it?"

"Nope."

She'd always loved this side of him, appreciated the gentleness and caring he'd always showed to her. Unlike most men, he never appeared uncomfortable or awkward around her, either. Nor was she intimidated by her mind. With Damon she'd always felt—normal. Even now when her world was once again in chaos, he made her feel, well, normal. She loved him for that.

She gave him a nudge with her elbow. "Get over it. I have."

"You have not."

He sounded mildly offended and she smiled. "It was a lifetime ago," she reminded him.

"Not that long," he argued.

She laughed at that. "Try four years."

"Hardly a lifetime."

True, but then the two nights she'd spent in jail had felt like a lifetime to her, so she supposed time was merely relative. But she had been over the moon for him back then, even when she'd been a kid and had herself a wild crush on the guy. Later when she was older and they'd starting dating, things got serious, and she'd fallen head over heels for him. She'd known he'd felt the same, too. They hadn't actually discussed marriage, but for the first time in her life, she'd felt secure in her relationship with another human being, probably because she didn't live with the constant fear that someone she loved would be taken away from her.

"No, not that, but our first kiss was definitely a lifetime ago." The first time she'd ever kissed him, it'd been an explosion of hormones and heat. She smiled wistfully at the memory. She had no desire to relive her youth, but reliving that one moment in time certainly wouldn't be a hardship. "At times like this, it's difficult to imagine ever being that young," she added.

"I know what you mean." He let out a sigh, dropped his feet to the ground and sat up straight. "Okay, I need to get some sleep and this is bugging the shit out of me. If you didn't kill Jonathan, who did?"

"If I knew that," she said, "I probably wouldn't have been the one they arrested."

"Did he have any enemies? Piss anyone off lately?"

"No," she said. "Jonathan was a people person. Everyone loved him."

"Everyone has enemies," he said meaningfully.

"Jonathan didn't."

But she did. A very powerful group of enemies who'd stop at nothing to ensure her continued silence. Again, why? Why not just shut her up for good? Or maybe, for shits and giggles they *had* killed Jonathan and were setting her up to take the fall. What if their plan was to sit back and watch Rosen flip the switch, thereby silencing her once and for all?

A bullet would have been easier.

She shivered again. For a woman who preferred simplicity and logic, her imagination was certainly running in overdrive tonight. Handy in the art world, but murder on the psyche at three A.M.

"You never answered my question earlier," Damon said.

"Which one?"

"Do you usually return to the office after your classes?"

The wind picked up, and she tugged the little cardigan tighter around her again. "Not as a rule."

Still looking at her, he leaned forward and rested his elbows on his knees. "Then why did you go back there that night?"

"To talk to Jonathan, who'd promised to be there, and because I had left my notes on the seminar I was preparing on my desk and I needed to work on them."

"It couldn't have waited until morning?"

She shrugged. "It could have, I suppose. But I had my slides at home and needed my notes to know exactly which ones I needed for my presentation."

"Your notes were on your laptop?"

She shook her head. "I work in long hand, then type up an outline."

"What time did you arrive at Artifacts?"

"About nine. Maybe nine-thirty. I'm not sure."

"And you usually go to the office at that hour?"

"No, but I was planning on taking a few days off to go to Chicago, which might have put us further behind on a couple of important projects, so I thought I'd check on a few things while I was there."

He stared at her long and hard, making her nervous. "Meaning Jonathan."

"Like I said, we'd fallen behind on a couple of projects."

"Because of Jonathan?"

She fidgeted with the buttons on her cardigan and nodded again. "The deadline to file on a couple of important bids, actually."

"I thought Linton was the one to bring in new business."

"As a rule."

He kept staring at her.

"He'd blown a couple of meetings with clients recently, so I wanted to make sure we were on track and the new proposals were done as promised."

"Why not just ask Linton about them?"

"I did."

"But . . ."

"He told me they were done, but I wanted to make sure."

"You were checking up on him."

She nodded.

"Was your business, your multi-million dollar business, in danger?" he asked. He spoke slowly, as if choosing his words carefully.

"No," she answered. "Not at all." At least not then. Not really. Of course she had a stack of messages in her purse that now stated otherwise.

"But it was important enough that you made an un-scheduled trip back to the office to follow up and make sure your partner was doing his job?"

"It wasn't as bad as you're making it sound."

"But it was important enough that you couldn't have waited until regular business hours? Important enough for you to arrange a meeting at a place where you knew no one else would be? Where you could get him alone?"

She didn't appreciate the accusation in his tone, or the implication that she'd actually gone and planned to kill Jonathan. "It's not like you're making it sound."

"Think how it'll look to a jury," he said. "Why couldn't it wait, Laurel?"

She might as well tell him the truth she hadn't wanted to face. Like it or not, he was, after all, her attorney. "Jonathan seemed to have lost his focus the past few weeks."

"Lost his focus, how?" he pressed.

"He'd been distracted, that's all."

"Distracted," he spoke the word slowly, as if savoring it. "Taking a lot of time off work?"

"Not time off actually," she said. "Just away from the office more than usual."

"So your business *was* in trouble."

She shook her head. "No, not really."

"And Linton was the reason. Which put the lifestyle you'd become accustomed to in danger."

She frowned. "You're twisting my words."

"He was stealing from you."

"No," she said adamantly. "Never."

"He was stealing from you, so you killed him."

She uncurled her legs and stood. How could he even think such a thing?

"Why are you doing this?" she asked, looking down at him. "I thought you were my friend."

"No, Laurel. I'm your attorney. Friendship doesn't enter into it now."

"That still doesn't give you the right to treat me like a criminal," she said, then walked back into her room.

As she suspected he would, he followed her. "You want to spend the rest of your life in jail?" he asked after closing the slider.

She let out a sigh and turned on the bedside lamp. "Of course, I don't."

"If I even decide to put you on the witness stand, what do you think Rosen is going to do to you up there? If there's so much as a hint of weakness in your story, he's going to rip you to shreds. If I don't put you on the stand, the jury will wonder what you've got to hide. I need to know everything you know."

She dropped onto the edge of the bed. "The truth is, I don't know what Jonathan was up to the past few weeks. He'd blown a couple of important meetings and couldn't, or wouldn't, account for his whereabouts. We'd even missed a deadline on an important restoration that was supposed to be his responsibility. I did try to talk to him about it, find out what was going on and see if I could help. But he kept insisting nothing was wrong, that I was just being anal."

"And you had no idea what might have been going on?"

She looked at Damon who had sat down next to her, and shook her head. "There's only one person who can answer that question," she said. "And he's not talking."

Chapter 12

DAMON KNEW HE'D be smart to get up off the bed. At the very least, he should put a respectable distance between himself and Laurel. Maybe then he'd stop thinking about her sweet scent, fantasizing about how much he wanted to kiss her again. He ached to touch her, longed to see for himself if her golden skin was as soft as it'd been earlier and not just a figment of his overactive, testosterone-fueled imagination.

He didn't move. His gaze dipped to her mouth.

God, he was so screwed.

"We should probably hire a private investigator," he told her, forcing his concentration back to the case and not to the way she'd moistened her bottom lip with the tip of her tongue. He cleared his dry throat. "If Jonathan was involved with someone, or something, we should know about it. Preferably before Rosen."

In fact, the more he thought about it, the more convinced he became that Linton could very well have gotten himself involved in something he shouldn't have been. He hadn't yet viewed any of the crime scene or autopsy photographs, but according to the coroner's initial report and the police investigative file, the body had been ravaged—stabbed numerous times. A murder that vicious was rarely a random act. Whatever Linton had been involved in couldn't have been good.

"It worked for Harrison Ford."

Damon frowned. "What are you talking about?"

"The one-armed-man defense."

"I don't get it."

"Dr. Richard Kimball. From *The Fugitive*. The one-armed-man defense," she said, although her voice lacked conviction. "Prove I didn't do it by finding the one who did, right?"

"Did you forget Kimball was convicted first, then escaped, with a death warrant hanging over his head, before he could prove his innocence?"

"Yes, well, let's hope it doesn't come to that." She stood suddenly and began to pace in front of the foot of the bed. "Do you really think a private investigator will have more success than the cops did in finding out who really killed Jonathan?"

"It can't hurt," he said. "They didn't exactly look too hard, now did they?"

"True." She stopped to face him. "But then all the evidence pointed to me, remember?"

"Evidence that not even Scanlon believes is accurate," he reminded her.

Damon agreed with Scanlon. Everything about Rosen's case against Laurel was too pat for his liking. Too slam dunk. He'd prosecuted dozens of murder cases during his tenure with the DA's office, and not one of them was tied up as neat and tidy, especially one as circumstantial as the state's case against Laurel. That fact alone raised a few suspicions in his mind.

Her lips momentarily tightened into a thin line. She shook her head. "No, that wouldn't work," she muttered to herself, then started pacing again.

"What are you thinking?" he asked her.

As if she hadn't heard him, she continued pacing. She

halted, stared off into space for a moment, then shook her head, and went back to wearing the carpet thin. He knew from experience her mind was elsewhere, attempting to pull together the pieces of a puzzle only she could see.

She came to an abrupt halt. "Footprints," she said with a snap of her fingers as she turned to face him again.

Uh-oh. She was thinking in shorthand. Her mind moving ten paces ahead of him. Luckily he understood her, knew how to slow her down and bring her back to his level. "Be more specific."

"Footprints," she repeated as if he were obtuse. "If you want to know where someone has been, just follow their footprints."

Not quite comprehending where she was headed, he motioned for her to continue.

"Electronic footprints," she clarified. "BlackBerry. Palm Pilot." She blew out a breath. "Footprints. An electronic paper trail, so to speak."

"That'll only be helpful if he kept a record of his appointments."

She grinned. "He did. He had a BlackBerry and kept it with him all the time. He used to say his life was on that thing."

"Okay. Good." It could work. In addition to a physical paper trail, specifically Linton's financial records, credit card statements, bank records, and even his phone records, all of which he'd have to subpoena, it might tell them what, if anything, he might have been up to.

"Any idea where this BlackBerry might be now?" If she said Linton's home, they were sunk. There wasn't a snowball's chance the family would allow him to search Linton's place to benefit Laurel. Not when they'd gone to so much trouble to make sure there wasn't a decent lawyer willing to handle her defense.

"It has to be at the office. That's the last place . . ." Her grin faded. Sadness flooded her eyes. "The last place he . . ."

She turned away and wrapped her arms around her middle as if she were trying to hold herself together. Sensing her need for comfort, Damon rose from the bed and went to her, gently turning her into his arms. "It'll be okay," he said, pulling her close.

She didn't cry, not that he actually expected her to shed tears, at least not in front of him. Laurel was the most stoic woman he knew. Emotional outbursts weren't her style. Keeping her cards close to her chest was, however, which made it difficult to know what was going on inside that mind of hers unless she let him in—which she rarely did.

But he'd known her for a long time and supposed he understood Laurel better than most people. He understood her stoicism stemmed from the fish-out-of-water existence she'd lived most of her life. He was no slouch in the intellectual department, but in comparing brain pans, his fell ridiculously short next to Laurel's. She was different. Unique. He could only imagine what it had been like for her growing up before she came into Conner and Evelyn's care. What she might have suffered emotionally. Being so different from the other kids had to leave emotional baggage. Kids were cruel under the best of circumstances, but give them something they couldn't possibly begin to understand, and their pubescent cruelty took on gargantuan proportions, especially to a very young girl far out of her social element.

With her head resting against his shoulder, she slipped her arms around his waist and hung on tight. "This is hard," she said, her voice tight. "With all the stupid bullshit I've had to deal with since the night I found Jonathan's body, I haven't even had time to mourn the loss of my friend."

He smoothed his hand over her back in a soothing gesture. "I know," he whispered. Discovering a dead body would be difficult under any circumstances, but when that body was one of your closest friends, coupled with being charged with the murder? The past few days couldn't have been easy on her.

In his opinion, she was holding up remarkably well. A lot of people would've had a complete breakdown by now, but not Laurel. She soldiered on in the face of adversity, just as she'd always done. Talk about grace under pressure. Laurel had it in spades.

She pulled back slightly and looked up at him. Sadness still shown in her eyes, but mingled with another emotion he couldn't quite decipher. Fear? he wondered.

"It's stupid, I know, but I don't think I want to hire a private investigator," she said quietly. "I don't want to find out that another person I trusted wasn't what he appeared to be."

"What do you mean?" he asked, wondering who had betrayed her. He supposed any number of the adults in her life could've been responsible, from the social workers who'd placed her in one home after another, to the various people she'd been sent to live with following her mother's death. Or maybe some guy had hurt her, although he had his doubts on that score since she rarely allowed anyone that close to her. "You do realize looking into Linton's past could mean the difference between a death sentence and freedom."

"I know that," she said. "I do. But I'd hate to find out I was wrong about him. Besides, it's just . . . it just seems so far-fetched. Like what? Jonathan was leading a double life that I didn't know about?"

"It's entirely possible." He loosened his hold on her and slid his hands up her arms to her shoulders.

"What if I don't want to entertain the possibility?"

The hurt in her eyes made him curious, but also resurrected the protectiveness he'd always felt toward her. An emotion he knew from experience could lead him right into a world of trouble neither of them needed.

That knowledge didn't stop his hands from drifting upward to cup her satiny soft cheeks in his work-roughened palms. "Look, Laurel. My job is to keep you alive. I'll do whatever it takes to ensure that happens."

The barest hint of a sad little smile curved her lips. "You know, for as much as I protested, I don't know if I could get through this mess without you."

He smiled. "Sure you could," he told her. "You're a strong woman, Laurel. Don't forget that."

Something flickered in her eyes, but this time he recognized the emotion. Desire. That other emotion in her gaze he'd mistakenly thought could be fear, hadn't been fear at all.

Man, was he ever in trouble.

"I am glad you're here, Damon," she said softly.

God help him, he had to kiss her. "Me, too," he said.

Tension radiated between them. Before he could debate the wisdom of his actions, he lowered his head and kissed her.

Telling himself kissing Laurel was nothing more than a measure of comfort for a friend in need because she was facing such a difficult situation was a baldfaced lie. The instant his lips pressed against hers, the sweet taste of her mouth fired his libido and blindsided him.

He didn't believe she'd actually meant to slide her body along his, or return the kiss in a way that defied the boundaries of friendship or that of a client and her attorney. There was no way in hell either of them had imagined for a minute the air around them would crackle with an energy that could only be described as sexual in nature, but when her lips moved beneath his in an erotic dance of seduction, his testosterone shot through the roof.

Heat stirred in his belly and burned hot in his groin as her tongue demanded entrance. She tasted sweet. And hot. So hot. Like mind-blowing, sweat-drenched bodies, and tangled-sheets sex. The kind they used to have.

God help him, he wanted nothing more.

He should stop the insanity, but he couldn't. He wanted Laurel.

Instead, he moved his hands, sliding them around her rib cage to chase down her back, settling on the curve of her bottom, pulling her closer.

He brought his hands up, gliding along her side and stopping on her rib cage again. With his thumb, he traced the underside of her breast. She trembled in his arms.

She slid her hands from around his waist to wreathe her arms around his neck, the movement creating more friction as their bodies moved together. Through the thin fabric of her top, the pebble hardness of her nipples brushed against his chest.

His cock throbbed. He knew he should stop. Stop before they went too far. He also knew he'd wake up in the morning with more than regret, too, if he didn't end this craziness—now. He'd wake up in bed with a beautiful, sensuous woman. A naked woman.

For the space of a heartbeat, he figured spending the rest of the night making love to Laurel would be worth every regret thrown at him. The temptation of having her in his bed again was too much for him to ignore.

He waited for common sense to prevail.

It didn't.

Thank God.

He held her close, and slowly guided them toward the bed, where he gently eased her down upon the mattress. She moaned into his mouth and arched her back, brushing her breasts against his chest. He groaned, then slid his hand beneath her top to cup her in his hand.

She immediately pulled away from him. He silently cursed the loss of contact with her body, and the fact that he wanted nothing more than to pull her back into his arms and finish what he'd stupidly started in the first place. Until she grabbed the hem of her pink camisole and yanked it and the cardigan over her head, then tossed them to the floor. She reached for him and pulled him down to her and kissed him. Hard, demanding. Pure Laurel.

She moaned in protest when he ended the kiss, but her protest quickly turned to pleasure when he captured her nipple in his mouth. A breath left her on a hiss of sound, and she dragged her fingernails up his back to dive into his hair.

His dick throbbed painfully within the confines of his jeans, each thrust of her hips against his driving him closer to madness. Damn, but he had to have her. Wanted nothing more than to slide into her silken heat, to make her his—again.

A relationship with Laurel was nothing short of complicated. Forget the fact that she was now officially his client—what they were doing was definitely unethical—but there was also a matter of geography. Long distance relationships weren't his style and rarely worked. He had no intention of moving back to L.A. for good and Laurel's business was here. Sure his heart had been pumping a little faster since he'd walked back into the courtroom this morning, but that didn't mean he was ready to start practicing law again on a regular basis. It'd been nothing more than the thrill of competition, the thought of kicking Alan Rosen's ass in open court, of putting the jerk in his place.

Ethics, geography, and the fact that Laurel had told him four years ago to take a hike. She'd said she'd wanted to see other people. He hadn't believed it. They'd been in love one minute and the next she wants to see if the grass is greener in someone else's bed?

It didn't matter why their relationship had ended. None of the above was conducive to a lasting union anyway, but how long would it be before she got tired of him again? So why not just take what she was offering now and wake up a little less stressed come morning? Because he wasn't that kind of guy. Dammit.

As much as it pained him to do so, he ended the kiss and rolled off of Laurel before things really went too far. He stood and scooped up her top and set it on the bed next to her. "I'm sorry," he said. And he was. Sorry he'd stopped. Sort of.

"It's my fault," she said, sitting to tug on her top. "I'm just tired. I didn't mean . . ." She looked at him, but he couldn't find an ounce of regret anywhere in the desire still making her eyes bright. "I didn't mean for that to happen."

Neither did he, but that didn't mean he hadn't enjoyed every spontaneous second.

She glanced pointedly at the clock on the bedside table. "Maybe we should try to get some sleep."

Like that was going to happen.

"I have to get my car from the impound lot in the morning," she added, "then meet Stacy at Artifacts by ten."

He took a step toward her. She looked as if she were about to bolt, so he grabbed hold of her hand before she could try. "You know what? I take it back," he said. "I'm not sorry. Just sorry we waited so damn long."

She shifted uncomfortably. Those regrets he'd feared slammed into him. Maybe he should've put a stop to things before they'd gone as far as they had, but dammit, he refused to apologize. Not for something he knew they'd both enjoyed.

He let her go. For now.

"Goodnight, Laurel," he said and walked out of her room. He hadn't gone two feet into his own when he heard her close the door to their adjoining rooms—followed by the distinct click of the lock.

Because she didn't trust him, he wondered? Or herself?

* * *

Fabrizio held the penlight between his lips as he methodically searched the contents of the safe, careful to return each item he examined to its precise location. With a good two hours left until dawn, time wasn't much of an issue. Once he finished with the safe, he had the offices and computers to search. He'd be out of here within the hour, with the assurance no evidence remained in existence to tie his client directly to Linton or the fraud he'd hired Linton to perpetrate.

Breaching the security system had been a simple matter for a thief of his caliber. Although rather sophisticated, the security system guarding the treasures held within Artifacts wasn't quite what he'd find in the Louvre, but he did have to navigate an intricate laser pattern once inside. He'd been prepared. He was always prepared.

All entering the building had required of him was picking the locks, electronically speaking, as they were guarded by a digital keypad. Cracking the safe hadn't even been a true test of his skill. A standard locking mechanism, not even digital, had only required the use of a stethoscope.

He removed the last set of disks from the safe and read the label on the clear plastic case—*Gates of Paradise*. He opened the container and quickly scanned each of the five CD's containing a series of numbers and dates written on the individual disks. He'd found what he'd come for and could return to his homeland in a matter of hours now. His work, in America, at least, was almost complete. He'd deal with Mendocini and his plan to defraud the people of Florence upon his return.

From inside the black canvas bag containing the tools of his trade, he pulled out five blank CD's and exchanged them for the originals, then returned the set of dummy CD's to the safe. At first glance, no one would even notice the original CD's were missing.

From his meeting with Omar, he knew there weren't supposed to be any other copies of the *Gates of Paradise* in existence, and Omar claimed to have paid the price for such a guarantee. For the benefit of security and the integrity of the work Artifacts performed, and because computers could easily be hacked into, the employees weren't permitted to maintain copies of the work they did on their computers. Once a job was completed, the programming was saved to disk and the original job obliterated from their computer systems. The *Gates of Paradise* restoration had already been completed, but he planned to make certain no other copies existed before he left.

He closed the safe and spun the dial, then gathered up the black canvas bag. With the assistance of his small can of aerosol spray, he carefully made his way out of the back room where they kept the safe, through the workroom, and into the office structure. There were no laser beams to contend with here.

The first room was totally vacant. He entered a second office across the hall where he turned on the laptop computer resting on the oversized oak desk, then searched the wall of bookcases and each of the drawers in the unlocked desk while the computer booted up. Chances were the police had already downloaded the hard drives of all the computers in the office as a part of their investigation, but he searched them anyway. As he'd expected, the hard drive showed no evidence to indicate the *Gates of Paradise* restoration had ever taken place. A few more keystrokes and he was confident no encrypted files existed, either.

He had one office and the reception area left to search, and then he'd be on his way, with no one the wiser to his nocturnal visit. The desk in the last office was locked, but he wasn't deterred. He fired up the desk top computer, picked the lock and began to rifle through the drawers. His hand stilled over a row of files when he heard a sound.

He waited, holding his breath and listening. All he heard was the sound of his own heartbeat thumping mildly in his ears. He'd locked the door behind him once he'd entered the building. He hadn't heard the turning of a lock or the jangle of keys, but he had heard something. Footsteps maybe?

The hair on the back of his neck rose.

He waited. And waited. No one appeared, no lights came to life. No alarms sounded.

Nothing.

Silently, he left the office and using the same method as before, used the aerosol can to highlight the red beams of light blocking his path as he made his way back through the workroom. He scanned the area, peering into the shadows, but found nothing out of the ordinary to cause him alarm.

Convinced no one lurked in the building besides himself, he returned to the office, finished his perusal of the files in the desk drawer, then scanned the computer's hard drive. Convinced it, too, was clean, he powered down the computer, gathered his canvas bag, then performed a thorough search of the reception area.

Clean. To the best of his knowledge, now that he had the disks, there was nothing to connect Linton to his client. The building was clean, as had been Linton's home and that of his business partner. Dr. Jennings' home had been a puzzle, though, as he obviously hadn't been the first one there. In fact, her home had been ransacked, telling him it hadn't been a professional like himself. He had nothing against the lady. His beef was with his own client and the deceased Linton, the ones responsible for the fraud against his beloved St. Giovanni's. He hoped for her sake, however, that Dr. Jennings understood she definitely had an enemy.

Confident his work here was completed, he headed back to the workroom to the exit. The door was still locked, convincing him all he'd heard had been the building settling. He opened the door a fraction and peered into the empty parking lot. As a precaution, he'd parked the black SUV he'd rented in the alley a block and a half down from Artifacts. With the assistance of a high-tech electronic device, after re-setting the alarm, under the cover of night, he slipped out the back door as easily as he'd broken into the place.

Keeping to the shadows, he crept silently along the back of the building toward the alley. He rounded the corner and came up against the lethal end of a pistol aimed directly at his heart.

Chapter 13

"WHY DID YOU STOP?"

In the quiet of her room, Laurel wrinkled her nose after saying the words aloud. Too blunt, she decided. Perhaps subtlety would be best.

She tugged the blankets higher to her chest. "You didn't *really* mean to kiss me last night, right?"

Ugh. That wasn't subtle in the least. In fact, she sounded pathetically insecure. She was no blushing virgin. She knew all about making love to a man, and especially how to please one—Damon in particular.

She inched the blankets up to her chin. She'd might as well pull them over her head and give in to pathetic and insecure.

Maybe instead of practicing what she'd say to Damon when she saw him, she should just forget the incident even occurred. Problem was, she'd thought of nothing else the rest of the night. What little sleep she had managed had been fraught with images. Erotic images. Images so hot and steamy, she'd woken up all achy and needy.

She fought the urge to pull the covers over her head. Unfortunately, she had a full day ahead of her and couldn't afford to hide out in bed. A day, she thought with a groan, she'd be spending with the most recent subject of her fanciful dreams.

With no choice but to brave the day—and face Damon—she reluctantly tossed the covers aside and hauled her butt out of bed.

So why had he stopped? Why hadn't he made love to her last night?

Because she'd been vulnerable, that's why, she thought logically. She'd needed a friend, and Damon had *always* qualified on that score. She'd been swamped with too many emotions crowding her at once, the loss of Jonathan, Damon's suggestion that perhaps Jonathan wasn't what she'd believed him to be, and the possibility that another person she'd trusted had betrayed her. Damon probably hadn't even meant to kiss her.

But why had he stopped?

But he had. And she'd been tossing and turning ever since. Just like the last time they'd made love, it had been all heat and hormones.

But they were no longer lovers and she had no business getting all hot and bothered. It'd been nearly four years since they'd last made love. What was wrong with her?

So if they weren't lovers, what exactly were they? Granted, he was her attorney, but they were friends first. Except friends didn't kiss the way they'd kissed. Friends could keep their hands off each other, and she and Damon obviously couldn't even manage that much.

She blew out a frustrated stream of breath. Last night, he'd kissed her as if he'd meant it. He'd kissed her as if he'd meant to do much more, and she'd encouraged him.

So you did.

She let out another sigh. Okay, so maybe she had. Big deal. *She* hadn't meant it. Not really. At least not in *that* way.

She looked at herself in the bathroom mirror. "God, you're such a liar."

The truth was tougher to admit—she'd wanted Damon last night, and if he hadn't come to his senses, she was certain they'd have made love. Being held in his arms had given her a sense of comfort she'd realized had been missing in her life for some time now.

Like four years?

She bit her lip.

As much as she tried, she didn't have a seriously logical explanation for what happened. Except that perhaps with Damon she felt safe. Not to mention turned on to the nth degree.

Did it matter that there was nothing practical or logical about the way he'd made her feel? She had a feeling she could attempt to dissect the situation fifty ways to the next millennium and doubted she'd ever come up with an answer that appealed to her pragmatic nature.

What was she thinking? She had no business letting kisses or heat or hormones get in the way of what was really important—like clearing her name. She was, after all, facing a possible murder conviction.

She frowned. But what if Rosen won? What if the ADA convinced a jury she had killed Jonathan? If convicted, she'd end up serving a prison sentence. Twenty-five to life. Or worse, certain death.

She turned on the tap, then splashed cold water on her face, which did nothing to alleviate the sudden chill gripping her. She, of all people, knew that life was too damn short, even under the best of circumstances. Hers could end up being cut ridiculously short if the prosecutor had his way.

What was she doing wasting time worrying about the practicality or logic of why Damon had kissed her or had stopped before they'd made love? Shouldn't she be enjoying the fact that she still held a certain kind of sensual power over him. She should be doing something about the fact that they still desired each other.

And dammit, she planned to do something about it. Now.

By the time she finished washing her face and brushing her teeth, she still hadn't worked up the courage to confront him. Her days were quite possibly numbered. She needed to do everything within her limited power to spend what time she might have left living to the fullest extent possible.

She ran a brush through her hair, contemplating her life thus far. Despite the circumstances of her youth, losing her mother at a young age, the series of foster homes and how socially inept she'd been growing up, she didn't feel as if she had a whole lot worth complaining about. Sure, she'd been humiliatingly awkward, but what kid sent to high school at the age of twelve wouldn't have been grossly out of their element? But she'd turned out okay. With Jonathan gone, her circle of friends might be virtually non-existent, but at least she didn't spend an hour a week on a shrink's couch.

Her life might not be perfectly balanced, but she had embarked on a couple semi-serious affairs since she ended her relationship with Damon. Her relationship with the rocket scientist from Jet Propulsion Laboratories had ended because he'd taken a fabulous job offer from NASA and had relocated. They'd even tried the long distance thing for a time, but as she'd expected, it hadn't worked out all that well.

Her next relationship had ended because she'd been a poor judge of character and the rat bastard had cheated on her. She'd vowed to make smarter choices in the future and had concentrated on her work. Her last affair had ended only four months ago, because although they'd had a lot in common and had been perfectly suited in many ways, she'd soon realized she didn't love the guy. In her opinion, without the possibility of a future together, there wasn't much point in delaying the inevitable.

She set the brush down on the counter and left the bathroom. She and Damon weren't exactly suited. They didn't have much of a future, either, she thought, slipping on the cardigan that matched her pajamas. Even if he did get her acquitted, there was the issue of their living arrangements. She knew from first-hand experience, long distance relationships were doomed to fail.

Besides, she thought, she also knew from experience she and Damon were polar opposites. He liked sports and she didn't know a batting average from a field goal range. He was into Garth Brooks, she preferred Bach. She watched the Sci-Fi and Discovery channels, he was more of a CNN and ESPN kind of guy. They didn't even vote within the same political party.

She sucked in a deep breath. Did any of it *really* matter? She wasn't exactly in a position to be on the lookout for a life mate with her future nothing but a big fat question mark. Could there really be any harm in reigniting the flame with Damon?

Why not? Life as she knew it could possibly end much sooner than she'd hoped. She loved him, but she was no longer in love with him, so he couldn't break her heart. And if by some bizarre twist she did end up with her heart in tatters, who cared? How long would she have to suffer anyway? Just long enough for all those death row appeals to be denied.

She crossed her room to the door leading to his and reached for the lock. Her decision made, she gave it a twist and yanked open the door.

The room was empty. She stood quiet and listened, then heard water running in the bathroom. Bravely, she followed the sound.

He stood in front of the sink, his firm, square jaw lathered in shaving cream, wearing only a pair of khaki trousers. As he drew the razor along the underside of his jaw, she admired the play of muscle in his back.

"Why did you stop last night?" she blurted. She could be a condemned woman before much longer. She didn't have time for subtleties.

Damon winced. Whether because of her unexpected question, or because he'd nicked his chin with the razor, or even a combination of the two, she couldn't be certain.

"Didn't anyone ever tell you it's not smart to sneak up on a guy with a sharp object in his hand?"

She crossed her arms then leaned her shoulder against the doorjamb of the bathroom. "Sorry. Would you answer the question, please?"

He ran the razor under the hot, steaming water, then tapped it on the edge of the sink before casting a quick glance in her direction. "What was the question?"

"You're stalling."

He negotiated the razor upward along his throat. "Uh-huh," he murmured.

She dragged the toe of her slipper along the seam where the plush carpet met the marble tile. "Are you going to tell me or not?"

"Shouldn't you be getting dressed?"

"We have time." It wasn't even seven-thirty. Besides, she couldn't get dressed until the hotel returned the clothing she'd sent out to be dry cleaned last night. "Why won't you answer the question?"

He looked at her in the mirror's reflection. "Why is this suddenly so important?"

"Because I wish you hadn't stopped."

The seductive darkening of his gaze bolstered her courage. She pushed off the doorjamb and stepped into the bathroom, coming up beside him. "At all," she added.

With his eyes locked on hers, he reached around her to

snag a hand towel from the marble counter. He kept staring at her as he wiped away the remnants of shaving cream from his face.

His silence threatened to burst her bravado bubble. "Say something, Damon."

He tossed the towel on the counter. "What do you want to hear?"

"That you meant what you said. That you weren't sorry."

The hint of a smile lurked around the corners of his mouth. "You have to ask?"

She nodded. She did have to ask. He knew that about her.

"Why did you stop?" she repeated. She had to know. Know that she wasn't imagining the desire, or that he'd wanted her last night as much as she'd wanted him and that he was only being noble or some other stupid reason. Not that he didn't want her.

"Because it seemed like the right thing to do at the time."

The huskiness of his voice warmed her.

Still, she frowned.

"Why?"

"Laurel," he said and smiled. "It's way too early for so many questions."

"I'm a scientist. It's in my DNA to question everything."

"Did you ever consider that not every question has an answer?"

"No."

He chuckled at that. "Then let me ask you something." He settled his hand on her waist and urged her closer. "Why did you come in here this morning?"

With the distance between them narrowed, her heart rate picked up speed. Her mind went blank.

"I'm still attracted to you, Laurel." His other hand landed on her hip. The heat of his fingers pressed into her, nudging her even closer.

Attracted. Not still in love. Big difference in her opinion. Hearing that should have filled her with a sense of relief. Instead, she felt a tiny stab of disappointment.

"It doesn't have to make sense," he added.

So says he. To her, things had to make sense. Be logical.

"The timing is lousy," he continued. "I'm your attorney. You're the last person I should be lusting after."

Lust? Okay. Lust she could handle. Lust was good and short term enough for a woman with a noose swinging above her head. Lust partnered quite well with attraction.

"I need to be concentrating on building your defense." He aligned their bodies and his hand slipped to cup her bottom.

Her hormones went haywire.

"Not fantasizing about making love to you."

Shouldn't she say something? She opened her mouth, but whatever she'd been about to say evaporated like steam the moment his lips brushed over hers in a feathery kiss. She didn't hesitate, and for once in her life, she didn't question, only lost herself in the heat of the moment.

She slipped her arms around his waist and pressed her body against the heated warmth of his skin. Her hands wandered the sculpted landscape of his back, enjoying the feel of muscle play beneath her fingertips.

Unlike him, she didn't wonder about making love to him. She already knew it'd be magnificent. The man was just too good in bed. Period. And goodness, could he kiss.

His tongue swept into her mouth and her toes curled inside her slippers. She didn't think about lists or clearing her name, but concentrated on the dampness gathering between her legs and the heat pooling in her belly.

His hand skimmed beneath her camisole and moved upward over her rib cage to cup her breast in his warm palm. Heat spiraled through her when he rubbed his thumb over her nipple. She groaned into his mouth as spikes of pleasure prickled along her skin.

He ended the kiss, but his lips traveled down her throat, his tongue trailing a fiery path to the slope of her breasts. He pushed her top up to expose her breasts, the warm moist air brushing against her heated skin. Then he captured the nipple he'd teased into a tight bud in his mouth, and logic no longer mattered, not when she was about to explode from the absolute pleasure of his mouth against her skin.

Desire tugged at her. Hard. She gripped his shoulders for support. She wanted more. So much more.

She heard pounding. Damon lifted his head. "Were you expecting someone?"

"Huh?" Wasn't that her heart pounding?

She heard it again.

"The door," he said, tugging her camisole back into place.

She looked at him, confused. "The door?"

He placed a quick kiss on her lips and left the bathroom. She sat dazed and heard voices in the distance. When he returned a few moments later, he carried her dry cleaning.

"Oh!" Heat crept up her face and she laughed nervously. "The door." Goodness, she couldn't remember when she'd last been confused in such a delicious sort of way.

"You'd better get dressed if we're going to pick up your car before meeting Stacy at the office."

She nodded. "Yes. Uh . . . thank you," she said lamely and pushed off the counter. "But we will finish this later."

She took her dry cleaning from him and ignored the cocky lift of his eyebrows. She hurried to the sanctity of her own room. She might have momentarily lost her wits amid the confusion and passion, but one thing she knew for certain—there was absolutely no question in her mind as to whether or not they'd make love. It was simply a matter of when.

She hung the cleaning in the closet and smiled. And the sooner, the better.

She parked the black SUV, a rental, across the street. She wasn't sure she'd have the nice ride for too long, but it sure beat driving her undependable and ancient Honda Civic. She appreciated the SUV because she had things to do today. Important things to secure her future. Her baby's future.

She entered the Olympic Boulevard office building, but wasn't prepared to trust the antiquated elevator not to get stuck between floors, so she opted for the stairs. She entered the stairwell and was immediately assaulted by the aroma of stale smoke and urine. Her stomach turned as she climbed the stairs to the third floor where Everett P. Sharpe's office was located. The bastard owed her a favor, and she intended to collect.

Not that she'd have much trouble in convincing Everett to do exactly what she wanted. As she knew all too well, ethics and Everett weren't exactly synonymous. Even if he had suddenly developed a conscience, which wasn't likely, she had the promise of a hefty fee to sway him. And if that failed, which she doubted, there was always the added insurance policy she'd brought with her—in the form of a .38 snub nose.

She reached the third floor and exited the stairwell. The air quality improved greatly, and she breathed easier as she walked the short distance down the dingy corridor to Everett's office. On the last door at the end of the hallway, the words Everett P. Sharp & Associates were painted in black block letters.

Associates? That was laughable. The cheap bastard ran a one man operation, answered his own phones, and typed his own letters. Everett hated parting with a dollar and wouldn't even hire himself a secretary to at least provide his potential clientele the façade of a reputable counselor-at-law.

A bell tinkled above the door when she opened it, announcing her arrival. The office was as she remembered it. Dingy white walls yellowed with age and a hideous shag carpet in varying shades of avocado and worn thin in places, lay the foundation for a reception area in serious need of a facelift. Except for an old worn leather love seat with duct tape hiding a tear on the arm and one on the cushion, a couple of hard plastic chairs, and cheap walnut veneer tables, the place was deserted.

A black metal picture frame held an old warped print of the coastline and hung on the wall opposite the ratty sofa. On the oblong coffee table sat a two-year-old-copy of *California Lawyer*, along with a few tattered back issues of *People* and *Entertainment Weekly*.

She wrinkled her nose. The place might look respectably clean, if old, but there was a musty smell that did nothing to help the roiling of her stomach.

"Be right with you," a voice called from a room somewhere in the back.

She didn't bother to wait, but left the shabby reception area and headed toward Everett's office. He was circling the desk as she entered. He stopped and stared at her, the color slowly draining from his face.

"What are you doing here?" His voice sounded strained.

"Everett P. Sharpe," she said slowly and gave him a once over. "Attorney to the scumbags."

A cheap gray polyester suit hung on his lank, middle-aged frame. The plain white shirt he wore, no longer pristine, needed ironing. The gray-and-mauve-striped tie was frayed on one edge. Black wing tips, in need of a shine, graced his ridiculously large feet. He didn't look like a lawyer, but a used car salesman, the kind that sold her her Honda.

"How have you been, Everett? It's been a long time."

He frowned, obviously not recognizing her. She wasn't surprised. She had changed since she'd last seen him.

Fear flashed in his soulless brown eyes. He should be afraid after the way he screwed her.

"Not long enough." He shoved a thinning hank of lack-luster brown hair sprinkled with gray away from his forehead with a trembling hand.

She glanced pointedly at his shaking hands. Nothing that a stiff drink probably wouldn't cure. "What's the matter, Ev? Not enough Irish in your coffee this morning?"

He tucked his hands in the pockets of his trousers. His frown deepened. "What do you want?"

She strolled casually toward the brown tweed guest chairs. "I need a lawyer," she said and sat in the chair closest to the grime-covered window overlooking Olympic Boulevard.

"I'm sorry," he said. "I'm not accepting new clients at the moment."

She flashed him a smile. "I have a feeling you'll change your mind when you hear what I have to offer."

Annoyance flashed in his gaze. "I doubt that."

"Sit down, Everett," she said, settling her purse in her lap. She felt for the handle of the pistol beneath the fabric of her bag. "We need to talk."

"I'm busy."

He didn't look busy. He looked hung over and nervous as hell. He should be. He owed her, and they both knew it. After the way he bungled the handling of her great-aunt's estate, robbing her of what should have belonged to her, he owed her big time. She'd promised him she'd collect one day. Well, that day had finally come.

"Then I suggest you get *un*-busy," she said in a threatening tone. "Or the State Bar just might learn of a certain financial discrepancy involving client trust accounts. You wouldn't want something like that to become public knowledge, now, would you, Everett?"

The color returned to his face, turning his usual sallow complexion mottled. "That's a lie, and you know it."

"Is it?" she asked with a careless shrug. "I suppose it doesn't really matter. The investigation by the bar association will be enough to cast doubt and suspicion. You probably won't be disbarred, unless, of course, they find you've been cooking the books."

When he said nothing in his defense, she gave him a pointed look filled with meaning he clearly understood. Everett had a habit of padding financials—in his favor. And she had the probate documents to prove it. At least insofar as her association with Everett P. Sharpe was concerned.

"Which is entirely possible," she continued. "Isn't it, Everett?" She opened her purse wide enough for him to see what she carried inside. "Perhaps they'll only suspend you while conducting their investigation. Imagine how that would impact your practice? Who's going to want to hire a lawyer that can't be trusted with money?"

"Get the fuck out of here," he said in a low, threatening voice.

"Shut up and sit down," she snapped at him. He really was beginning to irritate her. "I have a proposition for you."

His gaze slipped to her bag, just as she'd hoped. "You can't come in here and threaten me."

Her smile was a slow, condescending one. "I never threaten, Everett," she said smoothly. "I merely make promises. And you know me well enough to know, I always keep my promises."

What little fight he'd managed to muster, waned. He let out a long slow breath. "What is it you want?" he asked again.

"Only what I'm entitled to," she told him. And she was entitled to plenty.

"Get to the point," he said irritably as he returned to his side of the desk. "I'm a busy man."

Busy screwing over his clients. "Does the name Jonathan Linton ring any bells on your cash register?"

"So?" he said with a shrug of his thin shoulders. "He's dead."

"Precisely. And I'm carrying his baby. The Linton heir."

That claim certainly got his attention. He appeared skeptical, but sat up a little straighter just the same. "No shit?"

"No shit."

"What's that have to do with me? I'm not exactly on the Lintons' list of retained counsel."

Everett wasn't exactly the sharpest knife in the kitchen, either. Was it any wonder he made a decent side line ripping off his clients?

"Jonathan's estate," she said. "It's mine. All that Linton money belongs to my baby." She rested her hand against her still-flat stomach. "Mine and Jonathan's baby."

His gaze dipped to where her hand rested protectively over her tummy. "You don't look pregnant."

"It's early yet. Start of the second trimester," she said. "I want what I'm entitled to, Everett. For my baby. And you're going to get it for me."

He surprised her by chuckling. "Are you nuts? You think you can just waltz in there and they're going to hand everything over to you because you claim you're knocked up with their dead son's brat?" He laughed again, more heartily this time.

She narrowed her eyes. "You're more stupid than I give you credit for," she said venomously. "I'm going to be rich. Very rich. And so will you when you advise the family that unless they provide for me and my baby we'll go public with a paternity action against Jonathan's estate."

"You *are* crazy."

"Crazy rich."

Everett leaned forward. "You know you're going to need proof."

She reached into her bag and withdrew the print of a sonogram. "Good enough?" she asked, setting it on the desk.

He picked up the film, but didn't appear convinced. "They're going to demand a DNA test. You know that, right?"

"They won't insist on a test that could endanger my un-born child," she said confidently. "Especially if I have a doc-tor who'll agree that this is a high risk pregnancy. But you tell them we'll agree to a DNA test once the baby is born."

She reached back into her bag for her cell phone. "Do I need to make that anonymous call to the State Bar?"

"How much exactly is in it for me?"

Greedy bastard. She knew she could count on him.

"Half your usual percentage. Consider it punishment for the shoddy way you handled my great-aunt's probate."

Wisely, he didn't dare quibble. "I'll see what I can do."

She suspected he would. He had more shady sources than a tabloid reporter.

The bell over the door jangled, signaling, she assumed, the arrival of his next client. She stood and headed for the door, then stopped and looked at him over her shoulder. "Oh, and buy a new suit, would you? Or Johanna Linton won't even let you through the gate."

Chapter 14

LAUREL'S HAND SHOOK so hard as she slipped the key into the lock, it took her three tries before she could open the door. Returning to the scene of the crime wasn't something she'd been looking forward to doing. The memories were too fresh.

"It'll be okay," Damon said from behind her.

His nearness gave her comfort. She knew he was the last person she should be depending on, but she couldn't help herself.

"I hope you're right," she said, but she had serious doubts. She hadn't been back to Artifacts since the night she'd found Jonathan's body.

With a twist of the knob, she finally pushed open the heavy metal door and walked into the workroom to disengage the alarm system. The building, which she and Jonathan owned, was an old storefront they'd converted into a minor show room and reception area with offices and a small conference room where they occasionally made presentations to potential clients. The back of the building, which had once been used to warehouse goods, had been converted into their workroom and storage area. Now the area was nothing but a big cavernous room that smelled of paint and chemicals, where a murder had taken place.

Surprisingly the workroom looked as it always did, with shelving and various work stations for the work they actually performed at Artifacts. She was grateful that there was no yellow crime scene tape strung around the worktable where she'd found Jonathan's body. As she walked across the concrete flooring, the only stains she could determine were from the various paints and chemicals they used in their work. There wasn't even a chalk line like she'd seen in the movies. She supposed if she looked close enough some of those red splotches might actually be blood splatters, but she was more than willing to go with the belief they were nothing more than drips of Titian Red.

She came to a stop a few feet from the work area where she'd found Jonathan's bloodied corpse sprawled on the floor beneath a large, oblong wooden trestle table. He'd been meticulously restoring a nineteenth century gilt frame for one of their small museum clients. "He must've been working on it when he died," she said to Damon.

"What makes you say that?" Damon asked, coming up beside her.

"Because," she said, pointing to a small lump of clay on a palette. "This is the type of clay we use for restoring antique frames. It has to be mixed and used right away because of how quickly it hardens."

Damon strolled closer to the table. "That could explain why he didn't notice his attacker until it was too late."

"What makes you think Jonathan was attacked?" No one had ever mentioned an attack. She hadn't really given it a lot of thought because she usually couldn't get past the thought that Jonathan was dead.

"I'll know more when I get the ME's report later today," he said, "but the police report indicated there were several stab wounds in his back. My guess is one of those wounds struck something vital, which made it easier for the attacker to overcome him the way he did. You didn't know?"

The image of Jonathan's ravaged body flashed through her mind. She shook her head to clear it. "No," she said. "If they could think a woman had killed him that way, then I guess it makes sense."

She turned away. "I'll go see if I can find his BlackBerry. Come on up to Jonathan's office whenever you're done here," she said, knowing he wanted to look around. She then hurried toward the door leading to the offices, anxious to escape the unpleasant memories.

The rest of the building was deserted, as Stacy wasn't due to arrive for at least another ten minutes. She went into her office and dropped her handbag on her chair, then crossed the hall to Jonathan's office.

She flipped on the overhead lights. As with the workroom, everything appeared to be just as he'd left it. His laptop sat closed on the desk, the file with the specs for the museum frame resting atop his inbox.

And no sign of his BlackBerry.

She sat in the chair and began searching the drawers. The top center drawer held nothing but a few pens and a stray paperclip or two, along with a handful of take-out menus from area restaurants and delis. In the top left drawer, all she found amid his personal stationery were a couple of empty note pads and half a book of stamps. The remaining drawers were similar, filled with a mixture of personal and business files, and proposals for restoration work they'd been waiting to hear back on, but which she now suspected would end up being awarded to other bidders.

In the bottom drawer she found a pair of chargers and the empty black leather case for his BlackBerry. But no BlackBerry.

Damon entered the office. "Any luck?"

She let out a sigh. "No," she said. "It's not here."

The heavy back door to the building clanged shut. Laurel

flinched at the sound far too reminiscent of the slamming of the metal bars of a jail cell.

"Where is everybody?" Stacy called out.

"In here," Damon called out, then looked back at Laurel. "You checked everywhere?"

"It's not here," Laurel said again. She plucked the empty case from the drawer. "This is all I found."

Stacy entered Jonathan's office. She'd dressed casually, wearing a short white denim skirt with a pair of gem-studded sandals and a teal silky tank top that showed off her early tanning efforts. "What are you looking for?" she asked.

"Jonathan's BlackBerry," Laurel said.

Stacy grinned and dug into her bag. "You mean this?" she asked, producing the BlackBerry.

Damon took it from her. "What are you doing with it?"

Stacy dropped her bag on the desk. "Jonathan gave it to me to sync with the master calendar I keep on the main computer."

"I thought for sure the cops would've had it logged in as evidence," Damon said. He started pressing buttons, powering up the electronic device.

Stacy's grin widened. "They probably would have, if they'd known it existed. Jonathan handed it to me as I was leaving that night, but I was too lazy to walk back to my desk so I stuck it in my bag and promised to have it back to him in the morning. No one knew I had it, and honestly, with everything that's been going on around here, I forgot about it until you mentioned it."

Laurel stood. "Thank you, Stacy."

"No problem," Stacy said. "I'll go pack up my laptop and grab a couple of files. I'll need to open the safe for the CD's on the two projects I want to work on at home."

"You really should just take some time off," Laurel told her, but she did appreciate Stacy's dedication, even if it all might end up being nothing but a big waste of time.

Damon took the seat Laurel vacated, his attention zeroed in on Jonathan's BlackBerry.

"I'd rather keep busy," Stacy said as she led the way down the short corridor to the reception area and show room. "If you don't mind, I'd like to take a stab at the proposal for the two Bruegel reproduction bids."

Laurel winced at Stacy's word choice.

"You know," Stacy continued, "I don't want you to think I'm an opportunist or anything, but you are going to need someone to help carry the extra workload now that Jonathan's gone."

Laurel walked to the front door and began gathering the pile of mail that had collected on the floor where the postman had pushed it through the mail slot. Two envelopes immediately caught her attention, and based on their size, they were more than likely negative responses to the bids she'd found in Jonathan's desk.

She held up the two envelopes and looked at Stacy. "What workload?"

Her assistant grimaced. "Once you're acquitted, it'll get better. You'll see."

Laurel didn't share Stacy's optimism—on either front. She finished gathering up the mail and carried it to Stacy's desk. "I don't think you're an opportunist."

Stacy sat and began sorting through the huge stack of mail. "Good," she said with a quick smile. "I know it's probably in poor taste to even bring it up, but I can do the job, Laurel."

"I know you can," Laurel told her. Stacy could perform magic with paints.

Laurel rested her backside on the edge of Stacy's desk. "We were just waiting to hire someone new to handle the administrative end of things. Jonathan and I had planned to give you an official promotion—and the pay raise to go with it."

"I like the sound of that," Stacy said with a laugh. She tossed the junk mail into the garbage can under her desk, then looked up at Laurel. "It's appreciated, too. Thank you for having faith in me."

Laurel offered Stacy a small smile in return. "Faith is something for which no empirical evidence exists," she said. "And in this case, doesn't apply."

Stacy blushed and turned her attention back to the mail. "Uh-oh. This looks official," she said and handed Laurel a small padded envelope.

Laurel read the return address. A Beverly Hills law firm. She tore open the envelope but before she could examine the contents, someone knocked on the front door.

"What the hell does he want?" Stacy said, glaring at the door.

Damon exited the office, Jonathan's BlackBerry in hand. "Either one of you know what or who 'JT' might be?" He looked toward the front door, and promptly slipped the BlackBerry in his pocket. "You'd better open it," he said to Laurel.

She dropped the envelope on the desk and went to the door. She turned the lock and opened it, stepping back to allow Detective Pete Teslenko entrance.

The detective nodded curtly in Damon's direction, then said to Laurel, "Dr. Jennings, would you come with me please?"

Alan Rosen jammed the receiver down on the telephone after checking his voice mail for the third time since arriving in the office less than an hour ago. Nothing. No word from the forensic accountants he had scrounging through Jennings's and Linton's financials. Even that prick Scanlon still hadn't returned his calls.

"Fat fuck," he muttered.

In front of him lay the report on blood evidence from the Linton murder he'd received from the crime scene unit supervisor late yesterday afternoon. He glared at the report for a moment, then pushed away from his desk in disgust and stood, turning to face the window. The mid-morning skies were still overcast, the dreary weather a perfect match to his increasingly foul mood.

His case against Jennings was falling apart. Not only had Metcalf shown up out of the blue to defend his personal ticket to the big time, but the blood evidence indicated a third party had more than likely been present at the murder scene.

According to the report, a third DNA sampling had been recovered from the murder weapon. The new evidence didn't necessarily prove Jennings hadn't committed the murder, but the presence of a third party sure as hell was enough for Metcalf to raise the question of reasonable doubt in the minds of the jury.

He was screwed.

There was no way he could prevent Metcalf from discovering the report on his own, so burying it wasn't an option, but that didn't mean he'd make it easy for the bastard. There wasn't even a legal argument he could make before the courts to suppress the evidence once Metcalf did learn of it.

No doubt about it. His case had just taken a serious nose dive and there wasn't a fucking thing he could do about it. Unless he could prove the murder was premeditated. But without something solid, like proof that Linton was stealing from Jennings, it wouldn't be easy.

His cell phone rang. He turned from the window, snagged the phone off his desk to check the display, and frowned. PRIVATE CALLER.

He still had no clue who'd called him yesterday afternoon. There wouldn't be a record of the call on his cell phone bill, either, other than to indicate an incoming call had taken place since the caller's number had been blocked.

He thought about letting the call go to voice mail, but suspected the caller wouldn't bother leaving a message. Someone was interested in the fate of Laurel Jennings, and Rosen had his doubts about that blocked caller being one of the Lintons. He'd been in constant contact with Johanna Linton and her brother-in-law Abe, the head of Monarch Studios, so the chances of the caller being either of them were slim. Besides, he'd personally called them yesterday to advise them of the latest turn of events. Neither had been pleased, and he'd been reminded again how much he had riding on a conviction.

He hit the call button before the fourth ring. "Rosen," he said.

"Good morning, Mr. Rosen."

The voice was the same. Deep, resonant, and completely unfamiliar. He sensed the trace of a New England accent, but couldn't quite place anything more than a general geographical location.

"Who is this?" Rosen demanded.

"Someone interested in your future," the caller replied.

Rosen turned to look out the window again at the gray morning skyline. "My future, or the future of Laurel Jennings?"

The caller chuckled, but Rosen could find no humor in the sound.

"You're a very astute man, Mr. Rosen. I like that."

Rosen frowned. "What do you want?"

"A conviction, of course," the caller said. "As do you."

"Why?" Rosen asked. "What's in it for you?"

"Let's just say both of our futures will benefit greatly when you obtain a conviction of Dr. Jennings. We'll leave it at that, shall we?"

He wasn't about to admit his case was circling the drain. If he had to go to trial today with the evidence he had, Jennings would be acquitted for sure. Thank God he had six weeks before trial. Six weeks to build a strong enough case against the Ice Queen to ensure she'd fry.

"Let's not," Rosen said. "Why are you interested in Jennings?"

"Check your e-mail, Mr. Rosen. I'm sure you'll find it quite interesting," the caller said, then disconnected the call.

He flipped his phone closed, returned to his desk, and went directly to his e-mail account. There was nothing out of the ordinary under his county e-mail address, so he tried his personal e-mail. Sure enough, a large PDF file immediately began to download into his in-box.

The return e-mail address gave him no clue as to the identity of his mystery caller. The address was an untraceable Hotmail account.

He began to read what he had been sent. The first page was a copy of a newspaper article from the *Boston Globe*. He read the headline:

RENOWNED SCIENTIST DIES IN CAR CRASH

"What the . . ." he muttered as he scanned the report. Scott Metcalf? Damon's old man? Well, that was interesting. But what did it have to do with Laurel Jennings?

He scrolled down to the next page, which started the official police investigation file. A smile slowly curved his lips. "Well, I'll be damned."

Interviewed by detectives as a "person of interest" was none other than the Ice Queen herself. He smiled. His case just might have sprouted wings, after all.

Laurel's steps faltered. She knew a crime scene when she saw one.

She glanced from Teslenko to Damon, then at the law enforcement milling around a white van. Someone swung open the passenger door and she read the official emblem: Los Angeles Coroner.

Not just any crime scene, she realized. A murder scene.

Oh God. What now?

Damon's fingers wrapped around her upper arm. "Wait a minute," he said. "Just what the hell is going on here?"

Teslenko ducked under the crime scene tape strung across the alleyway, a mere block and a half from Artifacts. All the detective had said when he'd shown up at her door less than five minutes ago was that Scanlon wanted to speak with her. Since the portly detective was unofficially on their side, she didn't see much harm in complying with the request. Now she wasn't so certain.

"I told Scanlon this was a bad idea," Teslenko complained sourly.

"I don't understand," Laurel said. "What is this about?"

Damon glanced at the ME's van then back at Teslenko. "You think just because a body was found near my client's place of business there's some connection?"

Laurel's eyes widened. "Am I being accused of something?"

They'd already passed a pair of police cruisers blocking the south entrance to the alley. In the distance, she noted a second pair of cruisers guarding the north entrance as well. The area was under full scale investigation. A murder investigation, and now she was right in the middle of it—again.

Teslenko ignored their questions and kept his attention on her. "This way, Dr. Jennings." He lifted the tape a little higher. "Please," he added.

She looked to Damon for confirmation. He let go of her arm and motioned for her to precede him under the tape.

She didn't want to look, but her gaze was automatically drawn to the black body bag on the ground as they neared the back end of the coroner's transport vehicle. A pair of technicians wearing bulletproof vests with big yellow letters on the back indicating they were members of the crime scene unit were busy photographing the immediate vicinity.

Damon's hand settled on her arm again. "Don't answer any questions," he told her.

Teslenko glanced at them over his shoulder, his mouth tightening into a thin line, his opinion clear. Too bad, Laurel thought. Damon's job was to protect her. She was, after all, his client.

She came to an abrupt stop when the technician photographing near the body bag stepped away. "Oh my God," she whispered.

Inside the unzipped bag was indeed a body. A man's body. A thin, lithe gentleman whose exact age she couldn't determine, but she figured him to be in his mid to late thirties. His skin, although pale in death, held remnants of a once deep tan. His raven black hair was slicked back, and his unseeing brown eyes were open. He'd been shot, if the gaping hole in his chest was any indication.

She shuddered but couldn't tear her gaze away.

Damon stepped in front of her in an attempt to block her view of the dead man. "What does this have to do with my client?" he demanded.

Teslenko jammed his hand through his hair. "I knew this was gonna be a mistake," he said irritably. He turned and motioned for Scanlon to join them.

"Doc. Metcalf," Scanlon said by way of greeting as he approached them.

Damon didn't bother to accept the hand Scanlon extended.

Scanlon urged them away from the body bag while motioning for Teslenko to stay put. "Thanks for coming, Doc," he said. "Did you know him?"

"No," she said. "I've never seen him before."

"What the hell is this all about?" Damon demanded once

they were out of earshot of the law enforcement personnel milling around the body.

"It could be nothing," Scanlon said. "On the surface, looks like a mugging gone bad. Could be, too, but I don't think so."

"What does this have to do with me?" Laurel hated that her voice trembled. She despised showing weakness in front of Scanlon, but especially his partner.

"That's what I'd like to know," Damon said. "Just because some random murder happened to take place within a block or two of my client's place of business shouldn't have you pegging her as the prime suspect. Unless you have some proof she was involved, then I'd tread carefully, Scanlon. You wouldn't want me filing harassment charges."

Scanlon frowned. "Cut me some slack, Metcalf. We're on the same side here."

Scanlon's admission did little to comfort Laurel. Once again she was being questioned by police for a crime she didn't commit. She'd be developing a complex before much longer at this rate.

"What have you got?" Damon asked the detective.

"DB, GSW to the chest. From the powder burns, looks to be close range. Probably a .38, but we won't know for sure until I get the ballistics report back."

"Who was he?" Laurel asked.

"Don't know. No ID on the body." Scanlon dug into the pocket of his jacket and pulled out a sealed plastic baggie. "This is all we found on him."

Damon took the evidence bag from Scanlon. She leaned closer and examined two small, metal objects, similar in shape and size to an Allen wrench or hex key. Rather than the traditional L-shaped end, these tools tapered down into a thin, blunt edge.

Damon handed the bag back to Scanlon. "Looks like lock picks."

The detective nodded and tucked the evidence bag back into his pocket. "With the break in at the doc's apartment and this happening so close to where the murder took place . . ."

"You thought I might know something about it?" Laurel asked, her tone incredulous. "That's ridiculous."

"It's nothing more than a coincidence," Damon said to Laurel.

"Not necessarily," Scanlon answered. "And I don't put much stock in coincidence, either. At least not on the job. No chance your place of business was broken into last night, was there?"

"We have a very sophisticated security system," she said. "But no, there didn't appear to be anything out of place. At least that I could tell."

"Good," Scanlon said, nodding his head. "That's good. I hate to ask, Doc, but where were you this morning between three and five?"

Laurel blushed. She couldn't help herself.

"She was with me," Damon said before she could summon an answer that wouldn't incriminate her. At least in the criminal sense.

Scanlon stared at her long and hard. She looked guiltily away.

"All right," Scanlon said slowly.

Laurel had the distinct impression he knew there was something they weren't telling him. He was a smart guy. He'd figure it out eventually.

A cell phone rang. Laurel hadn't bothered to bring her purse, so she knew it couldn't be hers. Besides, her cell phone was still dead since she had yet to replace the charger that had been destroyed when her condo had been ransacked.

Scanlon slipped his phone from his pocket. "Must be yours," he said to Damon.

Damon frowned. He reached into his pocket and pulled out Jonathan's BlackBerry.

Laurel struggled to hide her surprise.

Damon calmly checked the display, then pushed the appropriate button. "Yeah." His frown deepened. "Give me five minutes." He disconnected the call then looked to Scanlon. "Are we done here?"

"Yeah. We're done," Scanlon said. "I'll be in touch."

Laurel waited until they'd passed beneath the crime scene tape. "Who called?"

"Stacy," Damon said. "She said to tell you the *Gates of Paradise* CD's were missing from the safe."

Chapter 15

DAMON CHECKED ONE last time the list of the safe's contents Stacy had printed off for him. "Everything else seems to be here," he told them.

Stacy flipped through the blank CD's. "I don't get it," she said. "The *Gates of Paradise* project was finished weeks ago. No one had any reason to even mess with the project disks."

"You're sure nothing else has been disturbed?" he asked. "Nothing else is missing?"

"Let me go check the files," Stacy offered, then took off for the office where the filing cabinets were kept.

"Any guess on where the originals might be?" Damon asked Laurel.

She stood with her backside pressed against a paint-stained work table. "Unless Jonathan had them, but like Stacy said, the *Gates of Paradise* project was completed weeks ago. There was no reason for him to have the disks."

Like Scanlon, Damon didn't believe in coincidences, either. Granted, Los Angeles was one tough city. A man murdered not two blocks away from Artifacts could very well be nothing more than just another random act of violence. But when an unidentified body turned up with only tools of a theft trade on him, and now there were important project

CD's missing from Artifacts, Damon didn't believe for a minute there wasn't a connection. Plus, someone had been looking for something at Laurel's place. He didn't like the way things were adding up.

"You think there's a connection, don't you?" she asked him.

He let out a long, slow breath. "It's hard to say," he answered noncommittally.

"Damon," she said, a note of impatience in her voice. "I'm not stupid."

"I know you're not."

"Then stop treating me like I'm an idiot."

"I'm sorry." He had no excuse, except perhaps his long-time habit of wanting to protect her. "Yes, I think there's a connection," he admitted. "The break in at your place. A dead body. Lock picks. And now this. Too many coincidences for me."

"Do you think he could've been the one that killed Jonathan?"

"Maybe," he said with a shrug, "but I have my doubts."

"Because who ever killed that man in the alley could also be Jonathan's killer?"

"Good question."

Stacy returned with a handful of files. "Here's everything we have on the St. Giovanni project," she said, setting the files next to Laurel. "It's all there."

Damon slipped the BlackBerry from his pocket. "Can you print from this thing?" he asked Stacy.

"Sure," Stacy said, taking the device from him. "Tell me what you want."

"Everything."

"You got it."

"Any idea who JT might be?" he asked as Stacy turned to leave.

"No," Laurel said.

"Stacy," Damon called after her. "What about you? Any idea who JT might be?"

"Not off the top of my head," Stacy said, and kept walking. "If anything comes to me, I'll let you know."

Laurel picked up the files Stacy had brought her and perused the labels. "So what do we do now?" she asked.

"I have to go to the ME's office to pick up the autopsy photos." He closed the safe, then walked across the work area to where Laurel stood. She looked up at him as he neared and his chest tightened.

"Take my car," she said. "I'll stay here with Stacy until you get back."

He settled his hand on her shoulder. "Lock the doors," he said, trailing his thumb along the edge of her throat. Her pulse beat rapidly beneath his touch. Without thinking twice about what he was doing, or even why he felt compelled to do it, he dipped his head and kissed her.

His body responded instantly to the pressure of her lips against his. Right or wrong, ethics be damned, there was no question in his mind. He wanted Laurel. Whether or not they would make love was no longer a question, only when.

"Oh! Excuse me."

They broke apart like two guilty teenagers at the startled sound of Stacy's voice. Laurel's cheeks turned pink, and she flicked at something on her skirt.

"I'm sorry," Stacy said.

"What is it?" Laurel asked, avoiding Stacy's inquisitive glances.

"I was thinking of calling an order into the deli."

"I've got to go," Damon said. "Keep the doors locked until I get back."

After an answering nod of agreement from Laurel, he headed for the rear exit.

"He's hot," Stacy said in a bad stage whisper.

"Yes, I know," Laurel answered quietly.

*   *   *

"Lunch," Stacy announced from the doorway of Laurel's office. "The conference room work for you?"

Laurel slipped the billing statements for the St. Giovanni project back into the appropriate file. She considered declining Stacy's offer, but then she wouldn't be doing much for that whole cultivate-female-friendships-item on her list of things she needed to change about her life. Best to take advantage of an opportunity while she still had the option.

"That'd be nice," she said. She closed the file and left her office. In the background, she heard the whir of the laser printer. A local Top 40 station played softly throughout the office speaker system. Normal sounds, she thought. Sounds of just another day at the office. All that was missing was the constant ringing of the telephone. She almost expected to hear Jonathan's voice drifting through the office as he talked on the telephone to a client.

She walked into the conference room and flipped on the overhead lights. A sudden pang of sadness pierced her. There would be no more Jonathan, she thought, schmoozing clients, as he used to say, or otherwise. Artifacts was just her now, and Stacy. The idea would take some getting used to—provided she even had a business left once all was said and done.

Laurel pulled a pair of steaming hot pastrami sandwiches, a couple of bags of chips, and two diet sodas from the paper bag that Stacy had left on the conference table. Stacy returned from the stock room with picnicware, then left again, returning moments later with the huge stack of unopened mail and her steno pad.

"I thought we could multi-task," her assistant explained when Laurel gave her a quizzical glance.

"So this guy that was axed," Stacy started as she carefully unwrapped the tin foil from her sandwich, "all the detectives found on him were some lock picking tools?"

"That was all Detective Scanlon showed us," Laurel answered. She tore open the bag of barbecue-flavor potato chips and snagged one.

"No mention at all of our missing CD's?"

Laurel shook her head and sat. "No," she said. "At least I didn't get that impression."

"I wonder why he wanted the St. Giovanni disks?" Stacy mused, then popped a corn chip into her mouth.

"We don't know that he stole them," Laurel reminded her.

"Oh come on, Laurel. That's just too freaky of a coincidence."

Laurel took a sip of her soda. "Then where are the CD's?" she asked, even though she did agree with Stacy. "Don't you think Detective Scanlon would have mentioned finding them on the body?"

Stacy dusted corn chip dust from her fingers, then popped the top on her soda. "You know what I think? I think whoever wasted the guy probably has our CD's."

That was a definite possibility, provided the two incidents were even related. At this point, all they had was the unsubstantiated supposition of two lay-women and what could very well be nothing but a very bizarre coincidence.

Laurel unwrapped her own sandwich. "But why?" she mused aloud. "What could anyone want with old project disks?" That was the part that made the least amount of sense to Laurel.

"And why that project, in particular?" Stacy added. "Nothing else was taken, and we have some important restoration and reproduction projects locked up in that safe. Corporate espionage, maybe?"

Laurel considered the possibility, then quickly discarded it. "If it were, don't you think all of the disks would've been stolen?"

"Good point," Stacy said before taking a bite of her pastrami.

Laurel let out a weighty sigh, wondering if they'd ever have answers. Or better yet, if what little information they did have would be enough for Damon to raise reasonable doubt within the minds of the jury and save her ass.

She could only hope.

"You know," Stacy said. "I can't help thinking that this whole thing might be related to Jonathan's murder."

Laurel had entertained the possibility as well. "Damon and I were discussing the same thing earlier."

A twinkle of amusement entered Stacy's gaze. "I didn't realize you and Damon were an item."

Surprisingly, Laurel didn't blush. "We are *not* an item."

Stacy scoffed. "Sure looked like it to me."

"He's my attorney."

"So?" Stacy shrugged. "Who cares. The guy is hot. And he's definitely got the hots for you."

The feeling was mutual.

A frown suddenly creased Stacy's brow. "I can't remember the last time a guy looked at me the way Damon looks at you."

Laurel found that difficult to believe. Stacy was young and attractive, not to mention vivacious and intelligent. She'd always imagined Stacy had a flock of men prepared to answer her beck and call.

"Maybe we should go over the mail," Laurel suggested, anxious to change the subject.

Stacy pushed the mountainous stack of envelopes out of reach. "The mail isn't going anywhere," she said, then frowned. "Why is this uncomfortable for you?"

Laurel shrugged. "I'm not sure what I'm supposed to say." Female bonding rituals were a little beyond her realm of expertise. "We aren't exactly discussing the correct chemical compound used for breathing life back into five-hundred-year-old frescoes."

"There's more to life than work," Stacy said, then popped another corn chip into her mouth.

So she was supposed to be learning. "Do you have a lot of women friends?"

"A few," Stacy answered. "You?"

"Not really." Zero, to be exact.

"And why not?" Stacy asked.

"Making friends has always been difficult for me," Laurel surprised herself by admitting. "There aren't any old friends from high school in my Rolodex because I was so much younger than the other kids."

"I imagine the atmosphere wasn't exactly conducive to developing long-lasting friendships."

"In all honesty," Laurel said, "all I wanted to do was escape. My first years of college were a little better, but only because of the maturity level of the student body. Still, I was a fourteen-year-old prodigy surrounded by young adults in the eighteen-to-twenty-two-year-old range."

"Not exactly a recipe for bonding, was it?"

"No," Laurel said. "Not really. By the time I was the same age as everyone else, I was already working on my first Ph.D."

"Which kept you separated from the herd," Stacy surmised. "That had to be rough."

"I survived," Laurel said with a shrug. "Except for Damon. He never treated me as if I were a freak."

"So what made you switch from science to art?" Stacy asked her. "Those two fields aren't exactly in the same stratosphere."

"I wanted a change," Laurel answered coolly. Finished with her lunch, Laurel pushed her plate aside. "Maybe we should go over the mail."

She wiped her hands on the paper napkin, then reached for the padded envelope she'd set aside when Detective Teslenko had shown up at her door. She examined the outside of the envelope, but didn't recognize the name of the law firm. The address, however, was in the same neighborhood as Artifacts. Curious, she shook the contents from the envelope. Another sealed envelope fell onto the table, along with a blue-backed legal document and a cover letter on the law firm's stationery.

Laurel stared at the envelope, almost afraid to touch it.

"Oh my God," Stacy leaned forward and frowned. "That's Jonathan's handwriting."

Laurel picked up the plain white envelope with her name written on the front. Carefully, she tore open the flap and removed the contents. She read the handwritten note, then passed it to Stacy.

"I'm sorry," Stacy read. "Love, Jonathan." She looked at Laurel. "Sorry about what?"

Laurel set the business card for a small local bank and the key that had been in the envelope on the conference table, along with a legal document indicating ownership of a safety deposit box now belonging to her. "I don't know," she said, "but I bet if we go open this, we might have a better idea."

The problem with following up a hunch on a case the brass considered closed was finding the time to do the leg work. Leg work that had to be performed off the clock, on a clock that never seemed to stopped ticking.

He'd bet his pension his newest murder investigation was somehow related to the Doc. Not that he believed for a second she was remotely responsible for the death of a thief found less than two blocks away from her place of business, but dammit, he knew in his gut there was a connection. Even Pete agreed with him on this one, which was saying something considering his partner's dislike of the Doc.

There wasn't much more they could do at this point and he and Pete were pretty much at the mercy of the ME's office now, waiting for the fingerprints to come back, hopefully with an ID. He didn't expect to learn anything new from ballistics, either. He and Pete had already determined the shooter had used a .38, and had been up close and personal, based on the powder burns on the DB's clothing. He couldn't even connect the body to the break in since the crime scene boys hadn't managed to lift a single, viable print from the Doc's apartment. All he had to go on for the moment was his gut, which had been churning with acid for the past two hours.

He'd missed lunch, so he popped a Tums from the roll he kept in his pocket, then changed lanes as he neared the freeway off ramp which would lead him to the Brentwood neighborhood where Jonathan's mother, Johanna Linton, still lived in a mansion owned by Monarch Studios. An arrangement he'd discovered by performing a simple internet search.

In Scanlon's opinion, people with money were a strange fucking lot, and the Lintons were no exception. Jonathan's father's will had revealed a few interesting facts. Like the provision for his once-studio-starlet wife, Johanna Purcell Linton.

The now-aging beauty had done well for herself when she'd caught the eye of Sol Linton, who'd been head of Monarch Studios during its heyday. His internet search had revealed a press-fueled scandal back in the seventies when the pair had married, some even going so far as to refer to the bride as an old-fashioned social climbing gold digger. Yet in the fifteen years of their marriage, there'd only been a few breaths of scandal surrounding the couple, most of which involved an occasional indiscretion on Sol's part.

Upon Sol's death, however, another media feeding frenzy had ensued when a hungry tabloid reporter had unearthed a copy of Sol's will. The family-owned studio and control of the Linton fortune had been bequeathed to little brother

Abe, not the grieving widow. There had been a provision providing for Johanna, allowing her all the wealth and privilege that being a Linton entailed, however her future would remain secure only so long as she never remarried. Apparently Sol hadn't even trusted his wife enough to name her conservator of the trust fund for their only son, Jonathan. Abe Linton had been the one in total control of the heir apparent's purse strings.

Not that any of the information he'd gleaned could be connected to Jonathan Linton's murder, but the family dynamic had been an interesting bit of information. And it made him wonder exactly how much control old Abe had exerted over Jonathan. Tight reins usually led to at least a few minor rebellions, particularly among the wealthy and privileged. And that was the type of information Scanlon was after. Leopards didn't rearrange their spots, especially spoiled rich ones.

His stomach grumbled as he pulled up to the curb in front of the Linton mansion. He probably should've stopped and grabbed a chili dog. Then maybe he would have thought to call ahead and make sure Johanna was even home.

He cut the engine and pulled his keys from the ignition. He left his vehicle and started up the concrete driveway to the enormous Spanish-style structure. There were no fancy wrought-iron gates to keep out unwanted visitors, or even dogs patrolling the grounds. Just a well-manicured lawn, half the size of a football field, and a trio of Mexican gardeners who paid him no attention, busy trimming and caring for elaborate plantings lining the long, circular driveway.

As he drew closer, he spied an older model white SUV parked near the stucco arches. The driver was seated behind the wheel, but as Scanlon approached, the driver fired the engine and started down the driveway in the opposite direction.

Scanlon tried to ID the driver. As if he'd sensed the police-man's hard stare, the driver turned and looked at him, then quickly sped away.

Recognition dawned. Everett P. Sharpe? What the hell was he doing here?

Not only was Sharpe far out of his neighborhood, the sorry excuse for a lawyer was way out of his league. Sharpe's clientele hardly stretched to Brentwood, but were usually nothing more glamorous than small time thugs, prostitutes and poor schmucks who couldn't afford a decent attorney.

Whatever Sharpe was doing here, couldn't be good.

Scanlon approached the heavy wooden front door and rang the bell. He pulled his badge from his pocket and held it up to the uniformed maid who answered the door.

"Detective Scanlon to see Johanna Linton."

The woman stepped back and showed him into the foyer. "Wait here, please," she said, then promptly disappeared.

His entire apartment would have fit into the foyer. Marble tiles he'd bet were imported and a grand sweeping double staircase were the main focal points leading to a landing above. The chandelier hanging above the entry was proba-bly worth more than his pension fund. He examined a paint-ing over an inlaid table and couldn't help wondering if the Goya was an original or perhaps a reproduction courtesy of Artifacts.

The maid returned. "This way, sir."

Scanlon followed the petite woman, past the staircase to a room near the rear of the mansion. A solarium, he believed the rich and greedy called them, which was nothing more than a fancy name for a sun room filled with flowering plants and wicker furnishings. The maid pointed toward Johanna Linton. Scanlon nodded his thanks, then the maid disap-peared.

Johanna Linton stood at a gardener's table at the east end

of the sun room, carefully trimming a miniature Bonsai tree. "Good afternoon, Detective," she said as he approached. She didn't bother to look in his direction, but kept her attention focused on her task. "Can I offer you something to drink?"

"No, thank you."

"Are you familiar with the Bonsai?"

"Not especially." His thumb was blacker than a chunk of coal. "I've been known to kill silk plants."

"An interesting species," she said, nipping at the plant with a pair of pruning shears. "They say the Bonsai is an art form. It's the meticulous shaping that transforms them into such aesthetically appealing horticultural masterpieces."

She set her pruning shears on the table, then turned to face him. He was struck again by her elegance and beauty. Even though he knew her age to be well into her fifties, she didn't look more than a facelift over thirty-five.

"But you didn't come here to discuss my hobbies, did you?" She elegantly began tugging on each of the fingers of her gloves to remove them. "What is it I can do for you, Detective?"

"I'm doing some follow up for the district attorney." The lie slid easily from his lips. "I was hoping you could answer a few questions for me."

Johanna motioned to a pair of white wicker chairs over-looking the elaborate gardens of the backyard. "Of course," she said, pouring a glass of iced tea from a pitcher on the round, glass-topped table between the chairs. "Anything if it'll help ensure my son's killer receives the justice she deserves."

Just the reaction he was hoping for. "You don't like Dr. Jennings much, do you?"

Her warm hazel eyes hardened. "She killed my son."

Scanlon didn't agree, but stating his opinion wouldn't

garner him the insight he needed. "Yes ma'am," he said. "I understand. What was your relationship with Dr. Jennings like before your son's death?"

She took a dainty sip of her iced tea. "I had no reason to dislike her."

"Were your son and Dr. Jennings involved?"

"You mean romantically?"

"Yes ma'am," he said. He already knew the answer, having gotten the information from the Doc herself.

She set her glass on the table. "No, although they might have dated for a brief time. But that would've been years ago."

"Was this before or after they went in to business together?"

"Before," Johanna answered. She gracefully crossed her legs. "Probably shortly after they met in graduate school."

He manufactured a knowing grin. "Jonathan dated a lot, did he?"

Her eyes warmed when she returned his smile with one of her own. "My son was a very charming young man."

He took that as the yes he'd been searching for. "Would you happen to know where I can find his most recent lady friend? Or perhaps you might know a name, or two."

Her smile abruptly faded into a thin line. "I'm afraid I wouldn't know," she said, her eyes turning glacial again.

He'd struck a chord, and a dead end. No way would she give up any more information, not with the icy waves he sensed coming off her.

Twenty minutes and several lame, leading nowhere questions later, Scanlon thanked her for her time and rose to leave. She walked with him to the door. "Hey, was that Everett Sharpe I saw earlier?"

Her hand began to tremble as she reached for the door.

"You're acquainted with Mr. Sharpe?" she asked, a distinct thread of caution in her voice as she opened the front door.

Scanlon grinned, he hoped amiably. "Oh, we go way back," he said, fabricating a half-truth. "I thought that was him, but I couldn't be sure. Can I ask how you know him?"

She hung onto the edge of the door until her knuckles turned white. "He was here to discuss a probate matter."

"Yes, well, good luck with that," he said. "Thank you again for your time, ma'am."

She said nothing more. The door closed before he hit the top step of the porch's landing on his way out.

"Probate matter, my ass," he muttered to himself as he descended the steps and started down the driveway. In other words, Sharpe was somehow involved with Linton. And he had every intention of finding out exactly what the piece of shit was up to, because whatever it was, it wouldn't be good—or probably even legal.

"What do you think's in it?" Stacy whispered.

Laurel stared at the still-closed safety deposit box sitting atop the gleaming surface of the mahogany table, almost afraid to find out. More proof that another person she'd loved wasn't what she'd believed him to be?

She hadn't known what to expect when she and Stacy had arrived at the bank less than an hour ago. But after verifying her identity to the clerk and providing the blue-backed document, they'd been taken to a vault containing the bank's safety deposit boxes. Once the appropriate box had been retrieved, the bank clerk had shown them to a private viewing room.

"I suppose there's only one way to find out," Laurel answered softly. She scooted to the edge of the chair and reached for the oblong metal container.

Stacy's hand shot out, stopping her. "Wait," she said.

"Do you think maybe you should wait for Damon? What if it contains some kind of evidence? The DA could accuse you of tampering or something, couldn't he?"

Laurel settled back in the chair. Stacy could be right. If the box did contain some sort of evidence, the prosecution could end up having it suppressed. On the other hand, he could also end up using it against her.

She bit her bottom lip, unsure how to proceed, or if she even should continue. The timing of the arrival of the key and the note from Jonathan with the legal document declaring her ownership of the safety deposit box was in no way coincidental. As the letter from the attorney had indicated, the envelope had been sent to her because Jonathan was dead. On his instructions, too, of that she was confident.

What did he tell his attorneys? she wondered. In case I die, send this to Laurel? How had he known it was even a possibility? Because he had been involved in something illegal?

"It could be hours before Damon returns," Laurel told Stacy. As it was, he probably wouldn't be all that happy with her for leaving Artifacts, once he received the message she'd left on his voicemail. The least she could do now was return with something that may be of value to her defense.

Like what? Jonathan's murder caught on video tape?

Laurel smiled suddenly. She might not know a lot about her assistant's personal life, but one thing she did know— Stacy liked her techie toys. "By any chance, is your cell a camera phone?"

Stacy returned Laurel's smile with one of her own. "Better yet, I can record video."

"Perfect."

She waited while Stacy searched her enormous handbag for her cell phone, then set it up to record.

"Okay," Stacy said as she stood and rounded the table so she was standing next to Laurel. "I'm ready when you are."

Laurel scooted forward in her chair and once again reached for the safety deposit box. The key slid easily into the lock and clicked when she turned it. The oblong metal lid popped open.

"Here goes nothing," she said. She took a deep breath and lifted the lid.

Stacy gasped. "It's money," she said. "A lot of money."

Laurel couldn't believe her eyes as she stared transfixed at stacks of bank-wrapped one-hundred-dollar bills. "There must be at least a couple of hundred thousand dollars here."

"What's that box?" Stacy asked, still looking through the viewfinder on her camera phone.

Laurel leaned forward and lifted the square black container from the safety deposit box and set it on the table in front of her. Stacy inched closer, zooming in, Laurel assumed, on the little black box.

Laurel snapped open the lid. Tucked inside the box were a set of CD's, all very clearly labeled *Gates of Paradise*.

Chapter 16

WITH THE LINTON autopsy photos and the report from the medical examiner along with the initial findings from the crime scene investigation unit tucked under his arm, Damon entered Clifton's Cafeteria, his purpose two-fold. One, he was waiting for Laurel to call him back to let him know she'd returned to Artifacts. That she'd even left irritated the hell out of him. She'd been annoyed with him earlier, accusing him of treating her like an idiot. He'd apologized, but dammit, he hadn't expected her to go and start acting like one.

What the hell was she thinking taking off with Stacy on what was probably nothing more than some fool's errand? She was Laurel's assistant and she trusted her, but the truth was, Damon didn't know her from Eve.

He'd told her to lock the doors for a reason. With Laurel being so damn smart, he didn't think he'd needed to spell it out for her, but apparently he'd been wrong.

The body count was rising. He didn't want to believe that she could actually be a target, but with everything going on, he wasn't about to take any chances with her life, either. Her place had already been so brutally ransacked, Artifacts robbed and quite possibly, the alleged thief found dead in the vicinity. Even a moron could see these were not unrelated incidents. And Laurel was a far cry from moron.

The hostess greeted him with a warm smile, but he spied his second reason for coming to Clifton's already waiting for him. "Just one today, sir?" she asked as he approached the podium.

"My party's waiting for me," he said with an inclination of his head in Scanlon's direction. At the hostess's nod, he crossed the busy cafeteria to where Scanlon sat waiting at a booth near the back, a half-empty glass of iced tea in front of him. Damon dropped the envelope marked AUTOPSY PHOTOGRAPHS on the table, then slid into the booth across from the detective.

Scanlon's gaze slid from Damon to the envelope and back again. "I'm a hungry man, Metcalf. Don't even think about ruining my lunch with a bunch of gruesome Kodak moments."

Damon flipped the envelope over as a harried waitress approached to drop off a couple of menus. "Can I get you something to drink?" she asked.

"Coffee," Damon ordered. He needed a boost, and iced tea wouldn't cut it. "And a chicken club, hold the fries."

"Make mine turkey with fries," Scanlon told the waitress, waving away the menu. "And I'll take his fries too."

"Your arteries must love you," Damon said once the waitress was out of earshot.

Scanlon reached for his iced tea. "Like you give a shit about my health," he fired back good-naturedly.

"Thanks for meeting me," Damon said. He'd called Scanlon when he'd left the ME's office. He needed to have a talk with the detective, needed to know if he could truly trust him. Laurel desperately needed someone on her side. Having that someone on the inside was even better.

Scanlon took a drink of his iced tea. "So what's up?" he asked, returning his glass to the table.

"Off the record?"

Scanlon's sigh was a long, weary one. "Why do you lawyers always have to make my job more difficult?"

The waitress returned with his coffee. "I have to protect my client, Gino," Damon said once they were alone again.

"I have a feeling I would've liked it better when the state was your client."

"The lines were more clearly drawn, that's for sure," Damon admitted, adding a packet of artificial sweetener to his coffee. Both of their jobs were a hell of a lot easier when they were fighting for the same causes. But that's why he'd called this meeting—to confirm they were still on the same side. The side of justice.

"What if I told you there might actually be a connection to Laurel and the body found this morning?"

"This is all hypothetical, I suppose?"

Damon didn't bother to appear innocent. The skepticism in the seasoned detective's shrewd gaze said he wouldn't buy it, anyway. "What do you think?"

Scanlon smirked and reached for his tea. "It wouldn't look good for her."

"She didn't kill him," Damon said, keeping his voice low. He leaned forward, bracing his arms on the table. "She really was with me last night."

"She could've snuck out in the middle of the night."

Damon shook his head. "Not possible."

Scanlon's left eyebrow winged upward. "You better be fucking your client, Metcalf, because unless her sweet little ass was pressed up against your fat hairy one all night long, I'm gonna think you're full of shit."

"Not exactly."

Not yet would've been more honest, because he was certain it'd only be a matter of time before he and Laurel made love again. They were supposed to be over, so why now, he honestly couldn't say.

He made no secret of the fact he was still attracted to her—even though she had dumped his ass with nothing more than a lame excuse and a see ya later, Pal. Not that the timing for an affair was any better now, or even optimum. Once her legal issues were resolved, he'd be on the first plane back to Bozeman.

Or would he?

"But we were having a conversation during the estimated time of death," Damon added.

"In the middle of the night?" Scanlon scoffed.

"When was the last time you had a decent night's sleep?"

"Touché," Scanlon leaned back in the booth. His knowing gaze said he knew exactly what he and Laurel had been up to in the middle of the night. "So what's the connection? Hypothetically, of course."

"A robbery. Something may have been taken from Artifacts."

"No shit?"

"A set of project CD's. They were allegedly locked in a safe and now they're missing."

"Any proof?"

Damon shook his head. "Nothing other than my client's word and a dead thief two blocks away. The originals were apparently replaced with a dummy set."

"Could be a coincidence."

Damon gave Scanlon a shrewd look. "For the record," he said, "I don't believe in coincidences, either."

The waitress arrived with their meal. "I'll be back with refills," she said with a brief smile, then disappeared again.

"We didn't find anything on the DB except those picks I showed you this morning," Scanlon said. He grabbed the bottle of ketchup and proceeded to drown his double order of fries. "No ID, not even a goddamn vehicle we could trace. I want to know how he got there."

"He could've parked elsewhere." Damon plucked a colorful cellophane-tipped toothpick from a quarter section of his chicken club.

"So far as we've been able to determine, there were no abandoned vehicles in the immediate vicinity, either."

"Maybe he was working with someone else," Damon suggested.

"And after he lifts the disks, he's gunned down by his own man?" Scanlon shook his head in mock disgust. "There's just no honor among thieves these days."

The waitress returned as promised to refill their drinks, then promptly left them alone again to care for her other customers.

"We should probably have the place dusted for prints," Scanlon suggested.

"Not a chance," Damon said. "All we need is for Rosen to get wind something is up. He'd have Laurel on trial for two murders before the lab could finish processing the crime scene."

"Good point," Scanlon said, then took a bite of his sandwich. "You know he's got a hard-on for your client. And since this meeting never took place, I'm gonna tell you he's getting damn nervous without an airtight motive. Son of a bitch has left half a dozen voicemails on my cell."

"What Rosen has a hard-on for is the DA's job." Rosen's ambitions drove him, not the law. In the end, Damon suspected, it would eventually lead to the ADA's downfall. He knew. He'd once made the same fatal mistake. Winning had become more important than justice.

"Word is Linton money just might finance his campaign."

Damon wasn't surprised. Wasn't he defending Laurel because of the Lintons' influence? Because he'd had no luck finding a single attorney willing to go up against the Lintons? "Provided he can secure a conviction. I'm going to do my best to make sure that doesn't happen." He only hoped that this time his best actually was good enough.

"He hates you." Scanlon polished off the first quarter of his club sandwich. "Passionately," he added around a mouthful.

Damon grinned. "Good. It'll keep him distracted."

"I can see you're worried."

Damon shrugged. "Rosen's competent enough, but he's got a one-track mind."

"Yeah, and it's filled with delusions of grandeur." Scanlon took a swig of iced tea, then added, "There's something else you should know. I saw Everett Sharpe leaving Johanna Linton's home today."

"Sharpe?" He should know that name, but couldn't immediately recall precisely where or why. During his tenure with the DA's office he'd dealt with too many criminal defense attorneys to keep them all straight. "What about him?"

"He's a scumbag with an office not too far from here," Scanlon provided. "He represents, for lack of a better word, small-time hoods, prostitutes, drug offenders, and drunks. I hear he's moved into bullshit nuisance value plaintiff claims lately, as well."

He knew the type. Too well. "Okay," he said after a moment's thought. "I think I know who he is. Incompetent as hell. If it's the same guy I'm thinking of, he should've been disbarred years ago."

"That'd be the one. A real piece of work. You wouldn't happen to recall if he handles any probate work, would you?"

"He used to do some," Damon said. "Apparently he fucked over a client a few years back. Something about an unknown relative coming forward. He tried to bury the information, never bothered to inform his client and caused a shit load of legal problems for the client."

"Looks like he's back for more," Scanlon said. "Johanna Linton told me he was there to discuss a probate matter today."

"I find it hard to believe Jonathan Linton would hire someone with Sharpe's less-than-stellar reputation when the family has half of Wilshire Boulevard and downtown already on retainer."

"That's what I was thinking. I'll go lean on him, see what bullshit squirts out of his ass." Scanlon's grin was anything but friendly.

Damon finished off his coffee. "Look Gino," he said, returning his empty mug to the table, "part of the reason I wanted to see you today was that I think Laurel could be in danger. Linton's been murdered. Someone trashed her place, obviously looking for something, then broke into Artifacts when they didn't find it. Now a set of project CD's has been taken. The DB this morning might not have been on her doorstep, but close enough. I think we need to consider the fact that someone else may be involved. She needs protection."

"What do you expect me to do about it?"

"Order police protection for her."

Scanlon's short bark of laughter held no humor. "And if I go to the brass with this, it'll be my ass."

"I know it's asking a lot."

"No shit. For one, the case is considered closed by the department. My visit with Johanna Linton was off the clock. So is my trip to Sharpe's office when we're done here. My ass is already on the line, Metcalf. If Rosen hears I've ordered police protection for a defendant he's prosecuting, I can kiss my badge good-bye."

Damon understood the risk Scanlon was taking by even

talking to him. He might unofficially be on their side, but he had a pension, and what was left of an unblemished career, to safeguard.

"Your client needs protection, then it's up to you," Scanlon added.

It'd been his job to keep Kendra Tarragona and her children safe, too. He'd made a promise and failed. "I can't be with her 24/7."

"Then hire a fucking bodyguard," Scanlon said heatedly.

Laurel would never go for it. She'd scoffed at his suggestion to hire a private investigator to check into Linton's background. "I need your help, Gino."

Scanlon muttered a string of curses. "All right. Maybe I can talk to a few of the guys on patrol. Call in a few favors and keep it quiet."

"Thanks," Damon said. It wasn't perfect, but better than nothing at all. "I appreciate it."

"No guarantees."

Damon spied the waitress and signaled for the check. "Understood," he said.

Damon's cell phone rang. He pulled it from his pocket and checked the display, recognizing Stacy's number. "Excuse me," he said to Scanlon, then hit the call button. "Where are you?" he said, his tone more harsh than he intended, telling him he was more worried about Laurel than he first thought.

"We're on our way back to the hotel, so meet me there," Laurel said. "And bring my laptop up with you. It's in the trunk of my car."

Scanlon started patting his pockets, then pulled out his own cell phone. "Scanlon, here," he said. "Hold on a sec." More pocket patting until he produced a small note pad and a pen. "Go ahead." He started jotting notes on the pad.

"Damon, we need to get in touch with Detective Scanlon," Laurel said.

"I'm with him now," he told her. "What's up?"

"The safety deposit box had two hundred fifty grand in cash and copies of the missing CD's."

"You're sure they were copies?" he asked. They could be the originals missing from the safe.

"I'll have to load them on my computer to be absolutely certain," Laurel said, "but the CD's are a different type than we normally use in the office. Stacy recorded everything on video with her cell phone."

"Send it to me when we hang up." He'd take a look at the video first before mentioning it to Scanlon. Laurel was in enough trouble, and for as much as he believed he and Scanlon were on the same side, he wasn't going to take a chance and possibly hand over evidence that could end up providing motive to the prosecution.

"You'll show it to Scanlon?"

"I'll take care of it," he said without making any promises.

Scanlon flipped his own phone closed. "That the Doc?" he asked Damon.

Damon nodded. "Hold on a sec," he said to Laurel.

"Ask her if the name Fabrizio Renaldi means anything to her?" Scanlon asked.

"I heard him," Laurel said. "Tell him no."

Damon conveyed the message to Scanlon. "Why?" he asked Scanlon.

"That was the ME's office," the detective said. "According to Interpol, our DB has been high on their watch list for years. He's a thief they've never been able to nail. High dollar type, too. Someone fell asleep at the switch, because they had no idea he'd even left Florence."

Damon relayed the information to Laurel.

"St. Giovanni's is in Florence," she said.

"The *Gates of Paradise*," Damon said, leaving no doubt

whatsoever in his mind there was now a solid connection to Laurel and Artifacts.

"Damon," she said, her voice filled with anguish. "What the hell was Jonathan up to?"

That's what he wanted to know, before anyone else showed up dead.

Less than twenty minutes after leaving Clifton's Cafeteria, Gino Scanlon and Pete Teslenko stepped into the elevator that would take them up to the third floor offices of Everett P. Sharpe. Once Metcalf had left, Scanlon had called Teslenko to meet him, then hung around Clifton's, doing more damage to his arteries with a hefty slab of coconut cream pie while he'd waited for his partner to arrive.

As usual, Teslenko had complained about Scanlon's obsession with a closed case, but had agreed to accompany him to Sharpe's office just the same. He'd wanted Teslenko with him for one very simple reason—intimidation. Not that it would take much to intimidate a coward like Sharpe, but Teslenko had perfected "the stare," the one that usually had suspects singing like pretty little yellow canaries. A few minutes of that look from Teslenko and he expected Sharpe to start whistling an informative tune.

The elevator rumbled to a stop, but it took a few worrisome heartbeats before the doors eventually opened. "This is a bad idea," Teslenko complained, stepping off the elevator. "All it's gonna take is a call to the watch commander from this weasel dick and our asses will be in a sling."

Scanlon followed Teslenko off the rickety elevator, then led the way down the corridor to Sharpe's office. "Don't sweat the small shit," he told Teslenko.

But Teslenko did have a point, even if he wasn't all that worried about Sharpe ratting them out to the brass. All he planned to do was lean a little heavy on Sharpe to find out why the guy was sleazing around the Lintons. Besides, the way Scanlon figured it, any ass chewing he and Teslenko might have to endure was worth the risk if it meant they could exonerate an innocent woman.

The Doc wasn't guilty of murdering Linton. Sharpe *was* somehow involved, however indirectly. He could smell it.

The bell over the door dinged when Scanlon and Teslenko walked into a deserted reception area. "Have a seat," came a male voice from somewhere in the back office area. "I'll be right with you."

Scanlon didn't bother. He motioned for Teslenko to follow him, then took off in the direction of the voice. They found Sharpe seated behind a cluttered desk on the phone in an equally cluttered office with dirty windows obscuring the downtown view. A diploma from Pepperdine University School of Law hung in a cracked frame above a pair of low bookcases jammed full of *California Reporter* addendums, along with the standard framed certificates from the state and federal courts declaring Sharpe held the esteemed honor of being sworn in to practice law before both jurisdictions.

Scanlon didn't bother showing his badge. From the apparent surprise in Sharpe's shifty, narrow-eyed gaze, he knew exactly who he was.

"I'll have to call you back," Sharpe said to his caller, and promptly hung up the phone. He shifted his gaze to Teslenko, who stood just inside the doorway, a hand on his hip, which conveniently pushed aside his jacket just enough to allow Sharpe a glimpse of the service revolver tucked safely inside Teslenko's shoulder holster.

Sharpe's Adam's apple bobbed up and down. "What can I do for you gentlemen?"

Scanlon walked up to the desk and braced his hands on the cheap, imitation wood grain. Leaning forward, he said,

"What's this I hear about you harassing Johanna Linton, Sharpe?"

The attorney's narrowed gaze widened slightly. "I did no such thing."

Teslenko shifted his stance and crossed his arms over his chest. "That's not the way we've heard it."

"Today was the only time I ever spoke to her." Sharpe's Adam's apple danced some more. "I had business there."

"I know your type of business," Scanlon said, giving Sharpe a hard stare. "Mrs. Linton wouldn't normally give you the time of day. I'm surprised she even let a piece of shit like you in the house."

"Like I said," Sharpe said nervously, "I had business there."

"Exactly what kind of business?" Scanlon asked the lawyer.

Sharpe sat up straighter. "I can't tell you that."

"Ah, yes," Scanlon said with a slow nod. He pushed off the desk. "Client confidentiality."

Teslenko made a sound that could've been a bark of laughter. "That's rich, coming from a guy who probably flunked Ethics 101."

"We're well acquainted with your type of client, Sharpe." Scanlon shoved a stack of files and loose papers aside and parked his ass on the side of the desk. "We've busted enough of them. They couldn't get a job scrubbing urinals for people like the Lintons. What were you doing there?"

Sharpe came out of his chair. "Unless you have a warrant, you need to leave." He tried to look smug, but with the nervousness of his jerky movements, failed to pull it off.

"Trust me," Scanlon said menacingly. "You don't want us to get a warrant. You're harassing one of the Hollywood elite, Sharpe. All it'll take is a phone call and I'll personally be the one to tear your office apart. Now, what were you doing at Johanna Linton's place today?"

"I told you. I had business there."

"What kind of business?" Scanlon pressed.

"I can't tell you," Sharpe said, his nasally voice almost whiny.

From the doorway, Teslenko stared hard at Sharpe. "Try again."

Sharpe shifted on his feet. "It's a probate matter."

Scanlon looked over his shoulder at Teslenko. "'A probate matter,' he says."

"Sounds like legal bullshit for extortion to me," Teslenko said, never taking his gaze off of the lawyer.

Scanlon turned back to Sharpe and grinned. "Not as big and dumb as he looks, is he? You trying to extort money, Sharpe? That's illegal, you know."

Sharpe's gaze darted between the two detectives, then finally settled on Scanlon. The lesser of the two evils, Scanlon figured.

Sharpe stood a little taller. "My client has a legitimate claim to the Linton estate," he told them, but the slightly discernable quaver to his voice belied his attempt at conviction.

"Yeah, right," Scanlon scoffed. He leaned forward, casually resting his arm across his knee. "I'm no lawyer, but I'm betting extortion could finally get your ass disbarred. Not to mention have you sittin' pretty in the county jail. But that wouldn't be much of a hardship, now would it? Considering you'd have a lot of friends there, and all. Who's your client, Sharpe?"

Sharpe's sallow complexion reddened. "You can't come in here and threaten me, Scanlon," Sharpe said angrily. "I'll have both of your badges for this."

Scanlon let out a long, weary sigh. "Let's try this again," he said. "Who's your client?"

Teslenko reached into the inside pocket of his jacket, once again revealing his service revolver.

Sharpe turned green, then breathed an audible sigh of obvious relief when Teslenko pulled out his cell phone.

Scanlon didn't bother to hide his grin. Fucking idiot. Like they'd really shoot the bastard. Tempting, but . . .

"Judge Gleason will sign a warrant for us," Teslenko said. "She likes me."

"You know, I believe she does." Scanlon kept his gaze on Sharpe. Far as he could recall, they'd never so much as spoken to Judge Gleason or her clerk. "Who's your client?" he asked Sharpe for the third time.

"I don't have to tell you shit."

"Make the call, Pete. And then place a call to the station to run a wants-and-warrants check on our buddy here. I'll bet we can at least come up with an unpaid parking ticket or two."

Teslenko started pressing numbers on his cell. "A cold beer says at least a dozen."

"You can't arrest me for unpaid parking tickets."

"Sure I can. I can do anything I want to, Sharpe," Scanlon said amiably. "Especially if those tickets have turned into warrants."

"All right," Sharpe said.

Teslenko lifted the cell phone to his ear.

"All right," Sharpe said again, louder this time. "I'll tell you, but you have to swear you didn't hear it from me."

Teslenko lowered his cell.

Scanlon waited. "I'm losing my patience," he said.

Sharpe took a deep breath, then jammed a trembling hand through his thinning hair. "Cara Caldwell," he finally answered.

Teslenko put the phone away.

"Where can we find this Ms. Caldwell?"

"I don't know." Sharpe shrugged his wiry shoulders. "She contacts me."

Teslenko opened his phone again.

"I don't have an address for her," Sharpe answered in an agitated rush, then looked relieved once Teslenko flipped his phone closed again.

"If she's a client of yours, then she's probably in our system." Scanlon slid off the edge of Sharpe's desk. "Better get those parking tickets paid up," he added as he turned to leave.

"Fuck you, Scanlon," Sharpe shouted after them as Scanlon and Teslenko walked out of Sharpe's office.

Scanlon ignored him.

"God, you're a prick," Teslenko said to Scanlon once they were inside the elevator.

Scanlon pressed the button for the ground floor. "Yeah, I'm gifted that way."

They rode down in silence. "So what now?" Teslenko asked as they left the elevator and crossed the foyer to the front door.

"We go to Rosen's office." God, he was tired, and Rosen was the last person he wanted to deal with at the moment.

"You're not seriously going to take this to him now, are you?"

"Hell no," Scanlon said. He followed Teslenko out of the building into the bright afternoon sunshine, instantly patting his pocket for his shades. "We've got to run by the jackass's office, because he's been calling me for the past two days. His last message insisted we come by his office no later than four o'clock."

"So what do we do now?" Teslenko asked.

"After we see what's crawled up Rosen's ass," Scanlon said, "we pull a rap sheet and find out who this Caldwell woman is and what 'claim' she thinks she has to Linton's money."

"She might not have a rap sheet," Teslenko reminded him.

Scanlon thought about that for a moment. "She's one of Sharpe's clients," he finally answered. "Trust me. She'll have a rap sheet."

Chapter 17

SHE HATED THAT bitch. With a passion.

She peered over the steering wheel, watching the bitch as she entered the Beverly Hills Hotel, not once glancing in her direction. For someone so smart, Laurel Jennings was pretty fucking stupid.

Jonathan had been smart. Too smart for his own good. Maybe if he'd been as stupid as Jennings, he'd still be alive. But he'd lied. Worse, he'd laughed at her. He'd deserved to die.

Fresh anger bubbled up inside her. She shoved a lock of hair away from her face, then gripped the steering wheel—hard. Jennings would get hers, too. It was the only way she'd have what should've already been hers.

She took several deep breaths in an attempt to calm her raging temper, then reached into her purse for her cell phone. She dialed Sharpe's number. She'd tried him earlier, but all she'd gotten was his answering machine. He'd better have been out conducting her business.

This time the prick answered. "Where the hell have you been?"

"Who is this?"

As if he didn't know. "Who do you think, asshole?" she snarled.

Through the phone line, she heard the creak of his chair. "Cara," he said. "I met with Johanna Linton earlier today."

"My, aren't you on top of things—for a change."

"The news isn't good," Sharpe told her. "She said there's nothing she can do. Jonathan's estate is held in a trust. Her brother-in-law is the one in control of it."

Anger continued to claw at Cara's insides. "A trust that belongs to me now," she said between clenched teeth. "To my baby."

"Unless you're willing to file an actual claim against the estate, there's nothing I can legally do."

The hell there wasn't. "Then talk to the brother-in-law."

"Do you have a clue who that is?" Sharp asked. "Abe Linton. He's the head of Monarch Studios."

Her turn had finally come and she was not about to be deterred. Not now. Not when she was so close to having everything she'd ever dreamed of having. For her. And her baby. "I don't care who he is," she said. "Make it happen, Everett."

"I can't just call up the head of a studio and ask for an appointment," he argued.

"You will if you know what's good for you."

"Look, maybe you—"

"No! You look," she fired at him. "I want what's mine. Handle it."

"I'll do my best."

Sharpe didn't know the meaning of the concept. Which didn't exactly fill her with a whole lot of confidence.

She pulled in a long, even breath, then exhaled slowly. "What about the business?" she asked, struggling for a calm she was nowhere near feeling. "It's worth a fortune. And I know for a fact it's not tied up in some stupid family trust."

"From what Mrs. Linton told me, it wouldn't matter if there were fifty heirs to Jonathan's estate. There was a death provision in the partnership agreement with Laurel Jennings.

So long as she's breathing, the business belongs solely to her."

Then she'd just have to make sure Jennings took her last breath, wouldn't she?

"Anything else?"

"No."

"Take care of this Everett. Do you understand me?"

"I'll try."

"Try harder," she warned, then disconnected the call.

She tossed the cell phone on the passenger seat. Sharpe was lying. The bastard.

She turned the key and fired the ignition. Cool air blasted her through the vents, but did little to calm her simmering temper. She grabbed hold of the steering wheel and shook it, letting out a low-ebbed growl of frustration.

Dammit. She really shouldn't be surprised Sharpe was lying to her. They all lied—eventually. They lied to get what they wanted, and once they had it, the story always changed. Jonathan had said he loved her and he'd lied. He said he'd take care of her, and he'd lied. And when she'd reminded him of those promises, he'd had the gall to laugh in her face.

She hadn't meant to kill him. But when he'd laughed at her, she'd lost her temper.

She'd never killed before, but she certainly was good at it. First Jonathan, then that character she'd caught coming out of Artifacts this morning. She hadn't known his name, not his real one anyway. She'd found an ID in his wallet, and while it matched the name on the rental car receipt in the glove compartment of the SUV, it hadn't matched either of the names on the two passports she'd found in the black bag that he'd carried with him. All she'd known about him was that he was a thief and he'd stolen a set of CD's from Artifacts.

She wanted to know the importance of those disks. She

supposed she really shouldn't care. Did it matter at all now that Jonathan was dead?

Probably not, she rationalized. She slipped the SUV into drive and pulled away from the curb. She had more pressing matters to attend to at the moment—like making certain Laurel Jennings took her last breath.

"It was a stupid move."

Laurel couldn't really argue with Damon, but she was getting a little sick of hearing it, even if he was right. Taking off with Stacy probably hadn't been her wisest choice considering there was a murderer on the loose, but what was she supposed to do? Sit and wait like a good little girl? Do as she'd been told? She'd done that all of her life and what had it gotten her? Nothing but a long series of betrayals.

"I know," she said for the third time. "I promise it won't happen again. Okay? Now can we *please* move on to a new topic?"

She would've much rather had a cheeseburger, fries, and a super-thick strawberry shake for dinner, but the oriental chicken salad she'd ordered from room service had been surprisingly satisfying. Still, comfort food would've been so much more welcome after everything she'd been through today. A dead body, a robber, the very real possibility that Jonathan had been stealing from her, and now Damon continuing to berate her for taking off with Stacy.

She didn't want to believe Jonathan could've been ripping her off. It made no sense whatsoever. Her deceased partner hadn't exactly been pauper material. But what other reason could there be for what she and Stacy had found in the safety deposit box?

She got up from the love seat in Damon's room and went to the mini-bar fridge for a bottled water. She should go back to her own room and look at the disks again. She'd done a cursory search and review but found nothing out of the ordinary thus far. Instinct told her she was missing something. What other reason could there be for Jonathan having those particular disks? The same disks that had been stolen from Artifacts?

"Why didn't you tell Detective Scanlon about the safety deposit box?" she asked as she opened the fridge.

"Motive," Damon answered.

Her hand stilled over the array of cold drinks. "Excuse me?"

"The last thing we want to do is hand Rosen motive. Granted, he does have some damning physical evidence that puts you at the scene, but most of what he has against you is still circumstantial. The presence of this unidentified DNA seriously weakens his case."

She straightened and looked across the room at Damon. "What DNA?" she asked. "And why am I only hearing of it now?"

"Because I only learned of it this afternoon," Damon told her. "It was in with the reports I picked up from the ME's office. There's no match in CODIS, but I'm betting Rosen thinks he can still get a conviction."

"Do you? Think he can still convict me, I mean?"

Damon shrugged his wide shoulders. "He's a good prosecutor."

Oh, that made her feel a whole lot better.

"What does Scanlon say about this other DNA?"

"He doesn't."

Laurel frowned. "But I thought he was on our side?"

"Maybe," he said with another shrug. "He might not have heard about it yet. Rosen sure as hell isn't broadcasting the news. There wasn't a single mention of it in any of the state's files."

"But Scanlon *is* on our side, right?"

"I believe that he is, but we can't forget that he's a cop first."

Which in her mind translated to they couldn't trust him. At least not completely.

Her irritation grew. She snagged a bottle of water and used her foot to shut the fridge door. "But I've already been arrested and charged with the crime," she said, twisting off the cap. "Because of the death provision in the partnership agreement, I thought the DA already had motive. Why would the money and CD's make a difference at this point?"

Damon set the sheaf of papers they'd been studying on the cocktail table, a print out of the information contained on Jonathan's BlackBerry. Other than several appointments with the unknown "JT" after hours that Laurel couldn't explain, none of the notations on Jonathan's calendar appeared out of the ordinary.

"Rosen will argue that the death provision in your partnership agreement was your motive for killing him, but if he can't prove premeditation, it might not be enough to convince a jury. At least not beyond a reasonable doubt," Damon explained. "This isn't a civil trial. He needs more than just a majority of the jurors to believe you killed Jonathan. He needs all of them to believe his argument."

Laurel tossed the cap into the garbage can and returned to the love seat opposite Damon. "And the contents of that safety deposit box can prove premeditation?"

"It could. The note from Jonathan doesn't help."

I'm sorry. Love, Jonathan.

Sorry for what? What the hell had he been up to?

"The physical evidence will be persuasive. Even if I can manage to explain it away, our argument is still going to be weak because there isn't a single witness who can confirm your alibi. I'm confident I can raise some doubt, but I don't know if it'll be enough. We come forward now, before we know why that cash was in the safety deposit box, or why Jonathan had a copy of the *Gates of Paradise* disks hidden, and you might as well skip the trial."

Do not pass Go. Do not collect two hundred and fifty thousand dollars. Go directly to the gallows.

Suddenly parched, Laurel took a long drink of the cool water. It did nothing to lessen the tightening in her throat or loosen the imaginary noose she envisioned looped around her neck.

Damon leaned forward. Compassion was clearly evident in his green eyes. "I know you don't want to believe Jonathan was stealing from you, Laurel, but after what you found today, you have to consider it a possibility."

"There could be several explanations," she said, but so far she hadn't been able to conjure a single one that sounded remotely reasonable. In truth, she couldn't think of a single reason for Jonathan to have that kind of money tucked away in a safety deposit box, or copies of one of their most important projects.

"You're sure you emptied the box?" Damon asked her.

"Yes." Emptied it, videotaped it, and counted the cash. She'd returned the quarter-mil to the safety deposit box, but she had taken the CD's with her.

"Maybe there was another note that you might have missed," Damon suggested.

"No," she said with a shake of her head. "The only note came with the key." A note in which Jonathan had apologized. For what? Stealing from her?

She stood and walked to the sliding glass door leading to the balcony to look out into the dusk-filled courtyard and the illuminated gardens below. Since her mother's death, the people she'd counted on most, the ones she'd trusted, had betrayed her. Damon being the rare exception.

Give him time.

She pushed that thought away. Paranoia didn't suit her. But then again, with her history, maybe she should proceed with a bit more caution in the future.

There was no reason for her to believe Damon would ever betray her. He was, and always had been, the one constant in her life. In actuality, she was the one guilty of betrayal. Did it count when the betrayee had no clue he was being betrayed? She knew his father's death had not been an accident. Even though her motives in keeping quiet were pure, she continued to perpetuate the cover up with her silence. Did that make her just as bad as the people responsible for Scott Metcalf's death?

She wasn't sure she liked the answer.

"How could I have been so wrong about Jonathan?" She understood she was socially stunted. A trait hardly uncommon for people like her who had spent their formative years with their noses inside textbooks. She'd developed book smarts, not street smarts. So maybe the problem wasn't with the people who'd betrayed her, but with herself for her inability to correctly judge the character of others?

She flinched when Damon's warm hands suddenly settled on her shoulders. She hadn't even heard him come up behind her. Still, she didn't pull away, but instead took comfort from the human contact. She might as well enjoy it while it lasted.

No, she thought. Not just any contact, but Damon's touch.

"We don't know yet for certain that he was stealing from you," he said quietly.

She knew an attempt to placate when she heard one. "And you don't know that he wasn't—yet" she countered. "I need to take a closer look at those disks. He had them for a reason."

And if she discovered Jonathan was stealing from her, then what? It wouldn't be the first time she'd been so terribly wrong when it came to judging character. She'd trusted Conner, and look how that had turned out. He'd arranged to have his best friend murdered.

Detective Scanlon claimed he didn't think she was guilty, and he appeared to be helping them, yet Damon didn't feel as if he could trust him with the information she'd discovered today. She'd trusted Jonathan, but now she couldn't help wondering if she'd made yet another error in judgment.

She blew out an unsteady stream of breath. "I don't know who to trust anymore."

Damon's hands slid down her arms, to her waist and around her middle. He pulled her against him until her back was flush against the width of his chest. He felt warm and safe. Another illusion? she wondered.

"Me," he said, his breath warm and enticing against her ear.

A shiver that had nothing to do with being chilled traveled down her spine. Her breasts tingled and a warmth spread through her tummy.

"Trust me, Laurel."

She fed the illusion by smoothing her hands over his wrists, then lacing her fingers with his. "I do," she said, but the words felt stilted on her tongue. Untrue. Another fallacy.

God, she hated herself. She wasn't being fair to him. He shouldn't offer her his trust. She didn't deserve it. However indirectly, his father was dead because of her. She had no proof, nothing that would prove beyond a reasonable doubt, as he was so fond of saying, but heaven help her, she knew who was responsible for Scott Metcalf's death. Or rather, knew who had *ordered* he be eliminated. A senseless waste of a gifted life to ensure her silence. And like a coward, she'd never come forward.

What good would it do anyway? Not only would more people be hurt, namely Damon, his mother, and Evelyn Tillman, but who would believe her? There were times she hardly believed the reality of her past herself.

"We'll figure it out," he said.

She desperately wanted to believe him, even if it were nothing more than another illusion. "Promise?"

His entire body stiffened a heartbeat before his arms fell away. She turned to look at him and immediately recognized the sadness and regret that flickered in his gaze.

"You know I can't do that," Damon said. His gaze clouded, and she easily imagined he was locked in the past, unable to shake the blood-soaked images from his mind. Promises were but whispers in the wind. Who knew that better than he?

He turned away from her. She wanted a promise from him now, but she knew him so well and knew he couldn't do it. Not even for her. Yet she understood, too. She knew from experience, he just didn't have that kind of power. No one did.

Once he'd have been arrogant enough to have made her that promise. But no longer, all because he believed himself responsible for the senseless death of a young mother and her four-year-old daughter. As he moved away from her, she saw the guilt and self-loathing in his eyes over the lengths he'd gone to in the name of so-called justice. Because of him, Kendra Tarragona's infant son had also been orphaned, all because he'd been incapable of keeping the promise he'd made.

"It wasn't your fault," Laurel told him.

Damon walked to the mini bar and poured himself a scotch, downing the fiery liquid in one swallow. The liquor burned his throat, settled into a ball of fire in his gut, and did little to squelch the guilt already simmering there.

"Oh really?" His tone dripped with sarcasm, but he was already beyond caring. "How do you figure?"

Undaunted by his surly attitude, she walked purposefully toward him, her long floral skirt swirling around her slender ankles. "You weren't the one who pulled the trigger, Damon."

Maybe not. But his hands, and his conscience, carried the blood-red stain of his ambitions just the same.

Reaching into the mini bar again, he snagged another micro bottle of scotch and poured the contents into the cut crystal glass. The booze wouldn't erase the memories, only dull them for a short time. For now, a brief session in dull worked for him.

Laurel joined him at the mini bar. The light scent of her perfume teased him. If alcohol wouldn't chase the memories away, maybe sex would. He looked at Laurel, at the absolute trust in her deep lavender eyes.

He tossed back the scotch.

"No one blames you for what happened," she said, her voice soft and filled with tenderness.

He blamed himself. That was enough.

"You did your best," she added when he remained silent.

"My best got that woman and her daughter murdered," he said eventually. "There's a little boy out there that now has to go through his life without a mother. All because of a promise I couldn't keep. Don't ask me to make promises, Laurel. I don't know how to keep them."

He'd been prosecuting one of the biggest cases of his career, a well-known drug dealer on trial for a double homicide of two undercover police officers. He had the murder weapon, a ballistics match, and the defendant's fingerprints on the weapon. He even had an eyewitness who'd been in the wrong place at the wrong time.

Kendra Tarragona, a pregnant waitress and single mother had been coming off the swing shift at an area family restaurant when she'd walked into the parking lot in time to see the defendant murder the two undercover narcotics officers. Unseen, she'd ducked down behind a parked vehicle and remained safely out of sight. Then, once the defendant left the scene, she'd called the police.

She'd given her statement to detectives, picked the defendant out of a series of mug shots which had led to the arrest of Wilson Walker Bullock. She'd even ID'd the shooter in an actual police line up. Kendra Tarragona had been his star witness in a double cop killing and she'd cooperated every step of the way—until the moment she'd changed her story on the stand.

Angry and frustrated, he'd done the unthinkable. "I threatened a witness," Damon admitted to Laurel. "I told her that I'd have her prosecuted for perjury if she didn't recant her testimony."

In addition to her statement, he had a sworn deposition and told her he'd easily make a perjury charge stick. Did she want to spend the next six months behind bars, have her children placed in foster care, while a known drug dealer and cop-killer walked?

Laurel inched closer and smoothed her hand down his back in a soothing gesture. "You couldn't have known what was going to happen," she said. "It wasn't your fault."

He made a sound filled with disgust and self-loathing. "Yes, Laurel. It was. I knew she was putting her neck on the line if she testified. With the threat of going to jail hanging over her head, she finally told me she feared for her life, and that of her two children, if she testified against Bullock. She'd been receiving threatening phone calls and had been followed home from work. She'd even noticed a dark sedan parked outside her daughter's preschool on two separate occasions.

"Without her testimony, my chances of a conviction were circling the drain. The evidence didn't mean shit because the defendant had a bogus alibi backed up by two of his thugs. Tarragona's credibility easily shattered their testimony. She was a single mother, a war widow, trying to put the pieces of her life back together. And I couldn't let it go."

"You did what you could," she said. "It wasn't like you lied to her."

"No, what I did was worse," he said. "I pulled strings to save my case. I managed to get my star witness into witness protection. Once she testified, the U.S. Marshal's office would take her and her two children into protective custody until they could be relocated, provided with a new identity, and given enough start up money to rebuild her life elsewhere. I'd promised her that she and her children would be safe, and it hadn't been enough."

"You had no idea—"

"I promised her," he said heatedly. "I gave her my word that she and her children would be safe. I made a promise I didn't have the power to keep."

Based on his promise, Kendra had reluctantly agreed to testify. With the testimony necessary to prove the state's case against the defendant, the jury had convicted Wilson Walker Bullock on two counts of murder in the first degree, with special circumstances for killing two of LA's finest.

"Kendra Tarragona never got a chance at that new, better life," he said. "While I was off celebrating my victory, Kendra and her daughter were gunned down in a drive-by shooting. The two U.S. Marshals who'd been taking them into protective custody were wounded, one when he'd used his body to shield Kendra's infant son that he'd been placing in the van."

"He saved that baby's life," Laurel reminded him.

Damon considered a third scotch. "And ended up in a wheelchair for his heroics." He dragged his hand down his face. "And the worst of it is, no one could prove Bullock was behind the hit."

"But he's still a resident of New Folsom Prison's death

row," Laurel said. "He's exhausting appeals and awaiting execution."

Not that he had anything to do with the jury's decision to send Bullock to death row. His last official act as an assistant district attorney had been to attend the double funeral for Kendra and her daughter. He'd gone back to his office afterward and tendered his resignation effective immediately. He hadn't hung around long enough to cover the penalty phase of Bullock's trial, but walked away without looking back.

"Until I showed up at your arraignment two days ago, I thought I was happy to never see the inside of a courtroom again," he said.

"I know," she said softly. "But once this is over, you can—"

He pulled away from her touch. "Can what? Go back to making furniture to occupy my time so I don't go out of my freaking mind from the boredom?"

There. He'd said it. Given voice to what had been nagging at him since his plane landed at LAX. He'd felt it inside the courtroom, too. That old hum in his veins, that surge of adrenaline he used to feel every time he faced a judge, a jury, or argued a point of law against a formidable opponent.

"What are you saying?"

"I'm saying I don't know if I can go back," he said. "I thought I could come here, do what needed to be done and walk away again, but . . ."

A gentle smile curved her lips as understanding lit her gaze. "But you miss practicing law."

Although all he'd done is make an appearance at Laurel's arraignment, he could no longer deny the truth. Those few minutes he'd spent arguing against Rosen to convince the judge to release Laurel on bail were enough to make him realize he'd merely been existing these past months. "More than you know," he admitted.

Whether or not he had the courage to do anything about it, though, remained unanswered. He'd lost his focus once. The law wasn't about winning, but justice.

She nudged his arm aside and slipped hers around his waist. "Would it really be so bad?," she asked, her voice as whisper soft as the unexpected press of her lips against his.

He urged Laurel closer. He wasn't about to make any snap decisions, but was fed up with constantly lying to himself. Like each and every morning when he crawled out of bed, telling himself he'd made the right decision in leaving.

"No promises," he said.

She nodded, then lifted her lips to his.

Slowly, he brought his mouth down to hers again. She trembled in his arms when he gently nipped her bottom lip. Her soft moan as he traced his tongue over the spot fired his libido.

He lifted his head to look down at her. Desire lined her gaze, along with another emotion he could only describe as trust. Trust he probably didn't deserve, but he was tired of denying himself what he wanted. Tired of living a lie. Not certain whether the scotch or the need rippling through him had finally dulled his common sense for good, he slipped his mouth over hers and kissed her deeply.

Laurel didn't much care if she were making a monumental mistake. Her life was a mess. She was an accused murderess. Her business was slowly dying off because of the publicity surrounding her arrest. The people she believed in and trusted betrayed her. Just once she wanted something wonderful and spontaneous. If she did end up being convicted of Jonathan's murder, was it so wrong for her to have at least one magically impulsive moment in her life to cling to?

She wanted hot. She wanted exciting.

She wanted Damon.

She clung to him as his tongue mated seductively with

hers. He tasted a little like scotch and a whole lot like man. A man, she realized with sudden clarity, that she'd missed so very much.

Tiny shivers of delight danced along her skin as he continued to tease her mouth, demanding a response she didn't hesitate to give. Her nipples beaded and rasped against the lace of her bra, the sensation adding to the heat Damon so effortlessly fanned into a raging inferno.

His hand came to rest on her hip. Through the thin, silky fabric of her skirt, his fingers pressed into her flesh. He rocked her closer until their bodies were perfectly aligned. His powerful legs grazed against her thighs, sending spirals of warmth shooting through her body. They ended low in her tummy, then wound down to where she ached to have him inside her.

She didn't question the desire exploding between them. Every time she kissed him, she'd felt this way. She'd felt this way for as long as she could remember and wasn't about to deny the passion for another moment. They might not have forever, but they had these few stolen moments, and that would have to be enough.

The realization saddened her.

He slipped one hand into her hair and gently cupped the back of her neck in his warm palm. He teased the side of her throat with his long fingers, tracing lazy patterns along her flesh, slowly moving forward and down to brush the swell of her breasts.

His thumb rhythmically smoothed along the scooped neckline of her pale lime-colored sweater, then dipped lower, beneath the lacy cup of her bra to tease her nipple. She trembled again at the deliciousness of his touch.

The fingers teasing her breast moved to her shoulder, and he gently eased her away from him. She looked into his eyes. A wealth of pleasure ribboned across her skin at the desire firing his green eyes.

"Make love to me, Damon," she whispered.

"Laurel—"

"Don't deny me," she said. "I think we both know better than most that life is just too damn short."

"You're sure about this?" he asked. "I can't make you any promises, Laurel."

She managed a small laugh. "I don't think an almost condemned woman is exactly in a position to be concerned with promises, do you?"

He opened his mouth to respond, no doubt to tell her he'd do his best that that didn't happen or offer her some other useless platitude about justice prevailing in the end. She didn't want to hear it. Not now. She only wanted to lose herself in the mindlessness of sex with Damon.

She placed her fingers over his lips, still damp from her kisses. "Don't say it," she told him. "Just tell me you want to make love to me as much as I want to make love to you. Tell me that for the next few hours nothing is more important than the pleasure we'll find in each other's bodies."

Chapter 18

LAUREL'S HEART THUNDERED. She wasn't asking for forever. Only the here and now, because it was all she had to give.

Damon reached for her hand. Something flickered in his gaze. Regret?

Her breath caught. No, she decided. He was *not* going to deny her. Deny them.

She advanced, but he took a step back.

"Laurel."

"I want you, Damon." She lifted her hand and began unfastening the buttons of his crisp white dress shirt. Her gaze dipped to his khaki trousers. "And I know damn well you want me."

The smile that slowly curved his lips sent her pulse careening out of control. He never could resist her. Thank heavens that much hadn't changed between them.

She yanked his shirt free of his trousers, then splayed her palms over his wide chest. "Make love to me," she demanded gently. She pressed her lips against his warm skin. "Give me something worth remembering for however long that might turn out to be."

A sound, somewhere between a groan of pain and a growl ripped from his throat when her tongue darted out and laved at his nipple. "Make a memory with me," she whispered against his skin.

She pulled back and looked up at him. Emotion filled his eyes. No hesitation. Only desire.

He held her gaze, held her mesmerized. "And no promises," she added, before she slowly lifted her top over her head.

She tossed the garment aside, then walked away from him, coming to a stop at the foot of the bed. With a flick of her fingertips, she unfastened her skirt and let it fall to pool around her feet. Her bra was next.

Damon's mouth went dry at the sight of Laurel standing next to the bed wearing nothing but a pair of lace panties that barely covered the essentials. He'd forgotten exactly how beautiful she was, and now his fingers itched to touch her again, to make her his one more time. His dick throbbed painfully. His body craved hers in a primal need to mate, to possess her in the most elemental way.

She overwhelmed him.

Unable to deny her, or his own need for her a second longer, he went to her and pulled her slender body against his, capturing her lips in a hard kiss meant to possess.

She moaned softly and wreathed her arms around his neck.

Gently he eased her down upon the mattress, surrounding her with his body. She moved enticingly beneath him as he slid his hands over her sleek curves. There would be no turning back. For tonight at least, Laurel would be his. They'd deal with tomorrow . . . tomorrow.

Her hands slipped beneath his open shirt, her gentle touch sweet agony. She drew him in, held him spellbound, obliterating everything but the fierce desire driving him. She wanted a memory. There wasn't a snowball's chance he'd deny her request now.

Dragging his lips from hers, he teased her with quick darting kisses along her jaw and down her throat. She wove her fingers through his hair and pulled him down, urging him to take her into his mouth.

He complied with her unspoken demand. She let out a hiss of breath and arched her back off the bed.

She wasn't the only one collecting remembrances to be recalled later. He did the same as his hand skimmed her hip, slowly moving over her body, reacquainting himself with every line and contour.

"Damon," she whispered sweetly. "I want you naked."

He was lost. His control slipped a notch.

Rolling away from her, he quickly shrugged out of his shirt. His shoes, trousers, socks and briefs hit the floor next. She lifted her bottom to remove her panties, but he stopped her and did the honors himself, slowly sliding the filmy scrap of lace down her long, slim legs.

God, she was stunning. Long lean lines, sleek curves. And for tonight, she once again was his.

Laurel opened her arms and waited impatiently for Damon to rejoin her on the bed. She held him close, could feel the beat of his heart against hers. She never wanted to let him go.

She drew inarticulate patterns over his back, loving the feel of his skin against her fingertips. She slid her hands down to his ass where she gently pressed her fingers into the muscle. Her senses scattered as he embarked upon his own sensual journey, using his tongue and fingers to travel over her body.

He moved his body lower, gently pressing open her thighs, then teasing her with a feathery brush of his fingers over her moist curls. She felt hot, cold. Dizzy.

She twisted the bedspread in her hands when he brought

his mouth down upon her and whirled his tongue enticingly around her swollen clit. Sensation tore through her. Every nerve in her body came vibrantly alive.

He gripped her hips, holding her while he continued to torment her with his tongue, using his fingers to drive her insane with desire. She'd die from the intensity. She just knew she would. Any second now, and she was a goner.

The sheer pleasure and sweet intoxication of his mouth and hands pushed her closer to the edge of oblivion until she couldn't breathe. Tension pulled her body tight. She was convinced she'd snap in two, until her world finally, blissfully exploded, spinning her so far out of control she cried out from the force of her orgasm.

Tiny tremors racked her body with sensual aftershocks. "Damon," she said, her voice ragged.

"Shhh," he whispered. "Let me love you." He rested on his elbows, holding his weight above her, his hands tenderly smoothing the hair from her sweat-dampened face. Passion burned hot in his eyes. "Let me make you come again."

And then he kissed her. Long and hard. Slow and with a promise of the prophecy his body would fulfill.

With agonizing slowness, he filled her. She wrapped her legs around his hips, pulling him deeper, taking all of his beautiful length. She moved against him, each thrust, each stroke of his body filling her with heat until she was mindless with the desire clamoring inside her.

He shifted, slipping his hand beneath her bottom, thrusting deeply inside her. Her mind spun away again. Liquid fire spread through her body. The tension, the promise of yet another incredible release taunted her, remaining a breath away.

She clung to him, digging her nails into his back as she reached for that sweet oblivion. He moved again, their bodies separating and she cried out in frustration.

A sexier than sin smile canted his mouth. "I want to watch you come for me," he said, his voice tight.

He settled onto his knees, then back on his heels before he pulled her to him, her bottom resting on his thighs, her legs wrapped around his waist, her arms around his neck. Their bodies joined, he held her to him with his arm banded around her, then slipped his free hand between their bodies and rubbed his thumb against her clit.

In what felt like seconds, her body exploded into a shattering orgasm. Spasm after spasm rocked her body. The world around her stopped spinning. She heard his own rough groan of pleasure as he drove into her one last time, burying himself inside her.

She collapsed against him. With great care, he eased her back onto the mattress, then moved them beneath the covers before he pulled her up against him.

She snuggled close and rested her head on his chest. Closing her eyes, she let the exhaustion claim her, smiling when she realized that it was his heart thundering in her ear.

The ringing of the telephone pulled Laurel from sleep. She sat up in bed, momentarily confused by her whereabouts— until Damon shifted on the mattress beside her.

The memory of their lovemaking came back to her and she smiled. Until the phone rang again.

The sound came from her room.

She frowned, wondering who could be calling her. Reluctantly, she left the warmth of Damon's bed and grabbed the first item of clothing she could find to slip into before hurrying into her own room to answer the phone. She picked it up mid-ring.

"Hello?" she answered, juggling the receiver while attempting to button Damon's shirt to cover her nakedness.

"Laurel? Oh thank goodness," the caller said in a rush. "We've been so worried about you ever since we saw the news. Are you all right, honey?"

Laurel turned on the bedside lamp. "Evelyn?" She glanced at the digital clock. It wasn't quite nine o'clock on the west coast, which meant it was nearing midnight in Boston. Her foster mother did suffer with night owl tendencies on occasion, or more appropriately, was a serious *Tonight Show* junkie.

Laurel eyed the clock again. Must be a commercial break, or the end of the opening monologue.

"I hope you don't mind, but when I didn't hear from you, I worried," Evelyn said. "Why are you in a hotel?"

"How did you find me?"

"Conner had the number."

How resourceful, she thought sarcastically. Not that she was at all surprised, but she couldn't help wondering exactly how Conner had learned she was staying at the Beverly Hills Hotel. Homeland Security? Justice? IRS? A man in his position possessed endless resources.

She gave Damon's shirt a tug before she dropped onto the edge of the bed. "I've been meaning to call," she told Evelyn, feeling a mild stab of guilt for not doing so sooner. Regardless of her feelings about Conner, they didn't extend to Evelyn. The woman had been a mother to her in every sense of the word, and Laurel loved her. She'd once loved Conner, too. She hadn't known her own father, who'd left her mother shortly after Laurel's birth. In fact, Conner had been the only real father she'd ever known. And his devotion to Evelyn was admirable. It was just too bad he'd turned out to be such a lying, conniving, and corrupt snake.

"Things have been a little hectic lately," she said. An understatement, but it was all she had by way of excuses she could safely relay without causing Evelyn more worry.

"Oh, I do understand, honey. I really do," Evelyn clucked. "I can't believe they arrested you for killing that boy. I hope you know we both believe you'd never do anything like that."

She appreciated the vote of confidence. Not that it'd make a difference to the DA, but still.

"Jonathan," she said. "His name is . . . was, Jonathan." And he'd been no boy, but a full-grown man with obvious secrets. She moved to the desk and booted up her laptop.

"How are you holding up?" Evelyn asked.

Laurel thought about that for a moment before answering. "Okay, I guess," she eventually said. That is, considering she was going on trial for a murder she didn't commit, her business was floundering, and her home was destroyed. "Life's a little stressful at the moment, though."

"I can only imagine," Evelyn said, her tone steeped in sympathy and compassion. "Is there anything we can do to help?"

"No," she said. "I'll be fine, Evelyn. Really."

"Do you have a good lawyer, honey?"

She had the best, at least in her opinion, but no way was she telling Evelyn, and by extension, Conner, that Damon was representing her. "Yes," was all she said. Not that her silence on the subject would make much of a difference. The court files were public record. Conner could probably access them with a click of a mouse for all she knew.

And then what? Her hands started to tremble.

The "what if's" were getting to her. What if the Institute was behind Jonathan's murder? What if this was another one of their well-orchestrated plans to ensure her continued silence? What if they killed Damon because he was representing her?

"I heard on the news tonight that your trial is in six weeks. We'll be there."

"No!" She gave a nervous laugh. "I mean, it won't be necessary. Da—my lawyer thinks the case won't even make it to trial."

Okay, so now she was out-and-out lying. She felt bad about it, too, and no doubt was doing a lousy job of it, as well, but she had a very good reason. As far as she was concerned, if she never saw Conner Tillman's face again it would be too soon, but more importantly, she didn't want him to know she was with Damon.

Evelyn, of course, was an entirely different story. It made her relationship with her foster mother complicated, but the "we" part of Evelyn's statement made her more than a little jumpy.

"Oh, honey, now don't be so stubbornly independent. You can't possibly believe we'd allow you to face something like this alone."

"I'm not alone. Stacy's here," she said, even though it was a stretch. Stacy wasn't her friend, but her employee. For the time being, at least.

Plus, she had Damon. For how long was anyone's guess, but she'd selfishly take what she could get. Until it became too dangerous. If that happened, then all bets were off. She'd face her dragons alone.

"I'm fine. Really," she assured Evelyn. "Besides, I'll probably never even see the inside of a courtroom." She let out a short breath. "Let's not talk about my legal hassles. What have you been up to lately?"

Thankfully, Evelyn took the bait, and for the next thirty minutes Laurel clicked through the programming disks she'd brought back from the bank and offered a series of "uh-huh's" and "how nice's" while Evelyn prattled on about the preparations of a big charity auction she was cochairing to raise money for a new no-kill animal shelter in the area. She heard the latest gossip on a few of Evelyn's friends and some other people Laurel couldn't actually place in her mind's eye. After such a long absence, was it any wonder certain memories had begun to fade?

When Evelyn mentioned Conner, Laurel rolled her eyes. She couldn't care less that the man had just gotten over a nasty cold. He could croak from pneumonia and the only reason she'd attend the funeral was to confirm the son-of-a-bitch was truly dead. She'd insist the grave be dug up in six months, too. Just to make sure. She wasn't about to take anything at face value where he was concerned.

After promising to call the minute she had more news, Laurel hung up the phone. Despite her best efforts, she still managed to harbor the occasional bout of homesickness, which was stronger than usual now that she'd spoken to Evelyn.

Since leaving Boston she hadn't been back. While she didn't regret her decision to leave, there were things about home she missed. Like Christmas, especially Evelyn's pumpkin-and-cream cheese roll the woman made by what seemed the truckload every holiday season. Oh, and what she wouldn't give for a slice of her warm, apple crisp or those delicious caramel tassies which were practically guaranteed to add a good inch to her waistline.

And the seasons. Lord, how she missed the kind of spring you could only experience after coming out of a long, cold winter. Fireworks over the harbor in summer and the crispness of the air and the smell of burning leaves in the fall. California was nice, but it just wasn't home. Anything she could possibly want was available to her, the weather was incredible most of the time, but in her opinion, the southern end of the west coast was really nothing more than one long endless summer with a few cooler evenings thrown in when the calendar declared it was supposed to be winter.

She couldn't go home. Ever. She'd accepted that fact a long time ago. Still, she longed for changing seasons, the sense of family Evelyn had worked so hard to give her along with the traditions that had somehow become her own. She missed home, and there wasn't a damn thing she could do about it.

She let out a weary sigh. God, she'd give just about anything to return to Boston. Not Boston, exactly, she realized, but back to a simpler time. Before betrayal had opened her eyes to a darkness she'd naively believed could only exist on the silver screen or in the minds of conspiracy theorists.

What she needed was something to shake off the melancholy mood she'd slipped into all because of a phone call that reminded her of a life that was no longer hers. She popped in another CD. Nothing like the possibility of more betrayal to shake off a serious bout of homesickness.

The CD booted up and she clicked on the spec sheet. Again, nothing out of the ordinary jumped out at her. Everything appeared as it should. Not until she clicked over to the coded files of the third relief panel did she notice anything strange. Buried within the codes was a symbol that didn't belong. Delta, a small triangle.

To an untrained eye, it would've gone unnoticed, but to someone familiar with the programming codes of computerized restoration, the small Delta was definitely out of place.

She moved the cursor over the triangle and clicked. The screen flickered and an entirely different program booted up. A few clicks and wrong turns later, she finally located a menu, where she clicked over to a spec sheet similar to the one she'd viewed earlier. With one major exception—She wasn't looking at the specs on a restoration, but a reproduction.

She studied the new spec sheet, convinced she was right.

The attached files of notes confirmed the ugly truth. A truth that revealed the depth of Jonathan's betrayal.

Her business partner, her dearest friend, the man she'd trusted with her most precious asset, her business, hadn't been stealing from her as so many had implied. Instead, he'd been paid handsomely to be a party to a fraud perpetrated not only on St. Giovanni's, but the people of Florence. According to the document she read, Omar Mendocini had paid Jonathan half a million dollars to recreate a set of relief panels. Panels that would replace the originals, which Omar Mendocini planned to claim for himself.

She continued reading and scrolled to the bottom of the page where she found a hyperlink over the letters "DL." She clicked on the link and a new document popped up on the screen—a letter to her from Jonathan.

Dear Laurel,

By now you can probably guess what it was I was apologizing for. I'm sure you can guess where the money came from, too. I truly am sorry. The $250,000 you found is your half, courtesy of Lorenzo the Magnificent's descendant, even though you didn't have anything to do with what I've done. What you do with it is your decision. Consider it start up money for a new beginning. Once word gets out, I'm sure there will be fallout and Artifacts' reputation will no doubt be ruined.

Please understand, Laurel, I didn't have a choice. You're going to be hurt because of my mistakes, and I apologize for that. I wish I could say I did it to protect you, but that'd be a lie. I did it to save my own ass, selfish prick that I am. And if you're reading this, then I was too late anyway.

Love,
Jonathan

"Oh Jonathan," she whispered. "What have you done?"

What could he possibly mean? Saving his own ass? From what? Or from whom?

"Laurel?"

She jumped at the sound of Damon's sleep-roughened voice. "I'm here," she called out to him.

He sauntered into her room, looking sleepy and rumpled and sexier than any man had a right to be. "What are you doing?"

"I know where the money came from," she told him when he came up behind her. He settled his hands on her shoulders and gently massaged, as if he knew the tension would already be gathering there. "I just can't believe he'd do something like this."

Damon leaned forward and read the note still on the screen. "What is he talking about? Who's Lorenzo?"

She let out a sigh. "He means Omar Mendocini, one of the board of directors of St. Giovanni's. He claims to be a direct descendant of Lorenzo de Medici, better known as Lorenzo the Magnificent. Apparently, Mendocini paid Jonathan half a million dollars to recreate the relief panels for the *Gates of Paradise*."

Damon moved to the bed and sat. "Why?"

"To replace the originals."

"But wasn't Artifacts hired to restore the *Gates of Paradise*?"

"Exactly. We were hired to restore the previously reproduced panels for the doors to the baptistery. It's not uncommon. The originals are, or were, stored in a hermetically sealed vault. Those are the ones Jonathan was paid by Mendocini to replace. He was paid to recreate them so Mendocini could steal the originals, the ones actually created by Ghiberti."

"But why?" Damon asked. "It's not like Mendocini could sell them."

Laurel shrugged. "Who knows," she said. "Prestige, perhaps? Maybe Mendocini felt they belonged to him or his family. Jonathan said he was a pretentious little prick, but I got the impression that while he came from old money, he didn't have much of it himself."

"Is it possible someone else is involved? Someone who bankrolled the fraud?"

"After this, I'd say anything is possible," she said. "What do I do with this information? I can't let something like this just die with Jonathan. The truth has to come out. The *Gates of Paradise* are too important to the art world."

She clicked on the printer icon and started sending the documents to the portable printer hooked up to her laptop. "At least we now know why Fabrizio Renaldi wanted the disks."

"Looking to erase any connection between Jonathan and Mendocini," Damon supplied.

She fed more paper into the printer. "Yes, but where are those disks now? Renaldi is dead."

"Whoever killed him probably has them."

She flipped through the pages that came off the printer and handed Damon the note from Jonathan. "Read the second paragraph."

"I did it to save my own ass," Damon read aloud. He looked over at her. "From what?"

She shook her head. "I wish I knew."

Damon read the note again and frowned. "You'd said yesterday that Jonathan had seemed distracted."

"I think we know why now."

"Maybe not. Maybe it was something else."

"Like what?"

"Maybe 'JT' knows the answer."

"Who's 'JT'?"

"I don't know, but Jonathan met with him, or her, several

times after hours the past couple of months. I'd have to check to be certain, but I think I remember seeing one or two meetings noted during office hours. When would you say this distraction with Jonathan started?"

She leaned back in the chair and mulled over Damon's question. "At least a couple of months. We received our first cancellation on a bid in February. Jonathan totally blew the deadline. He hadn't even started the job. If I'd known about it, Stacy or I could've covered for him. He said it was just one of those things, it fell through the cracks."

"Did you notice anything different about him?"

"Like what? He was using drugs or something? No, not Jonathan. He abhorred drugs. He rarely took an aspirin if he had a headache."

"My guess is he owed someone a lot of money. It's just a guess, but I bet we wouldn't be too far off base thinking it just might be this 'JT' character."

Her insides churned and breathing suddenly became difficult. To suspect Jonathan might have betrayed her was one thing. To have the evidence of his duplicity in her hands was enough to make her feel ill.

She stood and walked to the sliding glass door. She needed air. Now. Tugging open the slider, she pulled in several deep breaths of the warm night air. Jonathan had betrayed her, not just her, but Artifacts. Their reputation was ruined. Once word got out, and she didn't doubt for a minute that it would, she'd be lucky to get a single new commission. She'd be willing to bet any remaining jobs would be cancelled as well. She was ruined.

"We'll give this to Scanlon," Damon said. "He already has a contact at Interpol."

"That'd probably be for the best," she said and turned to step away from the door. The sheer curtain fluttered in the evening breeze. And then she heard a popping sound, followed by the distinct ping of something connecting with the sliding glass door.

"What the hell?" Damon said and came up off the bed.

She heard a second pop just as she reached for the sheers to pull them back. Shock swept over her as she stared at the spider web of cracked glass. "How on earth?" she murmured.

"Get down!" Damon shouted as a third shot rang out, followed by the shattering of glass when the door exploded in front of her.

Chapter 19

THE BITCH WAS like a fucking cat with nine lives. Cara hated her. Passionately. As long as Laurel Jennings was breathing, she'd be denied all she was entitled to—and dammit, she was entitled to plenty. Jonathan owed her. He'd lied to her, and now he owed her.

She slipped behind the wheel of the black SUV, pissed off beyond belief at herself for missing her target. The skirt of the maid's uniform twisted around her hips and she angrily tugged it back in place. With a high-pitched screech, she threw her bag against the interior passenger door. She grabbed hold of the steering wheel and shook it hard, letting out a string of vile curses. When that didn't work, she pounded her fist on the passenger seat and let out a howl of frustration.

She needed a bigger gun. One with a longer range. Or better yet, she'd wait until she was real up close and personal with the bitch. Then she wouldn't miss.

But how to get close enough to put a bullet through the bitch's cold heart was the problem. And now that she'd missed her target, her chances of getting her alone were going to be next to impossible. That stupid detective would no doubt order police protection for her now. Plus she had Metcalf to worry about, too. Now that she was getting dicked by her "lawyer," the bitch would never be completely alone.

Fuck! She slugged the passenger seat again. She should have killed the bitch when she had the chance.

She sucked in several deep breaths in an attempt to calm her soaring anger. She'd find a way. She had no choice in the matter now. Her future, her baby's future, depended on her holding it together and not fucking this up.

She jammed the key into the ignition and fired the engine. In the distance, she heard the wail of sirens. She shifted the SUV into drive and pulled away from the curb, her mind already spinning with possibilities.

She drove to a gas station with a mini-mart about a half dozen blocks away and parked near the Dumpsters. Snagging the small duffle off the back seat, she crossed the parking lot and entered the mini-mart in search of the restrooms where she changed out of the maid's uniform. She bought a cappuccino, tossed the maid gear into the Dumpster, then climbed back into the SUV.

She took a sip of her french vanilla cappuccino. The SUV would become too hot to drive for much longer. By tomorrow, she'd better dump it just to be safe. But damn, she was enjoying the nice ride. So much nicer than her undependable whooptie mobile.

She sipped her drink and thought of Jonathan. She thought of what it had been like, before things became ugly. Before he'd laughed at her.

Why had she believed she could trust him? Hadn't she been screwed over enough to know better than to trust a man? But she had trusted Jonathan because he'd been so different than the rest. He'd treated her with respect, surprised her with gifts, like the wool coat or the eighteen-karat-gold belly button ring among other little trinkets that showed his affection for her. Other than his little gambling addiction, which he managed to keep hidden from her for months, she'd believed him to be different—honest. She'd been such a fool. She'd believed he truly cared for her, but he hadn't. It had all been a lie. In the end, he'd been no better than the rest of them.

Except this time she hadn't taken it. This time, she'd done something about it. She'd stood up for herself. And dammit, she would have what was coming to her.

She set her cappuccino in the cup holder, fired the ignition and pulled out of the parking lot. She drove back to the Beverly Hills Hotel convinced she'd find a way to end Laurel Jennings for good. She had too much at stake to stop now. And failure? Well, that just wasn't an option.

Scanlon tossed the pizza crust into the empty box, then took a long pull on the half empty beer bottle. "You know, Pete," he said and set the bottle on the table with a thud. "I've chased plenty of dead ends during my career, but this Caldwell has them all beat. How is it possible for someone to just disappear off the face of the earth without a trace, then suddenly reappear out of the blue? And what the fuck is her connection to Linton?"

Teslenko stretched his arms over his head. "She was thorough, that's for damn sure."

"It's gotta be identity theft," Scanlon suggested. He leaned back in the cheap vinyl kitchenette chair and rubbed his rotund belly. "With all the new regs since 9/11, she'd be lucky to rent an apartment without proper ID."

"Or open a checking account, buy a car. You name it. We need to figure out whose identity she stole. And how the hell do we find that out with a trail that's been cold as ice for two years?"

Scanlon drained the last of the beer from the long necked bottle. He wished he had an answer because this case was giving him an ulcer. "Sharpe?" he suggested.

Teslenko leaned back in his chair and yanked open the

fridge, pulling out two fresh bottles of Corona. "Don't hold your breath, partner," he said, handing a cold one to Scanlon. "He's not exactly your number one fan."

Scanlon nodded in agreement. Not that he gave a shit. Sharpe could go pound sand for all he cared about the incompetent excuse for a lawyer.

"What I want to know is what kind of claim Caldwell thinks she has to Linton's estate," Teslenko said. "All I keep coming back to is the oldest trick in the book."

"Pregnancy?"

"What better way to get your hands on Linton money than to provide them with a new heir apparent."

Teslenko had a point. It wouldn't be the first time a woman stooped to extorting money from some poor schmuck by getting knocked up. But Linton wasn't just any guy. He was connected and loaded, or rather his estate was worth millions.

The kitchen clocked ticked away the seconds. Maybe they should call it a day. It was nearly eleven and they'd spent the past four hours going over every last shred of documentation they could find on Cara Caldwell and Jonathan Linton and had nothing to tie them together other than halfbaked theories and supposition. Teslenko's argument was the best they'd come up with so far since they'd starting looking into Caldwell and Linton's backgrounds. And so far as they could tell, Linton was so clean he squeaked.

"Well, one thing I can't figure out is why Caldwell is using Sharpe to do her dirty work for her," Scanlon said. "Especially since he screwed her over once already."

Five years ago, Sharpe had been retained by Cara Caldwell to handle the probate of Edith Caldwell's estate, a greataunt by marriage. Edith Caldwell, who'd been married to Cara's grandmother's half-brother, Lester, hadn't bothered with a will and had passed away intestate. Cara had been the only living relative, or so everyone believed, until a blood nephew showed up and claimed the estate belonged to him. According to the laws of succession, since Cara was not related to Edith by blood, but by marriage, she was excluded from the estate and everything went to the nephew.

The problems for Caldwell started because Sharpe didn't bother to inform his client. Caldwell believed she owned the Huntington Park property located in southeast Los Angeles, and when she attempted to mortgage the two bedroom bungalow, she'd been arrested on a series of charges, including fraud. The DA's office had eventually dropped the charges, primarily because Caldwell had acted in what she believed was good faith. Because of Sharpe, the legal hassle had to have been a nightmare for her.

"Probably figures the incompetent son-of-a-bitch owes her," Teslenko said. "Lemme see that mug shot again."

Scanlon picked up the mug shot of Cara Caldwell taken several years ago and handed it to Teslenko. She was young in the photo, barely twenty. Hardly the kind of woman he'd have associated with Linton, though. Rich fucks like Linton usually swam within their own moneyed gene pool.

Teslenko handed the photo back to Scanlon. "She look familiar to you?"

Scanlon studied the mug shot. "Not really." There was nothing remarkable about Caldwell. Straight brown hair, shoulder length, light brown eyes, pug nose and a bow-shaped mouth. A pretty girl, but not striking. She could be anyone.

"Huh. I guess not," Teslenko said, tossing the photo onto the table. He glanced at the clock above the stove. "I've had enough for one night."

"Yeah, me, too," Scanlon agreed. Chasing leads on a closed case, having another murder case dumped in his lap, one unofficially connected to the closed case he couldn't let go of, plus having his ass royally chewed by Rosen added up to one hell of a long day.

At least they'd found out what bug had crawled up Rosen's ass. Apparently the ME had reported a third DNA sampling found on Linton's body. It still galled him that Rosen had the nerve to rip him and Teslenko up one side and down the other for fucking up his case against the doc. Like they'd had anything to do with it.

The doc had bigger problems, and he wondered if Metcalf was even aware of them yet. Despite the findings of a third party's DNA, which gave Metcalf a good argument for reasonable doubt, Rosen still had what he thought could be his ace in the hole, provided he played it right before the jury. The problem was, Rosen was the type to twist the evidence in his favor.

Jennings had been a person of interest in the death of Metcalf's old man. The death had eventually been ruled an accident due to lack of evidence but that didn't mean shit, especially to an ambitious lawyer like Rosen determined to win a conviction. But from the file Rosen had shown him today, even he had to wonder what had really happened in Boston four years ago. There was more to Scott Metcalf's death. He could smell it.

He had enough to worry about. In addition to finding a connection between Linton and Caldwell that could prove Jennings was indeed innocent, he had a bigger problem. He'd accepted an invitation to his daughter's house on Sunday afternoon to celebrate his granddaughter's third birthday.

"I need to sleep on all this anyway," Scanlon said. "Let it stew a while."

They had learned a great deal about Caldwell, until the time she apparently disappeared into thin air two years ago. She had a rap sheet, but no convictions. Her most recent brush with the law came from a stalking charge which had been dropped when she'd agreed to voluntarily check herself into the funny farm. It was also the last bit of information they had on the woman. After her stay in the county psych ward, Cara Caldwell had simply ceased to exist.

"Let's say your hunch is right and the doc isn't guilty of offing Linton," Teslenko stood and chucked the empty pizza box into the garbage can. "You think Caldwell is the murderer?"

"I don't know," Scanlon admitted. "She's never been convicted of a felony. That could explain why nothing came up in CODIS when the ME's office checked the third DNA sampling."

"Let's stop by the loony bin first thing tomorrow," Teslenko suggested. "We could get lucky."

"Good luck," Scanlon said as his cell phone rang. "Without a warrant, it'll be next to impossible to get those shrinks to talk to us."

He snagged the phone from the charger and checked the display. "It's Metcalf," he said, then flipped open the phone. "Scanlon, here."

He looked over at Teslenko, who glanced at the clock above the stove.

"We're on our way," Scanlon said to Metcalf, then snapped the phone closed.

Teslenko frowned. "What now?"

Scanlon reached for his jacket and shrugged into it. "Laurel Jennings," he said. "She's been shot."

Laurel couldn't stop shaking. Her entire body trembled. The paramedic attending her had said something about shock, but she couldn't be certain since no one single thought stayed with her long enough for her to decipher much of anything other than the stark fear still radiating off her in chilly waves. All she knew for certain was that she felt frozen from the inside out.

She tried not to pay too much attention to what the paramedic was doing to her right arm, which stung like the devil.

So did her bare legs, but from all those little pin pricks digging into her from the glass fragments embedded into her skin, rather than a gunshot wound. Damon had said it was a flesh wound, just skimming the surface of her skin. Even the paramedic told her there probably wouldn't be any muscle or nerve damage, as the bullet had merely grazed the fleshy part of her upper arm. It still hurt like hell.

Uniformed cops, a pair of detectives from the Beverly Hills police department and a team of county crime scene investigators swarmed her hotel room and the courtyard below the balcony where they believed the shooter had fired off three shots at her. Damon spoke in hushed tones to one of the detectives but kept glancing worriedly in her direction. She offered him up a reassuring smile she was nowhere near feeling.

"We'll have to transport you to the hospital," Ramon, the first paramedic said. He was so young, she thought. He barely looked old enough to be out of high school, but he had a gentle touch and a compassionate nature.

"They'll want to take x-rays," his partner, Ken, who was older by a few years and a more seasoned paramedic, told her.

Her legs alternated between stinging and tingling, but she didn't dare touch them or the huge sheets of gauze they'd laid over the top. Instead she balled her free hand into a fist and tried not to think about what she was convinced were thousands of tiny shards of glass embedded into her skin.

"Don't worry," Ken said. "They'll give you something to relax you before they start plucking glass from your legs." He was easily the biggest looking guy in the room. He resembled more of an offensive lineman than one of LA's bravest. The sleeve of his blue uniform shirt stretched against the width of his enormous biceps. The guy didn't just lift weights. He probably bench pressed pick-up trucks. For fun. He might not have a neck, either, but he did have kind eyes and an easy laugh. He'd even made Laurel smile a couple of times despite herself.

"That's good to know," she said in between the chattering of her teeth. "I've never been into that whole shot of whiskey, bite on a bullet thing."

The younger paramedic checked her blood pressure again. "Eighty over fifty," Ramon said. "It's dropping. We'd better get those legs up."

The big guy came forward and stooped in front of her. "Laurel," he said, his voice the epitome of calm. "I'm going to carry you to the gurney so you won't have to strain the muscles in your legs by walking. That way, you hopefully won't pull the skin. It might hurt a little when I move you, but if you relax, it won't be so bad."

She nodded. "Okay," she said. "Just tell me what to do."

Ken looked over his shoulder for his partner, who was busy clearing a path to the gurney they'd left in the corridor. When he received a nod from the younger man, he moved in and spoke in the same calming voice. "Okay, Laurel. Put your good arm around my shoulder."

She managed a tentative grin. "My arms aren't that long."

He chuckled, the sound oddly reassuring. "You ready?" he asked once she looped her arm over his shoulder.

He did have a neck, after all, she thought. Her fingers brushed against his nape. "Um, no."

"What's the problem?"

"Uh . . . I'm not wearing any . . . uh . . ." Heat scorched her cheeks. "You know."

Her knight-in-blue smiled. "I'll take care of it," he said, then gently removed her arm from around his wide shoulder.

He signaled for his partner and explained the situation. With the efficiency of a drill sergeant, Ramon cleared the room and brought the gurney inside. Damon hadn't been too thrilled about being booted from the room, she noticed, but that was just too bad. Just as soon as she had a minute alone with him, she'd be booting him from her life.

Again.

She didn't know what she was going to do insofar as her defense was concerned, but she'd figure out something. There was no way in hell she'd allow Damon to remain with her for another day. She didn't know which of them had been the actual target, but she had only one suspect in mind. A suspect who'd proven beyond a reasonable doubt in her mind that they meant business.

The Institute was behind the shooting. She was convinced of it. There was no other explanation that made as much sense to her. Although she still didn't know who had killed Jonathan, there was a definite connection between Jonathan, Mendocini, and the dead thief so she no longer believed the Institute was responsible for Jonathan's murder. Jonathan had needed money for some reason, and a lot of it. He didn't do drugs, and she'd bet the toxicology report would prove it.

"Better?" Ken asked, interrupting her thoughts.

She shivered. "Yes," she said. "Thank you."

"Okay," he said with an easy smile. "Let's try this again."

She looped her arm around his shoulder. Without so much as a grunt of protest, he slipped an arm beneath her knees and held the other under her bottom, easily lifting her from the chair. With one small adjustment, he carried her to the gurney Ramon had brought into the room, and gently placed her on top of the mattress.

Once they draped a sheet over her and elevated her legs slightly, it took a little ingenuity for them to strap her in without causing her too much pain. But that was nothing compared to the emotional anguish ripping through her of having to send Damon away.

Better to send him away, she told herself, than to know he'd been murdered to ensure her continued silence. She couldn't think of any other way to guarantee his safety.

What about telling him the truth?

Ramon tucked a blanket around her shoulders and she absently smiled her thanks. The truth? The truth had been the reason Scott's life had been ended.

She'd known it would come to this eventually, she just hadn't expected to feel as if someone had ripped her heart right out of her chest. She closed her eyes against a fresh wave of tears.

They'd been on borrowed time. Or living in denial, she wasn't sure. But she did know that forever had never been in their future. Once her trial was over, he'd have returned to Bozeman. She'd known that. For her, she'd either be spending her last days behind bars, or if she was lucky, rebuilding her life. So if she'd known all that, why the hell did it hurt so much?

Because she'd done the stupidest thing a woman in her position could've done. She'd let her defenses down. She couldn't say she'd fallen in love with Damon because the truth she'd been avoiding these past four years wasn't that simple. You couldn't fall in love with someone if you've never truly fallen out of love with them. And for that reason, she had no choice but to send him away from her.

"We're going to Cedars," Ken said. "Is there anyone here you want to ride along with you? Someone I should tell to meet us there?"

"Yes." Her heart twisted another degree because it was only temporary. After tonight, she'd really be all alone. "But I do need to speak to Damon first, if that's okay."

Ken gave her a warm smile, then went to the door and called for Damon while Ramon checked her blood pressure again. "Ninety over sixty," he said, readjusting the stethoscope around his neck. "Better."

Ken returned with Damon. Somewhere between the shots fired at her and the cops arriving, he'd tugged on a T-shirt and a pair of sneakers. His thick, black-as-midnight hair was mussed. She resisted the urge to smooth it.

"They're taking you to Cedars Sinai," Damon said. He reached for her hand, but stopped himself when he saw the IV tubing. Instead, he settled his hand on her arm and gave her a gentle squeeze. "I'll be right behind you in your car."

"I'll need some clothes," she said. "Something loose. One of those skirts I bought, and maybe a sleeveless top."

He leaned toward her and smoothed his hand over her hair. The worry in his eyes ripped another piece off of her heart. "Laurel—"

"Not now," she whispered around the lump lodged in her throat.

He gave her a weak grin. "We'll figure this out," he said, then brushed his lips over hers in a feather-light kiss.

The door to her room stood open. In the corridor, she heard the sound of raised voices, followed by the distinct shout of her name.

"Laurel!"

"It's Stacy," she said. "Go tell them it's okay."

Ramon, who'd stepped away to give her a moment of privacy with Damon was back at her side, ready with the stethoscope to check her blood pressure again. "We really need to get you to the hospital," he said.

Damon frowned. "Did you call her?"

"No," Laurel said.

"How did she know to come here?" he asked.

"I have no idea."

Damon went to get Stacy and the paramedics moved her from the room into the corridor. From her half-sitting position, she got a good look at the crowd that had gathered. Several uniforms, detectives wearing suits, and even a few guests stood with their doors open to peer into the hallway.

Stacy rushed forward. "Oh my God," she said, her voice an octave higher than usual. "Laurel, are you all right?"

"I'll be fine," Laurel reassured her. "Ride with me to the hospital?"

"Of course, I will," Stacy said, her tone chipper. She kept pace with the paramedics as they wheeled the gurney down the hallway to the elevator. "I've always wanted to ride in an ambulance."

"How did you know to come here?" Damon asked Stacy from his side of the gurney.

Stacy's eyed narrowed slightly. "I was on a date with a reporter from the *Times*. He has a police scanner."

Someone pushed the button for the elevator. It dinged almost immediately, but when the doors slid open, the car was occupied. "Detective Scanlon," Laurel said, surprised to see him and his partner.

"What are you doing here?" Stacy said, her tone no longer warm and friendly, but cold as ice.

Laurel was no expert on jurisdictional issues, but she was fairly certain a pair of detectives from the LAPD weren't on official business at a Beverly Hills crime scene.

"Doc," Scanlon said with a brisk nod by way of greeting. His partner, she noticed, didn't even bother to acknowledge her, but gave Stacy a sharp look. "I heard you had some trouble tonight."

"Seems to be her middle name lately," Stacy said with an edge to her voice.

Laurel didn't argue with that assessment, or question Stacy's attitude toward Scanlon and Teslenko. Her assistant wasn't exactly a fan of the two detectives who'd arrested her for Jonathan's murder. She'd seen it once before. Earlier today when Detective Teslenko had shown up unexpectedly at Artifacts.

"We really need to go," Ken said, then wheeled the gurney into the elevator car. Stacy stepped in beside her, as did Ramon.

"I'll meet you there," she heard Damon call out before the elevator door slid shut.

Laurel let out a long slow breath, closed her eyes, and tried to relax. Damon would meet her at the hospital. She'd have time to speak with him alone then. In the interim, she needed time to think and work out in her mind exactly what she was going to tell him, what sort of lame excuse she'd give him this time that he wouldn't believe.

"Does it hurt much?"

Laurel opened her eyes and turned her head to look at Stacy. "More than a little," she said.

The look in Stacy's eyes didn't convey the smile on her face. "Look at the bright side," she said. "Maybe they'll give you good drugs; then you won't care what happens to you."

Chapter 20

DAMON PULLED A small weekender bag from the closet, set it on the dresser, and placed a soft, patterned skirt inside to bring with him to the hospital for Laurel. From the drawer he selected a pair of lacy panties and a matching bra. He drew his thumb over the lace of the bra in his hands. So delicate, he thought. Like Laurel. Like life.

He knew she was going to be okay, but that didn't stop him from worrying. There was no question in his mind about it. Someone had been trying to kill her. But why? How was it related to Linton? Or was it because of the *Gates of Paradise*? And most important, what was to prevent them from trying again?

He added the undergarments to the bag. He'd been sitting right in this room when someone had fired three shots at her. He couldn't help feeling responsible for her, yet he clearly understood he was being illogical. He didn't have the power to protect her. No one could—a lesson he'd learned the hard way.

Teslenko stopped just inside Laurel's room through the adjoining door and propped his shoulder on the frame. "It isn't official yet," Teslenko said to him as he moved aside to let Scanlon into the room, "but the word is the shooter used a .38 caliber. My guess it's the same gun that took out Renaldi yesterday."

"Yesterday," Damon said. "Is it that late already?"

"Quarter to two," Scanlon said and lowered his bulk into the vacant chair. "We should talk."

"Okay," Damon said. He added a red cotton button-down top into the bag and zipped it up. He'd come back for the rest of her things later. Regardless of the assurances of the hotel's manager, no way would they be staying another night. "I don't have much time. I promised to meet Laurel at the hospital and that was almost two hours ago."

He'd have gone to her sooner, but he'd been questioned over and over again by the two Beverly Hills detectives. They were nothing if not thorough and would be putting Laurel through the hoops at ten o'clock the next morning.

He grabbed the weekender bag by the leather handles and motioned for Scanlon and Teslenko to precede him into his room. Closing the door behind him, he twisted the lock. Law enforcement had finally cleared out, and the hotel staff had done what they could to restore order to Laurel's room, including boarding up the broken glass door. He was still moving them out of here. Maybe they could rent a condo on the beach for a while.

And do what? Play house?

Why not? he wondered. Would that really be such a bad idea? He liked to think not, but Laurel might have other ideas.

He dropped the bag on the floor next to the love seat. "Something to drink?" he asked the detectives.

"No, thanks. We're good," Teslenko said.

"Speak for yourself," Scanlon said and strolled over to the mini-bar fridge. "Mind if I help myself to a soda?"

"Help yourself," Damon said, but Scanlon had already popped the top on a can of Diet Coke.

Damon strode to the dresser and slid open the top drawer where he withdrew the documents Laurel had printed off earlier. After they'd realized what had happened and that the place would be crawling with law enforcement, she'd asked him to take her laptop and the documents to his room for safekeeping. He'd agreed.

He pushed the drawer closed, then walked back to the seating area. "I should take this to Rosen, but I don't trust him not to twist it and use it against Laurel." He handed the documents to Teslenko.

"What's this?" Teslenko asked as he scanned the spec sheet on top.

"That is a spec sheet for the reproduction of the relief panels for the east doors of the baptistery of St. Giovanni's, better known as the *Gates of Paradise*," Damon explained. "Artifacts was hired by St. Giovanni's to restore the reproduction. That should've been the end of it, except Omar Mendocini, one of the board of directors, paid Linton to reproduce a set of the panels. Those panels he planned to replace on the original doors and keep the originals for himself."

Scanlon sat in the chair opposite the love seat. "The doc mentioned that project when I gave her a ride home the other night."

"What does any of this have to do with Linton's murder or the attempted murder on Dr. Jennings?" Teslenko asked. "You think this Mendocini took out Linton and is gunning for Dr. Jennings now?"

Damon leaned forward and braced his elbows on his knees. "It's possible, but I doubt Mendocini is behind either incident. There's a letter there from Linton to Laurel. He was paid a half a mil to help Mendocini perpetuate the fraud. It's my guess that Renaldi was working for Mendocini. If he hadn't been at Artifacts, he might still be alive."

"So there really was a theft at Artifacts?" Scanlon asked.

"I'm afraid so," Damon admitted. "The original set of disks of this project were stolen from the safe."

"Dammit, Metcalf. Why didn't you tell me this earlier? We could've preserved what we could of the crime scene and had it analyzed right away."

"Because, it's more complicated than a simple robbery." Damon snagged his cell phone from the cocktail table, pressed a few buttons and handed it to Scanlon. "Push play when you're ready."

Teslenko moved closer and looked over Scanlon's shoulder. "Well, I'll be damned," he said when the video stopped running. "That's a lot of green."

"Two hundred and fifty thousand dollars worth," Damon told them. "In the letter from Linton that Laurel discovered tonight, he explains that this is her half of what he was paid by Mendocini."

"Partners to the end," Teslenko said, his tone dripping with sarcasm.

"She had nothing to do with the fraud," Damon shot at him.

"Easy now, boys," Scanlon said. "How did the doc know it was there?"

Damon let out a breath and rubbed at the tension gathering in his neck. "She received a letter from an attorney. When I was at the ME's office, then busy meeting with you," he said and looked over at Scanlon, "she and Stacy went to the bank and found the safety deposit box. The attorney sent her all the appropriate legal documentation she needed to access the safety deposit box. The key was tucked inside a handwritten note from Linton. All it said was, 'I'm sorry. Love Jonathan.'"

"No mystery what he was apologizing for," Teslenko said and finally took a seat. "I hate to be the one to tell you this Metcalf, but this information doesn't exactly exonerate your client."

"Rosen would call it motive," Scanlon added.

"I know all that," Damon said a little too sharply, his irritation still running high. In his opinion, it just gave the DA one more reason to prosecute Laurel for Linton's murder. He might not have been ripping her off, but once word got out, Artifacts would be ruined. That was plenty of reason for Laurel to want to kill Jonathan. The only problem was, Laurel didn't do it. He knew that as well as he knew he'd take his next breath.

"So what do you want us to do with it?" Teslenko asked.

"Laurel wants the information given to the proper authorities," Damon said. "She knows it's going to ruin her business, or what's left of it, but she says the *Gates of Paradise* are too important to let this thing stand."

"I can contact Interpol and get the ball rolling," Scanlon said. "But you know Rosen's going to jump all over this thing. It's just one more reason for her to have killed Linton."

"I'm sure he will," Damon said, "but I plan to argue that she didn't know about it until after Linton's death. I'll go directly to Yates with it if Rosen won't listen to reason."

"But can you prove that she didn't know about the money?" Scanlon asked.

"We have the digital date stamp on the video—"

"Which could've been altered," Teslenko interrupted.

"But the documentation from the lawyer wasn't mailed until the day of Jonathan's funeral," Damon concluded. "That's enough for reasonable doubt, in my opinion."

"Could work," Scanlon said, then chuckled. "God, I'd pay to see Rosen's face. As if the DNA evidence wasn't enough to put him on the warpath, he's seriously gonna pop a cork when he gets a load of this."

Damon looked at Scanlon. "Did you find anything out at Sharpe's office today? What was he doing out at Johanna Linton's place?"

Teslenko made a sound of disgust. "Dick head."

Damon agreed.

"He didn't say specifically, but the dirt bag swears his client has a legitimate claim against Linton's estate."

"Who's the client?" Damon asked. "What claim?"

"We're still trying to determine the claim, but we're leaning to the oldest trick in the extortion handbook for now."

"Pregnancy?"

"That'd be the one." Scanlon reached into his jacket pocket and handed Damon a copy of a woman's mug shot. "Does the name Cara Caldwell ring any bells, Metcalf?"

Damon studied the photograph. There was something hauntingly familiar about the young woman, but he couldn't place where he might have seen her before. Working in the DA's office, he'd dealt with countless defendants, witnesses and victims. A few of them remained forever burned in his memory, but this woman wasn't one of them.

"I can't be sure," he said and handed the mug shot back to Scanlon. "Let me guess, she's never been convicted so no DNA to match with CODIS."

Scanlon looked at his partner. "He's good, isn't he?"

"For a lawyer?" Teslenko answered with a shrug. "Not too bad."

"You think she's the one who murdered Linton?" Damon asked.

"She's a definite person of interest," Teslenko offered. "Problem is, we don't know who she is."

Damon frowned. "I don't understand."

"What he means is," Scanlon said, "that after her stint at the funny farm, she disappeared."

"We suspect she assumed a new identity," Teslenko explained. "She's kept her nose clean, too, because we didn't come across any AKA's."

AKA, or also known as, occurred when a fingerprint match came up under another identity. Damon once prosecuted a guy involved in a confidence scam with twelve different aliases. The guy had been good, having employed the services of a prominent plastic surgeon to alter his appearance.

"Can I see that mug shot again?" Damon asked. Scanlon handed him the copy and he stared hard at the photograph of Cara Caldwell. He wasn't imagining things. There was something familiar about her, but he couldn't quite figure out what it was or how he knew of her. "She's familiar—sort of."

"I had the same impression," Teslenko said. "But nothing I could put my finger on, you know?"

Damon stood and handed the mug shot back to Scanlon. "I need to get to the hospital," he said. "If I think of anything, I'll be in touch."

"Metcalf."

Scanlon spoke, and Damon noticed neither detective had taken the hint. They were both still seated.

"Sit down," Teslenko said. "You need to hear this."

Slowly, Damon sat. He looked from Teslenko to Scanlon. "What is it?"

"Rosen," Scanlon said. "He's got an investigation file that he plans to use at trial."

"Something that pertains to Laurel."

Scanlon nodded.

Teslenko leaned forward. "I saw the file, Metcalf. Rosen showed it to us. It's from the Boston DA's office."

"How much do you know about the investigation surrounding your father's accident?" Scanlon asked.

Damon shrugged. "As much as anyone," he said. "But my father died four years ago. I don't understand what it has to do with Rosen's case against Laurel."

"Did you know that she was a person of interest in the investigation?" Teslenko asked.

"Sure," Damon said. "She was one of the last people to see him alive. She worked for him. He was her supervisor."

Some unspoken communication passed between Teslenko and Scanlon. "I'll bet you didn't know that although the case was ruled an accident," Teslenko said, "there's a retired detective from Boston Rosen plans to bring out to testify at the doc's trial that he didn't believe the case was an accident. Or more accurately, that he believes that your girl knows more than she was willing to talk about."

"A cop with a hunch," Scanlon added. "Pain in the ass every time."

"Don't I know it," Teslenko said.

"The only reason I think he's digging up old cases, is to rattle your ass during trial," Scanlon said. "Especially one that hits so close to home."

"Thanks for the heads up," Damon told them. "I'll handle it."

I can't stay here.

Laurel's tearful statement spoken that cold night in Boston four years ago came back to him. He'd asked her why? Begged her to tell him why she was leaving Boston, but all she'd say was she couldn't stay. She'd quit her research job at the Institute and claimed she had an opportunity to study art history under some renowned professor of the Renaissance waiting for her in California. Only she hadn't even been specific about that no matter how much he pushed her for more information. He'd been young and hot-headed and hadn't looked much beyond his own bruised ego at the time.

To be honest, he hadn't really known what the hell she was up to, other than she'd enrolled in the art history program at UCLA and then suddenly was going into some kind of art business with Linton, whom she knew from her days at MIT. A damn pathetic waste of her amazing talent, in his opinion. She was a gifted scientist, not some art flunky.

Then he'd gotten a bad idea and hadn't been able to let go of it. He'd been working in a general practice firm in

downtown Boston when he heard from his buddy, Joss
Jacobs, who'd been with the public defender's office back
then, that the Los Angeles County district attorney's office
was hiring, so he'd sent off his resume. He'd been hired, relocated to California but by then it was too late. Laurel
hadn't been all that happy to see him and when he'd pressed
the issue, she claimed she no longer loved him, suggesting
they'd both be better off if they moved on, met new people.

He'd known in his gut she was lying to him. Or maybe
his ego wouldn't let him believe that she could've fallen out
of love with him. He thought about the way she'd made
love to him tonight. Neither of them had spoken those three
little words, but he didn't doubt for a second what they
once had was as strong as ever. Why else would he have
come charging to her rescue the minute he'd heard she was
in trouble?

"Rosen's case is crumbling and he's scrambling," Teslenko
offered.

Damon stood. "Don't worry about it," he said. "I'm not."
But Laurel would when she learned of it.

Why? Because she had something to hide? Did she really
know more about his father's accident than she'd told the
authorities? And if so, why in the hell would she hide it
from him of all people?

"Where's Damon?" Laurel asked. She looked around the
emergency room parking lot of Cedars Sinai Medical Center,
but didn't see her Jag in the immediate vicinity. "I thought
you said he was waiting?"

"He is, but at the hotel," Stacy said, then glanced nervously around the area. "I'm over here. It's not too far."

She hoped not. Her thighs weren't stinging nearly as badly
as before they'd brought her into the emergency room, but
they were still plenty sore. A very patient, young intern had
painstakingly removed the glass fragments from her flesh,

doused her with an antibiotic cream, and covered each of her tiny wounds with bandages. Of course, the aches in her thighs hurt nowhere near as bad as the steady throb in her arm, and the Percocet they'd given her, along with a small dose of Ativan to calm her, hadn't yet begun to touch the pain.

With her arm in a sling and a pair of too large doctor's scrubs for clothes, she carefully walked behind Stacy to the big black SUV near the edge of the parking lot.

"I should've brought the car to you," Stacy said when Laurel reached her side. She unlocked the door and held it open. "I didn't think. Sorry."

"That's okay." Laurel struggled to lift her leg high enough to climb inside the Escalade's plush interior. Her still raw skin pulled tight with the movement and she winced in pain. "What I wouldn't do for your little car right about now," Laurel told her with a thin smile. "Or mine."

Stacy gave off a laugh that held a definite level of nervousness. "It wasn't ready yet, so they let me keep this another day." She helped Laurel into the seat, then fastened the seat belt for her.

Laurel settled back into the soft, buttery leather passenger seat to wait for Stacy to climb in behind the wheel. The exercise of walking across the parking lot must've sped things up, because the Percocet started to kick in, taking the edge off her pain and making her drowsy.

"I appreciate your help tonight," Laurel told Stacy after she fired the ignition. "Thank you."

Stacy said nothing, just backed out of the parking space, then drove silently through the parking lot toward the exit. As they neared the exit, Laurel spotted a silver Jaguar ahead, pulling up to the gate of the parking garage. She sat up straighter and looked more closely. Sure enough, Damon sat behind the wheel. He had the window rolled down and was pulling a parking ticket from the automated attendant.

Relief poured through her at the sight of him. She knew she shouldn't feel that way, but couldn't have stopped the acceleration of her pulse if her life depended on it. Actually, his life did, but she couldn't get past the relief of seeing him.

"Stacy, could you stop?" she asked before they reached the attendant's gate. "Damon's here."

Stacy kept driving.

"Stacy?" A tingle of fear climbed up Laurel's spine. "Stacy did you hear me? That's Damon pulling in over there."

Stacy turned her head to look at Laurel. Pure venom lit her golden brown eyes.

"Stacy? What's going on?"

"Don't call me that again, you stupid bitch," Stacy said hatefully. She punched the accelerator and whizzed right past Damon who didn't even glance in their direction.

"What are you talking about?"

"Cara," Stacy said heatedly. She zipped out of the driveway, made a right, and hit the gas. "My name is Cara. Cara Caldwell."

Laurel reached for the door handle, but it was useless. Not only was Stacy driving way too fast, but she'd apparently switched on the master lock, preventing Laurel from opening her own door and escaping. She tried the window, but it was locked as well.

She attempted to think, to devise a plan to escape this madness, but the drugs she'd been given were now working in full force. She felt fuzzy and out of touch, her thoughts muddled.

"What happened to Stacy?" she asked, but the question came out wrong, so she tried again. "Who's Stacy?"

"Stacy Owens was a means to an end," said Cara or Stacy or whoever the hell she was. "A convenience I took advantage of."

"But we checked your background," Laurel said. "We

had to because of the work we do." The bonding agency wouldn't provide the security bonds necessary for them to conduct business without a detailed background check of each person who worked at Artifacts. The investigator's report indicating no criminal background existed was filed in Stacy's personnel file. She even had copies of Stacy's transcripts. How was this possible?

Her eyes were starting to get heavy. Passing out was not an option. She needed to see where she was being taken so she could tell Damon. Damon would save her. Didn't he always?

"You checked Stacy Owens's background," Cara said. "Not mine."

Laurel frowned and tried to concentrate. "But you have an art degree from Michigan State," Laurel said. "You can't fake that."

Cara laughed. The sound sent another chill chasing down Laurel's spine.

"God, you're fucking slow on the uptake," Cara said. "*Stacy* has an art degree from Michigan State. I just happen to be very artistic and creative."

"You stole another person's identity?" Laurel couldn't believe what she was hearing, or that she and Jonathan hadn't realized Stacy wasn't who she claimed to be. But then, they'd never had any reason to suspect something wasn't right. Or had Jonathan?

Laurel sucked in a sharp breath. "You killed Jonathan," she said.

"He deserved to die," Cara said venomously.

Cara made a right turn, but Laurel couldn't make out the street name. She spied the sign for Interstate 10 just as Cara switched lanes and headed for the on ramp.

"He lied to me," Cara said. "They all lie. That lawyer you're fucking will lie to you, too."

No, not Damon, Laurel thought. Or did she say it aloud? She was too groggy now to know the difference, but Cara made a sound that could've been a humorless laugh.

"Let me out of here," Laurel said, but her words, mildly slurred now, had little effect on her captor. Cara just punched the accelerator and sped up the on ramp.

Chapter 21

"WHAT DO YOU mean she's been discharged?" Damon demanded. He nailed the emergency room receptionist with a harsh glare. "You're absolutely certain she's not here?"

The woman frowned. "Yes, I'm sure," she said, her tone haughty. "She left about fifteen minutes ago."

"How did she leave?"

The receptionist shrugged her shoulders. "I wouldn't know, sir."

Something wasn't right. Laurel would've called him. "Where's her doctor? Let me talk to him."

"I'm sorry, sir, but that's not possible. Privacy laws prohibit the distribution of information on our patients unless the patient specifically designates someone to receive the information." She gave him a sardonic grin. "And it ain't you."

Damon's frustration climbed another notch. "I'm not asking about her medical condition," he said. "I just need to know where she went."

"I wish I could help you," the woman said and turned to assist another patient or family member.

Damon knew she didn't give a rat's ass. He could be a

stalker for all she knew, or the one who put Laurel in the ER in the first place. He walked to the exit and stood under the glare of the fluorescent lights under the canopy wondering what to do next.

Stacy! Stacy had gone with Laurel to the hospital. She probably drove Laurel back to the hotel. He frowned. But wouldn't one of them had called to tell him not to bother coming?

He pulled out his cell phone, checked the listing of numbers recently called and highlighted the number for Stacy's cell. He punched the call button, but it went directly to voice mail. She'd either turned off her phone or her battery went dead.

He thought about calling Scanlon, but what for? Because he was feeling antsy about Stacy taking Laurel back to the hotel and not calling him first? And what the hell had Stacy been doing at the hotel tonight anyway?

Geez, he was losing it. Suspecting suspects where none existed.

With nothing else to do but return to the hotel and wait, he walked across the lot to Laurel's car and climbed in behind the wheel. Damn. It just didn't make sense that Laurel wouldn't have called him, or had Stacy call him.

Stacy, he thought and frowned, recalling the mug shot Scanlon had shown him of Cara Caldwell. Little about Stacy Owens resembled the Caldwell woman. Stacy had short, bouncy reddish curls, where Caldwell's hair was medium-length and a mousy brown. Caldwell had a little pug nose and a bow shaped mouth where Stacy had a perfectly straight nose and full lips. Stacy even had well-defined cheekbones where Caldwell's just sort of blended into the structure of her face.

It was the eyes, Damon thought. They were the same. The best plastic surgeon in the country could alter the shape, but they couldn't change the intensity of someone's gaze. "Holy shit," Damon muttered.

No, he couldn't be right about this. He just couldn't, but reached for his cell phone again anyway and dialed Scanlon's number.

He picked up on the third ring. "This had better be fucking good," he groused. "I have to get up in less than four hours."

"Stacy is Cara Caldwell."

Damon heard a rustling sound. "You sure about this, Metcalf?" Scanlon sounded more alert now.

"Not a hundred percent, but close," he said. "Gino? She has Laurel."

Scanlon swore again. "I'll call Pete. Do you know what they're driving?"

Damon thought for a moment. He'd seen a vehicle parked next to Laurel's Jag this afternoon when he'd left Artifacts to go the ME's office. "Black," he said finally. "An SUV. That's all I know."

"Come on, Metcalf. Think harder. I need a make or model so we can put an APB out on the vehicle."

"Big," Damon said. "Late model. Escalade, maybe a Navigator. I'm not sure, but it wasn't foreign."

"You're sure a lot of help," Scanlon complained. "How soon can you be at the house?"

House, code for police station. Damon started the car and backed out of the parking slot. "I'm on my way," he said. At this time of the morning, there'd be little-to-no traffic. "Less than twenty. What are you going to do?"

"Put on some goddamn clothes and find a gallon of strong, black coffee. I have a feeling it's gonna be a long fucking day."

A pretty young cadet poked her head into the room where Damon sat around a makeshift conference table with Scanlon,

Teslenko, a Lt. Bellamy, and the watch commander who came on duty three hours ago. "You the ones looking for a Black Cadillac Escalade?" she asked.

"Could be," Scanlon said. "What have you got?"

"This just came in," she said and handed Scanlon a report, then left.

Damon still hadn't been positive whether the vehicle he'd seen parked beside Laurel's Jaguar yesterday had been an Escalade or a Lincoln Navigator. It'd been nearly six hours since he'd realized Laurel was missing, and so far, they'd come up with nothing. Uniforms had been sent to watch Artifacts and Laurel's condo but so far, nothing. They'd even called in assistance from the Beverly Hills PD and requested the hotel be watched, but so far, all they'd had was dead silence on all fronts.

"Luxury Rentals has reported a Black Cadillac Escalade stolen," Scanlon said. "Customer was supposed to return it yesterday by noon. When they attempted to run the credit card for the additional rental time this morning, it was rejected."

"Renaldi?" Teslenko asked.

Scanlon shook his head. "Says Marcello Gallo, but the passport photo is the same as our DB."

"I'll let Interpol know," Teslenko offered.

"They're probably the reason the credit card was rejected," Lt. Bellamy said. "If Renaldi is on their watch list, they'd have most of his aliases on file."

Damon liked Bellamy. He'd worked with him on a couple of cases back when Bellamy had still been a detective. The guy was smart and well-respected, and he was also a good cop who'd risen through the ranks the old fashioned way— by a lot of hard work.

"I'll go put out a fresh APB to notify all the officers on duty," the commander said.

Teslenko laid a hand on Damon's shoulder. "We'll update the third watch with anything new during roll call later, too. We'll find your girl, Metcalf."

Third watch wouldn't come on duty for hours yet, but Damon appreciated the detective's diligence just the same. In fact, he had no complaints whatsoever about how Scanlon and Teslenko were handling the case with one exception— they still hadn't found Laurel and had zero leads on where Stacy might have taken her.

He took a sip of cold coffee from the Styrofoam cup and tried in vain not to worry. Laurel was tough. She was strong emotionally when it counted. She wouldn't crumble under the strain. And she was damn smart. If she could find a way to escape Stacy or Cara, that is, she would—provided she was physically able to do so.

He didn't know what kind of shape she was in physically, and that had him downing more of the too strong coffee than was wise. He looked over at Teslenko, whose attention was momentarily on the pink baker's box of donuts on the table in the corner. "It was you," Damon said.

Scanlon and Bellamy both looked at him. "Pete," Damon said with an inclination of his head in Teslenko's direction. "You sent me that fax. About Laurel."

Teslenko snagged a maple bar from the box. "I don't know what you're talking about," he said, but refused to look in Damon's direction.

"The hell you don't," Damon said and straightened. "'Isn't this *your* Laurel?' It was you." Damon leaned forward, resting his elbows on the table. "You're not quite the prick you want everyone to think you are."

Teslenko managed a small grin. "Get over yourself, Metcalf," he said and sat back at the table again. He took the stolen vehicle report and studied it, ignoring his partner's shocked stare.

"Well, I'll be damned," said Scanlon. "Pete does have a heart behind that badge."

"Don't count on it." Teslenko shot Scanlon a look of annoyance. "She needed a friend. Even I could see that."

Raised voices filtered down the hallway. Alan Rosen appeared in the doorway, looking as if he wanted to hit someone. His narrowed gaze zeroed in on Damon. No doubt his primary target.

"What the fuck is going on here?" Rosen shouted. "You're supposed to be working for the state, not the defense."

Lt. Bellamy stood. "Mr. Rosen, would you like to have a seat."

"No, I don't want to sit down," Rosen thundered. "I want to know why you people are fucking with my case."

Damon stood, his own patience tested to the limit. "You have no case, Rosen. My client is innocent."

"Where have I heard that before?" Rosen fired at him.

Damon took a step toward Rosen. Teslenko stood suddenly, blocking Damon's path. "The evidence against Laurel was nothing more than circumstantial and you know it."

"The hell it is," Rosen countered. "Physical evidence is all I need to put that bitch behind bars where she belongs. We've got her fingerprints on the murder weapon. Not to mention her DNA all over the body. And don't forget, she has no alibi."

"And you have no solid motive," Damon shot back.

"I've got ten million reasons why she iced Linton."

"It's a bullshit case," Damon stepped around Teslenko and faced Rosen. "One any decent ADA wouldn't have bothered with. But the Lintons had you, didn't they? What did they promise you in exchange for a conviction? Financial backing for your political campaign?"

Rosen's complexion reddened. "Fuck you, Metcalf."

"Hit a nerve, huh?" Damon said and walked away before he did something stupid—like beat the jerk to a bloody pulp. God, he'd have loved to have plowed his fist through Rosen's perfectly capped teeth and politician's smirk, but he wouldn't put it past the son-of-a-bitch to bring him up on assault charges. And what good would he be to Laurel then?

Lt. Bellamy braced his hands on the back of the chair in front of him. "You have no case against Laurel Jennings, Mr. Rosen. You're after the wrong person. She's not responsible for the murder of Jonathan Linton," he said in a calm, reasonable tone. "We think we know who is, and just as soon as we have her in custody, you can go after your conviction."

"I'm not dropping the case against Jennings," Rosen said.

"Of all the . . ." Scanlon muttered. "Look, you jackass. Jennings is missing."

"That's it," Rosen said. "I'm filing a motion to have her bail revoked."

Damon's temper took flight again. "On what grounds?" he demanded hotly.

"She didn't skip," Scanlon said. "We think she's been kidnapped. And you could help us out here instead of being your usual pain in the ass. Give us any information your office has on Cara Caldwell."

"Caldwell?" Rosen looked momentarily surprised. "I handled that case. A stalker, but we didn't file charges because the judge gave her an out. She's a nut job. What does she have to do with Jennings?"

"*You* handled the case?" Scanlon scrubbed his hand down his face. "Who was the complainant?"

"I don't know. Why?"

"Christ Rosen, use that pea brain for something other than making other people miserable, would you?" Teslenko said sarcastically. "Stacy Owens? Sound familiar?"

"I dunno," Rosen said. "Maybe. Why?"

"Stacy Owens is the admin assistant at Artifacts," Damon offered. "We think it's the name Cara Caldwell is using."

"Well, it's not Stacy Owens," Rosen told them. "She disappeared not long after the charges against Caldwell were dropped. If I remember right, I think her landlady said she moved back to Michigan."

Damon sifted through the papers scattered over the conference table. "Look at this. Is this the Stacy Owens you remember?"

Rosen took the photocopy of the driver's license photo from Damon and studied it. "Yeah, that's her."

"Dammit," Scanlon slammed his hand down on the table. "Caldwell can't be Owens."

"Look again," Damon told Rosen. "Are you sure?"

Rosen snatched the photo from Damon's hand. "That's her," he said, his tone filled with irritation. "The eyes look a little different, but that is Stacy Owens."

"Plastic surgery?" Teslenko suggested.

"There's one on every corner in this city," Scanlon said.

"To look like Owens," Damon said. "Thank you, Alan. I appreciate it."

Rosen didn't bother to acknowledge the sentiment. "I won't drop the charges until Caldwell is in custody."

"Fair enough," Damon said.

"I'll have my secretary send over anything we have on Caldwell," Rosen said, then turned his attention to Lt. Bellamy. "Do you have a three-county-wide APB out on Caldwell?"

Scanlon grumbled something that caused Bellamy to shoot him a warning glance. "Yes, she was last seen driving what we believe is a stolen black Cadillac Escalade."

"Your second murder charge against Caldwell," Teslenko

said. "We believe she's the shooter in a case now involving Interpol."

Scanlon quickly explained the murder of Fabrizio Renaldi, Renaldi's connection to both Mendocini and Linton, as well as the attempt on Laurel's life.

"You should make it a statewide alert," Rosen said. "Caldwell has connections in San Bernardino County. A cousin, I think."

"You wouldn't happen to have an address?" Bellamy asked. "Or a name?"

Rosen rubbed his fingers back and forth over his forehead. "Jerome Turner," he finally said after a few tense moments.

"JT," Damon said.

Scanlon shot him a quick glance. "Excuse me?"

"JT," Damon said again. "It was a notation no one could explain in Linton's BlackBerry. He had several meetings with him, most of them after hours."

Scanlon looked at Teslenko. "I'm on it," Teslenko said and left the room.

Within minutes they were studying a mug shot of Jerome Nathanial Turner, a two-bit thug with long stringy hair and a bad complexion, and a rap sheet longer than Damon's arm. Petty crimes mostly, a few drug charges, most of which the San Bernardino County DA's office had either dropped or were pled down to a misdemeanor. He was currently under investigation for running an illegal gambling operation. Last known address was in Blue Jay, a small bedroom community in the San Bernardino Mountains.

"I'll contact the Berdo County sheriff's office," Bellamy said.

"We're out of here," Scanlon said, slipping into his jacket. Teslenko was right behind him.

"I'm coming with you," Damon said. Gambling. So that's who Linton had gotten involved with, a two-bit bookie.

"Metcalf." Rosen put a hand on Damon's arm and shook his head. "It's not a good idea. Let them handle it."

Damon shrugged off Rosen's hand. "I'm going." He gave Scanlon a hard stare. "I either ride along or I meet you there."

"Shit," Teslenko shoved his arms through the sleeves of his corduroy sport coat. "I hate lawyers."

"You hate everybody," Scanlon said.

Teslenko gave Damon a pointed stare. "With good reason."

"Fine," Scanlon said. "But you get in the way, Metcalf, and I'll plug your ass myself with my service revolver."

Damon didn't care what Scanlon threatened. Laurel needed him and dammit, he'd be there. He saw no reason to change the status quo at this stage of the game.

A game, he thought as he followed Scanlon and Teslenko from the room, that he prayed they wouldn't lose.

Laurel felt as if every part of her body were screaming in protest at being abused. Her arm throbbed to the point of distraction. One of her legs felt as if it were on fire, and her head pounded mercilessly. Her shoulders were stiff and she groaned as she slowly tried to sit. Her sling was missing and she whimpered when she inadvertently jerked her wounded arm.

She didn't know where she'd been taken, but she was freezing. The paper booties the ER nurse had given her last night before leaving the ER did zilch by way of keeping her feet warm. She swung her feet to the cold stone floor. A thin blanket covered her, and she attempted to pull it around her shoulders, but her arm began to throb in protest so she gave up.

She couldn't even rub her arms or legs to generate warmth. Gingerly, she touched a hand to her thigh. Even through the blue scrubs she wore, she felt the heat. Infection, she thought. Just great. Without antibiotics, she could end up in serious trouble if she were unattended for too long.

She looked around and tried to get her bearings. The room was dark, but small shafts of light streamed in from hastily boarded windows that were high in the walls. A basement, she determined, then explored further with her gaze. Sure enough, she spied the shape of a steep staircase in the far corner of the room.

How on earth had Stacy, or Cara as she insisted on being called now, gotten her down the steep staircase alone? Thanks to the medication she'd taken at the hospital, she'd eventually passed out during the drive to only God knew where, so she had no clue. Cara was a petite thing. No way could she have gotten her down here all by herself.

Carefully, Laurel stood. The room swayed and she reached out with her good arm, her fingers coming in contact with thick cobwebs. She drew her hand back and grit her teeth. God, she hated bugs. Spiders in particular.

The low ceiling provided a fairly respectable hand hold to help steady her, cobwebs aside, as she made her way across the dank space toward the staircase, careful not to jar her bad arm. Aside from the cot she'd woken up in, the room appeared to be empty.

She reached the staircase and peered toward the top in the darkness. Nothing. She climbed three stairs before she saw a thin line of light beneath the door, a door which she was positive would be locked. But she had to try just the same. She needed to get out of here before Cara came back for her.

She stilled midway up the staircase. She heard voices. A woman's voice. Cara, no doubt.

Less than a minute later, she heard the crunch of gravel coming from outside. Footsteps. A man's footsteps by the heavy sound, followed by the slamming of a car door. A car started, idled for a couple of minutes, then drove away.

Was she alone? She'd only heard one set of footsteps, and she was fairly certain it'd been a man. But the voice she'd overheard had been a woman's voice. She figured it was safe to assume she hadn't been left unguarded.

She retraced her steps down the staircase, careful not to make too much noise. She reached the bottom and looked around. The room was nothing but dark shadows, something that could prove an advantage.

She bit her bottom lip. What she needed was a weapon. Her search of the room proved futile. As she'd suspected, aside from the cot, the room was empty.

She looked to the boarded windows. Without the strength of both of her hands, she doubted her ability to pull one of the boards loose, but she had to try. She couldn't just sit here and wait for Cara to dole out whatever fate she had planned for her.

One more person she'd trusted who'd betrayed her. She couldn't think about that now and pushed the thoughts aside. If she were lucky, she'd have plenty of time to wallow in self pity later.

She tried the first window, but the boards were all secure. Same with the second and the third she tested, as well. The fourth window farthest from the stairwell finally showed some promise. She tugged on one of the wooden planks, and it gave slightly.

She was sweating. From fever or exertion, she couldn't be certain, but she wasn't about to give up the one slim chance of hope she had now.

She tugged again. The nail creaked and groaned, but

wouldn't give completely. One more hard tug with her good arm and one side of the plank fell loose.

A small ray of sunlight burst into the room. She nearly cried out in relief, but slapped her hand over her mouth to stifle the sound. She squinted against the sudden brightness and grabbed hold of the plank where it was still secured on the other side. Now able to get a good look at where to apply the right amount of pressure, she wiggled and pulled and tugged on the plank, slowly working the board free.

Her arm burned from the exertion. She bit down hard on her lip and she kept moving the plank back and forth until the nail finally gave and the wood plank broke free.

Breathing hard, she rested her head against the cold concrete wall. The coolness of it felt heavenly against her heated skin. She had fever, of that she was absolutely certain now. And she was parched. God, what she wouldn't give for a cool drink of water. Her throat felt like seared meat.

She set the plank on the floor next to her feet. With what little light she did have, she tried to take a look at her thighs, which were burning up to the touch. She loosened the tie on the scrub bottoms and pulled them away from her body. She winced when she saw her left leg, which was definitely swollen and red. She tried not to panic. It could be nothing more than a miniscule glass fragment that had been missed by the intern last night and was attempting to work itself out.

With supreme effort, she tied the scrubs tight around her waist. She shivered, but she no longer knew whether it was from the cold or the fever. It didn't matter, she tried to open the window. It wouldn't budge. She looked closer, and it had been nailed shut. Even if she could slide it open, she doubted she'd be able to shimmy through such a small opening as it was no bigger than eighteen-to-twenty inches square.

She walked over to the cot for the blanket, stopping to steady herself only once. As much as she'd have loved to pull the thin blanket around her for warmth, she carried it to the window. If Cara came downstairs and saw the light pouring into the room, she'd know something wasn't right. Laurel needed the element of surprise to gain the upper hand.

She carefully threaded the blanket through the thin crack in the two remaining planks. The dark gray material would no doubt be noticeable from the outside, but she'd heard the car on the opposite side, so maybe she'd catch a break. God knew she needed one.

The blanket in place and the room once again pitched into darkness, she picked up the plank and made her way to the side of the staircase to wait.

Laurel didn't have any reference for time. She had no clue how long she remained hunched in the corner by the staircase waiting for Cara to show. But the second she heard the throw of the bolt on the door above, she was instantly alert and ready.

Light spilled down the staircase and she slowly stood. She bit hard on her lip against the pain as she raised her arms above her head, readying her weapon.

She heard the thunk of footsteps on the stairs. And she waited. Waited for her quarry to draw closer.

A heavy boot clumped on the bottom step. Without a sound, she took a step forward and brought the plank down hard upon the back of her captor's head.

Laurel let out a cry of pain as fire shot up her arm. But that didn't stop her from drawing the wood plank back up again and giving her captor's head a second hard whack that crumpled her to the cold stone floor.

She heard a groan and wasn't sure whether it was from her or the body lying on the floor at her paper-slippered feet.

She wasn't about to wait around to find out. Ignoring the
pain in her arm and the hammering in her head, she dropped
the plank and moved as fast as she could up the stairs. She
burst out of the basement and into a small kitchen and
came to a stop. Seated at a round wooden table was Cara—
with a gun pointed directly at Laurel's heart.

Chapter 22

"HAVE A SEAT, Laurel."

She wanted to cry. She'd worked so hard only to come face to face with the wrong end of a pistol. Only she refused to shed so much as a single tear. Like Cha-cha had said her first night in jail, don't let the bastards know they're getting to you.

"You hungry?" Cara asked.

"A glass of water would be appreciated," Laurel said stiffly.

Cara rose and walked to the fridge in the corner, all the while keeping the gun aimed at Laurel. She returned with a bottle of Coke, twisted off the cap and set the bottle in front of Laurel.

"Thanks," she said, then drank greedily. Water would have been better since she suspected she was dehydrated, but she'd make do. At a time like this, wet and cold was wet and cold. After she downed nearly half the cola, she set the bottle on the table and looked at Cara. She was no longer Stacy to her, she realized. The woman seated across from her was another person entirely. Stacy was long gone.

"What do you want?" Laurel asked.

Cara grinned, "What's mine. I want what Jonathan promised me."

"Whatever Jonathan may or may not have promised, he didn't promise it to you. He promised it to Stacy."

"It doesn't matter now. It's mine and I intend to have it. For our baby."

"Baby?" Laurel couldn't have been more stunned by that bit of news. She hadn't even realized Jonathan and Stacy were having an affair. Perhaps if she'd paid closer attention she might have noticed the typical signs, but the truth was, she just hadn't. She didn't pay much attention to anything but her work. Work had always been her salvation, her place to hide, she realized. Because that's exactly what she'd been doing since she'd left Boston. Hiding.

No more, she thought. She just couldn't do it anymore. If she escaped this mess only to end up dead because of things she had no control over, so be it, but she'd remain silent no longer. Silence wasn't living, and too many people had already been hurt because she'd been too afraid to come forward with the truth.

"That's right," Cara said smugly. "Our baby. Mine and Jonathan's."

Laurel tipped her head slightly to the side. "I didn't know you and Jonathan were having an affair. He never mentioned it."

"We wanted to keep it a secret."

Laurel pursed her lips and slowly nodded, then looked Cara straight on. "We? Or you mean Jonathan wanted to keep it a secret?"

"It doesn't matter."

"Apparently it mattered to Jonathan if he didn't even tell me about it," Laurel said with a smirk. "We shared everything, Cara. Surely you know that."

"You tried to control him. Just like that family of his."

"He couldn't marry you, you know," Laurel said. The woman was unhinged, she saw that clearly now. Now if she could only distract her long enough to get the gun away from her, she might actually live to see another day. "His family wouldn't hear of him marrying someone beneath him."

Cara's eyes narrowed to slits. "He paid for that," she said. "Just like you will."

"Why me? I didn't do anything to you. I gave you a job. A good job, too. You could've easily made a better life for yourself."

"You don't know anything about my life," Cara sniped at her.

"Sure I do," Laurel said, keeping her tone measured and even. She was an academic. Most of her life had been spent studying, and that included basic psychology. She only hoped what she learned in books could be applied to real life. "I know what it's like to be shit on by fate."

"What do you know?" Cara laid the gun down on the table. She looked away, her gaze on the café curtains fluttering from the open kitchen window over the sink.

"I know more than you think I do," Laurel said. She watched Cara closely, but her hand remained on the gun.

Cara looked back at Laurel. "He lied to me," she said. "He said he loved me."

"In his way, he probably did. But you know how men are," Laurel added with a shrug.

Tears welled in Cara's eyes. "I didn't mean to kill him," she said, her voice suddenly thick. "But he laughed at me when I told him I was pregnant. He told me to get rid of it because it wasn't his."

Laurel didn't know whether to believe Cara or not. The Jonathan she knew wasn't a cruel person. Unfortunately, she knew better than most, that people weren't always what they seemed, and that included Jonathan.

"He couldn't marry you, Cara. His family, they're very powerful people. They would've stopped it."

"I did love him."

"I understand."

Cara looked at her then, and she saw a glimpse of Stacy in her eyes. "I didn't mean for it to go like this," she said. "I lost my temper that night. I couldn't believe he would treat me that way and I just lost it."

Laurel sat quietly, keeping her eye on the gun still clutched under Cara's grasp. "What do you know about the man that broke into Artifacts?"

"I killed him, too," she said. "I saw him coming out of Artifacts. He didn't take me seriously, either."

A mistake Laurel was determined not to make. "What were you doing there at that time of night?"

"I don't know. I'd been to the cemetery to see Jonathan. I guess I felt closer to him at the office, so I went there."

"Who is that downstairs?" Laurel asked. She intentionally shifted her gaze to the open basement door, hoping to distract Cara.

Her ploy didn't work. Cara simply shrugged. "Jerome. He's my cousin. Worthless piece of shit for the most part," she said. "But lately he's been doing pretty good with some gambling business. Jonathan owed him money."

"Yes, I know," Laurel said, to which Cara appeared mildly surprised. "It was all on the disks we recovered from the safety deposit box yesterday." Not all of it as she implied, but Laurel easily pieced the rest of it together. Jerome was no doubt the JT referenced on Jonathan's BlackBerry.

"So the cops know to come here," Cara said absently. She looked back at Laurel. "That complicates things."

"It doesn't have to," she said. "I'll help you, Cara."

Cara laughed then, a humorless chuckle. "Sure you will."

"I will. I promise. I know what it's like to have people you trusted betray you. I know how much it hurts."

Which was why if she made it out of this mess alive, she was going to tell Damon the truth. It was enough that she lived her life in constant fear, she could no longer keep the truth from him. He deserved to know what really happened to his father. And maybe, just maybe, as he was so fond of saying, justice really would prevail in the end.

Cara didn't have time to answer as the sound of sirens approaching drew closer. She stood and walked to the kitchen window and lifted the curtain with the nose of the gun. "They're here," she said.

Cara turned back to Laurel, pain so evident in her eyes. "I'm sorry it had to come to this," she said, then aimed the gun directly at Laurel.

Detective Scanlon was the first one to burst through the back door leading directly into the kitchen, followed by his partner, then Damon. A group of uniformed officers in full riot gear charged the front door.

Laurel's heart nearly stopped at the sight of all those weapons aimed at her, but the red laser beams on her chest nearly undid her. She reached for the chair and sat.

"I couldn't stop her," she said. "I thought she was going to shoot me, but at the last second she pointed the gun at her temple and pulled the trigger."

Scanlon signaled for the other two officers to search the basement.

"I might have killed him," Laurel said.

Damon came to her side and pulled her close. "I didn't care whether I did or not," she said. "I just wanted to get out of here."

"It's okay," he said.

"He's alive," one of the officers called up from the basement, giving her a mild sense of relief in an insane moment.

Damon smoothed his hands over her hair and cupped her face in his hands. "Are you all right?"

"I think I need a doctor," she said, then before she could utter another word, her world went black.

* * *

Damon sat with his head in his hands, his elbows propped on his thighs while Laurel slept amid the steady beep of the monitors. She'd been rushed to the local community hospital after she'd collapsed in his arms. She had a fever caused by a staph infection. Luckily, she'd had no signs of blood poisoning and would be fine just as soon as the doctors managed to get her infection under control.

He was exhausted and still wrestling with the news Laurel had given him yesterday evening. He didn't blame her. God knows she did the only thing she thought she could've done, but dammit, she should have told him the truth a long time ago.

They'd wasted so much time. Time he had every intention of making certain they made up for, just as soon as she was well enough.

He'd called Alan Rosen with the facts as he knew them. Rosen had left a couple of hours ago, and Laurel hadn't been too keen on trusting the ADA who'd been out to get her, but Damon felt kind of bad for the guy since his case against Laurel had fallen apart. If Rosen wanted a career-maker, then he certainly had one now. What the ADA planned to do with the information was up to him, but Damon felt confident that Conner Tillman's days as head of the Institute were numbered. There wasn't much he could do about the Institute itself, or the men who were behind scenes. They were powerful men, but in Damon's opinion, not completely untouchable. A prosecutor as ambitious as Rosen would find a way to see justice, and his own ambitions, served.

"You look terrible."

Damon smiled as he looked up to find Laurel smiling at him from her hospital bed. "You should talk, Mr. Wizard. You're not looking so hot yourself right now."

"Better than you."

He grinned. "Wanna bet?"

She wrinkled her nose. "Bad turn of phrase," she said.

Damon winced. "Sorry," he said and meant it.

Her gentle smile returned. "Is it really over?"

Damon nodded. "For the most part. You know you might have to testify at some point if Rosen gets his way."

"I know." She let out a sigh. "Will you be there?"

He stood and walked to the bed. "Wild horses, baby."

She frowned. "Are there really wild horses still in Montana?"

"You'll just have to come see for yourself."

She let out a gusty sigh. "Is that the best you can do, Metcalf?"

"What do you mean?"

"That's a lousy marriage proposal."

He took a step back. "I thought it was pretty good."

She turned her head away from him. "Shows what you know."

He tucked his fingers beneath her chin and gently turned her face toward his. "Marry me, Mr. Wizard."

She smiled. "I've been thinking about it. Artifacts is history now anyway. There's no reason for me to say in L.A."

He frowned. "That's a lousy acceptance to my proposal."

"What are we going to do in Montana anyway?"

He gave her his best wicked grin and braced his hands on either side of her pillow. "I can think of a few things we could do to occupy our time," he said, then leaned in for a kiss.

When they eventually came up for air, Laurel offered a few suggestions of her own that stirred his blood. One or two in particular made him wish to hell she wasn't in a hospital bed.

Laurel toyed with the edge of the sheet and looked up at him, worry in her eyes. "I'm sorry about Cara," she said. "I had no idea she was going to turn the gun on herself."

"There wasn't anything you could do," Damon reassured her. "She had a history of mental instability."

"Yes, I know, but I feel responsible. The least I can do is pay for her funeral."

Damon nodded. He disagreed, but Laurel had a good heart. It was part of what he loved so much about her. A heart that had kept them apart for too many years because she'd felt she was doing the right thing by protecting him. He planned to spend the rest of his life reminding her that he was the one who was supposed to do the protecting. Not that she'd buy that no matter what colored bow he tied on it, he thought.

Her gaze clouded again. "I do love you, Damon."

He kissed her again. "I know you do."

She let out a gasp of breath and frowned at him. "And?"

He chuckled. "I love you, too."

"Better," she said, then wound her good hand around his neck and pulled him in for a deep kiss, one filled with all that was in her heart.

Don't miss Jennifer Apodaca's
EXTREMELY HOT
available now from Brava . . .

"YOU REALLY BELIEVE that one kiss would get you in my bed, don't you? You think you can live up to your own legend?"

"One way to find out." He put his mouth to hers.

She stood immobile, her arms hanging down at her sides, her hands clenched in determination. As if she wanted to prove to them both that she wasn't susceptible to the combustible chemistry sizzling between them.

Luke took the challenge. He slid his hand off her neck and into her thick, soft hair. Then he spread his other hand over her lower back and pulled her into his body.

She resisted for a long second, then she softened with a frustrated sigh. Her mouth slid open as she exhaled, her rigid spine eased against his hand and she put her arms around him.

Surrendering? God, he hoped so. Then her tongue touched his and lust swamped him. His blood pumped fast and hard while his dick throbbed. He sank his tongue deep inside her, tasting Ivy, a flavor so real and intoxicating that it made him forget about statues, jobs, fathers . . . His entire world narrowed to the woman in his arms.

"No!" Ivy jerked her whole body away from him. She ran her hand over her mouth, her gaze losing the haze of desire and icing to frustration, maybe anger. Then she grabbed the doorknob, pulled open the door, and said, "Time for you to go."

What the hell just happened? He reached out to touch her, to reconnect.

Ivy smacked his hand away and glared at him. "Leave."

Damn, he'd been doing a good job of seducing her. "Ivy, you liked the kiss as much as I did. Don't lie."

She shoved her hair back out of her face. "So what? I don't think with my hormones, Sterling. You're just another dime-a-dozen bad boy."

Ah, that was it. She was tough, he'd give her that. Which just made her all the more interesting. Intriguing. Sexy. "You don't mind using bad boys to get what you want." She'd used his Urban Legend persona often enough on her radio show to prove her points. To tell the world what a bastard he was without ever having met him.

Her mouth thinned and her eyes narrowed. "Are you suggesting I sleep with you to get you to back off?"

He shook his head. "I'm not backing off whether you have sex with me or not."

She made that female noise in her throat again. "God, you're annoying. I can't believe all those ditzy Urban Legend fans actually fall for your bull. I liked you much better in your Clark Kent character."

He couldn't help it, he laughed. She'd been the one person who had gotten him to break character, and she'd been intrigued by him in spite of herself. Drawn to him. "Yeah, well, this is me, sweet cheeks." He leaned toward her. "I'm not a bad boy."

She put her arm against the edge of the door as if she were amused by his ignorance. "No? Then what are you?"

"A bad ass."

A light flared like a crystal star in her gaze. "The difference?"

Ivy York was such a pretender. That flare in her eyes told him how very much she liked dangerous men. He suspected it was because, deep down, Ivy possessed the same drive to survive and to succeed, a need to prove to the world that it couldn't destroy her. To answer her question, he said, "A bad boy throws tantrums and punches for no reason other than he's a spoiled brat with a man-sized cock."

Her lips twitched. "With you so far, *Urban Legend*."

She managed to make Urban Legend sound like something right out of a garbage can. He leaned his body closer. "A bad ass takes care of business and gets the job done." He slid through the opened door, thinking she could chew on that for a night.

"Hey, Sterling."

He turned at the top of the stairs and caught his breath. She stood silhouetted by the porch light in her black tank and tiny shorts. Her breasts jutted out with perky nipples, while her shorts cupped her hips where he longed to bury his dick. Her blond hair flowed down around her shoulders and damn it, she was hot. "What?"

Her smile was slow and sensual. "You really are a legend . . . in your own mind." She shut the door.

Take a look at Sylvia Day's
PASSION FOR THE GAME,
available now from Brava!

"DO NOT BE fooled by her outward appearance. Yes, she is short of stature and tiny, but she is an asp waiting to strike."

Christopher St. John settled more firmly in his seat, disregarding the agent of the Crown who shared the box with him. His eyes were riveted to the crimson-clad woman who sat across the theater expanse. Having spent his entire life living amongst the dregs of society, he knew affinity when he saw it.

Wearing a dress that gave the impression of warmth and bearing the coloring of hot-blooded Spanish sirens, Lady Winter was nevertheless as icy as her title. And his *assignment* was to warm her up, ingratiate himself into her life, and then learn enough about her to see her hanged in his place.

A distasteful business, that. But a fair trade in his estimation. He was a pirate and thief by trade, she a bloodthirsty and greedy vixen.

"She has at least a dozen men working for her," Viscount Sedgewick said. "Some watch the wharves, others roam the countryside. Her interest in the agency is obvious and deadly. With your reputation for mayhem, you two are very much alike. We cannot see how she could resist any offer of assistance on your part."

Christopher sighed; the prospect of sharing his bed with the beautiful Wintry Widow was vastly unappealing. He knew her kind, too concerned over their appearance to enjoy an abandoned tumble. Her livelihood was contingent upon her ability to attract wealthy suitors. She would not wish to become sweaty or tax herself overmuch. It could ruin her hair.

Yawning, he asked, "May I depart now, my lord?"

Sedgewick shook his head. "You must begin immediately, or you will forfeit this opportunity."

It took great effort on Christopher's part to bite back his retort. The agency would learn soon enough that he danced to no one's tune but his own. "Leave the details to me. You wish me to pursue both personal and professional relations with Lady Winter, and I shall."

Christopher stood and casually adjusted his coat. "However, she is a woman who seeks the secure financial prospects of marriage, which makes it impossible for a bachelor such as myself to woo her first and then progress from the bed outward. We will instead have to start with business and seal our association with sex. It is how these things are done."

"You are a frightening individual," Sedgewick said dryly.

Christopher glanced over his shoulder as he pushed the black curtain aside. "It would be wise of you to remember that."

The sensation of being studied with predatory intent caused the hair at Maria's nape to rise. Turning her head, she studied every box across from her but saw nothing untoward. Still, her instincts were what kept her alive, and she trusted them implicitly.

Someone's interest was more than mere curiosity.

The low tone of men's voices in the gallery behind her drew her attention away from the fruitless visual search. Most would hear nothing over the rabble in the pit below and the carrying notes of the singer, but she was a hunter, her senses fine-tuned.

"The Wintry Widow's box."

"Ah . . ." a man murmured knowingly. "Worth the risk for a few hours in that fancy piece. She is incomparable, a goddess among women."

Maria snorted. A curse, that.

Suddenly eager to be productive in some manner, Maria rose to her feet. She pushed the curtain aside and stepped out to the gallery. The two footmen who stood on either side to keep the ambitiously amorous away snapped to attention. "My carriage," she said to one. He hurried away.

Then she was bumped none too gently from behind, and as she stumbled, was caught close to a hard body.

"I beg your pardon," murmured a deliciously raspy voice so near to her ear she felt the vibration of it.

The sound stilled her, caught her breath and held it. She stood unmoving, her senses flaring to awareness far more acute than usual. One after another, impressions bombarded her—a hard chest at her back, a firm arm wrapped beneath her breasts, a hand at her waist, and the rich scent of bergamot mixed with virile male. He did not release her; instead his grip upon her person tightened.

"Unhand me," she said, her voice low and filled with command.

"When I am ready to, I will."

His ungloved hand lifted to cup her throat, his touch heating the rubies that circled her neck until they burned. Callused fingertips touched her pulse, stroking it, making it race. He moved with utter confidence, no hesitation, as if he possessed the right to fondle her whenever and wherever he chose, even in this public venue. Yet he was undeniably gentle. Despite the possession of his hold, she could writhe free if she chose, but a sudden weakness in her limbs prevented her from moving.

Her gaze moved to her remaining footman, ordering him silently to do something to assist her. The servant's wide eyes were trained above her head, his throat working convulsively as he swallowed hard. Then he looked away.

She sighed. Apparently, she would have to save herself. Again.

Her next action was goaded as much by instinct as by forethought. She moved her hand, setting it over his wrist, allowing him to feel the sharp point of the blade she hid in a custom-made ring. The man froze. And then laughed. "I do so love a good surprise."

"I cannot say the same."

"Frightened?" he queried.

"Of blood on my gown? Yes," she retorted dryly. "It is one of my favorites."

"Ah, but then it would more aptly match the blood on your hands"—he paused, his tongue tracing the shell of her ear, making her shiver even as her skin flushed—"and mine."

"Who are you?"

"I am what you need."

Maria inhaled deeply, pressing her corset-flattened bosom against an unyielding forearm. Questions sifted through her mind faster than she could collect them. "I have everything I require."

As he released her, her captor allowed his fingers to drift across the bare flesh above her bodice. Her skin tingled, gooseflesh spreading in his wake. "If you find you are mistaken," he rasped, "come find me."

Keep an eye out for Lucy Monroe's
DEAL WITH THIS
coming next month from Brava . . .

THE BEST PART of the tour by far was Jillian Sinclair. The worst part was the effect she had on him.

He found himself standing closer to her so he could get more of her elusive scent. She didn't wear perfume. The springtime freshness was too subtle for that. Probably her shampoo, but even knowing the fragrance was something so mundane did not diminish its addictive appeal. Of course, the fact that the unmistakable feminine musk underlying it was all Jillian, did not help.

Alan wanted to nuzzle right into her neck, and various other enticing places, and just inhale. Okay, and then maybe taste and touch . . . shit . . . he wanted this woman.

"Alan?"

"Huh?"

Jillian was looking at him questioningly. "I asked if you wanted to see more of the technical behind the scenes stuff."

"Yeah, that would be great."

Jillian knew more about the technical workings of the sets and the show's production than he would have expected. He took copious notes on everything she said. "I feel like I'm taking Film 101."

She laughed. "Bored?"

"Not at all. Just surprised you know so much."

"I never went to college, you know? I took some classes on acting though, but for the most part—boring. Having someone else tell me how to do what I love best just didn't work for me. I found I liked knowing how everything worked more. So, I took classes on set design, editing, prop design . . . you name it, I've probably taken at least one class on it."

"So, you really are a jack of all trades."

"Well all trades related to the film industry."

"Do you have dreams of directing one day?"

"Yes. And eventually, producing. I'm supposed to direct two episodes next season. It's part of my contract."

"That's great."

"Yeah, I'm pretty excited." She led him out of the prop room. "If this show goes for enough seasons, it will be my last full-time acting gig."

"Moving to film?" he asked and promptly tripped on one of those big black cables.

He fell toward Jillian, her hands automatically coming out to steady him and his grabbing onto her. They ended up with her leaning on the wall, him leaning against her with one of his hands on her hip and the other her shoulder.

It was the perfect position for kissing and his body perked up, hormones screaming at him to take the plunge.

Reason prevailed and he managed to apologize rather than lock lips.

"No problem. Are you okay?" she asked, both of her hands planted firmly against his chest.

She wasn't pushing him away and he wasn't quite up to the task of stepping back. Yet.

"Yes. I forgot to watch for the cords."

"It's one of the first things you learn."

"It would have to be."

"Yeah . . ." she swallowed and licked her sweet bow lips. Damn.

"Maybe you should hold my hand and guide me," he said in a low voice that he usually reserved for the bedroom.

Double damn.

"If it will make you feel safer." Her voice was huskier than normal too, and her pupils had almost swallowed the emerald green of her irises.

Triple damnation. She was turned on.

He willed himself to step back.

Nothing happened.

She stared up at him, silent but for the short little breaths she took.

His head began to lower while his libido cheered but his brain shouted at him to go to the men's room and soak his head under a cold faucet.

Her mouth opened slightly, ready for his to descend.

"Miss Sinclair?" It was Ralph, the security guard. "I just got off the phone with the Prop Master. He wanted to request that you not tour his room."

Alan found his lagging self-control and sprang backward.

Jillian sidestepped and moved toward the security guard. "I don't know what he thought we would do."

"Probably break something. He's pretty protective of his stock."

Jillian made a little growling noise. It was cute. "Yes, I know. He's quite the *artiste*," she muttered aside to Alan. "We just won't tell him we already toured the room, yes?"

"Whatever you say."

"If he asks, I'll tell the truth," she said on a sigh.

"Let me know if he asks."

Her brows drew together. "Why?"

"So, I'll keep our stories straight."

She groaned. "I hate subterfuge."

"I know."

That made her eyes widen, almost with fear. Like the idea

of him knowing her worried her. The woman was a 3-D Chinese puzzle and he planned to have all the pieces put together before this case was over.

"Thanks, Ralph."

"No problem, Miz Sinclair."

She turned back to Alan, her smile almost too bright. "So, what were we talking about?"

"I had asked if you planned to do movies once this series has run its course."

"Maybe . . . I'd like to do a movie or two, but mostly? I want to work behind the camera, and I'm hoping I can make that happen in a full-time way."

"What's stopping you?"

"From directing? Experience. Mostly. From producing, which is my real love . . . the green stuff. It takes a lot of seed money to build a name as a producer, not to mention some killer scripts."

"Another reason to rent out rooms in your house."

She laughed. "That's mostly to cover living expenses. My friend Amanda has almost all of my acting income in an aggressive investment plan. She's helping me realize my dreams."

"She sounds like a good friend to have."

"We've always been there for each other."

"I've got a brother like that. He's my best friend."

"That's great. That you're close to your brother like that. It's the way family should be."

"Do you have any siblings?"

"Yes. A younger brother. I haven't seen him in a while."

"Why?"

"It's hard to get home. He's talking about coming to visit. He might even transfer to the University of Vancouver next year. Our parents aren't too happy, but I'd love it if he lived closer."

"I hear that. My brother and I do a lot of IM-ing, e-mails, phone calls . . . it helps. But sometimes, we just have to get together face-to-face. Even if we didn't want to, Sir would insist on it."

"Who's Sir?"

"My grandfather. He raised us since our parents died when we were teens."

"And you call him *Sir*?"

"He's got his quirks, but he did a good job with us."

"I'm sure he did."

"What about you? You're originally from Southern California, right? I bet you call your parents by their first names."

Jillian laughed, but the sound was edged with something not in the least humorous. "No way. We had a very traditional home. At least once my mom married my stepdad. I had to call him Dad even though my own father is still living."

"That must have been hard."

"It was, but not because of any feelings of disloyalty I felt toward Scorpio. The truth is, he never played much of a parental role."

"Scorpio, the painter?"

"Yes."

Well, he knew where Jillian got her red hair from. But she didn't seem to have much else in common with her famous father. Scorpio was legendary for his affairs with young, gorgeous women and throwing parties that rivaled the decadent depravity of ancient Roman orgies.

"I guess you were lucky to have a stepdad then."

"You'd think so, wouldn't you?"

"You don't." He was getting tastes of Jillian's secrets and they only made him thirstier for more.

"One thing I learned growing up is that appearances can be and are often deceptive." She sighed. "Not that I think living with Scorpio would have been better. Sometimes, life doesn't give you any good choices. But you know? I realized after moving out that it could have been a lot worse too."

Despite his temporary insanity that prompted his request she hold his hand, Alan kept his distance for the rest of the tour. If Ralph hadn't shown up, Alan would have kissed Jillian senseless. He couldn't believe his own behavior. No matter how strongly she impacted his libido, he was not some rookie agent to be derailed by a pretty face. Or even a beautiful face. And intriguing personality. And charming personality. And the same sense of humor as his own.

Practically growling with frustration at himself, Alan forced out question after question about how things worked and who did what on the set and in the studio.

True to what she'd told him earlier, Jillian had enough knowledge to give him elucidating responses to every single query.